Abandoned by the Alpha

The Alpha King's Breeder
Book 15

Bella Moondragon

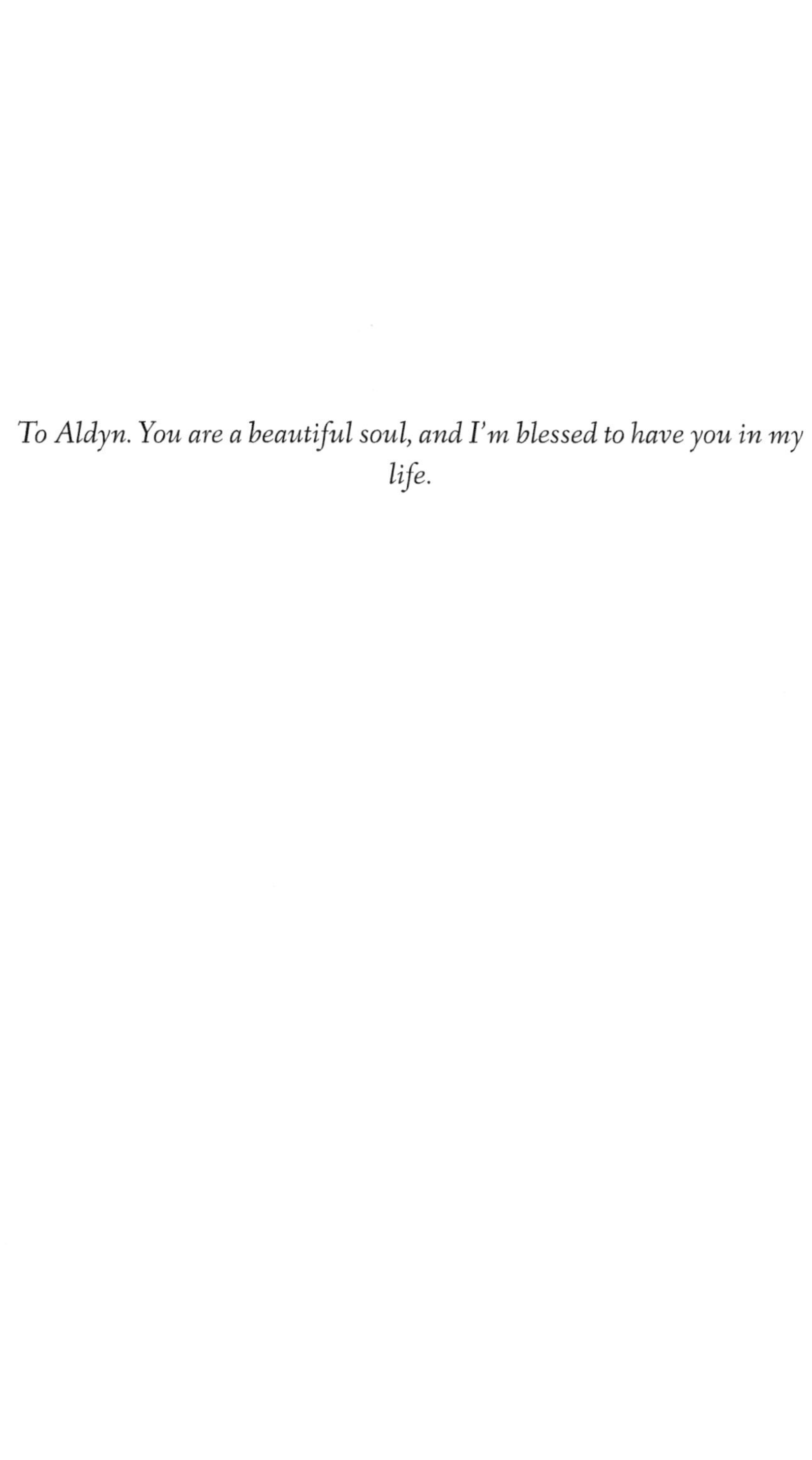

To Aldyn. You are a beautiful soul, and I'm blessed to have you in my life.

Contents

Chapter 1

Seeing Her Again

Blake

I love a straight line.

I like a natural, expected curve. I like a perfectly sharpened pencil against graph paper, the rhythmic pull of an eraser swiping away at flakes of lead. I like a solid foundation built on the back of flawless trigonometry–something static, impenetrable, and utterly flawless.

I like solid, well-built rooms in shades of muted gray. I like clothes that feel weightless, soft, without a tag scratching my neck or the feeling of fabric rubbing my skin. I like exactly three foods–a rare steak. Nectarines. One specific brand of granola that I'll stop eating if the recipe even remotely changes. I like a single cup of coffee in the morning–black and bitter. No cream. No sugar. No frills.

No color. No emotion. No feeling. Nothing unexpected. Nothing that'll draw my mind out of the carefully crafted funnel of resistance I've crafted where I'm safe and secure, unbothered and unburdened.

But... noise...

I flinch as another shrill voice wafts from the radio attached to a nameless warrior's hip across the cavernous grand foyer. The static makes my skin crawl even from this far away. I roll my neck, closing my eyes as prickles make my skin erupt in gooseflesh beneath the tailored tuxedo draped over my body, snug like a well-fitted glove. My reflection in the mirror, however, is stoic and unbothered–a mask of indifference, just how I like it.

"Bad news," Mom says, her voice cutting through the static weaving through my brain.

I look up at her as she carefully steps down the marble staircase in too-high heels and a dress of rich lavender silk–her signature color. Her white-blonde hair is pin straight and twisted in a low, regal bun pinned to the back of her head. The Luna Queen of Crescent Falls in all her glory, truly, her jeweled fingers sliding down the banister as she picks her way to my side. "Dad isn't coming. He's stuck up north, he says, still in a meeting with the chancellor of Wellington."

"He's always hated the symphony," I reply, and she rolls her violet eyes before coming to a stop at the bottom of the staircase. Two warriors appear at her side, one handing her the silken clutch that perfectly matches her gown while the other helps her into a luxurious white fur coat that rests just below her ankles.

"Well, there are things you can't train out of a man, and apparently taste in music is one of them," she says with a knowing, sly smile, eyeing me with interest. "I'm surprised you agreed to come with me tonight, given your affinity for the club scene. What did Brie call you? A club rat?"

"That sounds like something she'd say." I turn back to the slightly rusted antique mirror and straighten my tie, smoothing the black fabric over my starched white dress shirt.

Mom's reflection hovers just behind mine as she adjusts the pearl earrings dangling from her earlobes. Her lifted, demurely excited expression flattens, however, as she strokes a pearl. "These belonged to your great-grandmother," she says in a near whisper, a pained tone that makes me turn to look into her face instead of her reflection. "Grandma Maddy gave them to me recently," she continues with a heavy sigh. "I miss her. Isla. I wish you kids would have had more time with her."

I barely remember my great-grandparents. I'd been... around four years old when they died. My childhood memories are hazy, to say the least, but I remember running circles around a plush, butter-yellow armchair in what we used to call the pink room at the palace in Moonrise. I'd been chasing... Aris, I believe, in a tight circle while Isla's laugh reverberated around the room and our grandmother, Maddy, half-heartedly tried to rein us back in, but she'd been enjoying the show as well.

I remember playing with Isla's rings while she told stories about what Crescent Falls used to be like, what it used to look like before the population boom that followed her rise to power. She became more than just a breeder; she became a queen. What was once a small city turned into a deep, writhing metropolis with buildings that disappear into the clouds around us as I drive my mother toward the performing arts center in the middle of downtown, the city washed in twinkling lights that reflect off glass skyscrapers and wet pavement.

There used to be a forest here–a deep, endless one. Roads were narrow and made of dirt instead of multi-lane highways and bridges that span miles, that span entire pack territories that linger beneath the shadows.

Crescent Falls is... too loud. Too mechanical. Too electric. It echoes even in the darkest hours of night–a constant hum of noise. The sound of life itself.

And for someone like me, it's too much.

It's why I bought my penthouse in the clouds, so high off the ground I can't hear the traffic, the car horns and the scrape of trains and trolleys. It's why I paid a small fortune to have a team come to install blackout blinds on the windows that keep the immaculately tidy, open space out of the glare of the lights. It's why the walls are gray, the couch is gray, the cabinets, doors, and floors are gray.

Getting to this place was a blur. I blink down at the concert program in my hands, sure I was just standing in the foyer of my parents' castle, and now I'm here, surrounded by incessant white noise that grinds through me, screeching through my head like a train coming off its tracks.

"Oh my Goddess," Mom says, popping each syllable like bubblegum. "Do you recognize her?"

I lean into her space to look at her program as the concert hall below our booth sizzles with noise while people take their sweet time finding their seats. The memory of her music greets me, embraces me, folds me back into myself, and I close my eyes in an attempt to let it sweep me away.

"Marianna Abbot? It can't be." Mom turns to the friends we're seated with–her friends. Other high-ranking Lunas, as well as Betas' wives, whom she invited to share the royal booth tonight for the finale of the concert season. I'm the only male present in the booth as it stands, and the women titter around me like little birds as the memory of Anna's violin fades and is replaced by the soft "Oohs" and "Ahhs" falling from softly painted lips.

"She is just gorgeous. How do you know her? Should I know her?" a Beta's wife, her name lost on me entirely, says directly behind me. The nameless, faceless woman leans forward to speak to my mother, her hand resting on the top of my chair. I flinch at her proximity, but she doesn't notice how I lean away just a touch.

"Oh, it's been years since I've seen her. She and Blake were the best of friends back in the day."

A half dozen sets of eyes turn toward me, but I ignore them, pretending to be invested in the crowd below.

"Second chair at her age? What a feat," another little bird remarks, her dangling diamond earrings clinking, the sound loud and grating enough to drown out the noise all around me. "She must be an angel on the strings. What does she play? Violin? Cello? What else is there?"

"Bass is the big one, right?" another laughs, followed by more giggles, an endless amount of noise.

I rise, murmuring something under my breath that is either a firm, audible, "Would you all shut the fuck up?" or a soft and polite, "Excuse me," as I side-step out of the booth and into the private hallway leading away from the space directly overlooking the stage.

The warriors guarding the hallway don't pay me any mind. I cut through a service door to avoid the light crowd still mingling even as muted applause rings out through the walls, and the orchestra tunes their instruments. A dank, dimly lit concrete stairwell is at once my salvation–silent, but slightly damp, the odor of mildew masking the scents of several thousand people and making it possible to catch my breath again.

I should have known. No, I should have checked. I should have read the program online like a normal person would do, wouldn't they? See what wordless songs would play? How long I'd have to sit in the dark until intermission when I could order a scotch, neat–a double pour. Triple?

I practically fall down the stairs in my haste to just... get away. From what is entirely lost on me. Two weeks ago, my mind was torn to absolute shreds. Like talons of iron raking through my gray matter, leaving festering lesions in their wake. I remember little about the after, the healing, the incessant sense of mystics hovering nearby, worrying over me–their lord and fucking savior.

But I do vividly remember the look on Soren's smug-ass-shit-eating-grin-wearing face when I'd sputtered Marianna's name.

Worse. Skye's name.

To his credit, which I hate to give him, he hasn't said a word to anyone about it.

To my credit, a few white lies about my head hurting has kept most of the family at bay, including Evander and Ryatt, who would love to see me strung on the palace gates for the stunt I pulled by hiding over a dozen Alphas over five Goddess-damned years without so much as mentioning a word about it to the family.

I shove through another door with no sense of direction nor time, my breath coming in quick gasps, and stare into the empty abscess of the basement level of the concert hall.

Flickering fluorescent lights quiver overhead. The heavy stairwell door slams shut behind me, sending a booming echo into the recesses of the space. Lockers line the walls, followed by a few cheaply made and recently replaced doors. Practice rooms. Bathrooms. A few empty offices. I pace as the sound of the orchestra tuning bleeds through the ceiling, past pipes and incredibly unsafe exposed wires.

I do not know where I'm going as I loosen my tie, one hand braced and sliding against the wall as I walk into the cover of shadows where a short, metal staircase leads to the wings of the stage. The gnawing, overlapping voices in my head fade, replaced by water dripping and the screech of tuning instruments. Normal noises. Noises that remind me I still have two feet planted in reality.

A woman stands in the shadows holding a violin. Her dark, almost black, hair trembles just an inch above her shoulders. She raises the violin to her shoulder, tilting her head, pulling an invisible bow across the strings.

I can *hear* the silent music. I can see it in my mind as her perfectly straight spine relaxes, her body rolling to a song branded in my chest. The memory of it hurdles back to me against my will. The dark hues of a basement level apartment with an old couch and a TV heavier than I was at sixteen. Cans of soda going flat on a coffee table. Her laugh. The polyphonic texture of her violin over the smooth hum of a recorded cello piece. The sonata, the allegro, the distinct movements, tastes, colors, and noise as I watched her expression adjust to every changing melody, every pluck of her fingers and smooth pull of her bow. It was everything. It was nothing. It was the loudest sound and the softest lullaby. It was my undoing. It always has been.

Captivating. She was always just as captivating as her music.

Marianna abruptly lowers her hand and turns to me, her blue eyes wide, adjusting to the shadows gathered between us.

"Blake?" she rushes out, glancing around. "What—what are you doing here?"

"I have no idea," I answer because it's the honest truth. "It was too loud upstairs."

Her mouth moves, but no sound comes out. "You're at the symphony. Of course it's loud."

"Why aren't you on stage with everyone else?" I haven't spoken to her in years. Not face to face, nor voice to voice. I've seen her smooth signature on various forms and documents. I've seen her input and opinions regurgitated in emails between me and the mediator I hired to handle... everything.

We had an agreement. An iron-clad contract. It was... her idea. Her decision.

Not mine.

But she was right.

"I'm—I'm filling in for the first chair of the string section," she says, tilting her chin while her cheeks burn a deep fuchsia. "I go on stage last."

"Congratulations." I'm not sure my stiff tone is appropriate. I'm never sure. I can't read the emotion behind her eyes. I don't understand why her eyes narrow and her mouth pulls into a tight line. She's not happy to see me, I think. No, I know it. She's confused as to why I'm here, alone with her, but that sliver of feeling casting a shadow on the left side of her face isn't something I recognize.

Because it's a... bruise.

"Did he do that to you?" I ask without a shred of hesitation, my voice as cold and smooth as ice.

She looks away, her eyes back on the stairwell where shadows dart in and out of view. I have minutes with her. Possibly seconds. Seconds to take in the faded mate's mark on her neck as she swallows, the column of her throat bobbing.

"Anna—" I take a single step in her direction.

Her entire body locks up tight. My hands curl into fists at my sides.

"Marianna, it's your cue," a shadow hisses from the top of the stairs, and she moves like lightning, disappearing without so much as looking over her shoulder.

That ache is back. That writhing, snake-like presence in my temples. That pinprick that entices me to consider the stars, at the tapestry woven into the heavens. That dull, throbbing pain that urges me to pull prophecies from the sky and make my own music with them.

But the last time I looked there, searching for Marianna... and me?

It ruined everything.

Chapter 2

Skye

Marianna

Skye watches me with feline intent as I mix chocolate powder into her glass of milk. Her favorite glass. The only glass she'll drink milk out of. She has a glass for juice and another for water, but those are tightly packed away as it stands.

The kitchen is in shambles, boxes stacked as high as my shoulders in some spots. I know she saw me slip her vitamins into the milk. I know she's going to curl her lip at me, giving me that... look. That look that reminds me who her father is, even if nothing in the world could ever make me forget.

"It's just protein powder," I say, setting the blue ombre glass with little painted daisies dancing around it on the table, which has just enough space carved out for her cereal bowl. The rest of the space is taken up by train tickets and moving manifests, which she's picked through, of course, sucking every insignificant detail into her mind like it matters to her in the slightest.

"There's already seven grams of protein per serving in my cereal," she remarks when I turn back to the sink to continue scrubbing... nothing. Biding time. Wasting time until the movers get here.

"There is," I agree, giving her a smirk over my shoulder. "You need it. You're a growing girl."

She shifts her weight on her stool, the only thing she'll sit on these days. She's a peculiar little girl, but she's *mine*. My little weirdo. My starling. My sweetheart. She's... particular. Strict and nosey. But she's *so* smart. So freaking *smart*. Scary smart, if I'm being honest. She eyes me coolly before taking an exploratory sip of the milk.

"See? Another ten grams of protein won't kill you. Plus, it tastes good." She's also the pickiest child I've ever encountered.

She begrudgingly entertains me and drinks her milk, daintily wipes her mouth with a napkin, and hops off her stool. Her dark brown hair falls to the middle of her back. She halts when I tsk. A few strands of her hair catch the morning sunlight dancing through the windows, turning them a deep red, the color of wine. A familiar shade she didn't get from me.

"Not so fast," I say, arching a brow as she slowly turns to look at me over her shoulder. "You need to make sure everything is out of your room, okay? Do a second, then third, pass. You'd be in pieces if we got halfway to Eastonia and you realized you left your stuffies behind, right?"

Because we're not coming back here. This little house is no longer home. She doesn't answer. She doesn't even nod. She just stares at me with those eyes that look just like his, with a mirrored expression I used to spend hours trying to untangle.

I'm used to Skye being silent. She kind of just exists around me and my mom, Leona, her *grammy*, the only other person she trusts in the world. Skye likes to read. She likes to draw and often sits in the center of the rug in the living room scribbling, an open book just a foot away, multitasking.

Math is her strong suit, however. Numbers are like a second language to her. She's leagues ahead of her class when it comes to arithmetic, so much so that I was accused of doing her homework for her, but I'm a musician. Math was never, and will never be, something I grasp past the most basic levels.

I watch her skip out of sight. A memory floods my mind, turning the kitchen to the basement level apartment I grew up in, to the dimly lit living room with wood paneling where a sixteen-year-old Blake poured over an algebra textbook, scratching his head as he watched me tearfully try to grasp the concept of exponential equations.

"Marianna," he said gruffly, scrubbing a hand over his face, "you're mixing up cosines and tangents. I don't understand how–"

I burst into tears twenty minutes into that first tutoring session. We didn't even know each other. I was fifteen and trying to take my exit exams so I could transfer to a better school, my sights set on Wellington University, but passing my algebra class was the one thing standing in my way. He'd answered a desperate ad that my mom hung on a streetlight somewhere downtown, and then there he was, the Prince of Crescent Falls, in my living room, trying to teach me math.

He'd sat there just... staring at me as I came apart at the seams. His expression didn't fluctuate while I blubbered about how I was going to fail, how I wasn't going to get into Wellington, how my future was doomed. He had no idea how to react.

Instead, he asked, "Are you going to be an engineer?"

"No? Why the hell would I–" I'd noticed the relief sweeping across his face as he closed the textbook, and my tears dried instantly, replaced by the overwhelming urge to laugh.

Blake was, and still is, an enigma. He's not the least bit empathetic. He just doesn't get it–emotions. Crying in front of him had confused him greatly, and that was our *first* interaction. But he... kept coming back week after week, kept trying, ever patient while I failed over and over again.

"I'm trying to get into their music program," I told him one day, watching him sip cherry cola as he thumbed through a practice test he'd designed for me.

"Why?" His eyes met mine and held for a few seconds longer than they normally did.

"Because I want to," I shrugged, rolling my eyes. "Why do you want to be an architect?"

"Because I want to."

"Why are you looking at me like that answer didn't suffice, then?"

He looked away, then back again, scanning my face like I was some creature from space, and he was the unfortunate soul who'd discovered me.

It took weeks, then months, for him to say more than a few words to me outside of *math talk*. I was the one who prodded, asked about his personal life, which sounded a whole lot like he didn't have one. He was a student at Wellington, the prestigious university two hours away by train, but commuted for some reason. He didn't live on campus. He didn't seem to go out much, no partying, no sports, no nothing. Blake liked being alone; that was clear. He liked quiet and order. He often frowned at my untidy handwriting and smears of pencil lead.

But he did like the cherry cola I purposefully kept stocked in my ancient refrigerator. He did like the hum of classical music drifting from the stereo next to the TV. He liked me.

He liked me enough to give up trying to tutor me and started using our twice weekly sessions to do my homework for me while I lounged on the couch picking through sheet music, my toes tucked under his thigh.

We would sit in silence together for hours.

Those two years were the most intimate of my life.

Things shifted, however, a few days after my seventeenth birthday. It was a horrible, rainy, utterly gray late spring evening, a Saturday, if I'm remembering correctly. I spent my weekends at the music shop a few blocks from my apartment, and while my mom worked her waitressing job, I sorted records and gave violin and cello lessons to little kids to make some extra money to help with the bills and such, but that night... I can't remember exactly what happened or why I'd ignored my phone, the three texts rotting into oblivion, but one moment I was tucked in a practice room, rolling through the allegro of a sweeping, dark and riveting melody, and the next...

"Why aren't you answering my texts?" Blake ground out, shutting the practice room door behind him in a huff. He looked completely undone–his normally swept back, gelled hair wild and ruffled, his shirt unbuttoned and damp. He smelled like water. Brisk and clean, like he'd been in the rain for a while.

I turned to him, my chin still pressed to the chin rest of my violin. "Blake?"

"I texted you *three times*," he said in a tone that I'd never heard him use before. The hint of panic was enough to release my grip on my bow and lower the violin to my side.

"Are you okay?"

"Are *you*?"

"I'm–I'm fine," I managed to say, but the look behind his violet eyes made my stomach tumble to my toes as he braced a hand on the wall and hung his head like he was struggling to catch his breath. He was dressed strangely, I remember. I watched him unclasp a button holding a thick cloak over his shoulders. I never asked about his family. To me, he was just Blake. Not the prince. But I knew he often went to Eastonia where his cousins lived and ruled. Things are different there. Magical. Hard to explain.

"Blake, did something happen? You look–you look like–"

"I'm sorry I interrupted you," he said, briefly looking into my eyes. "I thought–it's nothing." He began to turn toward the door, but I stopped him, tapping my bow against his upper arm.

"You can stay, if you want." I tilted my head toward a stool in the corner. "I'm practicing my piece for my audition for Wellington's arts program. I'd kinda like your input."

His voice was like gravel when he replied, "I know nothing about music."

"And I knew, and still don't know, anything about quadratic

equations," I replied, and he looked amused for a fraction of a second, but then he sat, and I played, and he looked so relaxed. So stunned–

"Anna, the movers are here!"

Mom's voice rips me out of my memories. I blink away tears I... I don't remember forming and wipe them off my cheeks with the back of my hands. Skye thunders down the stairs, tearing for the front door. Mom and I call her our little house cat because she likes to sit in the front window and watch the world go by but also is exceedingly interested in strangers who show up in our cracked driveway, despite numerous conversations about safety and not talking to people she doesn't know.

But she skids to a stop in front of me, her violet eyes catching mine, and she furrows her brows.

I sniffle, shaking my head as I rub my cheeks. "I'm fine, Skye. Just a little sad."

"Because you love this house?"

"I do," I tell her with a squeeze of her narrow shoulder. "I did, I mean."

"Will we have windows like this at our new house?" She points to our view of... suburbia, I suppose. It's nothing special, but light dances into the nearly empty living room, and I sigh.

I crouch so we're eye to eye. She looks like me. She has my thick dark hair and heart-shaped face. Her eyes are big and slope downward toward her button nose, and she inherited the high, chiseled cheekbones my mother blessed me with. A dainty chin. A widow's peak. A shorter than average stature. Yeah, she's my daughter, and it's easy to see.

But where my skin tans easily and holds a golden bronze hue, she's fair. Her skin is dusted pink from running up and down the stairs, and freckles dot the bridge of her nose.

Her eye color is unique. It's Blake's. His contribution to her complicated genetics.

Skye might look like me, but her expressions were written by him. The slight narrowing of her eyes. That twitch of a smile. The smirk. The dead, hollow look she often wears when she's trying to understand someone else's big emotions.

"You're going to love it in Moonrise," I tell her. "I promise."

"Will you?" she asks, holding my gaze for longer than she usually does.

This move isn't about me. Sure, I'm accepting first chair of their absolutely stellar philharmonic, but the season doesn't start until this fall, which means I have the summer to settle her into her new life, which includes, hopefully, a new school. We'll see. I'm working on it.

"I think I'll like it a lot. I've heard it's beautiful there. I've heard there are flowers everywhere, and there's a big lake."

She perks up, still inspecting my face, trying to gauge what I'm feeling because she can't make sense of it. She can't decipher the tired look behind my eyes. The uncertainty. The fear.

"Grammy says there's magic in the air there," she says, her voice tilted and bright. "Is that true?"

"It is."

"Grammy said people like me live there."

My stomach pinches, but I keep my face neutral as I nod... even if it hurts. "There are." I smooth her hair away from her face and count the freckles on her nose. "I think you'll like it better than you've ever liked it here."

She turns her head to the door as male voices drift inside, followed by boot treads and the smell of sweat and cardboard.

"Stay out of their way, okay? Go find Grammy. We're going to leave for the train station soon."

She rushes out of sight as the movers funnel into the house. I fold my arms under my chest and look around, taking in the house and its details for the last time, my chest painfully tight as my eyes roam over the rug in the living room, over the coffee table with the cracked corner.

I watch a mover step toward it, reaching for it, but I say, "You can leave the table here. We're not taking it with us. Leave it–leave on the side of the driveway? Maybe a neighbor will want it."

He nods, picking it up like it weighs nothing. Like it wouldn't have hurt someone to crack their face against that corner.

My fingers find the nearly healed bruise on my cheekbone, and I close my eyes and breathe.

Chapter 3

She's a Secret

Blake

I haven't been back to Moonrise in over two weeks. It wasn't my idea to stay away this long, even though, almost a year ago now, Maeve badgered me into splitting my time between Eastonia and Crescent Falls. I didn't realize back then how often I'd actually find myself gravitating back to Moonrise, to Eastonia in general. She was right, which I'll never admit to her face, but coming back after two long weeks away, being fussed over by my mom, walking on eggshells with my dad over my idiocy... his words, not mine... it's good to be *home*.

I click the cursor on my laptop, staring at the untouched funds in a massive bank account I set up seven years ago, give or take a few months. The amount *has* changed. Grown with interest. Rarely a single dollar spent.

I run my hand over my face and check the page again, clicking through the account details, trying to paint a picture of what, if anything, Marianna has spent this money on... but there's nothing recent to show.

It's not the only account she has access to. Anything with my name on it–any personal accounts not tied directly to my family–is accessible to her at any time.

Sometimes a charge will come through that I can route back to a children's clothing store, or a bookstore, or five dollars spent at an ice cream shop, but those are far and few between.

I never miss them, though. I always wonder what ice cream flavor they shared, what clothes she bought the daughter I chose not to know.

My office door opens with a crack, and the shadow stretching through the midday sunlight belongs to Soren, unfortunately, but just like Maeve, he never knocks and likely never will.

He's dressed casually in jeans and a white T-shirt, his chestnut brown hair swept back away from his face, which he hasn't shaved in a while. He looks a little beaten down, but I suppose having a two-week-old baby will do that to a man. I wouldn't know. I wasn't there when Skye was that little.

He lingers in the doorway for a moment, waiting for my reaction to his intrusion into my space like he actually gives a damn.

"Do you need something?" I ask slowly, shutting my laptop.

"I heard you were back." He leans on the door to close it, and I straighten a touch when the lock snaps into place. Bastard. "We need to talk about what happened."

"Have you spent the last two weeks overthinking this?" I move my laptop to the side, clearing the space directly in front of me, before meeting his eyes. "I'd think you'd want to spend time with your child and your mate instead."

Soren takes several calculated steps in my direction before smoothly sitting in the armchair in front of my desk. He rests his ankle on his knee, splayed out, relaxed. He stares directly into my eyes until I look away.

"What do you want me to say, Soren?"

"I want to know what Hannibal did to you in there. While you've been resting in Crescent Falls, tucked tight in your childhood bedroom, by all accounts, I've been here, trying to take care of Maeve and Fallon while Ryatt, Evander, and every other Goddess damned man in this family breathes down my neck."

"Consider yourself lucky this is the way things went for you. Had hell not frozen over, your reception into the family might not have been met with such grace."

"Listen," he says, leveling with me, "I'm not going anywhere. Maeve is my mate. We have a daughter. I live here now, and you're going to have to get used to that. Everyone else has."

I bite the inside of my cheek as I move my favorite pen back to its spot.

There're many things I could say. I could admit that I don't like being confronted like this. I could say I don't like other people, especially other men, in my space. I could say that Soren doesn't deserve to be here, but that's not true, is it?

I've known him for five years. In fact, unfortunately, my relationship with him, at least based solely on blind trust, has been the closest relationship I've fostered since Marianna.

I trust him. I hate it, but I do. I know he loves Maeve. I know it's deeper than the mate bond for him. I know what he sacrificed for months to keep her safe. I know it tore him apart, and now he's adjusting to a new life with his mate at the helm, totally and completely at her whim and mercy.

It's a lot for a man like Soren, giving up that control. Letting someone else take the reins.

"Hannibal was looking for something, but I don't know exactly what it was, so I shielded everything. Every memory, every line of thought. He was trying to dig past those shields and–"

"Boiled your brain?"

"To put it in layman's terms, yes. If you think I've spent the last two weeks drinking scotch and smoking cigars, enjoying time off, you're wrong. I've been barely lucid."

"But you're lucid now," he says matter-of-factly, arching a brow. "You look fine to me."

"And *how are you?*"

"Don't fucking act like you care how I am in the slightest." He smirks. I can't tell what that means. He might be teasing me.

I grit my teeth, meeting his eyes. I remember seeing him for the first time and being so startled by his appearance that it took me aback, and I had to regain my composure before approaching him, asking him to become a murderer for hire. One of his eyes is nearly white. The lightest, softest gray in existence, while the other is split between a dark, bright blue and deep, steel gray.

"How is Fallon, then?"

"She's fine. She sleeps, eats, and poops, and that's all." He shrugs, but the smile he's biting back is undeniable. If I were a different man, I'd smile along with him. But his face changes, that smile gone in an instant, and he asks, "How's *yours*?"

My heart quakes as my chest tightens. This is the real reason he's here, and we both know it.

"What have you told Maeve?"

"About what you babbled while your brain was falling out of your ears? Nothing. I gauged whether she knew, but that was it. She thinks I'm criminally insane for even suggesting you have a kid. I danced around the details when Ryatt and your grandfather Isaac, who didn't leave until three days ago, by the way, grilled me over every second I spent on that island. No one knows, and I kept it that way for your sake, but I'm keeping it a secret from my mate as it stands, and I can't do that for very much longer."

I fold my hands in my lap, unsure where to even begin, or if I even want to.

"You need to tell me the details."

"Why? So you can go tell the world about my past transgressions? I'm sure the media would love to spin the story of the royal prince's bastard daughter."

"Is that what she is to you? A bastard? A *mistake*?"

"She wasn't planned, if that's what you're asking."

"You're only twenty-six," he reminds me, draping his arms over the armrests. "You said she's... six? So you were a teenager when she was conceived?"

"She just turned seven last week."

Soren shrugs, giving me a hard look. "Do you have a relationship with her?"

"With her–or her mother?"

"Either–"

"Neither."

Soren exhales deeply as he scans my face. I can't tell based on his expression what he's feeling. I've never been good at that. He could be furious or sad for me. He could be confused or excited, and I wouldn't know.

"Why not?"

"It wasn't the right time for me." A lie.

"So, you, what? Abandoned them?"

Real, unfiltered rage bubbles up, simmering through my blood. "No. I didn't abandon them–"

"Start from the beginning, for fuck's sake."

"I don't understand what gives you the right to know in the first place," I growl, and he grins at me then laughs.

"I'll fuck off right now," he says coolly, "and go tell *Maeve*. I'm giving you a chance to clear the air between *us* first so I can have your back when the family rains hell on you for keeping this a secret. Because no one knows, do they? Not your parents, not your grand-parents, not anyone on Maeve's side of the family?"

"No. They don't know about her."

"Why not?"

"Because we agreed to keep *me* a secret in the equation." I bristle as the words leave my tongue like it's even remotely close to the truth. "For her safety. Their safety."

"From what?" He laughs.

"The press."

Soren, to his credit, seems to understand this aspect of it, at least. Ever since the day Maeve brought him onto the balcony with their daughter, the press has been going ballistic, trying to find any snippet of information they can on Soren, the consort, or whatever the male equivalent is, to the Queen of Eastonia. The family has been busy squashing rumors, some of which have truth, about his past and origins. A new persona was created for the public to gnaw on, something tame compared to who he is and what he's done.

But he knows if he leaves the castle, he'll be bombarded with flashing cameras and shouted questions. It would be relentless. Overwhelming. Enough to drive a man mad. So, he's stuck in this castle until the chaos dies down, which could be weeks, if not months.

Welcome to the family, I suppose.

"I know what you're going to ask, so I'll make this as clear as I can," I say calmly. "Skye was born when I was nineteen, and Marianna was eighteen, and only her mother knew about the pregnancy. We had a brief fling." Another lie there at the end because the truth of what we were–what she was to me–it's far more complicated. "That fling resulted in a child, but by the time she found out, we'd already broken up. It was mutual."

I stay perfectly still, holding his gaze in the way I trained myself to, a way that makes it look like I'm okay with this... intimacy between us.

"And then what?" he asks, unimpressed, maybe even reading through the fault lines beginning to crack open behind my eyes.

I lick my lips, finding them dry. "Marianna wanted them both to have a normal life, and I agreed. I ensured that they were taken care of financially. Marianna moved on, found her mate, and married. The rest is history."

He blinks a few times before chuckling, "Yeah? So you don't even have a relationship with your own daughter?"

"I met her shortly after she was born." I was there. I was in the room when she came into the world, and the woman I loved saw her for the first time. It's a memory that I guard with my life, the very memory I was desperate for Hannibal not to see. A memory I was willing to die for.

"So she's got a mate–a husband, no less, and yet you wanted me to take her and put her and your daughter into hiding? You said she'd understand and that she'd know what to do–"

"Yes."

He leans forward, motioning in annoyance with his hands. "Blake, come on. You've got to give me something to work with here."

"What would you like me to say?"

"Anything that's going to make it easier to continue hiding this from my mate," he says slowly, his tone almost pleading. "You've backed me into a corner, man. I don't appreciate it."

"I am not in Skye's life, and that was Marianna's decision. I'm honoring her wishes–which were to keep my distance, so I am. Bringing my family into the equation would bring harm to Marianna, whose only priority is giving Skye a normal, easy life." The fissures widen as regret storms through my system. "Skye is seven now. This coming to light will only bring harm to her. She'd never be able to step out in public again without guards. She wouldn't be able to go to the park, or even to school, without people running over each other to get a glimpse of her."

"Denying her your side of the family isn't harming her?"

"It's not."

He pauses for a beat before asking, "Is she like you?"

I close my eyes. *I fucking hope not.* When I open my eyes again, he's still looking at me. I can't give him an answer because I honestly don't know. "She's happy and safe with her mother, and I'm respecting Marianna's wishes. That's all that matters. I–I was tortured, that's true." My jaw works as I look for the right words to convey what it felt like... dying. Slipping away into an abyss I couldn't swim out of. My only thought had been Marianna. Her face, her skin, her scent. Her fingers tracing my cheekbones in the quiet, cool darkness of the backseat of my car—the one night we let go, and let things be.

Just for a moment.

"Hannibal wants me for something. He needs me. I wanted you

to let me die because then her memory, her location, the fact that... we have a daughter who may, if the Goddess sees to punish us, have powers similar to mine. If I had died, he wouldn't have ever found her. He couldn't use them against me. That's why I told you to leave me behind and hide them."

Soren watches me closely then exhales deeply, his gaze downcast to his lap.

"So what now, Blake? You keep this secret from your family forever?"

"Do not tell Maeve."

"I... I won't, but *you* need to tell her soon. For my sake. She'll fucking kill me for keeping this from her, and you know that. You know her. She will find out sooner rather than later on her own."

"It doesn't matter. They don't live here in Moonrise. They'll never cross paths."

Chapter 4

Welcome Home

Marianna

"I think she likes it," Mom says over my shoulder as we watch Skye scurry from room to room in the townhouse I found for rent only a mile from the exterior wall of the castle. Cream-colored plaster walls and narrow, but brightly lit, hallways connect three bedrooms upstairs. Sunlight dances across dark wood floors, dust motes hanging in suspension. It smells like flowers. Wisteria and bougainvillea are already trying to bloom in the snug front garden lined with a pale stone wall, where the bright green spring grass has been freshly mowed in time for our arrival.

It's a quiet street, based on what the realtor told me. Cars aren't allowed, and there's a village square just a block away with a grocery store, bakery, and a park. Everything we'd need is within reach, secured by a gate separating us from the rest of Moonrise, which is apparently one of the safest cities in the Allied Kingdoms and great for young families.

Skye peeks her head out of one of the bedrooms and stares at us. "I want this one."

"It's yours, honey." Mom smiles, shrugging her shoulders. She squeezes my arm before turning for the stairs, her salt and pepper curls bouncing around her shoulders.

I follow Skye into the room she just claimed. It's a corner room with ceiling height windows that open halfway up, letting in a cool, slightly chilly early spring breeze. She's on her tiptoes, drinking in the sunshine and the view as I lean on the doorframe to watch her for a moment. I love witnessing the way she explores the world. It's so... innocent. When she was younger, she was adventurous and brave. Nothing scared her. Now, she's more docile. A bit withdrawn, if I'm being totally honest, like she sees the things she used to love in a new, darker hue.

Maybe that's just growing up.

Or maybe she's as different as I knew she'd be.

I had six years with her that were my own. Six years when her eyes were blue, like mine, before they slowly changed into the sharp violet tinged with gray in the center. I had six years when she spoke to me and told me stories, when she sang songs and danced in the sunlight. I had six years before she started folding into herself, into her head, which I know is now full of starlight.

Just like him.

The past year changed everything in so many ways.

"The movers won't be here until two days from now," I say, and she whirls, somewhat startled by my presence. "Grammy thinks tonight would be a good night to camp in the living room. We can lay out blankets and pillows and read books until the moon rises," I continue, smiling, but Skye just stares at me, calculating a response.

"What are we going to eat?"

"Whatever you want. We have to order out because none of our kitchen boxes are here yet. What do you think? Pizza?"

She nods and then flutters past me, chasing rays of sun down the hallway.

I linger near the window for a moment. My eyes roam the front garden before lifting to the wall in the distance, tall enough the trees lining a yard a few houses away don't reach the top, and then higher, to the gilded, sparkling windows of the massive palace blocking the scattered clouds.

My stomach tightens and then relaxes as I take a single, but restorative, breath.

"So, any word on the new phone?" Mom asks as she unpacks a bag of groceries–snacks, mostly, nothing that has to be cooked. I glance around the kitchen, which is painted a soft robin's egg blue, with white cabinets, a large refrigerator, and an island of white marble with a stovetop and an oven beneath it.

"I'm going to go pick it up in an hour or so. I'm sure I'll be there for a while setting up a new number and such."

Mom nods, popping open a bag of chips, which Skye snatches on her way out of the kitchen to continue sitting on the front steps watching the neighborhood. "You haven't spoken to him, right?"

"Dean?"

"Who else?"

I lean against the wall, praying my cheeks don't heat. I didn't tell her I ran into Blake last week during the concert. She doesn't need to know, I guess. It wasn't important. It was a weird coincidence, and... as I played through a solo, I glanced at the royal box, and he wasn't there, so it didn't matter, even if my chest still feels like it's caving in.

I hadn't seen him in seven years. That's a long time. That feels like a lifetime.

"I haven't."

She licks her lips. I feel her gaze inspecting my face before she turns to the fridge to unpack milk and juice. "He broke the restraining order by texting you so much–"

"I'm aware. I never responded."

"I just worry he might know that you left Crescent City," she says with a bite in her voice. "That's all."

"I left my old phone behind. You know that."

"But–after the concert, the success of it? You being you and blowing everyone out of the water?" She glances at me over her shoulder. "Someone will write about it–some critic doing their due diligence who lets the world know it was your last season with the Crescent Falls Philharmonic."

"No one other than Michael knew about my offer from Moonrise," I reply, but she shakes her head, and she's right.

"You should talk to the courts here and have the restraining order... broadened."

"It doesn't work like that, Mom. He'd have to come here first and... threaten me." My mouth dries out around the words.

She turns back to me, humming under her breath when Skye sprints inside again to fetch a juice box before darting back outside.

"Look, I'm safe. He doesn't know where I live, and this is a gated community. I already told the warriors at the guard station that he's not allowed, and they took that seriously. I practically gave them my life story!"

"He nearly killed you," she says under her breath, her eyes watering.

My stomach sinks. "Mom, he can't hurt me anymore, okay?"

She glances at the faded bite mark on my neck before turning away again, lifting a bag of grapes from the grocery bag.

I glance at my watch. "I'm going to go into town. I'll bring Skye with me to explore, giving you some time to rest."

"Just leave her here. She'll keep me company. She's taking stock of all the neighbors right now."

I purse my lips then relent and gather my purse from a hook near the front door. Skye has already disappeared into the backyard when I leave, walking casually through the exclusive village of Wisteria Way, past the guarded security gate, and into the city center, which is sprawling and packed but beautiful. The sun beats down on the top of my head as I walk along winding streets and pass unfamiliar shops. New scents tinkle my senses. Shifters, I know. Witches are different and smell new and strange. Like herbs and spices, not rain and deep, endless wilderness. A festival is being set up, it seems. Banners and streamers of red, pink, and silver hover over the street.

The phone store doesn't give me a hard time, thankfully. Before I know it, I have a new number for the first time since I got my first phone as a teenager, and I park myself on a bench in the center of some little park with a pond and fountain and spend an hour signing into my email, my bank account—*his*—bank account.

I stare at the money in that account for several minutes before clicking out. I've never really touched it. It's not my money, regardless of what Blake said when he gave me all the information, all the cards, all the pin numbers and data. It'll be for Skye one day. I've been doing fine on my own... lately. Not always. But my new salary as first chair and the sign-on bonus allowed me to put my mom and daughter into a beautiful new home in a safe, absolutely lovely neighborhood in a city that shines like gold.

My new job doesn't begin until this fall, a few weeks before the start of the symphony season, so I have time. Time to settle, to put down roots.

Time to figure out what to do with Skye.

I slump onto the bench, trying to become one with the etched stone. When I finally peel myself from its surface and find my way home, picking up a few pizzas and cream soda, Skye's favorite, it's nearing sunset. Wisteria Way is bathed in sunlight the color of ripe tangerines when I push through the wrought-iron gate and step onto the path leading up to my new front door, which is painted blue, the same color as the shutters and the tiles on the roof. An envelope sticks in the door jamb. I pluck it free on my way inside.

Skye rushes me, bouncing on her toes to peer at the pizza boxes. She gasps excitedly when she sees the ice cold, frosted bottles of cream soda, and I give her one, smiling as real, unfiltered joy lights behind her eyes.

Sweet girl.

My girl.

Mine.

Mom and I are busy arranging pizza on paper plates when I finally remember the envelope. "I didn't think we'd start getting mail yet," I murmur around a bite of pepperoni and cheese on a thin, delectable crust. I shove past the memory raging to existence of me at seventeen, laughing in the passenger seat of Blake's car while we ate pizza in a darkened parking lot. He leaned over the center console to swipe a smudge of grease from the side of my mouth, and... didn't stop leaning. Didn't stop until his lips brushed mine for the first time, and I...

"Did you see who left this?" I ask, my voice trembling just a touch as I slide my finger through the adhesive and pull out a note. Just a note. I scan the words, and the pizza feels like a lead weight at the bottom of my stomach all of a sudden.

"What is it?"

"Just–it's nothing. A welcome card." It's a bold lie.

It's a fucking summons. A summons I knew was coming because those creepy women in their white and silver robes haven't left me alone for the past year...

There are very few things my mom doesn't know about me. It would be hard to keep secrets given that it's only been us since I was just a little bit older than Skye. My dad wasn't like Dean or Blake. He didn't leave us–not willingly. He died. It's that uncomplicated. One day, he was here, and then he was gone, and it was just me and Mom left to navigate a world that wasn't very kind to us.

We were protected, of course, by our Alpha in the pack my father belonged to, but it only went as far as that. Crescent City is a huge place. Crescent Falls is even more enormous, with dozens of Alphas. Mom moved us out of his territory to be closer to her job, a waitress gig. We moved from a house in the wooded suburbs of the city center to an apartment in the neutral zone, and she saved every last penny to ensure I could still go to school for music one day. She never let me give up on that dream.

Even after Skye came into our lives.

She knows about me and Blake. She knows I was desperately, painfully in love with him. I like to tell myself she assumes it was that untouchable, fiery teenage lust and not something deeper. She knows

I loved Dean at one point, too, before I came to my senses and saw him for what he truly was, and still is. Dangerous. *A monster.*

But the one thing she doesn't know is why Blake and I didn't stay together, even when we found out about Skye's existence. She doesn't know why he left or that I made him do it.

She doesn't know the depth of what Skye is going through right now.

To her, Skye is just our little girl. Our precious, quiet, socially troubled angel.

She has no idea Skye is a mystic and has powers beyond belief, and I see it developing in real time, and it scares the hell out of me.

"Are you okay? You're looking a little pale." Mom lays a hand over my forehead. "Jeez, Anna. You're all clammy and flushed! What's wrong?"

"It's just the sugar," I lie, motioning to the empty bottle of cream soda on the counter. "It's homemade, I guess."

Mom doesn't look convinced, but the note is now crumpled in my fist, and I know, without a shadow of a doubt, this is the moment I've been dreading.

But I waste it again, telling her I'm going to go shower instead.

Chapter 5

Not This One

Blake

Stained glass inlaid with millions of moonstones filters silver hued light across marble tiles as my footsteps carry through the cavernous network of hallways in the temple. It's a busy day here in the center of the spiritual mecca that both priestesses of the Goddess and the mystics call home.

Women in silver robes walk in pairs, clutching books, talking in quiet tones. Some wear masks of crystal while others, normally much younger women in training as acolytes, wear veils of white fabric to cover their faces. The priestesses are more laid back, often wearing plain clothes within the temple, sometimes covering their hair with veils, but otherwise they're a great contrast to the white and silver of ordained mystics and their younger counterparts, the acolytes, who have yet to don their crystal masks.

Everyone, however, stops to bow and curtsy as I walk down the long, wide hallway with a cathedral ceiling that makes even the softest whisper boom.

My noise canceling headphones drown out what they murmur at

me, but it's the same as it always is. The same two words repeated over and over, from mouth to mouth, as I leave them in my wake.

The tight headphones sent a hint of classical music through my brain, just loud enough to keep the chorus of unintelligible voices at bay–the stars themselves–always chattering back and forth even in the middle of the day when they should be sleeping, but I digress.

I step through a doorway that leads out into a sprawling, tidy and wondrous courtyard. More women in robes kneel as they pick weeds from a garden. Some are sowing garden beds, preparing to plant this year's crop, whatever that'll be. Archways lead off the temple into the rectory, which blooms with more hallways of white marble and a lot more chatter. This section of the temple isn't open to the public, which means these women are more comfortable taking off their veils or masks here, and thankfully, after several years of my comings and goings, they don't jump out of my way to don their masks and hide their eyes anymore.

A trio of acolytes whispers in a sunlit corner, their bodies draped in pale blue and white robes. I pass, ignoring them, but they trail me with their eyes, giggling. Acolytes come in all ages–some young, some old. It doesn't matter. They all have the same power–reading the stars to pull prophecies from the sky, and that can develop at any point during their lives, and they're always called here, called *home*.

Another courtyard, much less formal than the first, greets me as I move through the rectory and back into the steady, unyielding spring sunlight. The larger of the two private buildings belonging to the temple stretches ahead of me. It's four stories high, cast in the shadow of the cathedral, but it's domed. The glass ceiling shines in a glare of sunlight. I cross under another marble archway and into the orrery, where my powers simmer and stretch against my will.

The foyer branches in eight different directions, leading to offices and classrooms. I walk straight, skirting around a bubbling fountain of carved moonstone, and fall back into shadows that lead to the room housing the orrery itself, where I find the woman I'm looking for.

Calliope turns to me as I enter the orrery and reluctantly remove my headphones. The classical hum is instantly replaced by a chorus of voices deep inside my head–pounding, screaming, laughing. The orrery before me turns and grinds. It's massive–ten times larger than the one my grandfather had built decades ago. Larger even than the orrery in Rifthold, which is under constant guard as it stands. Smooth, flawless brass keeps models of stars and planets suspended under the glow of the glass ceiling. mystics move around the marvel of ancient engineering with notepads, scribbling away while they try to decipher the erratic movements of the stars compared to the slow crawl of each planet in our solar system, prophesying.

But the mystical voices in my head grate on my gray matter, making my ears ring. My powers whirl, trying to decipher what the voices are hoping to tell me even while I forbid them to act.

I hate coming here, but this is... where I belong, unfortunately.

The voices fade when the Dame of the mystics, their leader, so to speak, takes a few steps in my direction with two other mystics at her side.

"High Lord," they say in unison, bending at the knees with their veiled heads bowed.

No one but the mystics call me High Lord. I'm not even sure what they mean by it. Occasionally, I'm addressed as High Priest, but only by them. To the Order of the Moon Goddess, the priestesses of the Church, I'm just Prince Blake.

But the mystics are something else entirely, despite being able to live in unison with their religious counterparts. It's a symbiotic relationship, I suppose. The mystics divine the stars and heavens, and the priestesses bear witness to their findings, relaying it to the world at large.

Here, I am king. That's plain. It's written behind their eyes, the rest of their expressions shielded by masks or veils.

"Any updates?" I grind out, narrowing my eyes to slits to stop from looking over their heads at the orrery.

Calliope rises first, shaking her head just once. "No, my Lord. Not today. Hannibal Arachnis is not in Eastonia."

"Then where is he?" I ask, my voice sharpened to a knife's edge but losing its luster with every syllable.

"No one has seen anything. It's not written in the stars," Calliope says in a monotone, high-pitched voice. I've never seen her face. She sounds beautiful, though, but they all do. They're a single unit of thought. Somewhere in their training —the same training I escaped from all those years ago, they merge, so to speak, losing themselves to the collective.

I don't know how else to describe it, but I know that while I can read the stars and decipher the movements of the orrery, like they can, I'm different. I can see and feel more, as well as manipulate the very fabric holding our world together.

I can reach into a mind and flay it open. I can stop time in a soul, cutting them off from reality for as long as my powers hold. I can make shields of stardust. I can travel through space and time at will.

I can see the day a person dies, but I can't change it. That's the one thing my powers can't do.

Not yet, at least.

I'm trying.

"He is not of our world, High Lord," Calliope says, her voice losing its fragility and turning to something husky and real instead of that practiced calm all mystics develop during their training. She sighs, turning her head ever so slightly to dismiss the other mystics, who go back to their work in silence. "He is not a being of this plane of existence."

"I am aware. What I need to know, what you and your people are meant to be doing, is finding him, where he came from, and what he *is*. It is imperative that we know as soon as possible, even if it's just a theory for now."

"He is ancient," she says, turning toward the spinning stars. "Immortal."

I stare at her, trying to gauge the flicker of emotion behind her tone. "Is he a *god?*"

"Likely," she says, turning back to me. "Like you."

I swallow, my throat contracting against the motion, against a knot that won't untangle. "The second there's a... break–a commotion–in the fabric of our plane, alert me."

She nods, tilting her head ever so slightly to the domed ceiling. "If that is all, my Lord, I have a meeting, and the new acolyte has just arrived. I must meet with her after she's been evaluated."

I nod, watching her silver-white robes ripple as she moves like water out of the room. I won't pretend I know everything about these strange beings. Some people think mystics have the souls of angels, and that might be somewhat true. They're not witches. Some are shifters, of course, given that we're the majority population-wise, but those gifts fade as their mystic abilities come into maturity. Mystics don't just appear out of thin air, like some of my family would believe. They're born, like we all are. They have parents and families who love them. New acolytes are rare, however. I know that much. Mystics seek each other out, like they can sense a sister outside of the fold.

I put my headphones back on and turn to walk out of the room, exhaling in relief and looking forward to going back to the palace to sit in my office, where everything is quiet and just how I like it.

A group of mystics lingers in the hallway I took to get here, and I decide to turn, following a different route out of the orrery. My footsteps echo, blocked by the music, as I move in and out of shadows. I take a hallway I've never been down before. It's wide and cavernous, slightly chilly with the spring air bleeding through the stone. The light grows bright when I near the foyer again, where stone benches line the hallway before the corridor opens to the foyer and the massive, sparkling fountain.

My powers surge. My heart thumps once before stopping completely. A woman sits on a bench with her face in her hands, her body convulsing with a silent sob.

I rip the headphones off my ears and break into a run. Marianna lifts her head, her eyes widening, her pupils blown so wide the cornflower blue of her irises shrinks until her eyes are black with shock.

"Blake?"

"What are you doing here?" I rush out, a feeling of dread tying my stomach into a knot.

She sucks back a sob, stammering, "They–they took her down the hall, and they said I couldn't come. I don't know where she is! They sent me a summons yesterday. I had to bring her. They haven't left me alone–alone since—" Another choking whimper steals her words.

My blood runs so cold I feel ice crystals moving through my veins. "Come here." I grab her arm, forcing her off the bench, and whirl us back down the hallway I just left. The act of touching her is... overwhelming to my senses. Warmth blooms, trying to gnaw through the dread coiling through my body like a snake. I'm jogging, resisting the urge to break into a run, but she's keeping up with me, just as frantic as I feel. I pull her to a stop in front of a door. The voices in the aether ring through my head like a death knell. My powers yank me toward the door, and I open it wide, unprepared for...

Her.

A little girl with red Mary-Janes kicks her feet as she sits on a wooden chair, staring at a globe of pure moonstone. Her dark hair ripples when she looks over her shoulder, her violet eyes shining with power.

"Mommy?" she says, her mouth widening into a smile I see in my dreams.

I brace my hand on the doorframe, my other still clutching Marianna's arm. Skye turns her gaze to me.

The last time I saw her, she was a newborn. Had just taken her first breath.

She looks like Marianna. A spitting image. As if just seeing her again isn't enough to absolutely shred me to fragments from the inside out, she has to look like Marianna, as well.

"No," I snarl, tearing my eyes from my daughter to look at the trio of mystics standing behind the table. "No. She's too young. Get out. We're done here."

The mystics glance at each other, none of them moving.

"I said *no*," I repeat so firmly I can taste the bitter cold ice on my tongue. I feel Marianna stiffening and sense Skye's eyes scanning my face. "Do not approach this child or her mother again. She is not an acolyte and will never be one. She is too young. Go away."

"Dame Calliope tasked us with her evaluation. She is gifted. She is powerful," they say in unison.

Marianna trembles. I can taste her fear like copper on my tongue, thawing the ice. It coats my mouth, and my dread turns to fury.

But Skye is totally unaffected, blinking at me with a slightly curious, but closed, expression.

"If I find out," I continue, my voice as cold and hard as steel, "that they've been bothered again, I will take action. Do not approach this child. She is too young for this. You have been warned and will not be warned again. *Out.*"

The center of the trio turns and walks out of the room through a side door, taking the globe with her, her sisters following with silent, unnerving steps.

Skye watches them go, her expression neutral. Maybe even a little bored.

Marianna takes an audible breath, and I realize with a start my hand is no longer on her arm.

Our fingers are now intertwined, and she's squeezing my hand.

Chapter 6

Seven Years

MARIANNA

I don't realize I'm gripping Blake's hand until his fingers loosen and fall away from mine. I tuck my hands behind my back, taking a deep breath to rein myself in while he stuffs his hands in his pockets– a very uncharacteristic motion that I notice, like he's nervous.

But of course he is.

He hasn't seen Skye since the day she was born, and I feel... awful about that now that I can see his face as he looks at her, seven years later, cautiously taking her in.

And Skye is looking right at him. She slides off the chair, her hands resting at her sides. She chose her outfit today. Denim overalls, a black shirt, her hair loose and falling down her back. The only pop of color she wanted was her shoes, which were a birthday present from her grammy in hopes Skye would start liking color again.

Skye inspects Blake from head to toe while I hold my breath for both of them.

I know Blake. I used to, at least. Maybe he's changed in the seven years we've been apart, but what hasn't is that immovable social anxiety that I can taste. Skye peers up at him, looking him right in the eyes–eyes exactly like hers.

Blake doesn't like new people. He's not a social butterfly by any means. Conversation is hard for him. He's a listener, not a talker. And if he does speak, it's guarded.

It took him years to open up to me. To joke with me, and when he did, he was so funny. So kind and charming.

But otherwise, he's emotionless. A void in a room full of people who are normal, I suppose, and able to just say something, anything, in the moment.

I look down at my daughter and finally understand some of her social quirks as well. She's just *his* daughter. That's all.

I pinch my jaw to try to relax the strain from gritting my teeth. Skye turns to look at me, noticing I'm not relaxed in the slightest.

Blake turns toward me, whispering under his breath, "We need to talk."

"I know," I reply, closing my eyes against the sensation of his breath lacing through my hair, tickling the top of my ear.

"Mommy," Skye says, her hand sliding into mine. "Can I have a coin to toss into the fountain?"

"I don't think it's that kind of fountain, honey–"

Blake turns back to us, removing his wallet from his back pocket, and cracks it open. Skye's eyes light with the promise of what ends up being every loose coin in the center zipper pocket, which he deposits into her waiting hand.

Skye immediately squeezes between us and tears into the hallway. I follow, breathless, about to call out to her to come back and say thank you, but she's gone.

"She can't get into trouble here. She's fine. They won't whisk her away again." Blake's voice is completely, utterly monotone–unaffected–but his eyes betray his true feelings as he strains to hear her receding footfalls.

He turns into the corridor, walking briskly, his eyes honed on

Skye while she skips ahead of him. I have to jog to follow his long strides, but when we reach the mouth of the foyer, and sunlight illuminates the wide, marble space, he stops, his shoulders relaxing just a touch.

I swallow my pride because I have to. This defensiveness, this choking feeling about Skye, and what's best for her... I have to set it aside for a moment.

Because I'm... terrified of how much I need him right now.

We watch Skye toss a penny into the fountain, leaning her body over the edge to watch it spiral toward the bottom of the crystal pool.

"When did this start? The summoning?" Blake asks, his eyes holding on Skye like he's in a trance.

I scan his profile, drinking in his new details. I hadn't gotten a good look at him at the concert, admittedly, because seeing him there, just feet away, had been a total shock to my system.

But here, in the sunlight, he's just as handsome as he was when we were younger and less burdened. Now, that youthfulness has bled into a hard, icy kind of attractiveness. A promise of violence, I suspect, that lingers in the muted dark circles under his hooded eyes. His cheeks are high and proud, and his nose is still perfectly straight and reminds me of those statues at the temple in Crescent Falls of the old warrior gods–high bridged and regal.

His jaw is sharper than it used to be and brushed with the beginnings of a dark, five o'clock shadow. His hair is still that dark brown tinged with a hint of wine red, at least in this light. In the shadows, his hair is nearly black.

He's grown a few inches, I think. He lost the roundness of youth, the baby fat, and is now lean and built, his shoulders broad. He flexes his hands, curling them into fists at his sides while he waits for my answer.

"About a year ago. I mean, she started changing a year ago."

His jaw tightens, but he doesn't look at me. He's still looking at her, and I give him space to do it, despite the tightening in my belly. I move to the other side of the archway and lean against a marble pillar, crossing my arms under my chest.

"The mystics," I continue, glancing at him, "began to appear a few months ago. I held them off for a while, and they respected that, but..." I close my eyes. "Blake, she's... she's struggling. She's been kicked out of three schools, and she just turned seven."

"I am aware of how old she is." His voice is cold. I guess I expected that, the ice in his tone. This was my decision, after all, keeping them apart.

I swallow past the knot in my throat. "I received another summons yesterday evening, and it said to come here in the morning. I thought I'd be talking to someone in charge, but they just... took her, and I didn't know what to do."

"I am in charge here," he says and looks at me for longer than a few seconds. He really looks at me, and I feel a blush, as well as a rush of guilt, spiral into damning heat when his violet eyes trace new lines, new divots and curves that weren't there before. He looks away, first down at his polished loafers, then slowly at Skye, who's now dangling her little fingers in the cool water, a pile of coins waiting for her wishes on the moonstone wall of the fountain beside her. "You shouldn't have come all this way for this. She won't be an acolyte. I won't let them separate you from her. You have my word."

"Is that what they would have done?"

"Yes," he says, and his chest relaxes like he's been holding his breath and finally let it go. "You shouldn't be here, Marianna. If they contact you again, let our mediator know, and I'll handle it. The mystics have no business in Crescent Falls–"

"I live here now, Blake." The words fall out of me before I can stop them. I wince when he looks in my direction. "I accepted a job that brought us here. With the philharmonic. It–it made sense to me to come. She's–she wasn't fitting in anymore." He bristles. I resist the urge to look away from him as I continue with quiet heartbreak, "I had to come here. I had to at least give it a shot, for her."

He closes his eyes and inhales before letting go of the breath. "Marianna–"

I lick my lips, cutting him off. "She has a hard time making friends. School has been damn near impossible for her. She can't handle it. She's so smart. She's–she's exactly like you when it comes to academics. She's years ahead of where she should be, and I think some of the administrators and parents saw that as a threat, but she's also hard to explain. I don't know how to explain it–"

"She's not a mystic," he says like he's trying to force himself to believe it. I think we both know that's not the case.

"No–yes–maybe that's what it is, but Blake, she's exactly like *you.*"

He looks at me, just the slightest movement of his eyes.

I lean away from the wall. "She's quiet now. I've been losing her for years. She's stuck in the stars. I didn't know how else to help her, but coming here felt like the right choice."

He looks like he's on the verge of showing a glimpse of emotion I'm not sure I'm ready to see.

"How long have you been here?"

"A few days. We're... we don't even have our furniture here yet. The movers are supposed to come tomorrow."

"I don't think it's wise that you stay."

"Blake," I grind out, "you don't get to make that decision for us. I have an interview with the Magical Arts Academy–"

"She is not a witch, Marianna."

"No, she's not, but–"

"Did he come with you?"

Now, I'm the one bristling. I glance at him, quickly looking away and settling my gaze on Skye instead as she lays out every coin he gave her, internally debating which coin she's going to toss next. "No."

He chews his lower lip, his body rigid. I know he saw the bruise. I could hear it in his voice when he asked if *he* did that to me. He never met Dean. Not once. I don't think I would have allowed it. I think if

Dean knew about Blake, things would have been far worse for me, honestly.

"He never touched her, if that's what you want to know. I... it was just me. He only ever touched me."

"He hurt you." There's a slice of pain in his voice.

"It's over. There's nothing else to say about it, but if you're going to give me a hard time about moving here, just know that I took Dean's proximity into account and decided to get as far away from him as possible." I exhale sharply, my nails digging into my skin as I continue to hug myself. "I was offered first chair, Blake. I wasn't going to give that up to keep her in Crescent Falls for you–"

"I don't live in Crescent Falls anymore," he says under his breath, his eyes locked on mine. "I live here, Marianna. I have for almost a year."

I didn't know that. I swallow, hating this ice between us, but I'm the one who put it there, aren't I? I had my reasons at the time. Good, solid reasons.

"She'll be around people like her. People who are different, who have different skills. People with magic–" I cut myself off, deciding I'm talking in a perfect circle, trying to convince myself more than him that I made the right decision.

"She doesn't have magic. It's something else entirely."

"Why are you acting like this is my fault for some reason? I'm trying to do what's best for her."

Blake holds my gaze, and I realize I never forgot how this feels. He doesn't just *look* at people. He looks inward, sees everything, feels it like it's his own emotions. It's a tangled net he can't break free of, but for some reason, he's always looked at me, held my gaze, held my fucking hand if I needed it, like I needed so badly just a few minutes ago. It's unnerving sometimes, but other times it's... amazing. It was amazing, at least, until I found out why he was doing it.

He finally looks away and leans against the wall, his normally steely posture slumping into something casual but not quite relaxed, like he's given up. "I'll ensure she gets into the academy."

"She can get in on her own."

"They don't accept mystics. But they'll accept her. I'll see to it myself. Where do you live?" His voice is still cold, still stern and somewhat steely.

"Wisteria Way," I say under my breath, feeling both hot and cold as I measure the space between us. Seven years. Seven long years without a word in person until the concert. Seven years without seeing his face. Now, look at where I am.

He licks his lips, nodding. "That's a safe neighborhood. That was a good decision."

"It was an expensive one, but I agree."

"You have access to my money anytime you need it."

"I know. I haven't–I haven't needed it." We look at each other, and I can finally see the way seven years of separation has festered between us. We're both walking on eggshells with every word we say.

"It was all I could offer you, and you never touched it," he says in a near whisper, and it's clear he's offended.

"I'm saving it for her. I figured you'd–you'd move on, have more kids, you know. She could go to college a hundred times over with those funds as it stands."

"I have no desire to move on," he says but then corrects himself quickly, "I have no desire to be mated or married, I mean."

"Yeah," I say, and it takes an incredible effort to add, "I see that hasn't changed, then."

And there it is, that knife wedged between us that's been cutting us to pieces since we parted ways.

He takes a breath, and after a beat, asks, "What do you think she's wishing for?"

"Cream soda," I say without hesitation, and the ghost of a smile tugs on his mouth.

My stomach hollows out and fills with guilt. "Blake... she doesn't know yet. About you."

"She doesn't have to know," he says, resigned, and adds, "Do not come back here without me, please. This place isn't safe for someone like her."

"Is it safe for you? You said you were in charge here."

"No," he answers, and meets my eyes for the first time in several minutes before bowing his head and turning into the light, the glare cloaking him from view as he walks away.

Chapter 7

Fancy Meeting You Here

"I think the couch looks fine right there," Mom says, kicking an empty moving box into a growing pile of dinged up cardboard. "But an armchair would be nice, don't you think?"

"One of those big, fluffy monstrosities?" I laugh, arranging framed photos on the mantle, my fingers gliding over an image of me, Skye, and my mom a few months after my daughter was born.

"I'd love something cozy to sit in while you're at work and I'm watching Skye do her homework. I'll start the hunt for one. I was just talking to our neighbor about a flea market held during the upcoming mating festival. I bet I'll find something there." She giggles, but her voice fades when she turns back into the kitchen to continue unpacking.

Skye is asleep upstairs, long tucked in for the night. Moonlight beams through the bare windows. I haven't put up the curtains yet. It's a beautiful, warm night with a soft, only slightly chilly breeze coming off the mountains. The moonlight calls to me, beckoning.

"Hey, Mom?" I round the corner into the kitchen. "I'm going to go out for a run. I'll be back in like... two hours. I want to explore a bit. There're tons of wolf trails all over the place here."

"I think you could use it. I won't wait up for you, but I put the spare key under the purple flowerpot on the porch."

I feel the shift before I've even walked back downstairs, now wearing just a robe to cover my bare skin. The early spring air might be unseasonably warm, but as my wolf powers submit to the moonlight, I can smell a hint of snow and ice coming in with the mountain breeze.

I shift in the front yard, leaving my robe in a heap on the steps, and zoom through the quiet streets near Wisteria Way. I'm not the only one shifting tonight. I pass a few neighbors in their wolf forms and the guards at the gate don't pay me any mind as I follow no set trail, no direction, and weave through the narrow cobblestone alleys of the inner city before reaching a bridge toward an older part of town.

The forest blooms ahead of me. I take a well-laid trail, picking up my pace until I'm panting, nearly out of breath. The trail splits into tighter wolf trails that weave through the woods, but I continue going up into the mountains until I lose the trail altogether, and it's just me and the breeze through my thick, black fur.

I'm about as average as a wolf can get. I'm not a trained warrior. I've never been hunting and don't have any skills when it comes to wolf-on-wolf combat.

But I like being out here in nothing but my fur, the moonlight guiding me until the forest thins, and the ground becomes soft grass and boulders.

In the shadow of a cliff, a large mountain pool of crystal clear water reflects the moonlight. The humidity in Moonrise is insane, even in the earliest days of spring. Back in Crescent Falls, this time of year? Goddess, it would still be freezing even as the winter grass fades into shades of bright green and soft yellow. I've heard Eastonia has hotter summers and more mild winters than Crescent Falls, too, which I'm looking forward to *immensely.*

But right now, I'm hot. My fur feels too thick for the warmth bleeding through the air. The breeze is below me now, not even touching the clearing and the perfectly calm water. It's... perfect.

I shift back into my human form, glancing around to make sure I'm alone, and then dive in. The water is still pretty cold, and I gasp as I resurface, then blow out a breath, smoothing my wet hair away from my face. My skin tingles as the heat in my body reacts to the sudden burst of chill, but the water feels amazing, smooth and silky against my naked skin. I swim into the shadow of the cliff and find a few large rocks resting below the surface of the water where I perch.

I lean my head against the rocks behind me, listening to the snow melt trickling down the cliff and into the pool, and watch the moonlight drift over the center of the alpine lake. It's not very deep, but deep enough my toes don't scrape the bottom unless I'm totally submerged.

My mind wanders over the day I had. The temple, the mystics, seeing Blake.

The thought of him curls through me, painful, but warm. It was like ripping off a bandaid, I suppose, but the wound beneath isn't close to being healed.

Blake broke up with me. That's the truth of it. He shattered my heart into pieces a few days before my eighteenth birthday. Then, two months later, I found out I was pregnant, and... I refused to tell him. My mom was the one who relayed the news.

So much happened between our breakup and her birth. So much that... wrecked me, and him, beyond repair. We were so young. So stupidly in love.

And when I found out about his powers?

I was scared of him, to be honest.

I think I still am, and it's why... it's why seeing Skye suffer is opening those old wounds again.

I don't know how to help her.

I didn't know how to help him.

I slip back into the water, sinking until it's up to my chin, but then movement catches my eye in the shadows, and another wolf approaches the pool. I slip back, silent, praying I'm shielded by the darkness as the dark wolf sniffs the water and jumps in.

Fuck. What do I do now?

A man appears, gasping just like I had as he breaches the surface, his dark hair glued to his head. His back is to me, but the water only touches his shoulders as he stands, swiping his hair back, murmuring a curse about the cold temperature under his breath, and his voice is...

I yelp in surprise, choking on the sound.

Blake slowly turns to face me, his eyes lit from within as he peers into the shadows.

"What are you doing here?" he asks.

"That's the fourth time in twelve hours you've asked me that question," I bite out, shivering but not from the cold.

He looks down his nose at me. "Technically, it's the second," he corrects. "And this place is on property owned by the royal family."

"I didn't know. I lost the trail."

He scans my face. I take a risk and step back into the moonlight. I doubt it's light enough that he can see the outline of my body beneath the surface of the water, but still. We're both naked. Totally, completely exposed to each other. It's ironic in a way.

He moves closer, stopping a few feet away. I can't move any closer to him, however. If I do, I'll fall into the deep end where he can clearly touch the bottom without an issue, but not me.

I feel my skin heating under his gaze despite the chill of the water lapping my breasts, the surface gliding just below my collarbones.

After several moments of appraising silence, he says quietly, "You're welcome to come here when you shift. I didn't mean–I didn't mean it wasn't allowed."

"I'm not royal, so it *isn't* allowed," I argue, surprising myself with the teasing glint in my tone.

He catches it, and the corner of his mouth ticks upward before falling flat just as quickly as it began.

I used to be able to get under his skin. It was my favorite thing to do when we were young, and he was still trying his hardest to get me to grasp any kind of mathematical concept. I'd bug him, pester him until he finally had enough, and that expression of indifference cracked, showing me who he really was.

But he's different now. More relaxed. Maybe it's his age. Maybe it's being in Eastonia.

Maybe it's me.

He drags his tongue along his lower lip before biting it–a motion I catch and shiver with the consequences. "Today was unexpected. I apologize if I was stern with you."

"You met your daughter today. I wouldn't have expected anything less."

"It wasn't Skye," he cuts in, slightly breathless. "Marianna, I haven't seen you in seven years other than briefly at the concert. You caught me off guard. I didn't know how to react. I still don't."

"I don't expect anything from you, just so you know. Skye doesn't know–"

"You've told me that already." There's the softest hint of pain in his voice, and it rakes through me, festering with guilt.

"I just... she hasn't asked. It's just me, my mom, and her. She hasn't asked about a dad... yet. And when she does, if she's old enough to understand, I have a plan."

"What is it?"

I honestly can't tell by his tone if he's even interested or not. His expression is guarded, but his eyes are withdrawn, hooded, and dark.

"The truth," I whisper with a shrug of my shoulder. "That me and... her dad couldn't be together."

He moves closer. I don't move back.

"I'd tell her," I continue, my voice wobbling as his proximity invades my space, "that it was a decision we made. It was a good thing. No one–no one got their heart broken."

"That's not even remotely close to the truth," he says in a near whisper.

I hold his gaze, forgetting how to breathe. There's barely a foot of space between us now. I can feel his warmth. I could easily reach out and touch his chest, run my fingertips over the smooth, taut muscle of his pecs, his shoulders.

The moonlight is overwhelming, reaching a peak, illuminating us in a soft, silver glow.

Maybe it's the moonlight. Maybe it's my tired, calm brain after running in my wolf form, my thoughts finally untangled, but I ask, "Do you want to know her, Blake?"

Whatever haze there was between us fades, and the chill creeps in again, but he doesn't move away. His face turns serious, shadowed, when he asks, "Is that wise?"

"I don't know. I have no idea. But she's yours as much as she's mine–"

"That isn't true, Anna."

Anna. The nickname funnels through me, turning me inside out. It leaves his lips in a whisper, a tone I remember so clearly even though years have passed since he last tangled his fingers in my hair, his body bent against mine in the too-snug backseat of his car, the windows fogged as he whispered my name, and...

"I'm a stranger to her. You've raised her on your own."

"You're her father, and you're here, in the same place as us–"

"I was in the same place as you for years–"

"We never ran into each other in Crescent Falls," I argue over the top of him. "Things were different there. You're the prince, and we never... we could never have crossed paths without guards or people taking pictures of you..." I feel my toes sliding off the rock keeping my head above the surface as I lean forward. "But we've run into each other twice *today*. If you're here, and I'm here, it's bound to keep happening."

He scans my face, trying to read my expression, trying to make sense of it. It brings back more memories of getting to know him, of those early days on the couch with math textbooks between us.

"I'd be okay with it. If you want to spend some time with her, I think it'd be good for her to be with someone like her."

He moves away, and I know I've crossed a line. The moonlit spell breaks, and my toes slide off the rock. I submerge before I can stop myself, and then his hands are clutching my waist, hauling me out of the cool water and back into the shadows.

I blink past the droplets hanging from my eyelashes, reaching up to smooth my hand over the planes of my face to wipe the water away, but his hands... remain. Just for a moment. Long enough for us to lock eyes while his thumbs rest against my hipbones.

He releases me and takes several steps away, turning into the moonlight, giving me his back.

"Blake–"

"We need to talk about this in a different way. A different place," he says low in his throat. His voice is tight, almost pained as he asks, "Can you come to the castle? I have an office there."

"I didn't–if you're not comfortable with this, with us–me and Skye–"

"No," he says firmly, shaking his head, looking at me over his shoulder. "That's not what this is. I'm not saying I don't–that I'm not accepting what you just offered, but we've had a contract in place for seven years. The terms are–"

"Well laid out. I know. You made everything perfectly clear when it was written." There's ice in my tone. He hears it, knows exactly what it means.

He grits his teeth, frustrated. "I can't talk to you about renegotiating those terms while you're naked," he says with force, like he's on the verge of losing control.

I shouldn't want him to, should I?

"My office would be more appropriate. We need to discuss the idea of her attending the academy, anyway."

"I'll think about it." I let the distance sink between us, growing heavy as he turns to face me again. I pushed him away once. I had good reasons to. I told myself it was for the best, that I could do this on my own. That I wasn't just punishing him for breaking my heart to pieces and… stomping it into dust.

"I'll make sure you're allowed entrance to the castle grounds. I'll be there when, and if, you're ready to talk."

I close my eyes and turn away when he pulls himself out of the water and shifts then stalks through the forest until he's out of sight, and the water becomes so cold it's unbearable.

Chapter 8

Just Walk Away

Blake

A maid sets a breakfast tray on the table in the corner of my office before bowing her head and scurrying out. Steam wafts from a carafe while the scent of coffee fills the room, and I rise, tucking my phone between my cheek and shoulder.

"It's just something I'm considering, Liam."

My brother sighs under his breath, his voice slightly filled with static when the connection buffers. "You're serious? Why would you walk away from–"

"I wouldn't be walking away from anything." I pour myself a cup of coffee, ignoring the breakfast spread I rarely ever touch. I normally don't eat until midday, but the kitchen begs to differ and keeps sending it anyway.

"You'd be abdicating, Blake. I mean, have you seriously thought this through?"

"That's why I'm telling you about it. I have, thoroughly."

"Do Mom and Dad know?"

"I haven't broached the subject yet, but I'm sure they assume something is going on based on how often I'm in Eastonia."

"You're there full time," he says, echoing a silent sentiment. Our parents know this is coming. They have to know by now.

"This would mean you would be Dad's heir going forward. You and Charlotte would be Alpha King and Luna Queen of Crescent Falls."

He pauses at the mention of Charlotte, his mate. Liam is only a year younger than me, born just after my first birthday. He and Charlotte met at Wellington a few years ago, and the bond just clicked. It was easy. Simple and uncomplicated. Maeve and Brie joked that he might've broken the family curse because neither of them got seriously injured or died, got kidnapped by an enemy, or started a war.

"Charlotte would be good at it," I tell him.

"I know she would, but it's something we'd need to talk about."

"You have time. It's not like Mom and Dad are my next call, nor am I going to tell them today." I lean against the wall near the window, sipping my coffee while scanning the forest and the neighborhood tucked next to the tall stone wall surrounding the castle grounds. Wisteria Way is my view from the office, of course. *Of course, it is.* The Goddess loves these games, doesn't She?

"What exactly would you be?"

"What do you mean?"

"When you abdicate? What's your title in Eastonia in Maeve's court?"

"I'm her royal advisor as it stands. I serve as a second when she's unable to do her duties, like now, while she's on maternity leave." I bring my coffee to my lips, wondering which pretty little townhouse Marianna chose.

"What about with the mystics? Don't they consider you their king?"

"I don't know if that counts for anything."

His soft laugh echoes down the line. "Mom thinks so. She says they call you *High Lord.*"

"They do." I sigh, turning from the window when the door opens without a warning knock, and Maeve strides in like she owns the place, making a beeline with a glare toward the chair she tried to steal from my office a few weeks ago. "Think about it. Call me in a few days after you talk to Charlotte."

"I will."

I hang up without another word and turn to my cousin, now seated behind my desk, Fallon resting in her arms as she swivels from side to side. "Can I help you?"

Maeve says nothing but arches a dark, manicured brow. She's dressed in a men's button-down shirt and gray sweatpants and looks very undone, but I'm used to that, I guess. She's always been surprisingly casual. She leans back in my chair and crosses her ankles on my desk, wiggling her bare toes.

My jaw tenses. Through gritted teeth, I ask, "Is Soren busy, and you're here in hopes of harassing someone else instead of spending your day pestering your mate?"

"I don't pester him," she says with a soft laugh. "But... I may have heard some juicy gossip from the High Priestess, however. She mentioned the High Lord of the Mystics got into a screaming match with three acolytes four days ago. Care to elaborate on what it was about?"

"No."

She levels a look in my direction. "*Blake*. What happened?"

"It's nothing, really. I objected to their evaluating a seven-year-old girl who may have seer abilities. She was too young to be an acolyte, and I put an end to it before they separated her forever from her mother."

Maeve purses her lips and looks down at Fallon, who's blissfully sleeping. After a moment, she says, "I've never liked the way they go about their training. I don't pretend to know the details... but...." Her eyes meet mine, searching. Scanning. Trying to look past my mental shields and see my memories of the time I spent there, a boy of fourteen.

"I've already begun the process of changing things, setting an age minimum for new acolytes.

Acolytes will have to be sixteen, at least."

"Do you think that's wise given some come into their powers far earlier than that? You did."

"I'm not like the other mystics. Someone of my caliber of power would be so rare, it's practically impossible."

"Unless they belonged to you. Your kids," she says pointedly, obviously digging. I'm aware that Soren scoped her out, and she didn't believe my situation could even be remotely possible, which is in my favor. Still, she's prodding a bit. I can sense it. So, I give her what she wants to hear.

I roll my lower lip between my teeth. "Precisely."

"Well, given that you seem keen on rotting in this office your entire life, and your progeny is destined to never happen, I guess I agree on the age minimum."

"Everyone under the age of sixteen will be admitted into a program at the academy."

Her brows raise practically to her hairline. "What? You really think you can convince those gnarled old witches who sit on the academy's board to let mystic children in? You know how witches feel about the mystics."

"Maeve, I have more money than the Moon Goddess," I say on a breath. "They won't need convincing when I give them a check for their troubles."

"You filthy dog." She laughs, not meaning it, I think. "They should name the program after you."

"I hope not," I mumble, turning to pour another cup of coffee, which is unlike me, but it's been a... strange couple of days, to say the least. I haven't been sleeping much. "But I will be paying for a new addition, a new wing to the school. A practice orrery. Something simple and meant for young learners."

"That's kind of you." She rolls her eyes like she doesn't believe I'm capable of caring about anything. She's probably right. There's only two things I care about, and currently, I'm wondering what they're up to today.

"It would keep families together, and after what I witnessed..." That's all I can think about. Marianna's tears in that hallway, her panic and fear. "I was planning on running it by you when I had a solid plan."

"Well, color me surprised. I didn't realize you had such a soft spot for children, Blake."

I narrow my eyes at her, but her attention is on Fallon, whose golden curls poke out of the swaddling she's wrapped in. Fallon is beautiful. Everyone in the family agrees. Her eyes are already starting to show signs that she'll carry Maeve and Ella's bright sea-green shade. But I can tell Maeve is tired. I don't think Fallon is the easiest baby.

Which makes me think of Skye and her shiny red shoes when she'd lifted on her tiptoes to toss a coin into the fountain. She'd lined up the coins by size and color, meticulously deciding which one to throw next, like every coin had a wish attached in varying degrees of significance.

I would have done the exact same thing.

"And she agreed, which is amazing given the short timing."

"What did you say?" I zoned out, apparently, and claw back to the line of conversation I missed.

"Marianna Abbot," she says with a smile, shaking her head. "Your old girlfriend, or whatever she was. *Your secret.*" She flutters her eyelashes at me, teasing.

"What about her?" My hackles raise, but she doesn't seem to notice how tightly I'm gripping my coffee mug. The only person who knew about my relationship with Marianna, at least that I liked her... no, that I was desperately, stupidly *obsessed* with her, is Brie, and thankfully she's the best at keeping secrets.

"She took a position here in the philharmonic! I knew the board was hiring a new first chair, but I had no idea she was the one they were chasing. You know how much money we give to the arts–"

"I'm aware. What about her?"

"Don't get so defensive, weirdo," she grumbles, sliding her feet off my desk. "She's coming to the castle tonight to play for us, well, to play at the party we're hosting to celebrate Patton and Jane getting engaged."

I totally forgot about that. Not the engagement–that came fairly quickly after they found out they were mates, during the two weeks I was gone, but the party tonight. *Fuck.*

"It was so last minute, but I called the director of the symphony, and he said Marianna was in town, had just moved here, and offered to try to set it up. Brie keeps talking about how talented she is, but I've never even seen her, let alone heard her play–"

"And she accepted coming here?"

"Yeah, she did. I mean, I didn't speak to her directly–"

"She wasn't forced into it?"

"What is your problem?" Maeve guts out, scoffing.

"Nothing," I say into my coffee mug, but her eyes are honed on my face, trying to pick apart the mask of indifference I keep trained around her–around everyone.

"It's just a small gathering, Blake, if you're worried about it. I didn't think you still had feelings for her, or whatever–"

"I don't. We were friends. That was all."

She hums like she doesn't necessarily believe it, and that's fine with me. It's none of her fucking business.

"Anyway, I did want to tell you that I'm taking Soren to Veiled Valley for a week or so. I'm not sure how long yet. He's cooped up here. I think he could use some air without the risk of getting trampled by paparazzi, so you'll have the castle to yourself. We're leaving tomorrow morning so we don't miss the party. And when we return, I think I'm going to take meetings again... slowly. The most important ones, at least."

She rises, brushing past me on her way to the door. "You'll still come to the party tonight, won't you? Patton desperately wants to be your friend."

"Even after I scrambled his brain?"

She frowns at me. "You can't just stay in this office every waking hour, Blake."

"Why not?"

She holds my gaze for a few seconds before turning with a huff, leaving my office door wide open in her wake.

I sink into my chair and drum my fingers on the desk before reaching for my laptop. Sunlight plays over the dark wood surface, casting a glare on the screen. For whatever reason, I search Marianna's name for the first time, finally losing control enough to give myself a glimpse into, at least, her professional life.

And it's... damning, to say the least.

She never went to Wellington, which was her dream, a dream I offered to pay for in full. She got a degree in music from the Crescent Falls College of the Arts, not a bad school, but not Wellington. From there, she fell off the map for several years before showing up again in the Crescent Falls Philharmonic Orchestra, working her way from sixth to second chair over the course of two years.

An article from Crescent Falls dated only two weeks ago highlights her last performance and mentions her acceptance into the philharmonic in Moonrise. A video I hesitate to click on for several minutes plays her solo.

I quickly shut it off, rise, and close my office door, locking it tight before returning to my chair. I connect my headphones to my laptop and lean back before clicking the video again.

Her violin sounds like water–smooth and... at first, cold. The sound bleeds into heat that moves through my body in waves before washing through the incessant voices in my head, the pull toward the stars.

Her music takes up every space in my mind, just like before.

Chapter 9

Space to Breathe

BLAKE

It's not a small gathering of people like Maeve said it would be. I should have known that this party would be a writhing mess of voices and lifted conversation bouncing from wall to wall in the formal ballroom, a space the size of a small city that puts the grand hall in the castle of Crescent Falls to shame.

It's well past 8:00. I sip a second glass of scotch, lingering along the far wall. Maeve invited her parents and several friends from Veiled Valley. Patton has a large group of friends in Moonrise, which surprises me even though I can't say I know the man very well at all yet. And, on top of a few high-ranking wolves and their partners, their mates, a large majority of the staff is here to celebrate one of their own—Jane—everyone dressed immaculately and enjoying the castle as guests instead of the people who keep it running like a well-oiled machine.

The most surprising guest is Uncle Ryan. I watch him move through the crowd toward my perch along the wall, nodding and flashing that charming smile at everyone who turns in his direction, but his eyes dart to mine, and he gives me a tight nod that silently commands me to stay where I am.

I bring my drink to my lips and sip when he reaches my side with a sigh. "So, how'd it go in Crescent Falls? I haven't seen you since... you had your brain scrambled."

I keep my eyes locked on the musicians playing mediocre string music on the platform at the opposite end of the ballroom. Marianna isn't here. Not yet, at least. I couldn't bring myself to ask Maeve what time she was supposed to show up, and I'm secretly hoping she doesn't.

"It was fine, like usual."

Ryan chuckles, "I know you're a grown man now, Blake, but you need to remember who my twin brother is. You scared the hell out of your dad."

"He's also a grown man," I reply, draining the rest of my drink. "I didn't go there to be coddled. I was there against my will. A prisoner. Cosette even came out of retirement to sit at my bedside and fussed over me for two entire weeks."

He smirks. "Gods, I love Cosette. How old is she now? Eighty?"

"Around there, I think." I glance at him over the hum of conversation. "Why are you here?"

"Am I not allowed to come visit?"

I narrow my eyes, and he rolls his back to the crowd.

"I brought Nora here for the weekend. She likes the art district, didn't stop talking about it all winter, and she's going to Veiled Valley with your parents after this for a few weeks to paint with Ella."

Another man edges through the crowd but doesn't smile or converse with anyone. Soren's expression is stern and slightly annoyed as he wades toward us, doing his best, I think, not to scowl when he tries to roll his shoulders in the fitted tux I'm sure Maeve forced him to wear tonight.

His expression lightens, however, when he sees Ryan but grows cold again when he sees me standing beside him.

Soren curses something under his breath. He comes to stand on my other side. Ryan gets called away by Evander, and I grab a third glass of scotch from a passing waiter. Soren takes one as well, and for a few minutes, we watch the crowd.

"Are you going to marry Maeve?"

"Are you always this blunt?" Soren asks with a rough laugh into his scotch. "I've asked a few times, but she keeps telling me no."

"Really?"

He nods, but the corners of his mouth lift into what I think is a smile. I have no idea.

"She doesn't think it's all that important, and to be honest, I agree. We have everything else. I love her. She loves me, for some reason. She's my mate, and we have a daughter. That's enough."

I shift my weight as the musicians silence their instruments, which were my only distraction from the noise of the partygoers. Now, their voices tangle with the voices constantly humming inside my head, showing me tethers to the tapestry of our world no one else can see.

"I think Kenna and Evander would prefer if you did marry."

"I think both are somewhat afraid of their own daughter and won't push the subject, even if I asked." He lifts his drink to his lips but doesn't sip. "And I have asked, just so you know. Evander gave me his blessing after a long conversation about whether this is actually what I want. Her–and her attitude."

I catch the amusement in his voice as he tips his drink back.

A soft hum of excitement drifts through the room as side doors open just out of sight. Claps ring out, followed by hushed murmurs. Someone cuts through the crowd...

"Shit," I hiss under my breath but not silent enough, apparently, because I feel Soren boring holes into the side of my face with his gaze. Marianna ascends onto the platform, gripping her violin.

Her shoulder length dark hair is pinned away from her face in a neat half up, half down style that shows off the curve of her glorious cheekbones and stunningly bright blue eyes. Her body is draped in a black gown that hugs curves I don't remember. Her fullness is... I'd felt it in the pool, of course, four days ago. Held her for a single moment and felt her heat, her skin.

I drain my third drink, letting the buzz I've been nursing for over an hour take on new life.

"Marianna Abbot, the new first chair of the strings section at our beloved philharmonic, is blessing us with a solo performance tonight," says the man who's been playing the cello all evening. He smiles at her. She gives the crowd a tight, slightly nervous, smile, her cheeks going even rosier under her soft makeup.

The rest of his praise is drowned out by the voices in my head—voices reminding me of her shortened tether to this world, her eclipsed string in the tapestry.

But I can't look away when she raises her violin and her bow, and the first notes ring out over the hushed crowd.

It's a joyous song—something sharp and lifted that captures the attention of the audience immediately. The music vibrates through the ballroom. The song dips into a flowing, almost gentle, melody that wraps its talons around my skull and sinks deep, quieting the voices and images I've spent the majority of life trying to silence.

In a grand, dramatic finale, she pulls her bow across the strings and the crowd erupts in applause, but I'm... transfixed.

The first time I'd heard her play was nine years ago, I think. I'd been in Eastonia, in Veiled Valley, spending a long weekend with Brie and her family to celebrate Aris completing what Ryatt and his late father called the Summoning, an ancient Shadowsynger ritual. That night, I felt off. Maybe a little uneasy. Marianna kept popping into my mind and wouldn't stop. Sure, I thought about her all the Goddess damned time back then. I had the biggest, most relentless crush on her that I didn't know how to act on, but that feeling was... different. I felt it in my chest, my entire body screaming to get to her, like something was wrong.

So I did just that and jumped back to Crescent Falls, which at my age back then took a serious amount of power I didn't necessarily have yet, and I found myself in front of a music store in the pouring rain.

She was in a practice room. I panicked, searching her shocked expression for any sign of harm, but she'd been fine.

She told me to sit down and played for me for the first time. I knew she liked music. I knew she could play the violin and had dreams of attending Wellington's prestigious music program, but I didn't really think about what her violin would sound like until I sat on that stool and... lost my mind.

And it felt amazing.

Another song starts while I wade out of my memories and back to the present.

"That's her, then?" Soren asks.

I glance at him, but his eyes are on the performance. "Yeah."

"What did you do, Blake?" he asks with a wry smile, his eyes meeting mine. "To fuck *that* up?"

I set my empty glass on a side table full of hot-house roses and leave the party, skirting around the back of the crowd gathered in the center of the ballroom to watch Marianna play. My heart pounds as the music fades, and the ballroom bleeds into a series of hallways, then the grand foyer, which is empty and so silent I can hear the blood rushing through my veins.

I sink onto the steps of the massive, branching staircase made of pure marble and hang my head, rubbing my temples.

I'm not sure how long I stay there in the quiet, but it's long enough for the clicking of heels to move toward me.

I straighten as soft voices drift in my direction. The musicians move through the foyer toward the door, led by a couple of royal guards. Marianna walks in step with the cellist, her mouth pulled into a tight smile that fades when her eyes slide to the side, finding me sitting on the stairs alone, like an idiot.

She murmurs something to the musicians and walks in my direction. I straighten further, stretching out my legs to look a little more casual than I feel about her approaching me right now, but she seems to pick up on that, her brows pinching together as she balances her violin case against her hip.

She doesn't say a word until the guards escort the other musicians outside, and the foyer descends into quiet again, the soft hum of music coming from the ballroom now more modern, recorded songs.

"Did you not like it?" she asks.

"What didn't I like?"

"The music I played. Was there something wrong with the songs I chose?"

"They weren't yours. You didn't write them. Your own compositions are so much better."

She frowns, swinging her case for a moment before sinking onto the step beside me. Beyond the crystalline windows stretching nearly seven stories to the domed ceiling, rain pelts Moonrise. I'm sure that outside of the thick, impenetrable walls, thunder is roaring through the valley.

"So this is where you live," she says almost to herself, glancing around at the shadows, the golden walls and marble details.

"Part time."

"What does that even mean, Blake? What are you doing here in Eastonia? You're the Royal Prince of Crescent Falls–"

"I'm abdicating."

Silence. The choking, heavy kind. It descends on us like a wet blanket.

"Why would you do that?"

I finally look at her–look down at her. She's sitting two steps below me, her gown fanning around her legs and the strappy black heels that complete the look. "I didn't feel like I belonged in Crescent Falls. I tried to, but my cousin convinced me otherwise, and now I serve in her court as her advisor."

"What about the firm?"

I let out my breath in a whoosh. I relax into the conversation like we're back on the couch again, in the shitty little basement apartment, and I hadn't fucked everything up yet. "They have other architects. I do some work there still, depending on the project, mostly as a consultant, but for now, Maeve needs me."

Another beat of sucking silence passes between us. I should... I don't know, say something. Tell her how wonderfully she played, how beautiful she looks.

"Why didn't you come to talk to me?" I ask without stopping myself. "After–after the lake–"

"Oh," she breathes, looking down at her lap. She opens her mouth to reply, but voices drift toward us, and I rise, extending my hand.

"I have an office upstairs. Do you have anywhere to be?"

"Home," she says with a light, unconvincing laugh. "Mom is with Skye. But, they're fine. Blake, we don't need to discuss this if it's not something you want–"

"Why would you think–"

Laughter echoes down one of the hallways in a warning that we're not alone anymore.

Chapter 10

Said Too Much

MARIANNA

I rise as Queen Maeve comes into view, holding the hand of the striking young man I'd noticed in the ballroom. It was hard not to notice him, honestly, with his multi-colored eyes and casual disposition, and it strikes me, quite suddenly, that this is her mate, the man the news can't stop talking about. Fretting about, more like it.

Blake rises, and I follow, my heart standing still as the Queen of Eastonia, dressed in a soft silver gown of lace that flows around her like water, turns the corner of the staircase and spots us with a start.

Blake narrows his eyes at her. The queen looks surprised to see him and then tilts her head in my direction for a moment before her head whips back to Blake with an expression I can only describe as... smug.

"Well, well, well," she grins. "Sneaking away from the party, Blake?"

"Speak for yourself," Blake says without a hint of emotion, even though I sure he meant to tease.

Queen Maeve turns to me as I step down from my perch, bow deeply, and open my mouth to thank her for inviting me here to play, but suddenly, she's in front of me, touching me, her hands gripping my own.

"You were *awesome*," she says, drawing out every syllable. "Brie's been talking about you for years, and I was so excited you were available to play tonight."

"Oh," I grit out as her heat funnels between our joined hands. I briefly look her in the eyes, and they're just as amazing as everyone says they are. A deep, vivid blueish green that I've never seen in the natural world. "Thank you, Your Majesty–"

"No, call me Maeve," she smiles, squeezing my hands until her mate clears his throat.

"Babe, are we going upstairs or..." He glances at Blake, lifting a brow. "Were you guys going upstairs?" There's a hint of something I can't decipher in his voice, an edge that forces tension between our little quartet.

Blake steps down to stand beside me. His hand brushes my lower back, but his fingers hover just above the low-cut fabric of my dress without touching me, but I can feel his heat, feel the way his fingers curl into a fist. "I haven't seen Marianna in a very long time and caught her as she was leaving for the night–"

"Oh, don't leave yet!" Maeve barks, giving me a stunning smile. "Please, stay! We have so much food and sparkling wine. The kitchen went a little nuts. They're about to bring out the punch, too!"

I glance at Blake, noticing the perplexed and entirely suspicious look behind his violet eyes, but then his gaze slides to mine.

"I–I can't stay, really, it–it wouldn't be appropriate," I stammer, raising my hands in surrender. "I was paid to play for you."

"And you've played," Maeve urges, her eyes wide and lit from within with... excitement. Her mate notices and furrows his brow, briefly looking in Blake's direction before rolling his shoulders and crossing his arms over his fitted tuxedo jacket. "Please? Oh, you have to, Marianna! Brie will be so jealous!"

"Oh–okay–"

Maeve beams and whirls to her mate, who sighs, extending his hand to her. They move back into the shadows toward the ballroom, where music drifts on a phantom wind, lacing the air with soft melodies that merge with the thundering rain just beyond the massive windows made of... crystal? I have no idea, but just standing here is overwhelming, and it's not because of Blake.

"I really don't have to stay," I tell him, swallowing past a knot of apprehension.

"I think you do," he replies, but he doesn't smile. His mouth is a tight line. He steps down, holding out his hand, and I take it, curling my fingers around his.

Despite the stern look on his face, he gives my hand the gentlest of squeezes and guides me back to the party.

His fingers don't leave mine, but his touch is light. We walk at a slower than necessary pace, like he's dragging out the few moments we have alone.

I'm correct about that theory, because in a shadowed alcove near a side entrance to the ballroom, he pauses and turns to me, pulling his fingers away from mine. "Maeve is being weird," he says quietly, his eyes on the crowd swaying to music and drinking to their heart's content. "She's not normally like this."

"Like what? She seems really nice. I met Brie once, remember? I can tell that they're sisters."

"Brie is actually adopted," he replies pointedly, which is news to me. I've never kept with the royal family, mostly because news of Blake could have been enough to send me over the edge into a dark, spiraling oblivion. "I doubt her affinity for kindness is nurture based. That's just who she is, but Maeve is tricky. I find it hard to trust her right now."

I can't help but laugh. "You're cousins. Of course you trust her–"

"Soren knows about you and Skye."

I blink up at him, furrowing my brows. "Who?"

"Maeve's mate."

"Oh–with the eyes?"

"Yes," he says in a whisper.

"But—are you friends with him?"

"No," he says quickly. "I don't—I don't have friends, especially not him."

"Well, I see that hasn't changed—"

"Marianna," he says, cutting me off as he closes the distance between us with a single step, "about a month ago, I was... in deep water, so to speak, as was he, and I said some things that I should have kept quiet. I know how you feel about Skye's safety and anonymity, and I want to keep it that way, for her sake *and* yours. If the press were to find out about her—about either of you? They'd have a field day. It would be chaos. You'd never have a normal life again."

Something twists deep in my stomach, a sharp pang of remembrance. A conversation we had just like this one but years ago, toward the middle of my pregnancy, when he showed up at my apartment, drenched, like he'd walked there through the rain.

"What happened?" I ask, banishing the memory of the absolutely gutting conversation we'd had almost eight years ago, praying those fragments fester and die for good.

"Nothing," he lies. He's never been good at lying.

"Blake—"

"We need to talk," he says, cutting me off, his fingers slipping back between mine. "Tonight, preferably, but Maeve isn't going to leave me alone about *you*, so I doubt that'll happen. Either way, this conversation needs to be had."

"Does she know we used to date?"

"Not to that extent. But she's scheming, and I don't like it."

"Do you want to... go to your office? It would be quieter there, I'm sure. Less listening ears?"

He considers the offer, his eyes searching mine and... holding, which is such an intense and unnerving feeling that quickly bleeds into... heat. A kind of intimacy I vividly remember and have... missed.

His eyes are exactly like Skye's, down to the silver star-like flakes around their irises, like the entire universe is just... there. Right within reach. A single blink away.

"No. Like I said, Maeve is entirely suspicious of me right now, and I have very strict rules about my space within the castle."

"You're saying I'm not allowed in your office?"

"*She's* not allowed in my office," he deadpans, but there's the smallest, teeniest glimmer of mirth in his eyes. "But she's never once respected that. She'll eavesdrop."

I look at the party again. The crowd is younger now that we've reached the late hours of the night. "So we don't talk about Skye right now," I tell him with a shrug.

"Not right now," he agrees.

"Then what do I do? Play–"

He takes my violin case and steps through a door directly to the side of us, tucking it just out of view. "Enjoy yourself. I think Maeve is jealous Brie got to meet you, and she never got a chance."

"Why would she be jealous? I'm a nobody!"

"You're not," he says low in his throat as he turns back to me. "You're tied to me, and she's curious. That's all. There's nothing nefarious about it other than new ammunition to use against me to get under my skin, which she has no problem doing."

I find myself smiling as our eyes meet in the shadowed haze of the alcove. Blake tucks his hands in his pockets and turns to the party, the distance between us growing so wide I quickly lose him to the crowd, leaving me on my own.

I don't know anyone here. Not a single soul other than Blake, who is now taking up residence near a drink table, leaning into what seems like a tense conversation with Soren, Maeve's mate.

Soren is looking directly at me, however. He gives me a tight smile, nodding his head in my direction, before turning to pour what looks like whiskey into a short, crystal glass.

"Thank the Goddess he left you alone for a second," Maeve says as she appears out of what feels like thin air. I nearly jump out of my skin, my hand flying over my heart.

Maeve is tall. The tallest woman I think I've ever seen. She exudes power, if that's possible. It falls from her, invisible to the naked eye, but I can feel it brushing over my skin like flakes of embers as she stands by my side, overlooking the party. She sighs heavily when she looks in Blake's direction and then chuckles, shaking her head. "Did you guys... date? Like boyfriend girlfriend date?"

"Us?" *What the hell do I say? What would he want me to say?*

"I just find it hard to believe Blake could talk to a woman without getting totally flustered."

"Oh, well, that is true–" I bite my tongue, my cheeks burning a bright, fiery red that's most definitely bleeding down my neck and flaring over the low-cut bodice of my gown.

"I knew it," she whispers, smiling to herself as she stares at Blake. "So, you were his girlfriend?"

"No," I rush out. Technically, it's the truth. We never had a conversation about that. What we had in those few weeks we were... taking our friendship to the next level... was brief and quickly turned strained. It wasn't that I didn't want to be his girlfriend or anything, but he... couldn't do it. "He tried tutoring me in math, actually. That's how we met."

I can feel her eyes scanning my profile but can't bring myself to look at her.

"Boring," she whispers to herself, and I fight the smile tugging at the corners of my mouth. "So, that's it, then? My sister made it sound like he was desperately head over heels in love with you."

That... absolutely crushes me.

"Mhmm," I manage to hum. "I mean, I don't know. He never said anything about it." He did. He did, in fact, tell me he loved me, but months too late.

Maeve grumbles something unintelligible over the music then straightens, clutches her breasts, of all things, and abruptly turns toward the archways lining one wall of the ballroom. "Shit, shit, shit–"

"Are you okay?"

"I'm fine." Her voice is strained as she peers into the darkened hallways leading off the ballroom into what I assume are the recesses of the palace. "I'm–our daughter is a month old, and I'm breastfeeding. I'm about to soak my gown, and it's lace from the Deadlands, impossible to replace."

"Oh, well, let's get you out of here–" I instinctually fist a stack of napkins from a side table as she hurries away. I follow, and I'm not entirely sure why, but she does look back to make sure I'm still within view before sliding through a side door and flipping on a light switch that brings a sitting room into startling focus.

I kick the door closed behind us. She sinks into a chair, accepting the napkins, which she promptly stuffs into her gown with a relieved sigh. "Thank you. I would have had to change, and it took me half an hour to get into this dress in the first place."

"It's fine. I've been there a time or two." I immediately regret opening my big, fat, stupid month.

Maeve's unnerving eyes meet mine. "You have?"

"I–I have a daughter." I shrug one shoulder, leaning against the door for support as my mind reels over what lies I can spin to get out of this and keep Blake safe. This is what he wanted. This is what he said needed to happen. His family couldn't know. Otherwise, the whole world would know about Skye, and... I agreed with him.

At least, back then. Back when I thought I could handle it all by myself.

"She's seven now, so I'm way past this." Another shrug. I tuck my hands behind my back, unsure what to do with them.

Maeve blinks up at me from the stool she just fell onto. "What's her name?"

Chapter 11

Do You Want To?

Marianna

I scrub my swollen, aching eyes with a groan as Mom clatters loudly in the kitchen a few feet away. It's barely 9:00 in the morning, but Leona Abbot has never slept in a day in her life and isn't going to start just because I'm nursing a hangover.

I don't even remember getting home last night. I don't really remember... anything.

"Tell me again, from the beginning," she says in what sounds like a near shout based on the way her voice ricochets through my throbbing brain.

"There's not much else to say." I groan, but the sharp smell of freshly brewed coffee yanks me back to my senses, and I open my eyes to Skye hovering in front of me, extending my favorite mug. "Thanks, baby."

"Skye, tell your mother to give me some details about her big night out with the QUEEN!"

I groan again, but Skye giggles and rocks on her heels, highly entertained by my predicament and her grammy's insistence to prolong my suffering.

"I made sure the queen didn't leak through her expensive gown, and in turn, she got me roaring drunk," I murmur around a sip of coffee. The caffeine leaches into my veins, thawing out some of the numbness. "I honestly don't remember the last... half of the night."

Skye, who has no idea what I'm talking about, continues to hover, not used to seeing me shriveled on the couch looking like death itself.

"Skye, sweetie, give these to your mother," Mom calls out from the kitchen, and within seconds Skye returns with two headache drafts clutched in her palm, and my journey to healing is well underway.

By the second cup of coffee, and after a mountain of bacon and eggs, I feel much better, but my head is still foggy when I step out onto the porch, gripping a third cup of coffee, to watch Skye inspect the ancient stone of the border wall around our front garden.

It's a cool, damp morning, which is... bliss. I wouldn't be able to handle the sun otherwise, not today, when my brain is leaking through my ears.

I don't remember a Goddess damned thing that happened after I returned to the ballroom with Maeve. Worse, I don't remember the conversation I had with Maeve in that little sitting room.

Dread fills my body, cutting through the last ribbons of hangover. I rarely drink. I wasn't part of the party scene as a teenager, and having a baby really limited my opportunities to do this in college.

The healing drafts start to fade, and my headache begins again with a promise of lingering all day, if not for the next few days.

"Gods, what did you do?" I grumble to myself, blinking into the gray haze of Wisteria Way.

Mom comes out onto the porch steps and sits beside me with a sigh, glancing in my direction. Her blue eyes scan my face, and I frown at her. "What?"

"I'm proud of you."

"For what?"

"Letting loose."

I roll my eyes back to Skye. "It was entirely unintentional."

"You deserved it, Anna. You've never been to a real party before–"

"It was a ball held in honor of an engagement for people I don't know, and I got drunk and have no idea whether or not I made a fool of myself in front of the royal family–"

A shadow passes our neighbor's gate. Skye straightens, standing on her toes to peer over the wall as...

Oh, great. Just... just great.

Mom rises, clutching the railing with one hand while she waves with the other.

Blake, dressed in slacks, a gray button-down shirt, smiles back at her, and... he's carrying my violin case.

I know what I look like. Hell. Hell frozen over, thawed out, and slapped into the microwave to further crisp while the insides become molten lava.

He pauses in front of our gate, his eyes on Skye as she peers up at him. I'm holding my breath, and beside me, my mother is, too.

Blake reaches into his pocket, withdrawing his wallet, and Skye is... holding out her hand. For coins. More coins, of course.

She beams at him before scurrying away like a little mouse with its hoard, disappearing into the backyard where she's been keeping a little pile of smooth, shiny rocks we found at the lake side yesterday– her treasure pile. The rest of the rocks she carried home are likely the cause of the incessantly painful rumbling coming from the washing machine.

Blake remains at the gate, his cheeks dusted a light pink in gray, overcast light. He meets Mom's gaze with an unsure, tight-lipped smile.

If I had the wherewithal to hold my breath, I would.

I take a sip of my coffee instead.

"Marianna left her violin at the castle," he says over a soft gust of chilly wind. My skin peppers with gooseflesh, and it's not from the cold. I didn't tell my mom I ran into Blake at the concert, or at the temple, and I sure as hell didn't mention he'd met Skye.

"Did you walk all the way here?" Mom asks, stepping toward the gate. "It's freezing!"

"It's not that long of a walk at all," Blake says, but his eyes remain on mine, scanning my face like he's trying to gauge how I feel about his intrusion into my private life.

"Come in, come in," Mom rushes out, opening the gate with a squeak that seems to echo against the clouds. The noise rips through my still faintly pounding head. "I just made another pot of coffee for Marianna."

"I'm sure you did," he says under his breath, his eyes meeting mine as he casually follows my mom into the house.

I stare after them, unsure of what I can do at this point. Mom's reaction to seeing Blake again after seven years isn't what I'd thought it'd be. Honestly, I hadn't given it much thought at all.

But Mom knows Blake. She has for a long time. They were both in the room when Skye came into the world.

Blake returns to the porch with a cup of coffee and sits beside me, grasping the steaming mug between his hands. I turn to the sound of Skye and my mom walking out from the backyard, my mom carrying her shopping basket and Skye skipping head with her coins jingling in her pockets.

"Bye!" Skye calls out.

"Bye, I guess," I say, narrowing my eyes at Mom as she shrugs, giving me a look, a little wiggle of her brows. I scowl, but she turns to follow Skye through the gate.

"So–"

"What was that about?"

"What?"

"Just–showing up here, my mom pouring you some coffee–"

"She offered–"

"She doesn't know you've met Skye–"

"I didn't realize you hadn't told her," he says before taking a light, exploratory sip of coffee. "When I brought you home a few hours ago, she was already awake, and we spoke for a few minutes."

"What?" My spine straightens as I stare at him.

"Your mom still wakes up at five like clockwork. I should have remembered," he says, taking a deeper sip from his mug. Then, he sighs. His eyes are on the gate, on the lilac bushes not yet in bloom on either side. "I think she was more surprised about seeing me with you slung over my shoulder than she was to find out I'd seen Skye."

"I was that drunk?"

"Yes," he says, meeting my eyes. He... doesn't look that well-off either. Dark circles line his hooded gaze, and his eyes are slightly bloodshot. "You were absolutely *housed*, Anna."

"I don't remember a Goddess damned thing," I grind out as my body flushes with embarrassment.

"I doubt anyone does. You weren't the only one, trust me. In fact, I bet no one made it out of that ballroom unscathed." He looks back at the gate. "There was a mishap with the punch bowl, I think. You had two glasses, and that was... enough."

"Was I drugged?" I gasp, but he chuckles lightly, shaking his head.

"No. Maeve is likely the culprit. She's not drinking right now for obvious reasons and ordered the punch a little stronger than she realized. I found her mate asleep in a stairwell on my way here, like he couldn't even make it back to their suite."

"No wonder I feel like hell. I remember my first glass. It was amazing. I didn't even realize it had alcohol in it."

"Which is probably why you feel like death right now," he replies with a nod.

"Did you drink it?"

"Unfortunately. You and I shared what would have been your third glass, and my fourth. I think sharing it is the reason we're still alive."

"Did we... did we do anything else?" My heart quakes, my blood pressure rising.

Blake searches my eyes and shakes his head. "No. I wouldn't have touched you when we were both so intoxicated."

"I know," I cut in as my cheeks flare with a blush I can't contain. "I'm sorry. I just–"

"You had fun," he assures me. "We all did, I think, based on what I remember."

Now we're both staring aimlessly at the wrought-iron gate, at the trembling leaves on the lilac bushes and the creeping wisteria vines the neighborhood is named after.

Another brisk breeze ripples through the yard, and I shiver, clutching my coffee mug, which has now reached critical levels.

"You should go inside and get some rest while they're gone and it's quiet."

I glance at his nearly empty coffee cup. "Do you want another cup of coffee?"

He doesn't look at me, but I can see the hint of hesitation flashing behind his eyes. Blake rises and follows me into the house regardless, picking up the blanket I've been wrapped in all morning so it doesn't drag on the floor behind me. While I pour two fresh cups, he lingers in the living room, scanning the family pictures on the mantel. I reach his side, and he accepts the fresh mug, but his eyes remain locked on a picture of me and Skye when she was probably around two.

"She looks like you," he says.

"I know. The cheekbones are apparently a dominant gene."

He smiles to himself–something light but reserved.

"Do you want to know her, Blake?" I ask, and the sun peeks through the clouds, streaming through the curtains to highlight his face. I see the years written clearly on his skin. Seven. Seven years apart, seven years of silence. It's a gaping sea between us.

"It's not up to me. She's your daughter."

"She's yours as much as she is mine. It feels unfair, given the circumstances. I... I want you to know her."

His eyes meet mine through the sunlit haze. "Are you sure? You know what I am."

"She's the same thing, Blake. I think I... I can't help her anymore, not with this. Not with her visions, her budding powers. I'm just a wolf. She's so much more than that and will grow more powerful as the years pass. You warned me this could happen, but I didn't listen back then."

"You had every right to be wary of me," he says low in his throat, a growl that reverberates under my skin. "You still do."

Silence settles between us, impenetrable. I'm not sure how to do this. Blake changed my life in so many different ways. Sometimes, on darker days, I wonder what my life would have been like if we'd never met. Would I have gone to Wellington? Would I have a different life than I do now?

But I wouldn't have Skye. She's... everything to me.

The worst part is that he can see that, can't he? The what ifs, the tendrils of whatever lifelines he can decipher?

"I took your life away from you," he says so quietly I almost miss it. "I made you a mother and made it impossible for you to follow the dreams you so carefully laid out."

"You gave me everything," I tell him, my voice just above a whisper. "Skye is the best thing to ever happen to me, and I need your help now. I really do."

He holds my gaze, his face etched with... sorrow. He drops his mask of indifference just long enough for me to see it.

"Do you want to know her? Do you want her to know you?"

Do you want to know *me* again?

I don't say those last words out loud. I can't. Seven years of pining, of immense regret, tangle through me as the front door opens, and Skye bounces in to show Blake the gumballs she bought at the store with his coins.

"Are you staying for lunch, Blake?" Mom asks, but Blake already knows that means he already has a plate at the table.

I meet his eyes and hold his gaze.

Chapter 12

At the Ball

Blake

The Night Before

Soren pours another glass of punch, bracing one hand on the table as the ladle scrapes the bottom of the bowl. "Shit, it's almost gone," he murmurs, his words slurred. "It's fuckin' good, though."

I squint past my blurred vision and spot Marianna in the small crowd as she moves in what I think is my direction, but there's three of her. Someone trips behind her, and Patton, who was just standing at my side, takes off in a rush to rescue Jane, who's now on the floor, tangled in her dress.

I'm not sure where the night went. One moment I was watching Marianna mingle with Maeve. Then, they disappeared, and reappeared, and the punch was served.

Music growled from speakers that sent smooth vibrations across the ballroom as conversations ran wild, and then... everything blurred. I think I danced at one point, which is incredibly unlike me. I think I might have actually danced with Marianna.

Everything got incredibly hazy after that first glass of punch.

"Where'd Maeve go?" My mouth feels incredibly dry. I take

another sip of the punch, wondering why it's not going down as easily as the first three cups. I'm not normally a sweets guy, especially when it comes to drinks, but this stuff is good. Too good. Stupidly, unexplainably good.

"I think she left," Soren slurs, looking around like he just realized his mate is nowhere to be found. "I mean, what time is it? It's gotta be midnight. Her parents are with—with Fallon. I just have one kid, right? I think—I think so?"

I check my watch.

"It's four A.M."

Soren scratches his head. "No, it's not."

I extend my wrist to him, and he looks down at my watch, blinking repeatedly like he's trying to clear his vision. A few yards away, Patton tumbles trying to untangle the fabric of Jane's intricate, fluffy gown, one of his shoes flying across the room.

Pressure on my forearm steals my attention from the drunken scene taking place throughout the ballroom, which is... more like a war zone now.

"I am so thirsty," Marianna whispers like it's a secret. "Blake, *help me*. I'm going to die of thirst."

"Here." I try to hand her the punch in my hand, but she just opens her mouth like a bird, and I pour it in, then pause. "Wait. Soren, what's in the punch?"

"Fruit? I dunno." He takes two stumbling steps away from the table.

"Who ordered it?"

"Maeve. She planned the whole thing." He laughs, waving a hand in dismissal, then stumbles away, trips over Patton and a man I don't know but who's friends with Jane, I suppose, and falls to the ground.

"We're not drinking any more of this," I hiss, taking the glass of punch away from Marianna's mouth.

"Where are we?" She sways into my body. I rope an arm around her waist, glancing around the room at the dwindling crowd of guests who should have dispersed... hours ago.

"*Shit.*"

Marianna starts to slump over my arm, her head lulling, but she grins, her eyes open to slits. "Blake?"

"Yeah?"

"Do you remember when we drove all the way to the coast and watched the ferries?"

"Yes," I whisper, looking down at her as the room spins out of control. Gods, she's beautiful. A soft, full, lovely weight in my arms. She turns to me, wrapping her arms around my neck to steady herself.

"Why didn't we just get a ferry and leave? We talked about it."

"We were going to go past Maatua. Past KiloKilo to sail the open seas." I smile, dreary, my body feeling more noodle-like than it ever has. Laughter rings out around the room in every direction, bouncing from wall to wall like music, but I know the music turned off hours ago. I think. Fuck, I can't even think right now.

"Why didn't we?"

"Because I would have had to stage a mutiny and steal a ferry, remember?"

"Sounds fun." She yawns, her cheek pressed against my chest. Her hair smells like nectarines. She must use the same shampoo she always has. I like that.

"Let's go to bed," she whispers around another yawn. "I'll walk you there because you're–you're so drunk." Her words slur into intelligibility.

"You don't live here, Anna. You have no idea where my room is."

"You do." Her hand rests on my chest, her fingers clutching my shirt, which is somehow unbuttoned halfway down. I'm not wearing my tux jacket anymore, either, and... I only have one shoe.

"I think we're in trouble," I say, blinking to clear my hazy vision. All around the ballroom, people are swaying to nonexistent music or sleeping on the cold tile floor.

Marianna murmurs something unintelligible, tightening her grip on my shirt. Her scent is overwhelming my senses, cutting through the alcohol clogging my veins. I want to carry her upstairs and into my bed. I want that so badly it hurts, but I forbid myself to even consider it, even if I were to just dump her on my mattress with the last of my lucidity and fall asleep face down on the floor.

When her knees start to give out, I pick her up, cradling her like a baby, and pick my way out of the ballroom, stepping over discarded shoes until I find my missing one.

"My shoes," Marianna groans, pointing into thin air. "Blake–"

"I'll get them." I swing her over my shoulder like a sack of potatoes. She grunts but quickly slumps back into semi-consciousness. I can't find her shoes anywhere, and by the time I breach the foyer, early morning light is already drifting through the windows, highlighting Soren trying to crawl up the grand staircase.

He gives up, lies down on the runner, and falls asleep.

"What the fuck is happening?" I murmur then turn for the door.

Moonrise is quiet this time of day. The town square outside the entrance of the castle shimmers in the hazy gray morning light. The beginnings of what will soon be a massive mating festival, always held in the spring, paint the normally gold and alabaster streets in shades of pink as I carry Marianna toward the guarded gates of the Wisteria Way neighborhood, less than two blocks away from the castle.

I'm out of breath, which is unusual, when I reach the security gate, my mouth full of cotton and drier than the middle of nowhere in Tarsian.

The security guards give me measured looks before rolling back the gate, nodding slightly, and I wave them off.

"Prince Blake," one of them says, "do you need assistance?"

I shake my head, mumbling an inaudible no before stumbling past the gate, trying not to fall over with Marianna still slung over my shoulder.

"Which house is yours?"

"The white one."

"They're all white," I growl, starting to feel a little bit more aware of my surroundings and our situation.

She points, but her arm quickly drops, and I spend the next ten minutes walking up and down the streets, trying to get her attention long enough to figure out which house is hers. They all look the same. Rows and rows of immaculate townhomes line cobblestone streets still damp from last night's storm. Toward the end of one street, along a row of homes closest to the exterior wall of the castle, a light switches on on the lowest level, highlighting a figure moving behind the curtains as they move through the first floor of the neat home.

I have a sudden burst of memory through the haze of punch rendering my mind utterly useless. There's one person in the entire world who takes pleasure in waking up before the Goddess, and it's Marianna's mother.

Leona steps out onto the porch wrapped in a robe when I reach the front gate. Her eyes, so like Marianna's, widen before she jogs down the steps.

"Blake? Oh, Goddess, is she all right?"

"I believe—" I wobble trying to unlatch the gate while keeping my arm braced against Marianna's thighs. "Something happened at the ball."

Leona stares at me for a moment, taking me in. I haven't seen her in seven years. I used to be at her house all the time. She took up an immense amount of space in my life for a solid two years. She knows me. She knows her daughter, too. Marianna doesn't party. She rarely drinks.

"Are you drunk?" Leona hisses, her eyes searching mine.

"*Very*," I gut out.

"Oh, Goddess, get inside right now!"

She bustles me inside where I quickly deposit Marianna on the couch, covering her with a blanket.

Leona hovers beside us, tsking, her face etched with what I

believe is disappointment, but then she smiles. "I never thought I'd see the day."

"What?"

"Marianna went to a party. There's a first for everything, I suppose."

Silence sweeps into the room. I feel it descending against my shoulders when I look down at Leona, who looks at me with an appraising gaze. "You've grown up, Blake."

"It's been a while."

"It has indeed."

I shift uncomfortably from foot to foot. "I can put her in bed–"

"I'm not risking you falling down the stairs, especially with her in your arms. She'll stay on the couch. I'll keep an eye on her."

Another heavy beat of silence passes. I should leave. I need to leave, actually, to not only clear my head but to find out what happened at the party, which was, by all accounts, supposed to be a classy engagement ball.

"I've met Skye," I say before I can stop myself, my usual filter failing completely. My head swims as I brace my hand on the back of the couch.

"She mentioned a tall man with purple eyes," she says, nodding in acknowledgement. "I only know one such man, so I figured it was you."

I wait for her to tear me apart, to rip me to shreds. She never has, even though I deserve it. I've *deserved* it.

"I forgot her violin," I whisper, wincing. "I'll bring it back in the morning."

"It's already morning, darling," she says with a knowing smile, her hand gently clapping my upper arm. "Go to bed, Blake. I'll see you in a few hours."

KENNA MOVES through the pink room, glancing between me and Soren, who's fuming, rubbing his aching temples as he casts icy glances in Maeve's direction. A handful of healing drafts made from Misty's tears cleared the worst of the hangover, but my head still pounds, radiating heat, and Soren isn't much better.

"I feel like I'm in a room full of teenagers," Kenna says, raising a brow as she stares us down. Fallon rests against her chest, totally oblivious to the tension in the room.

Maeve pours Soren another cup of coffee, and rain patters against the balcony a few feet away. "I had no idea someone brought homebrew to the ball. Otherwise, I would have put my foot down. The ballroom is completely trashed."

Soren sighs heavily, giving her hand a little squeeze before she walks away, retrieving Fallon from Kenna. "I'll talk to Beckett, that bastard. I'm sure it was him."

"We're lucky no one died," Kenna says sharply. Her eyes betray her tone, however. She's amused. Thoroughly. I find it odd that I can tell. I find it even odder that I'm not completely distracted by the voices and visions that normally dance through my brain without an off switch. They're quiet today.

I doubt it was the home brewed liquor because, admittedly, I've tried that. Tried to drown them out using a bottle of whiskey. It normally makes the voices louder and more demanding.

It's almost 10:00 in the morning now. I haven't slept. That also makes the voices and visions more vivid, but now they're... gone.

My head is practically empty save for the innate desire to be elsewhere.

"It was so nice meeting Marianna," Maeve says to Kenna, but she briefly glances in my direction. "Blake really fumbled the ball with that one, if you ask me."

"What's that supposed to mean?" I ask, arching a brow.

"I might have cornered her and asked what kind of relationship you had with her, and she said you were just *friends*. You know she has a daughter, right? I guess she separated from her mate a few years ago. I've never even heard of that happening. Maybe you still have a chance, Blake."

My stomach tightens, but I keep my eyes on Maeve as she drops into conversation with her mother.

Maeve still has no clue about Skye. That's probably for the best.

I rise, checking my watch, and say, "I have somewhere to be."

Chapter 13

She's Like Me

BLAKE

Skye has said four words to me over the course of the afternoon. It's not weird, I suppose. She doesn't know me. She's only seven, too, and doesn't yet understand that we're the same, and our view of the world is strikingly different compared to the people we love.

Leona didn't give me a choice about staying for lunch, which Marianna and I didn't have the stomach to touch as it stands. She's currently in the house with Leona, doing what, I don't know, but I'm sitting on the grass with my seven-year-old daughter who doesn't know anything about our connection, and maybe that's a good thing. I don't really think she'd care, to be honest.

What she cares about is rocks.

She hands me another rock which I dutifully split into pieces with the hammer resting against my thigh. She hums her disappointment when there's not an agate inside, which is what she's looking for, I think. The pile of rock discard is growing to the point it'll wreck a lawnmower, but I don't know how to tell her we should move onto something else, and neither Marianna nor Leona seem keen on interrupting us.

"Let's try this one. It looks promising," I tell her, picking through the basket of rocks she keeps hidden under the shed in the corner of the yard. She brought them over for me, which makes me wonder if I should feel special because she seems to guard the basket whenever Leona or Marianna's voices drift from the kitchen window just a few feet away from where we're kneeling in the grass.

Another hum of disappointment follows, and she turns back to the basket, but I hold out my hand. "Can you see which ones have agates?"

Her violet eyes meet mine, quietly searching for understanding. My powers started to emerge at her age based on what my mom, Sarah, told me.

"I bet if you dream about your rocks tonight, the dream will show you which ones have crystals in them."

Recognition flares behind those too familiar orbs of violet—the same as mine. The same as her paternal grandmother's. "In my dreams?"

Three more words. It's progress. "Yeah, do your dreams tell you things sometimes?"

She nods, unblinking.

"Do they tell you if it's going to rain the next day? Can you taste it?"

Another nod, but her lower lip wobbles into a smile.

"Do your dreams show you... what's going to happen the next day? If your mom is going to read a specific book at bedtime or pack a specific lunch before you leave for school?"

Her mouth widens into a grin, showcasing a missing tooth. "Yep. Why?"

"Well, that's a very long, complicated thing to try to explain," I reply, wondering if my tone is appropriate for a seven-year-old whose head is likely just as stuck in the stars as mine was as a kid. I used to be rambunctious, downright annoying, according to Uncle Ryan. I was loud and rough, always wrestling and goofing around with my cousins and my brother, but that changed almost overnight, and so did my eye color. I curled into myself. I grew quiet. Damn near silent, unable to differentiate the world of my dreams and the one my feet were planted on. When those first signs of power faded... things changed. Rapidly.

Marianna and I need to talk about this. I need Skye's history. I need to know when these things started happening, especially since there's been no one in either Skye's nor Marianna's corner when it comes to her developing powers.

Maybe I should be here.

"Do you see people you know in your dreams or strangers?"

"I saw Dean," she says, and my heart drops into my stomach. "Hitting Mom. I saw it in my dream. I told my dream to stop it from happening."

My blood rushes with a sudden promise of violence. I try to not let her see it, see the pain and fury behind my eyes. "Did you stop it from happening?"

She studies me for a moment, those tiny silver stars lighting from within. "Do you see strings in your dreams?"

I nod. "A lot of string. String that forms a... blanket in the stars."

"I don't see a blanket."

"You will one day."

"And then I can stop Dean from hitting Mom? Not just in my dreams?"

Fuck. She feels it. She has to know that feeling, that ache to get inside someone's mind, that pull to pluck and bend those strings—those lifelines beginning to glow into existence within her young powers. It's only a matter of time until she figures out how to use those gifts. Scrying is probably the most useful, but that takes practice. A lot of dedicated, committed practice.

Taking over someone's thoughts, their minds, is second nature. I was controlling Liam by the age of twelve, using my gifts to trick him into doing my chores.

She's likely very close to that already.

"Yeah, you'll be able to do that." I swallow hard, the fury over the mention of Dean and the confirmation he did, in fact, put his hands on Marianna sweeping through me in waves.

"Mom is scared sometimes." She rifles through the basket of rocks, plucking three of them into her palm.

"Of what?"

"Lots of things."

"Anything in particular?" I shouldn't be using her to pry. I fucking know that. I can't help it.

"Dean. I used to call him Mean Dean. He didn't like that, but I liked it."

I roll my lower lip between my teeth, glancing at the kitchen window. "Did he ever touch you?"

"Nope. He didn't like me. He told Mom I was weird and should be *combitted*."

"Committed?"

She nods. I see red.

"Mom didn't like that, and she told him to leave, but he kept coming back. She's scared of him. Dreams about him. I can see her dreams, too."

This is starting to border on inappropriate, but I have no idea how to turn the conversation in another direction.

"You're Blake?"

"I am."

"She dreams about you, too. Good dreams. I like those dreams."

I close my eyes, sighing around an ache beginning to bloom to life in my chest.

"You like pizza then, like me. In her dreams, she dreams about eating pizza in a car with you, which is so silly. Grammy would never let me eat pizza in a car! It would be too messy." She giggles, her nose wrinkling in a way that reminds me so much of my mom and twin sisters, Briar and Celeste, that for a moment I have to pause and just... look at her.

"I'm like you, Skye."

"You have dreams like I do?"

"All the time."

"Then you're a weirdo, too?"

I think about it for a moment. "Yeah, I am."

She grins again, giggling, and hands me the rocks.

All three are agates.

My phone rings while she's inspecting the crystals. I rise, walking up onto the back porch as Evander's voice echoes into my ear, the connection spotty. "Are you coming back to the castle anytime soon?"

"I have a few meetings at the temple. I likely won't return until you've already left for Veiled Valley."

"I'm not going back to Veiled Valley. I'm taking Soren to the Deadlands. Another of the Viper's men who's been on the lam was just apprehended there by Endovian warriors and passed off to Ryan. I need you to meet us there, look into his mind, see what you can find out because I'm willing to bet he's not going to tell us anything about her operations or Hannibal's location."

I look down at Skye, watching her lift the agates to the pockets of sunlight drifting through the clouds.

"I can make a brief trip. Tonight. I'll be in Silverhide by nightfall."

"We only need you for a few hours."

I hang up. Evander isn't one for drawn out goodbyes anyway. He's always been all business. I like that about him.

Marianna walks out onto the porch looking better than earlier today, but her eyes are still rimmed red as she bunches her hair into a bun and looks down at Skye.

I slide my phone into my pocket. "Are you feeling better?"

"More alive, I guess. I'm never going to another ball at the palace again." Her laugh is soft and unserious. "The punch was great, though. Do you think the kitchen staff will give me the recipe?"

"You'd need to get your hands on some bootleg alcohol first, and

I'm under the impression you've never done anything illegal in your life."

She arches her brows, humming a laugh. "I've run a few red lights here and there. I left Crescent Falls with a few unpaid parking tickets, too."

"I'll have to inform my father, seeing as you're now a fugitive."

She smiles again. Gods, I'd give anything, say anything, to see that smile all the time.

That's also when I feel that ache again. That incessant, unyielding pain that weaves between my ribs, squeezing tight. Guilt. Rejection. The works.

Marianna and I are over. The end of our relationship was sealed in ink, our names signed on a dotted line on a contract seeing to the welfare of the child we created–a perfect blend of her and me.

"Have you been breaking rocks all afternoon? This is her favorite thing to do. She'll be out here for hours."

"She's looking for agates."

"She sometimes gets lucky. We have a few on the mantle."

"She will only find agates from now on," I say, turning to look at Marianna.

She understands what I mean immediately, giving me a grim, somewhat withdrawn nod.

I step closer to her, my hand hovering over her arm, but I can't bring myself to touch her. "I was around her age when I started dreaming like she does. She's having visions, Marianna."

"Of what?"

"The future, most likely. Tangled events that may happen. Some things are static, like the weather. Whether it'll be cloudy when she wakes in the morning or if she should bring her raincoat to school. Whether she's getting cereal or oatmeal for breakfast."

Marianna nods, her eyes locked on Skye as she organizes her rocks.

"Other things are going to be... a lot for her to see and understand." I finally touch her. My fingers curl around her forearm, and she's cold, a chill rippling over her skin while I continue, "Things like... a strange phone call you take that changes her schedule. Leona running late coming home from the store. Getting displaced from school."

Marianna inhales sharply, her eyes meeting mine, filling with tears. "She knew she was going to get kicked out of school?"

"I'm not sure, but maybe. She's too young to really understand it yet." I take her by the arms, turning her to face me while I lean in, not wanting Skye nor Leona to overhear. "I'm concerned about her ability to see into your mind. I wasn't able to do that to people until I was a teenager."

Marianna rubs her temple, squeezing her eyes shut. "How do you know she's doing that?"

"Because she's looking into your–your timeline. Your tether, I call it. The thread of your existence–"

"Blake, I can't make sense of this. You know that!"

I exhale sharply, wincing as I try to untangle this situation and make it clear what's happening to Skye, but it's nearly impossible.

"She had a dream about us eating pizza in my car."

She blinks, tilting her head like she doesn't quite understand.

"That night I drove you to that concert in Moorn, and we had to camp out in the car during that storm? She saw that and saw us eating that disgusting pizza in the front seat. She's accessing your memories."

"Did she–did she see anything... else?" Her cheeks burn a fierce red as her expression shifts to panic.

I lean my forehead against hers, closing my eyes. "I'm assuming she's seeing the first memories of herself–where her tether started... which was that night. I doubt–she doesn't understand what she's seeing, but you need to be better about shielding your mind."

Marianna closes her eyes and sighs heavily. "And how the fuck am I supposed to do that, Blake?"

"I'll teach you. It's not as difficult as it sounds. We'll work on it, and I'll keep working with her–"

She steps away from me, closing her arms over her chest.

"Is that what you really want?"

"There's no one to teach her what she needs to know."

"The mystics–"

"Will break her, Marianna, like they nearly broke me."

She stares at me, her brow pinched in confusion, but I wave away her silent question and turn to clutch the porch railing instead, hanging my head.

"You asked if I wanted to know her, and I do. I want to know her. I can, at the very least, determine the best course of action because she *needs* to be trained. It's not an option. She is dangerous, Marianna, you have to understand that." My words are harsh, and I know it. Her face crumples as she bites her lower lip like she already knows this, has seen it coming to fruition. "She could easily break someone beyond repair–"

"I understand–"

"I don't think you do. I need to be very clear about what this entails. She's going to see things she's not going to like about people– strangers *and* people she loves. It's not going to make any sense to her, but these visions are going to get worse, progressively worse. And then she's going to figure out how to manipulate the things she's seeing, trying to make things better, trying to make things happen, and it will have consequences. I have to step in. I have to break our contract. It's time."

"What happens now? You tell your family?"

"I don't know yet–"

"Is she safe?" she asks, shivering. "Blake, is she safe? You just told me you were–you were in a compromising position–"

"She is safe. I will keep you both safe."

Marianna starts to shatter. She tries to hold herself together, but I can see the indents her nails are leaving on her forearms as she hugs herself.

"I need you to trust me, Marianna."

My phone rings. It's Evander again.

I let it go to voicemail.

"Can you trust me again?" I ask, holding her gaze.

She nods.

I pull my phone out of my pocket. "Come to the palace tomorrow morning, alone. We'll begin your training then. You go first, then her."

Chapter 14

Break Him

Blake

I walk out of my haze of powers onto a level, gravel road lined by farmland. Streaks of deep navy and fading violet paint the sky as stars twinkle into view, a masterpiece I'd stop to inspect if I didn't have somewhere to be. Along either side of the valley, houses built along the mountainside shine like their starry counterparts, and a few farmhouses are spread out, but the animals in the barns and sheds are silent, sleeping.

Silverhide is one of the most beautiful places I've ever seen. It's quiet here. Calm and restful, even during the rush of spring planting and the fall harvest. Ryan turned this valley into a utopia, and his pack is happy, healthy, and prosperous, but they still live as simply as possible. I get it. Sometimes I long for a life like that–something normal. Something still and calm.

Quiet. Always quiet.

A soft spring breeze carries the scent of snow still lingering on the mountaintops as I walk toward the center of the village where the farmhouses bleed into trios of cabins, then buildings made of stone stacked close together, housing stores and workshops.

The pack house rises in the center of what this pack calls the village center. A bonfire that never burns out glows, casting amber hued light across my boots as I move through the shadows.

My cloak fans out behind me in the breeze when I reach the door to the pack house and pull it open, met by a blast of heat from within and several murmured, male voices tangled in low conversation.

"Blake," Andrew, one of Ryan's many best friends, greets me with a nod and a stiff clap to my shoulder.

"Where's Evander?"

"The kitchen in the back." He clicks his tongue, shaking his head. "It's getting messy back there."

I roll my lower lip between my teeth as I scan the room. I know all the faces, all the names, all the men Ryan keeps close. When they were my age, they left everything they knew behind to come here for a different life outside of the modern restraints of Crescent Falls. It was a pilgrimage back to their wolfish roots.

I nod at Andrew in thanks and slip through the group of men gathered around long wooden tables. I feel their gazes as I open the door to the kitchen where group meals are made twice a day–breakfast and supper. The kitchen is large for that reason and modern in comparison to the rest of the village. At least, it's been that way for the last ten years or so.

The sleek modernity of the space will make cleanup easier after this is all said and done.

Stainless steel blinds my senses. I close the door behind me, inspecting the individuals arranged at different points around a man tied to a chair, his face beaten, swollen, and bloody.

I scan the knuckles of Ryan, Evander, Soren, and to my great surprise, Cole, finding them intact. This man wasn't beaten here. Not yet.

I eye Cole warily, wondering if he can see the lingering flash of confusion behind my eyes, but he gives me a tight nod, bracing a hand on a worktable as he leans beside his medical kit.

I realize then that Evander means to keep this man alive, at least until I'm done with him.

The man spits blood and growls at Soren, who smirks, rolling his eyes to mine. "Blake."

"Soren." I match his bored tone as I come to a stop beside Evander and unclasp the neck of my cloak, draping it over a work-bench. Ryan postures nearby, his arms crossed over his broad chest. He's taller than both Cole and Soren by a fraction of an inch but takes up much more space as he widens his stance, glowering down at the thin, somewhat scrawny and desperately underfed and unkempt man in that chair.

"You're a fuckin' leach," the man croaks, his words directed at Soren. "Traitor." He spits at Soren's shoes, but he doesn't back away from the assault.

"Traitor to what, exactly?" Soren arches a brow. "Being the Viper's little pet? I never was."

"And I was only a runner," the man grinds out, glancing at Evander before quickly looking away. "I rarely came within ten feet of that bitch. You know it. You were one of her big dogs, her favorite. I was nothing."

"Where are the rest of you hiding?" Soren asks, pacing in front of him. "Tarsian?"

"I dunno. Can't remember much. Been spending the last of my money on booze these days."

Evander lets go of an impatient sigh, his eyes sliding to mine, and gives me a quick nod.

My turn.

"What exactly has he said so far?" I ask the group, ignoring the prisoner completely.

Ryan replies, "Nothing we didn't already know."

"His name is Kurt," Soren adds. "He's a runner for one of the Viper's clients in the dark market, running contraband–drugs, miner-als, the like–over the border of the Roguelands and Tarsian."

"Which means I don't know shit about the Spider," Kurt adds, teeth bared in a snarl. "I can't tell you shit. I never worked with him or for him."

"But you had buddies on that island off the coast, didn't you?" Soren asks, tilting his head to the side and smiling cruelly down at Kurt.

"Yeah, well, so did you, you fucking traitorous dickhead. Where are your little friends, huh? The Viper's slut? What's his name? Or the thief from up north? Beckett and Patton, right? Then you got Louis and Maverick on your side. What's your game, Soren? Huh? Take over her business with the royal fucking family behind you?"

Soren crouches and smiles at him, going so far as to tuck the man's grayish brown hair behind his gnarled ears. "You were a runner, but it goes beyond contraband, doesn't it, Kurt? You were a messenger. You had high clearance within her operations in Twin Rivers, and all we need to know is where her clients and the other den leaders are hiding. That's it."

"I. Don't. Know," he says, exaggerating each word, and Soren sighs, looking bored, as he rises.

Evander takes me aside, walking me to the corner of the kitchen, just out of earshot from the prisoner. "We've apprehended a dozen of these men over the past three weeks during your absence," he begins, his voice a low whisper. "All of them have some type of memory loss we can't account for. They know their names, what they did for the Viper and the other den leaders, but any locations on other den leaders or clients who used their services are gone."

I hold his gaze. "I see."

"Have you or the mystics seen anything about Hannibal?"

"No."

He nods, gritting his teeth in frustration. "Our current plan is to flush out the den leaders. We know most have moved to Tarsian at this point and are in hiding. Their men are on the loose and much easier to catch, but Soren is familiar with this guy. He worked for the Viper, running messages between the den leaders. He doesn't remember a Goddess damned thing about their locations, though."

I nod again. "I'll take over now. Clear the room."

Evander turns and motions to Cole, Ryan, and Soren, but Soren doesn't leave with the other men. Instead, he perches on a workbench, his ankles crossed as he peers down at Kurt with a void expression.

"You don't need to be here for this," I murmur, cuffing my sleeves.

"I'd like to be. I'm awfully curious." There's a glint of mischief in his eyes that I don't miss.

"Suit yourself." I move in on Kurt, ignoring his sudden jolt of fear and loud, tangled protests. I roughly clap my hand against his forehead, forcing his head back as my powers surge forward, and his scream of pain when I tear into his mind fills my ears then shudders out like someone just blew out the flame of his existence like a candle.

His thread is thin and insignificant. No ties, no mate, no children. It weaves where it shouldn't have been, marking a few deaths that have had ripple effects in the lives of others. His thread is a muted stain in the tapestry–trivial. Unimportant. His death won't make a difference in the current flow of things.

His mind, however, is a tangled mess of broken memories. Surface images, like faces and images of the places he's gone, are still there, but the details are hazy, like someone cut them away, and blood pooled, soaking the fabric of his mind beyond recognition. I dig through it until I meet a vast nothingness.

Entire memories, which I imagine as shining globes of thought I can reach out and touch, are gone. His mind is as empty as a baby's would be, honestly. There's nothing here, like he's a fresh body, a new soul.

"Fuck." I snarl then put more pressure on his head until his neck is bent at an angle that could easily kill him if I make even the slightest movements.

I feel Soren approaching me. I ignore him and his morbid curiosity as I dig, and dig, finding nothing of substance. I follow his thread from beginning to end and see... nothing. Nothing, nothing, *nothing*.

I can do this to a person–break their minds, erase memories, manipulate what's already there.

So can Hannibal, it seems. He tried to do this to me, but he's not as good at it as I am. He couldn't break past my mental shields. I showed him lies, fake memories, my only weapons against people like him, and other people like me, rare as those are.

"He's bleeding," Soren says beside me, emotionless. Blood drips from Kurt's ears and nose.

"Do we need him alive?" I ask, gritting my teeth as my powers shudder, warning me of the possibility of depletion. Being in someone's head like this is... incredibly hard on my powers. It's far easier looking at someone's reflection in the stars instead, but this provides so much more information... usually.

"I doubt it–"

I pull back before Soren even finishes the sentence, my powers latching onto what's left of this man's mind, and pull his thread from the tapestry, snapping it.

Kurt slumps, his eyes glassy with a quick, painless death. It's probably more than he deserved.

Soren crosses his arms over his chest, his lips pressed together in an appraising fashion as he inspects the dead body being held upright by rope, and shrugs. "That wasn't as messy as I thought it'd be."

"What did you think would happen?" I grumble, moving past them to wash my hands, which are coated in Kurt's sweat.

"I thought his head would explode."

"It did, just on the inside." I feel ice in my veins that doesn't thaw when I run my hands under warm water.

It takes all of twenty minutes to explain my findings to Evander, who is obviously frustrated by the lack of information I have to give him. The showdown that took the Viper's life happened just under a month ago, and moves are being made in the defense all over Eastonia. His armies are moving, positioning themselves along the coast. Smaller factions of Ghosts, and Soren's rag-tag legion of rogues in the Roguelands, are sniffing out the last frays of thread connected to the Viper while also hunting down other den leaders who are now hiding like their lives depend on it—because they do. Evander isn't keen on keeping anyone alive, and his daughter gave him the green light to do as he pleases, which means everyone is dying.

"I need to be back in Moonrise by dawn," I say to Evander as we walk around the exterior of the pack house where a few additions have been made, and a room has been carved out for me to sleep in. "Is there anything else you need?"

"No," he says but then glances over his shoulder at Soren, who's following behind us, taking in the sights of Silverhide in the glow of the moon. "We're going to Veiled Valley tomorrow morning, as well. Kenna is coming back to get us at first light."

He squeezes my arm in farewell before dipping into the shadows. I imagine he's staying at Ryan and Aviva's place with Cole, whose services were deemed unnecessary after all. I wonder if he's disappointed he's not stitching anyone up right now.

"Not staying with the father-in-law tonight?" I ask dryly as I step into one of the shed-like additions and switch on a light, which illuminates a... bunkhouse. Twin beds on either side of the room and not much else.

"I offered to sleep here instead of taking up what I believe is Nora's bedroom at Ryan's house." He drops a backpack on his chosen bed and sits, stretching out his legs with a soft groan.

I eye him before dropping my cloak on my bed for the night and sit as well to unlace my boots. Silence settles for several moments before Soren says, "That was rather impressive, not gonna lie."

"Thanks."

"It takes a lot of power, huh? I noticed the ice starting to line your eyes, just like Maeve."

"It's called—"

"A depletion event, I know." He lies down flat on his back with his hands resting on his chest. "Trust me, I know a lot about that."

"I'll be fine by morning, but I will not risk ruining my day tomorrow trying to spirit back to Moonrise on limited reserves."

"What's the hurry?"

I eye him wearily as fatigue echoes through the marrow of my bones. I don't... I'm trying not to like Soren. I have to keep reminding myself of that. I shouldn't feel like I can trust him, I think. I don't seek him out for company. I don't seek company. I never have.

But he knows a lot more about me than anyone else, including details about the two people who mean more to me than my own life.

"I'm training Marianna in the use of metal shields starting tomorrow. Your respite from the palace is actually going to work in my favor, seeing as your mate won't be snooping around."

"Maeve is so curious about what you've got going on with Marianna," he chuckles and then sighs, amused to the highest degree. But then he turns his head and holds my gaze. "You good with this? Marianna, the mother of your secret kid, being around again? You made it sound like she wasn't a huge fan of yours."

"Things were difficult when Skye came into the picture."

"But that's changed."

"Not really–"

"You were all over each other at the ball." He laughs, looking back at the ceiling. "From what I remember, at least, she did drag you onto the dance floor, and you let her. You looked peaceful. You weren't being a dick for once."

"This isn't something we're going to discuss. You and I aren't friends."

"Suit yourself." He chuckles and rolls over onto his side, his back to me. "But mental shields? You're sure she can grasp it? That's elite Ghost warrior training you'd be putting her through."

"I don't have a choice," I murmur, lying down and closing my eyes. "Neither does she."

Chapter 15

Lie to Me, Honey

Marianna

The front gates of the palace are heavily guarded every second of the day. I clutch my purse to my side, dressed in tan slacks and a cream-colored sweater—less casual than normal—in hopes that I'll get in without a huge fuss. I double checked to make sure all of my IDs are in my wallet, and as I remove my sunglasses and peer at the security gate, I still feel an overwhelming sense of dread.

It was easy enough to get into the castle for the ball because a driver was sent to fetch me. I didn't have to come through the front gate that night. Now?

I inhale, holding my breath as I walk toward the warriors stationed outside the massive, towering wall of alabaster stone, but they don't even look in my direction.

Not until I make a move for the foreboding metal gate that prevents anyone from seeing what I know is an ethereal garden and the steps leading up to the palace.

The security post is the size of a small house, and while the guards on either side of the gate turn to me, giving me slightly menacing looks of warning not to come any closer, another guard steps out of the post and arches his brows, waiting for me to explain why I'm here.

I fumble with my purse, my cheeks burning red, and not from the warm morning sunlight dancing over the ancient cobblestone beneath my loafers. "Um, my name is Marianna Abbot. I'm here to see Prince Blake of Crescent Falls. We have a meeting this morning. He didn't really give me a time to arrive–"

The guard lifts a radio to his mouth and turns from me, motioning to the other guards to move out of my way. Without another word to me from anyone, the gate cranks open, revealing streaks of bright green and the first early spring blooms that line a wide, steep staircase made of pure white marble.

My mouth dries out as I nod my thanks and step into the front garden. The gate closes behind me with a screech that settles in my bones, making my teeth rattle.

Bees hum, bouncing from bloom to bloom. Little butterflies dance through the bushes, and tall, trembling grasses in shades of emerald and wheat. I start to ascend the stairs, tripping over my own feet.

My leg muscles are burning when I finally reach the front door, which towers over my head by two stories and is squished between even taller windows made of stained glass with moonstones and gems scattered within. It's a work of art, this palace. I can't believe it spent thousands of years underwater.

The doors open before I have a chance to... I don't know, knock? Ring a doorbell? A smiling young woman in a cream colored uniform steps outside, her hands resting over her stomach. "Miss Abbot?"

"Yes, that's me."

"Perfect. We've been expecting you. Follow me, please."

I do. Four stories later, my legs on the verge of giving out completely, I'm ushered down a wide, sunlit hallway on the fifth floor, which overlooks the forest directly behind my backyard on Wisteria Way. The maid pulls out a set of keys and opens a door, saying calmly, "This way, please."

I nod, swallowing hard, and step into what I know without a doubt is Blake's office.

It's a sharp contrast to the finery of the castle, which is dressed in shades of gold, white, and the occasional touch of crimson. Here, the large, open space is shrouded in tones of gray and black, everything sleek and modern. A large desk made of black wood takes up a huge area of the far reaches of the room. Ceiling height bookshelves made of tinted glass span the walls, and only a smidgen of sunlight breaches thick gray curtains covering the windows.

"His Highness doesn't normally take a tea or coffee service this time of morning, but I'll bring one up for you," the maid says and promptly leaves, closing me into the room by myself.

A few doors are spread along one wall. I have no idea where they lead, but Blake isn't here. "Blake?"

I look around and decide to test a few of the doors, but they're all locked. So I finally sit down in a large black armchair in front of his desk while toying with a loose string on my brand-new sweater. The maid returns with a coffee tray, which I help myself to. A steaming cup of what ends up being very strong coffee will not calm my nerves, but it's something to do.

I wait for twenty minutes, wondering if he's forgotten he asked me to come here, but as I'm bringing my coffee to my lips, my mouth suddenly fills with the taste of... metal. I lower my mug, padding my fingertips over my lower lip, wondering if I bit myself and I'm bleeding and that's where the strange, coppery taste is coming from, but then a burst of energy rockets through the room, and a dizzying spell of violet hued magic appears with Blake at its center.

I scream, spilling my coffee all over my lap and sweater.

Blake steps out of the haze, ripping off his thick navy blue cloak, and rushes to me. "Fuck, I'm sorry. I'm–are you okay?" He guides me out of the chair, holding me at arm's length to inspect the dark stain on my sweater and the coffee seeping into my slacks.

What a great start!

He chews his lower lip, his eyes lifting to mine. "Come with me."

"What the fuck was that?" I ask as he takes my hand and moves toward one of the doors along the wall. The lock slides out of place with a flick of his wrist, no need for a key. My stomach tumbles to my shoes.

The door opens to a narrow hallway with off-white walls and smooth, creamy carpet. Windows let in sunlight and a soft, cool breeze. He keeps his hand firmly clasped around mine. The hallway leads to a tidy, immaculately clean living room.

It's his apartment. His suite in the castle. It smells like him here—that brisk, cool scent of winter and snow that makes my body react with a wave of heat I can't tamp down.

He pulls me into his bedroom, and that heat expands to something dangerous and damning, and I feel it, see it in the way he slowly inspects my expression, that he can feel it, too.

We haven't really been alone like this in years. Just us in a space with no distractions, no whispered voices or prying eyes.

"I'm sorry," he repeats, stepping away to open a drawer in his dresser. He pulls out a T-shirt and hands it to me then rifles for a pair of pants for me to change into that will somehow fit when he's twice my size.

"My pants are fine, I think," I whisper unintentionally, unable to raise my voice any higher. Adrenaline courses through my body as his magic lingers on my tongue.

I grip the shirt and meet his eyes. "What—what was that? When you got here?"

"We call it spiriting or jumping. I can move from place to place using my powers," he explains in a calm, monotone voice that surprisingly settles me. "It takes some practice, but I think Skye will also have the ability when she comes into her wolf." He motions to a bathroom. "You can change in there. I can send the sweater down to the laundry to be cleaned."

"It's fine—"

"It's not," he cuts in. "I wasn't sure if you'd come today, and I was... running late. I was in Silverhide last night, and my powers...."

He cuts himself off, shaking his head as he turns from me and walks toward the door. "We can start the training here, in my suite. It's more private than my office."

"Okay–"

He slips out of the room, and I turn to the bathroom, my heart in my throat and my lungs refusing to expand.

I barely slept last night, not after our conversation about Skye. I knew Blake had powers. It was… part of the reason I pushed him away when we found out I was pregnant, after he'd already broken up with me, but still. It had come as a shock, even knowing some members of the royal family were… different. Special.

I change into the fresh shirt that brushes the middle of my thighs, then I step out of his room. I lay my stained sweater over a wood-backed chair in the sunlight, and Blake, nursing a cup of coffee as he fans through a handful of paperwork, looks over at me.

He notices me edging out of his bedroom and extends the papers to me, reaching for the pen tucked in his shirt pocket. "This is the new contract I had drawn up last night before I left. Our mediator has been sent a copy to review as well. I have my lawyer on my schedule for tomorrow, so we can review it and sign it together then, but I figured you could look over it now–"

"We don't need another contract," I cut in, and his arm slowly falls to his side. He looks confused, maybe a little unsure. "You're not going to… take her from me, are you?"

"Marianna," he says in a near gasp before he reigns himself in. His tone is deeply offended as he grinds out, "No, I would never do that to you. Either of you–"

"Then we don't need a contract. She needs you now. I understand that. We can weather whatever comes next, whether you want her to know the truth about who you are to her or not."

He swallows. I watch the column of his throat bob as my words sink in. "I haven't had a moment to give the prospect of telling her I'm her father any thought yet. I will decide soon, however."

"I'm not asking you to give me a timeline–"

"I don't know how to do this," he interrupts me, his voice stern and cool. "I don't want to hurt you by not being... a warm, empathetic father figure in her life–"

"She's neither warm nor empathetic." I laugh, unable to help myself. "She won't understand what that even means, Blake. When I said she was like you, I meant she was like *you*. Not just because of your powers. She's quiet and curious. She doesn't like big shows of emotion. It makes her shut down." Just like him. Exactly like him.

He nods along, running his fingers through his hair like this conversation is leaning toward being uncomfortable for him.

I choose not to say anything further.

Blake clears his throat, tosses the papers on a coffee table, and motions toward the couch soaking in the sun. "Let's do this, then."

I sink onto the cashmere soft cushions. He sits beside me close enough that our thighs touch, and his scent wraps around me, that mark on my neck that doesn't belong to him tingling in warning.

I ignore it. I have to.

"What does this entail exactly?"

"Lying," he deadpans, smoothing his hands down his thighs, down the finely knit fabric of what I realize are dressy black slacks. He's always been so put together. There isn't a causal bone in his body. "You need to lie to yourself, make up memories of things that didn't happen, and use those to block me from being able to see things that did take place."

I shake my head, chuckling in disbelief? "Is it that easy?"

"It sounds easy. It's not. You have to... make yourself believe in those lies. They have to feel totally, completely real."

"How does that stop someone from being able to see into my head, though? They still would. They'd just be seeing something I made up."

"This is a concept that predates me. Warriors, especially in the Ghost army, are trained to do this. It's a type of mental shield at play that keeps battle plans hidden in the event they're captured and to trick enemies. If someone like me, with powers similar to mine or magic able to access someone's thoughts, were to use them against another person, that person's metal shields, the lies and deceit, would be a distraction from the truth. The assailant would feel like they've seen what they needed to see and not dig any further."

"How does this help Skye?"

"She mentioned Dean," he says, and it crushes me.

I nod, closing my eyes. I feel his fingertips brush over my forehead before he tucks a lock of my hair behind my ear. "Lie to me, Marianna. Show me something that didn't happen."

Chapter 16

Those Are My Memories

Blake

Eight Years Ago

Marianna pants, gripping my arm to hold herself upright as we sludge through mud so thick it sucks my shoes into its murky depths. A layer of water runs over the mud, making what was once a dry dirt parking lot shimmer in the shadow of the festival taking place a few hundred yards away. Music drifts toward through the relentless sheets of rain hammering over our heads, and I stumble, nearly dragging her down into the mud.

"BLAKE!" she howls, laughing hysterically. I catch her around her middle and yank her upright, cursing under my breath.

"I'm never going to let you forget that this was your idea. I told you it was going to rain. Epically."

"Maybe you should be a meteorologist instead of an architect? You have a knack for it. You're never wrong." Her giggle laces through me, sending a flush of warmth across my wet skin.

Her boots keep getting stuck in the mud. My car is still a quarter mile away, thankfully parked on a hill overlooking the absolutely swamped festival grounds, but this is taking forever.

"Get on my back," I command, motioning at her to hurry up as lightning flares, followed by an enormous crack of thunder that makes my teeth rattle. "Come on!"

She heeds my command, wrapping her arms around my neck with her ankles crossed over my stomach. "I'm getting mud all over you, just so you know."

"Oh dear, and I was *so* clean to begin with."

"Was that sarcasm, Blake? That's new! Have you been practicing?" She tightens her grip around my neck.

"You're lucky I sometimes enjoy your presence, Anna."

"I think you always enjoy having me around." She rests her chin on my shoulder, humming a soft laugh. Her scent cuts through the rain, floral and warm. She nuzzles her face against my neck to shield her eyes from the spray of the storm, and her eyelashes fluttering against my skin makes me grunt with a sudden tightening in my jeans I'm struggling to ignore.

It takes twenty minutes of carrying her like this to reach my car, a sporty SUV low enough to the ground that it's going to be impossible to cross the now washed out bridge leading back to the highway, which I realize in a matter of minutes after reaching the car and pulling into traffic, both of us wet and shivering as we watch warriors trying to direct festival traffic back to Moorn.

"What are we going to do?" Marianna asks, her soaking wet hair dripping onto her shoulders and running down her arms.

"There's a grocery store nearby in a strip mall. We can park there. They might have dry clothing inside." I whip the car around and drive back in the direction we came. It's a mess everywhere. The sky is painted an angry black that splits with lightning every few minutes. All of the hotels are full for the night, which we find out as we sit in the front seat of my car, dressed in matching touristy T-shirts with a box of the worst pizza I've ever had in my life resting on the console between us.

Marianna busies herself by flicking through the radio stations.

"There's no availability at any of the hotels nearby," I breathe, gritting my teeth as I scan my phone. "Not a single fucking room."

"So? We'll just sleep in the car." She opens the pizza box, frowns, and serves herself a slice. "At least you have a nice car. We can fold down the back seats and sleep back there. You'll fit if you bend your knees a bit."

"Barely," I mutter. I don't want her sleeping in a car overnight. I run my hand over my face, debating my next move. If only I had the ability to jump. I'm not quite there yet, and I'm not going to risk it with Marianna with me. I could hurt her, I'm sure. Accidentally pull her to pieces, lose her somewhere in the void–

"What are you thinking about?"

"I'm thinking how much I hate the fact that you'll be sleeping in a car overnight."

"Why? It's not like I'll get in trouble or anything. Mom knows we're here. Also, I already texted her about the weather."

"You deserve a bed, not the back of my car."

"It's an *SUV*," she teases. "A *luxury* model, *Prince Blake*. It's like camping but better. Less bugs."

I eye her wearily, resigned to suffering, I suppose. I watch her take a bite of her pizza. "You should eat something."

"You look like you'd rather be eating dirt," I reply, and she laughs around a bite.

"It's totally raw in the middle," she admits, struggling to swallow. "But I'm starving."

"You're a mess." I laugh, and she grins at me. She's just... beautiful, even in a stupid shirt that says "*I Love Moorn*" and sweatpants two sizes too big for her. Her hair starts to dry in messy waves as she stares out the window at the somewhat empty parking lot. The store lights flicker out, and darkness descends.

I turn the car off.

"Did you have fun, at least?"

"I did. I had fun knowing you had fun."

She gives me a knowing smile. "You know, Blake, you're actually a really good guy. I wish you could see that."

"What do you mean?"

"You act like you're so–so unlovable. So different. It's okay to be weird."

"You think I'm weird?"

"You are weird. A total weirdo," she teases, but her eyes hold mine a little longer than usual. "You're a nerd, Prince Blake."

"So are you."

"I am fully aware of that, trust me. I'm proud of it." She finally takes a bite but doesn't break eye contact. Something shifts in my lower belly, an ache of want I've been trying to ignore since the moment I met her a year ago, and she totally, completely, upended my life.

We've been friends for months now. Sometimes I think she likes me more than that. Sometimes she... flirts with me, I believe. It's hard to tell. Lately, the past couple of weeks especially, we've been... together most of the time.

It's killing me, more so now as I watch her lips close around her pizza.

I want to tell her how I feel, but I don't know how to even begin. I've never done this before. I've never had feelings like this before. I've never really had a friend outside of Brie and Liam.

I don't want to ruin it with Marianna. She's the only good thing I've had in my life since I returned from training with the mystics. I'm not ready to risk falling into that darkness again.

"Blake?"

"Yeah?" My throat is entirely too dry. The word comes out in a rasp.

"Can I ask you something?"

"Of course."

She licks her lips, tossing her pizza slice back in the box.

"Wait, you have–" I lean toward her and swipe a splotch of

grease from her cheek, but my touch lingers against my will. Her eyes hold mine, searching.

She keeps her gaze locked on my face as she leans into my touch, and it's...

"What did you want to ask me?"

"I *like* you," she says, but her expression tightens, like she's worried I won't feel the same way. "I–I *really* like you."

I almost laugh.

But I kiss her instead.

She kisses me back.

Enthusiastically.

BLAKE

Present

I pull out of her mind with a sharp sigh as tingles of memories flood my body, awakening a feeling I've kept guarded for a very long time.

"Marianna, that wasn't–that *happened*," I tell her, meeting her eyes as she looks up at me, slightly breathless. "That wasn't a lie."

"I tried," she admits, her eyes glassy with my powers still swirling but fading around her irises. "I thought–if I changed how–"

"It has to be a completely made up memory," I cut in, my voice low and strained as I try to banish the internal agony clawing at my heart.

"Try again. I'll get it this time. I just need a minute–" Her nose starts to bleed. I quickly grab a tissue off the coffee table.

"No, we're done for the day." I rest my hand against the back of her head, tilting it back to blot the blood away. She's woozy, which I expected. "Why did you choose that memory?"

"I was trying to think of something to–to guard it with."

"Why?"

"Because it's one of my favorites." Her tone is soft as her weary eyes meet mine, finally returning to that vibrant blue I fell in love with all those years ago.

I flex my jaw, but I can't find the words I need to convey just how jarring that was for me to relive. That night changed everything. Absolutely everything changed. I look at her, my hand still supporting her head. "A month ago, someone tried to break into my mind," I tell her, releasing her slowly. I rise, discarding the tissue in a nearby wastebasket, and pace to the window overlooking the forest. "He got close to seeing you. I was guarding the same memory–memories, honestly, of you."

"Why was someone trying to break into your head?"

"I'm still trying to figure that out." I close the curtains. Her head is probably hurting, and the light will make it worse, for sure.

"Can you tell me what happened?"

"It's not important," I tell her, turning to face the couch. I sit on the opposite end, further away from her than before, and let the distance between us settle the familiar, absolutely choking feelings of desire still washing through my system. "Skye will need to go through this training as well, and to be honest, I'm thinking that I need my parents' help with you both. My mom is like me. Her powers are... similar. There are a few differences, but at their roots, they're the same. She trained me when I was a kid. She can help both of you."

"Did you just change your mind about training me yourself?"

"Yes," I admit. I can't decipher the emotion playing behind her eyes, but my powers are itching to get back inside her head, to follow her tether to our world to see if it still... binds with mine.

But I glance at the scar on her neck then quickly look away.

"Why?"

"I don't know if I can help you. I'm too close to you, too familiar. You don't feel threatened by me. We have shared memories. I was watching that scene play out from my perspective, Marianna, not yours. We're too close."

She rises. "Are you already going to push me away again?"

"Anna, no, that's not what I meant–"

"Why did you end things with me? After the concert?"

I stand, too. "I don't want to have this conversation right now. I was just inside your head, and you're not thinking clearly. My powers are still subduing–"

"Why did you break up with me? You never–you never even explained why."

"Please–"

"I need to know. Otherwise, I can't do this. I want to be there for Skye, but if you're going to be picking through my head, I need to know that I can trust you not to fucking hurt me again, Blake. This is–this is incredibly intimate."

Tears wet her eyes. I hate it. My entire body screams to get close to her, to fix this.

I can't tell her the truth, the reason why I've done so many unspeakable things... in her name.

Things no one knows about. Things I've lied about, spun into some narrative that keeps her out of the equation.

All based on something I saw when I looked at her thread in the tapestry... which was... *short.*

Because of me.

Her phone rings. She doesn't move to grab it from her purse. Her eyes hold mine, heartbroken, maybe even furious. The ringing dies out.

"Blake, please. Why did you end things?"

"I didn't want to hurt you."

"But you did–"

Her phone buzzes several times in a row. With a scoff, she moves to her purse and slides it free, but the look on her face as it falls makes my body tighten with concern.

"Are you all right?"

She grows so pale I can see every fine blue vein running beneath her skin.

"Marianna?"

"I need to go. I'll–I'll wait to see what our mediator says about the new contract." Her voice is laced with vitriol as a single tear slides free down her cheek.

"Marianna!"

She disappears down the hallway. I hear a door slam shut in my office–and then silence.

Chapter 17

He Only Cares About Himself

Marianna

I'm not even out of the castle before my body succumbs to an immense wave of regret. I brace myself on the banister of a sweeping marble staircase curving down to the third floor, squeezing my eyes shut as I sink against the steps.

What is wrong with me?

I'm literally criminally insane, aren't I? Blake is trying to help us, and I'm actively boxing him out, and for what? Unrequited feelings? A lingering ache of rejection I haven't been able to dim?

The idea that had he just... grown up, been a fucking man about this... I wouldn't have been through what I had to go through the past four years.

It should have been him by my side. It should have been his mark on my neck.

My phone buzzes repeatedly. My body curls with dread as I hang my head between my knees, resisting the urge to scream in frustration.

Female voices drift toward me from the hallway below. I lift my head as a trio of women in strange outfits walk past the base of the stairs. Their pants are made of what looks like leather but thin and seamless, held together by loops woven with braided string. The leader of the pack is obviously the young woman in the middle. She's incredibly tall–as tall, if not taller–than Queen Maeve. Thick, impressively curly dark brown hair turns a deep red in the sunlight as she notices me, one of her eyebrows lifting in confusion when she sees my... tears.

She motions for the other two women to keep walking, saying, "I'll meet you in the weapons room downstairs. Don't let the guys taunt you into sparring, okay? The clinic is already sick of many of the guys they've been patching up the last couple days." Her voice is deeper than I expected. Husky and warm, almost seductive for someone her age. She's young, maybe an older teenager, but as she turns her body toward the stairs, toward me, I realize this woman is... not only tall, but insanely, impressively, muscular.

Her taunt biceps flex as she grips the banister, her thigh muscles strain against her strange leather outfit while she gives me a sympathetic smile. "Are you okay?"

Thundering footsteps surge behind me but stop abruptly. The woman looks up, and her pinched brow relaxes as she breathes, "Hey, Blake."

Blake exhales like he's out of breath. "Lexa. I didn't know you were in town."

"I brought some of the girls. We heard the warriors were bored, and their captains asked if we'd give them a show." She shrugs, drumming her fingers on the marble railing. "And we did give them a show. Most of Captain Leed's battalion is currently in the clinic getting stitched up."

Blake sighs, unimpressed, but I'm watching the woman closely, perplexed. She's gorgeous. I've never seen someone who looks like her. She's exotic in a way I can't put my finger on. Her skin is a deep bronze, but she has millions of freckles. Tiny braids are woven through her thick curls, some adorned with carved beads and small shells. Her eyes are a deep, stormy blue flaked with amber.

She smiles wickedly at Blake before inspecting her nails. "Captain Johnson's battalion is next. They're waiting for us downstairs. Apparently, they learned a thing or two watching us spar with Leed's band of idiots and decided they want weapon play instead of hand to hand combat."

"I'll make sure the sparring area is... cleaned when you're done."

She smiles at him again, but then her eyes slide to mine. "Are you good?"

"She's fine," Blake says sternly–sternly enough that I bristle.

Lexa gives him a skeptical look but edges off the stairs and disappears around the corner. I rise, but Blake is suddenly beside me clutching my coffee stained sweater in his fist.

"Can we please talk for a moment? That's all I need," he grinds out in a low grumble. "Please."

"I don't think there's anything else to say–"

"I broke up with you," he whispers, his body closing on mine, "because I scared you. Because you looked at me like I was a monster, and I am, and I couldn't handle the idea of ever hurting you with my powers. I was young and stupidly in love, Marianna. I was also young and untrained. I handled it poorly. I know that. I didn't explain what was happening to me, but I thought I was doing the right thing, and looking back on it, I probably was." I close my eyes, my chest quaking as he continues, "I warned you about what Skye could become. I hate that this is happening to her–to us, Marianna. I will make it better, but you have to trust me. I didn't end things between us because I wanted to. I ended things because I had to. There was no other way forward for us."

I take a step away from him. He straightens, his face etched in cold shadow–his mask of bored indifference a heavy contrast to the force and depth of what he just said to me. I wish he'd just show it, for fuck's sake. The hurt. The anguish.

He never will. It's not his style, is it? He wraps those feelings up tight, hoarding them away, pushing everyone as far away as he possibly can.

I wish I had the same ability.

"You moved on, and I was happy for it when I found out you'd found your mate," he says with only a flicker of emotion behind his voice that betrays the words.

"I wasn't–Dean marked me before I knew for sure," I admit, meeting his eyes. My tears have dried. I feel weightless as I get lost in his gaze, which flashes with silent rage.

Blake is speechless for a moment. "He imprinted on you?"

I nod, wringing my hands before gripping the banister for support. "Can't you just look into my mind and see everything for yourself–"

"I will not do that to you," he cuts in sharply, his eyes dark and deadly serious. "Ever."

"Sometimes I wish you would," I whisper, closing my eyes as I take a deep breath and start walking away.

He doesn't follow me this time. We say nothing about what happens next, whether I'll continue training with him or if he's going to tell his family our secret–about our daughter. I also left my sweater at the castle. He was still gripping it when I left him on the stairs, and the shirt he loaned me?

It smells like him.

I reach my house after an entire hour of walking aimlessly around Moonrise in no set direction. My shoulders are flecked with the glitter that was falling from the streamers being lifted and arranged for the mating festival that begins this weekend when I walk into the house, passing Mom, who's sitting in the new armchair she wrestled me into buying.

"Anna?"

I close myself in the bathroom. I strip out of my stained clothes and take a lukewarm shower, standing directly below the spray of water as my mind fizzles with the last of Blake's magic. Dressed in a towel, I pad back downstairs, barely dry, my damp hair dripping down my shoulders and back, and Mom is in the same place she was before, but now her book is in her lap, her eyes honed on my wet steps into the kitchen.

"Where's Skye?"

"Out back breaking rocks," she says matter-of-factly, her voice growing closer as she moves into the kitchen. "Where have you been?"

"With Blake." I gulp an entire glass of water and turn to her, arching a brow.

She rests her hands on her hips, mimicking my expression. "Why?"

"He was helping me train in mental shields. He said it was necessary to ensure Skye couldn't continue breaking into my thoughts and memories. It didn't go well." I swallow hard, my mouth immediately going desert dry again. I turn to the sink, filling the glass again.

Her footsteps are light on the floorboards behind me. "Have you... talked to him?"

"Of course. Being in someone's presence usually means having to carry on a conversation to some degree."

"Anna, you know exactly what I mean."

I turn to her, leaning my hips against the counter. "What do you want me to say? That he suddenly wants to be in Skye's life? That he's back? That everything is suddenly going to be all right again?"

Mom searches my eyes, her expression dimming, new lines crinkling around her eyes. "I never understood why–"

"We broke up?" I laugh, but it's bitter. "Oh, he just explained that fully. Trust me. He broke up with me because he thought I was scared of him–"

"You were–"

"He lies, Mom. Blake has never told me the full truth about anything, and that hasn't changed, which he just proved. Blake is only interested in protecting himself–"

Mom barks a shrill laugh that rings through my bones. "From what?"

"Feeling! Feeling anything!" I whirl back to the counter and discard my glass in the sink.

"He's a young man, Marianna. You've always had such high expectations of him. Too high–"

"He never told me he had powers, Mom." I whirl back to her, my eyes going glassy with sudden tears. "Not until he looked inside my fucking head and didn't like what he saw."

She searches my gaze, her brow pinching in confusion.

"Yeah, that's what happened. He used his powers on me and decided he didn't want to be with me anymore with no explanation, no reason why. He left, cutting off contact. Then I found out *I was pregnant.*"

Now her eyes are growing wet.

"I'd just turned *eighteen.*"

"I am aware–"

"And you," I sneer, losing my grip, "found him and told him–"

"You were having a baby, Marianna. He needed to know."

"It wasn't your decision to make."

"I am your mother. Do you really think I was going to sit there and let you suffer alone? Because you were suffering, Marianna. Immensely."

She doesn't mean through the pregnancy. No, I was... severely depressed. Those few months before Blake found out were hell–like I'd been dropped into a pool of depthless water I couldn't find my way out of. It was like he was branded on my body, and I couldn't shake his memory.

"He pushed me away because he knew–" I suck in a rattling breath, "he thought I wasn't enough, you know? People like him, powerful people, people with standing–"

"He did not end things with you because of our low rank!"

"He's a mystic, Mom!" I shout. "And I'm just a wolf. That's what this is about, clearly. I wasn't good enough for him. I was a good time, an easy mark. He shoved me to the side when I found out about his gifts, and his play was over. That's what happened."

"Is that what he told you?" Mom is in utter disbelief and angry... but not at Blake. Her eyes are wild and narrowed on mine. "You can't actually believe that."

"He told me he loved me," I admit. "Just now, at the castle, when I cornered him after he told me we were too close for him to train me effectively. We had too many shared, overlapping memories. And then he told me he was stupidly in love with me back then and scared–"

"Which is exactly what he felt–"

"Like you know–"

"He told me as much," Mom says, her voice nearing a shout. "Within minutes, I might add, of finding out he was going to be a father at such a young age, Marianna. I've never seen someone look so devastatingly worried, and he wasn't worried about himself. He was worried about *you*."

I shake my head as my mind spins out of control. That deep ache of anxiety reels and riots through my body, threatening to drag me into the abyss.

"He was worried our baby would be like him!" My voice cracks over the words as the first tears trickle down my cheeks. "That's all. He–he knows how dangerous he is, and now look at us, Mom. Skye is the same. He's only around now because I can't help her. You can't help her, and we're losing her every second that passes. You have to know that."

Mom shakes her head.

I shrug, closing my eyes. "Blake will never care about anything other than keeping who he really is a secret from everyone, including me. That boy we knew, Mom, he's gone. He's as good as dead."

"You're delirious, and you need to go lie down–"

"Mommy?" Skye's voice carries on a soft breeze coming through the open back door before she comes into view, her violet eyes the same shade and shape as the man she inherited them from. She looks from me to my mom, her face shadowed by confusion. "Grammy?"

"It's alright, sweetie. Mommy's not feeling well." Mom cuts me a sharp look as she guides Skye out of the room.

Guilt nearly drags me to the floor.

I close myself in my room, change into a shirt and shorts, and sit on the edge of my bed. My purse rests on top of my dresser, my phone sticking out just enough I can see the blinking light telling me I have... hundreds of notifications.

It's not work. It's not from the academy. It's not old friends from Crescent Falls trying to check in on us.

Which means I'm not as safe here as I hoped I'd be.

Chapter 18

Something's Happening

Blake

Veiled Valley is shrouded in rain clouds as I walk through the castle, met by a welcoming gust of warm air. The spirit of the house is usually happy to see me compared to others. I've often wondered where it came from, why it chose this place to make its eternal home.

It follows me through the castle while I make my way to the office Ryatt keeps here, despite being a few months into his retirement, which I think was Ella's idea more than his.

Sconces light my way, flickering on with each step I take up a winding stone staircase older than anything in Moonrise. Veiled Valley has been around since the dawn of time, I think. So long, in fact, I can't see its origins in the tapestry weaving between the stars.

A blond young man steps out of a room carrying a stack of books. He flinches when he sees me in the shadows, then sighs, shaking his head. Silver eyes meet mine in the flickering haze of amber-hued light as he greets me, saying, "Shit, Blake, I didn't know you were going to be here tonight."

"Neither did I." I step past Aris, taking notice of the iron cuffs inlaid with sapphire and black diamonds. He never takes them off, and I know that in battle, those gems glow. He went through his trials in the cave beneath Veiled Valley, the same cave where Ryatt found the sword he still wears despite, technically, passing it down to Kenna. I've always found this side of the family to be slightly odd and secretive, if I'm being honest, especially when it comes to their ties to the ancient line of wolves they belong to—the Shadowsyngers.

Aris follows me, however, keeping in step as we turn another sharp corner and meet another spiral stone staircase. "Did you come here for a vacation like Maeve?"

"No. I doubt I would have chosen Veiled Valley if that were the case."

He smirks. "What's wrong with Veiled Valley? You can just walk out of the gates here without being totally bombarded by people, unlike Moonrise."

"I honestly prefer Maatua," I admit, which seems to shock him. I doubt he's ever seen me in swim trunks lying out in the sun. "Your grandfather summoned me here. I plan to leave once he's given his directive." My cloak swishes as I turn to Aris. He's a year younger than me, unmated, and turning into quite the warrior from what Evander told me. He can also shift into both a fox and a wolf, like his father, which is so rare that they may be the only ones in existence as it stands, other than Aris's maternal grandmother, Amanda, who still lives in Moonrise with her mate, Granger, and the rest of Evander's many siblings. They have an enormous family at this point. Brie, Maeve, and Aris have at least ten, if not a dozen, cousins on their paternal side.

And then they have us. The tangled web made up of Isla and Maddox's grandchildren and great-grandchildren.

"Well, if you change your mind, I'm meeting Maeve and Soren out for a night on the town later," he says, turning toward an archway at the top of the stairs. "They're out to dinner right now, and none of us were invited. Mom says it's because they haven't had a chance to go on a real date yet, and they already have a kid. Seems a little backward to me." He smirks and then disappears into the shadows.

I suck my lip between my teeth and move in the opposite direction, hiking another short staircase to a tower that houses a private suite for Ella and Ryatt. It's less than a quarter of the size of the wing of the castle in Moonrise now inhabited by Maeve and Soren, but it feels more like them, if that makes sense. Dark wood and emerald walls greet me when I step inside, passing a foyer, then a formal sitting room, walking a straight line toward the grand archway that melds into an angular office with walls the color of burnt sapphire. Ryatt sits in an armchair beneath a window flooded with rain. His eyes scan my face when I breach the archway and come to a stop a few feet away from him, my cloak swishing to a stop around my boots.

"Sit down, Blake. There's something I need to discuss with you."

"I won't be here for long. I have business in Moonrise."

He motions to the armchair across from his, which holds Ella's scent. I wonder if they sit up here in their old age and gossip about the family. I would if I were them.

He doesn't take no for an answer, ever, so I sit, but my back remains straight, barely grazing the plush cushions. "What do you need? I've already explained my current findings about Hannibal and his coven to Evander."

"I don't care about that. There's little we can do as it stands if the man is no longer in Eastonia." He drums his fingers against his thigh, glancing away from me for a moment. "I've spoken to your grandfather recently and wondered if you'd be willing to talk to me about your plans for Crescent Falls."

"My plans? For what, exactly? Crescent Falls is in a boom—it runs on its own—"

"That's not what I meant."

I ignore the twisting sensation in my gut. "You want to know if I'm going to be king one day?"

He gives me a short nod.

I weigh my options. I could easily dance around the question and deflect, but why bother?

I'm tired. Every thought and action these days is... not about my job, my birthright, nor my family. Not this one, at least.

Just her. Just them.

"I will not be Alpha King of Crescent Falls."

Ryatt stares at me, his silver eyes inspecting the dead, hollow expression I wear so well to mask everything I've ever felt. He doesn't seem surprised by my answer in the slightest.

"You seem unsurprised," I note, finally relaxing into the chair.

"You're right. I'm not surprised in the slightest. Isaac had his doubts." When he catches the briefest glint of confusion behind my eyes, he amends, "Not about your ability to rule. In fact, he thinks of it as a great loss. You are the most like your great-grandfather out of everyone in the family, who was a great king. The best Crescent Falls has ever had, and your reign would have been an incredible one."

"Did you call me here to try to convince me otherwise?"

"No, the opposite."

Now, I'm confused. Thoroughly. "I haven't announced my plans to my parents, and I would appreciate the chance to do so before others find out and spread the news to them."

"This conversation is not leaving this office," he replies. "You have my word."

"Is that all you needed?"

"No."

My jaw flexes. "Why am I here, Ryatt?"

"The mystics call you their king."

The mask slips, and I roll my eyes. "I really wish they wouldn't."

"You are in a great position of power within the temples across Eastonia."

"I'm not here to play chess, Ryatt."

"I understand that you..." He holds my gaze, tapering off. Fear washes through me for several seconds while I wait for him to say something about Skye, but he continues, "I understand you have no interest in further training with them, and I understand why—you don't need the training, and you never have, which I told your parents back when you were fourteen. You should have trained with Arthur, here, in Veiled Valley, learned the history of the mystics and their kind instead. But you cannot deny the power you hold over those–those beings." He motions in a dismissive manner. "And our kingdom–Eastonia–where I'm under the impression you mean to make your home–has been occasionally fooled by them, or worse, blindsided by their actions when a mystic falls into the wrong hands."

"You're talking about the Draven Coven."

"Draven, Arcane Umbra, and whoever comes next, yes. I am not going to deny the risk of a mystic falling into step with someone–something–like Hannibal Archanis. I'm not going to sit here and pretend everything is all right and that there's not a chance he doesn't already have mystics working for him, given that every foot soldier that fell under the Viper's command had their minds picked apart. Only a mystic can do that. Am I wrong?"

"Hannibal himself has the ability," I admit. "It was him. He wiped their minds, and I believe it was simple. The Viper, and den leaders like her, use fear to create a hive mind among their warriors. Soren was an exception, which is why he was so danger-ous, such a huge risk to them, but they benefited from his abilities. I'm under the impression that every single warrior that has ties to Hannibal in some way now has no recollection of their time under his control."

"Then he's a mystic, as well?"

"He's something like us. But I believe... I believe he's something like... Logan and Kieran."

Ryatt closes his eyes for a moment. "Soren mentioned this to me."

"The ears–"

"I am aware, and both Arthur and Misty are at work–"

"They will not find anything in our history about people like Logan and Kieran."

"Why not?"

"Because they never lived in Eastonia. They're from somewhere else, somewhere outside of our kingdoms, our maps, and the best thing we can do is prepare for history to be rewritten, and for war."

"You're sure?"

"I am." I rise, my skin tingling with a sudden sense of... knowing. I feel slightly unsteady as Marianna's image flashes through the fragmented visions and voices constantly at play behind my eyes. "And I already know what you're going to ask about the mystics. I plan on choosing a few to train directly under me, a few trusted individuals who can look beyond the hive mind they were trained to live within. They will be the ones who give us the first glimpses of enemies on the horizon."

"You've been hard at work, Blake."

"I like to keep myself busy. Excuse me." I give him a short bow and leave, my boots thundering down staircase after staircase as the voices and images yank my mind from side to side, trying to decide what to show me and why. Usually, it's easy enough to ignore them. I have my ways. My headphones, my music, an all-consuming video game and the like, but right now, even the soft echo of EDM music as I walk through the arts district of Veiled Valley isn't doing a Goddess damn thing to ease my mind.

I pass a restaurant and then backtrack as a couple comes into view. Soren meets my eyes through the glass, cursing, but Maeve gives me a shocked, then annoyed, look.

The voices fade, which likely means I'm supposed to be here, at this restaurant, interrupting what I think is Soren and Maeve's first official date.

"Do not sit down," Maeve snarls, trying to keep her voice low so as to not alarm the other patrons scattered through the tight little restaurant.

I ignore her, sliding into a seat between them.

Soren sighs, motioning to a waiter. Maeve's eyes narrow on her mate as he orders another round of scotch for himself and a glass for me.

"What the fuck are you doing here?" Maeve sneers, reaching

under the table to violently pinch my thigh. "We finally, finally have a night alone to be normal and you–"

"Do you feel anything amiss? Anything whatsoever?" I ask her, holding her gaze.

Her furious expression shifts to concern. "What do you mean? What are you seeing?"

"I can't make sense of it," I growl, unnerved–too worked up by my powers to keep the mask on any longer. I'm sure my real feelings are showing because even Soren stiffens, his eyes locked on my face. "I was here to see Ryatt. He summoned me. Then I started to feel– started to see–" I look at Soren, who stiffens further until he's totally rigid, hackles raised in what I assume is solidarity, unless he's about to lunge over the table and kick my ass for interrupting this date.

"Something's wrong with Marianna," I say, more to myself than anyone at the table. "But I don't know why I'm here, why the voices called me... here..."

"Where's Skye?" Soren asks.

"Skye? Marianna's daughter?"

"My daughter." I meet Maeve's eyes. "She's my daughter."

"Blake?" Maeve gives me a skeptical look, but my eyes blur with a vision–something happening in real time. I can feel the cool spring breeze in Moonrise as a man walks up Marianna's street under a cloak of darkness. Blood drips onto cobblestone where the security guard groans, trying to claw his way back to the gate. The man stops in front of Marianna's house and looks up as her bedroom light turns off.

"Fuck," I growl.

Soren rises, slaps a hand on my arm, and we disappear into the aether.

Chapter 19

You'll Have to Kill Me First

Marianna

Skye's asleep with her body curled around three of her favorite stuffed animals when I step into her room and shut off the nightlight casting stars all over her ceiling. A soft breeze whispers through thick curtains I quietly pull closed before tucking her in for what feels like the hundredth time. I've been on edge all day. It's been... the worst day. First, Blake. Me shoving another wedge between us. Then, fighting with Mom... with Skye overhearing. After the fight I went down to the lake and tossed my phone into the water in a rage, then shifted, running over all of Moonrise until the sun began to set, and I slunk home to sit at the table with my mother and my daughter. My dinner was served cold. I deserved it.

I gently close Skye's bedroom door while the mark on my neck aches. It's a deep pain that makes my throat and shoulders sore and is relentless, but also, unfortunately, familiar.

Dean wasn't faithful. I'm not sure he ever was. Our relationship was fast and furious and ended in a crash, but he marked me before I could fully pull away when I realized he wasn't the man I thought he was. That sealed things. We married. I moved Skye and Mom into his pack territory. I was young, stupid, and flailing, trying to find my footing in the world and he was... a Beta. He had power and influence.

He used it.

He wasn't going to let me go, and for the nearly two years we were together, I spent most nights tossing and turning in bed as the mark he left on my neck ached and burned while he cheated on me numerous times.

That wasn't the worst of it. Not even close. I was done months before he started threatening Mom and Skye. I'd already ended things, moved back to the inner city and out of his pack territory. I had local authorities involved. I spent another two years trying to rebuild a life without the crushing weight of him in it. He was supposed to stay far away from me.

Three months ago, he showed up at my house after his Alpha got a visit from royal warriors for interrupting one of my practice sessions with the Crescent Falls orchestra. He'd been thrown out of his pack. It wasn't his first transgression against his Alpha.

I did try to warn him that his bad behavior would catch up to him, and most of it didn't have to do with me. Still, I was the target of his rage, and I still wore his mark on my neck.

He put a few more marks on me that night. Bruises. A fractured cheekbone. A dislocated shoulder. The works.

I scrub his memory from my mind and close myself into my room, busying myself by replacing the worn out strings of my violin. My laptop is open beside me on the bed playing a soft litany of classical music I plan to rework and add to the set list for the upcoming season while another screen shows a few unread emails– promotions, ads, a return email from what I hope will be Skye's new school this fall giving me a date and time for our admission meeting.

My chest feels impossibly heavy as I pluck the strings, adjusting their tightness. My neck continues to burn until it's to the point I can't ignore it anymore, so I step into the bathroom where I dig through my skin care products to try to find something somewhat calming.

My reflection in the mirror is... messy. Haggard. Tired. I scrub my hand over my face before giving up and pressing a cool rag to my neck and walking back into my room where I shut off the lights and walk to the window to pull the curtains closed but... a shadow moves into view below, lingering at the gate.

"Blake?" I narrow my eyes, trying to squint through the darkness. It's a dreary, overcast night. Even the faint glow of the streetlight two houses down doesn't illuminate the shadow of a tall, lean man now reaching for the gate.

I pull on my robe and pad downstairs, sliding my feet into my slippers. "Blake, it's the middle of the–" My voice cuts out as my feet come to an abrupt halt on the footpath leading to the gate.

The face scowling down at me isn't Blake's. The smooth, handsome curve of Blake's jaw is replaced by a scruffy, unkempt beard in shades of deep red and blond. The wild eyes aren't that stunning violet. No, they're black with rage.

Dean unlatches the gate and steps into the yard.

"You're not allowed here," I manage to say as my neck burns like someone is pressing a boiling hot metal rod to my skin. "You need to leave. Get out of here!"

"You really fucking thought you could just walk away, huh?" Dean's dark blond hair is cast in shadow, dirty, like he hasn't bothered to take care of himself. I doubt he has. He lost everything over the past six months because he couldn't leave me alone, because he slept with his Alpha's sister, so I've heard, and now owes an incredible amount of money to his pack, a fine he incurred upon being exiled.

But a wolf is more dangerous as a rogue. He has nothing to lose.

And I've always been his target when he's like this. Drunk out of his mind.

"Get back," I grind out, teeth bared. "Get off my property, you disgusting bastard!"

"Eastonia, huh?" He looks around, smirking, taking several determined steps in my direction. "What did you think would happen when you left, Marianna? You'd be free? You still wear my mark. You'll have it forever, you fucking worthless bitch. You're mine. I should have locked things down a few months ago."

"What do you mean?" I snarl, backing up the porch steps. I have to get inside. I have to lock the doors and call the guards at the gate for help. "You need to leave. I'm going to call the guards to come—"

"They're busy. I made sure of that." His sick, demented smile burrows through my stomach, twisting like a knife. I glance down at his bloody hands and feel my body careen toward the door before my mind has a chance to catch up with what's happening, but I'm a second too late.

Dean lunges, grabbing me by the hair. I scream, but he cuts it out with a hand to my mouth. He doesn't bother opening the door. He kicks it in in one switch motion, like he's done this before. Broken into someone's home.

Lights flicker on upstairs, and my fear is replaced by a sucking, all-consuming kind of dread.

"You're going back to Crescent Falls with me," he shouts in my ear. "Without your fucking mutant daughter, that's for Goddess damned sure."

I try to squirm out of his grip, biting down on his hand, but he just laughs and shoves me so hard I fly into the mantle, my forehead crashing against the wooden surface. The framed pictures and Skye's agates tremble with the impact, but I catch myself on the wall and sway toward the foot of the stairs where I will remain.

I will not be moved from the spot, no matter how hard he hits, no matter what happens, I will not allow him to get upstairs.

Glass shatters when he swipes his hand over the mantle. Every frame falls to the ground, Skye's agates fracturing in a shower of delicate stone. I close my eyes as he rages, screaming obscenities in my face about me, about my daughter, my mother...

"Marianna," Mom's voice is soft but clear from the top of the stairs.

"Call the guard station."

"They're not answering. I called our neighbor–"

"You belong to me," Dean grinds out, his mouth against my cheek–hot and furious. Pain radiates through my lip when he hits me hard enough to split it, and my ears ring, but I block out the pain. All I'm thinking about is Skye and what she'll see, what she'll hear.

He punches me in the stomach. I remain upright, gripping either side of the banister. He'll have to kill me to get me to move.

I've been a terrible mother. I let this man into our lives to wreak havoc. She's seen it. She saw my face the day they came home to me unconscious on the floor of the living room, bleeding. No wonder she started to shut down. It was my fault. All my fault. I failed them. I don't know where I started going wrong, but it was my fault.

Another blow to my stomach has my grip on the banister weakening. Dean is out of his mind, his stench of booze filling the room, mingling with what I know is my blood.

His knuckles smash against my jaw. My teeth crack as a wave of pain like I've never felt before nearly sends me to my knees, but I won't move. I will not let him upstairs. I will die here before I allow him to get to Skye, which is what he really wants, isn't it?

She has always been in his way. She was my priority, not him.

He grips my neck as his words blur. I can't hear him anymore. I can barely register the room when I open my eyes to slits, seeing nothing but destruction and him taking up space. He squeezes until black spots shimmer around the edges of my vision.

"You're mine. You stupid slut."

My mouth fills with the taste of copper. A smooth, silent cloud of violet and stardust settles throughout the room before two men appear. One is dressed in jeans and an undone button-down shirt–casual. Soren's always been casual, down to the faded, worn down blue ball cap he's wearing backward as he races toward us and lands a vicious blow to the side of Dean's head.

Dean lets go. I gasp for breath. Mom's thundering footsteps merge with Blake's as they race toward me from different directions.

I see a single glimpse of Blake's face before my vision starts to fade. His eyes are wild. A desperation, utterly astonished expression cuts through his mask of emotional void, and then that gaze turns... murderous.

"Get her upstairs now," Blake thunders. Mom's arms hook under my armpits, and then she's dragging me up the stairs.

I open my eyes as Blake watches us, his face twisting in brutal, unyielding rage.

"Blake," I whisper, tears blurring my vision. "Blake–"

He turns away and stalks out of sight. I hear something crash, then Soren flies into view, tumbling onto the ground with an arm locked around Dean's neck. Dean is out of his mind and on the verge of shifting, but he's too drunk to get his wolf powers to bend to his will.

I stick out a hand before Mom can drag me around the corner at the top of the stairwell. Blake kneels, his black as night cloak flaring out behind him, but Dean goes suddenly still, his eyes flaring with magic.

Blake isn't touching him.

Soren lets Dean go and pants as he moves away, sporting a righteous black eye. Mom and I are still as stone, watching as Blake looks at Dean from head to toe.

"Blake?" Soren says, uneasy, glancing at Blake and then down at Dean.

"I'm not doing it," Blake says, confused, then Dean arches his back and screams bloody murder.

I brace a hand on the wall and turn toward Skye's bedroom. The door is open, and she's sitting on the edge of her bed, squeezing her favorite teddy bear to her chest.

Her eyes glow like vibrant violet stars.

Chapter 20

The Binding Spell

BLAKE

I slowly place my fingertips against Dean's forehead as he writhes, spasming as... his mind is torn to absolute shreds. It's sloppy. Untrained. Memories sprint toward my powers, blooming into images that make my blood boil. Him hurting Marianna over and over again. The memories split and shatter before my eyes, but it's not my doing.

I pull out of his mind and rise, my eyes on the two women standing shellshocked at the top of the stairs.

"Go to them. Go!" Soren barks, pinning an increasingly frantic Dean to the ground. I catch Soren's gaze, and he nods, a silent camaraderie expanding in the space between us. He's not going to let this man get back to his feet.

I'm at the top of the stairs in an instant. Marianna is kneeling at Skye's side, begging her to wake up, to stop, but Marianna's words are slurred as blood drips from her swollen, split lips. Bruises fan over her cheekbones and both eyes, and her nose is definitely broken. I grip the doorframe so tight it cracks to stop myself from returning downstairs to smash Dean's head in with my boot, but Leona is suddenly at my side, her hand gripping my arm.

She pulls me out the haze of murderous rage and back into reality, where my daughter is...

I step out of Leona's hold and kneel in front of Skye. Her nose is bleeding, and her arms are as cold as ice when I smooth my hands over her skin before gripping her, saying calmly, "Stop."

She trembles, tears flooding down her cheeks. I can't even look at Marianna right now. Otherwise, I'll go absolutely, unapologetically feral and kill Dean so violently even the most skilled crime scene cleaners won't be able to ride this house of his blood, but I feel Marianna's presence beside me, her hand flat against my lower back.

"Skye, you have to stop," I say as ice forms behind her eyes, her skin going frosty. But it's useless. She doesn't know what she's doing. She has no idea what she's capable of, but I do.

She's killing him. She *wants* to.

I can't let her do that. She's seven. She's just a kid.

I caress her cheek, leaning my forehead against hers, and close my eyes.

Her powers are... everywhere. They're just... bouncing, pinging off Dean's memories and thoughts, wrapping around those glowing, spherical structures like talons before popping them like bubbles. I can feel her fear in her powers as she empties his mind, but her powers are so young, so excitable and untrained. She has no control over anything she's doing. It's an emotional response. Something I know so well. Something I had to train out of myself over the course of years until I was a shell of the person I was when I was her age.

The more I feel, the more dangerous I am... to myself and others.

I smooth my powers over hers, imagining them like a hand, reaching, gathering, finding the strands of violet and stardust and collecting them like a ball of string.

"Stop," I whisper as my powers surge, but she won't.

Marianna whimpers beside me, scooching closer, laying a hand on Skye's thigh. "Please, baby. It's time to wake up. You have to wake up now. Please–"

The tapestry flares to life. It takes me by surprise. She shouldn't be able to access this yet, to travel through the planes of our world, to read between the stars, between the worlds of the living and the dead, but I'm watching her figure it out in real time, and I can't... I can't let it continue.

"No," I breathe and yank on her powers, pulling her out of Dean's mind in a final, desperate push.

But she's done... so much damage. I can see that. I can feel it as my own powers retreat, and the tapestry begins to blur.

And she... my daughter, my *powerful* daughter... finds his tether to our world, his lifeline, and plucks it free of the tapestry in her final act of vengeance before my powers pull her out of Dean's head.

The room erupts around me in startling clarity. I scoop Skye into my arms. She's freezing, turning to ice in real time as her powers reach a critical low. She's too young to be doing this. She doesn't have her wolf yet to keep her warm, to balance her conflicting magic. "Blankets! We need–blankets." Leona appears at my side and takes Skye from my arms, wrapping her in a thick robe. Marianna struggles to her feet but can't manage it, and I catch her before she doubles over, her hand pressed to her stomach as she hisses in pain.

"Is–is she okay? Skye? Skye!" Marianna's voice drops in anguish that cuts me to the bone. I steady her while she babbles, trying to reach for Skye, but a figure hovers in the doorway–two people. Soren and... Maeve.

Maeve drops the hood of her cloak and looks around the room, first at Marianna, then Leona, and Skye.

She stares at Skye for several seconds, stunned into silence, then her eyes turn to mine. "They both need the clinic. I'm taking all three of them there, now."

"Marianna and Leona can't handle the jump. They've never done it before," I rush out, shaking my head with a hand extended in Skye's direction. "Take Skye. She's–she's depleting–"

Maeve doesn't waste an instant, and Leona doesn't hesitate as she transfers Skye into Maeve's arms, who cradles Skye, her eyes scanning her face, her still open eyes. Her powers fade, and Maeve... turns back to me.

"This whole time? This is what you were guarding?"

I nod, my mouth going impossibly dry. Marianna leans her head against my shoulder, panting in pain. Soren starts forward, leaning in to murmur something to Maeve, and then she just disappears in a haze of crimson smoke that fades from the space as quickly as it came.

I look at Soren, meeting his gaze. He gives him a short, simple nod to confirm that the man downstairs, the man who terrorized Marianna, Skye, and Leona for years... is dead.

"I've got guys on their way to deal with the body," he says under his breath. "Take them to the castle–"

"I'll stay behind for now," Leona cuts in. "To deal with the guards who come. They'll want to know–"

"There will be no guards," Soren says, giving her a tight smile. "This is royal family business now. You're protected."

"And you can't stay here," I add, gathering Marianna into my arms. She feels lighter than usual. "We need to go."

Leona glances between us, her big blue eyes swimming with emotion I can't decipher. Relief, I think, takes up the most amount of space. She places her hand against her chest and breathes deeply before nodding. "I'm going to pack up a few things they'll want."

"That's fine. Soren, will you escort her to the castle when she's done?"

He nods.

Marianna is barely conscious. I move through the night, past the security gate where a guard is slumped, bleeding, trying to wave me down for help. I swipe a hand in his direction, and his eyes briefly light with my powers as they erase the memory of what happened to him. He'll call for help, but by the time backup arrives to see him safely to a clinic either in town or at the castle, Soren and his friends will have already cleaned up the mess and disposed of Dean in their own way.

I have to give Soren credit. He's not as bad as I wanted to think.

I shield Marianna with my powers–something I believe stems from our ability to jump from place to place–making us both invisible to wandering eyes. I move under a cloak of darkness around the backside of the palace where the clinic entrance rises into view. I drop the shields the second I reach the wide, glass doors, and within moments, I'm rushed in by witch nurses who take Marianna away, leaving me in the foyer slightly out of breath, my mind tangled by conflicting feelings I couldn't put into words if I tried.

I don't know what to do, so I follow them, weaving through sterile hallways and into a room with white walls that smells like astringent and the fresh, cotton scent of the nurse's uniforms. I barely hear what the healer says to me, what her nurse underlings convey and relay in layman's terms. I just stand there in the door and look at Marianna, a bloodied mess, and think about how I'd found her gripping the banister, using her body as a physical shield to stop Dean from going upstairs.

I'd been a few minutes too late to stop this from happening completely.

I'll carry that regret for the rest of my life.

Only when a familiar voice sounds out directly behind me do I break out of the haze and turn away from Marianna.

Maeve stands in the hallway looking grim, still wearing her crimson cloak and the casual, but pretty, dress she chose for her date night with Soren that was brutally called off.

"Where's—"

"Skye is asleep upstairs in one of the guest rooms. Leona is with her now."

I scrub my hand over my face and step into the hallway. One of the nurses closes the door to Marianna's room behind me like they've been waiting for me to leave this entire time.

"Blake–"

"I can't. Not right now. I can't talk about this right now–"

"I'm fucking sorry, okay?"

I peek through my fingers at her, taken aback by her tone. Maeve isn't a soft, understanding person by nature. She's as cold as me, but instead of curling into herself, she lets her chaos show. But right now, she's wary. Her eyes are lined with dark circles and full of what I can only describe as sorrow.

She steps closer, gritting her teeth before sighing, "She's seven, Blake. You've been hiding her–them–for seven years? Why?"

"Why do you think?"

She searches my eyes, finding an answer, I suppose, because her shoulders slacken. She doesn't say I hid them to keep them safe, that I hid them so other people wouldn't know and find them, let the media terrorize them forever. No, her voice is soft as she says, "You thought Skye would turn out like you if you stuck around, huh?"

"I guess it wasn't within my control after all."

"You're a fucking dumbass," she says low in her throat, but her eyes are teasing. "*Stupid idiot.*"

"Do you have anything nice to say? I've had a long, terrible night."

"You need to come to the gallery," she says, her expression tightening. "Now."

"I'm not leaving her here by herself."

"I've already given the command to have her moved into the same suite her mom and Skye are staying in. Once she's stable, she'll be taken there. For now... I might have fucked up." She winces and then purses her lips.

"What do you mean?" I'm on edge for multiple reasons now. I don't like the look in her eyes.

"When you and Soren stole away from the restaurant without a word about where you were going, I went back to the castle in Veiled Valley and told my mom what happened, and... Grandma Ella just happened to be returning from Maatua with... your grandma."

"No–"

"And now they're all here. Uhm." She knits her fingers together, looking surprisingly guilty. "They know."

"Gods dammit, Maeve!"

"What the fuck else was I supposed to say when I felt Soren beating the ever living fuck out of a man through our bond in the middle of the Goddess damned night, Blake? Riddle me that! The three of them followed me back to Moonrise and demanded answers when I showed up here again with a little girl with the same eyes as you and Sarah. Maddy is–Maddy is beside herself–"

"My parents don't know about her yet–"

"She's beside herself with worry about you and Marianna, Blake. They're in the gallery. I made them wait there for news, and now you need to explain what's going on before Maddy has an aneurysm, okay?"

I turn back to Marianna's room, but Maeve grabs my wrist.

"Please? We're already preparing for war, Blake. No more secrets. No more schemes. We don't have that kind of time or freedom anymore."

The door to the room opens abruptly, and the healer steps out, looking incredibly upset. I stiffen, and Maeve bristles beside me.

"Are you her mate?" the healer asks, and not even remotely kindly.

"No, I'm not," I gut out. The words sink, foul tasting.

"Where is her mate then? I need to speak with him. Warriors are going to be alerted–"

"Alerted to what?" Maeve chimes in, narrowing her eyes at the healer. "Is she all right?"

"No," the healer snaps back, disgust lacing the word. "She's under a binding spell, and it's wreaking havoc on her body. She won't heal. I can't break it. It's coming from her mark."

Maeve's jaw goes slack. I glance between the women, utterly confused. "What is going on?"

"That fucking bastard," Maeve whisper snarls, shaking her head. To the healer, she says, "Keep her stable. I'll be with you shortly."

She grips my arms and tears me away from the door while I try to dig in my heels.

"Enough, Blake. Things just changed. We're dealing with dark magic now. You need to go to Crescent Falls as soon as fucking possible."

Chapter 21

Death's Door

BLAKE

Kenna gazes down at Marianna, who blinks up at her, her eyes cloudy and unfocused when Kenna's faint healing powers ripple through her, healing bruises and gashes. We moved her to the apartment upstairs–a random guest suite on the fourth floor–an hour ago. I've been bouncing between her room and the room where Skye is still fast asleep under the watchful eye of Leona, who hasn't slept a wink tonight, and the first signs of morning are already shimmering through lace curtains lining the windows overlooking the city.

Kenna clicks her tongue, silently motioning for Marianna to turn her head to the side so she can get a better look at the mark branded on her skin. It's terribly inflamed–rotting, to be honest. Marianna winces deeply in pain when Kenna prods the swollen skin with her fingers.

Maeve paces behind me with Fallon tucked against her shoulder. My cousin shakes her head, her face twisted in fury.

The healer who discovered what they're saying is a curse, a woman named Minerva, is standing on the other side of the bed with her arms crossed, her expression a mirror image of Maeve's–anger.

"I've never seen it actually used before," Kenna says as she glances at Minerva. "You're one-hundred percent sure?"

"I can smell it," Minerva scowls, her eyes red and bloodshot. "It's a curse. Any type of binding spell is a curse."

"I'm aware," Kenna says tightly. "What I don't understand is how an average person would be able to get their hands on the potion or the individual ingredients needed to even begin this process. And the spell–"

"Can someone please explain," I grind out, losing the last grip I have on my already worn-thin patience, "what the hell is going on?"

Marianna's eyes scan the room looking for the source of my voice. She's a mess–a beautiful, strong, brave mess–but in tatters all the same. Kenna's healing gifts aren't nearly as strong as Misty's, but Misty isn't here. So far, whatever she's doing is working on the superficial wounds, but the mark...

"This is insane," Maeve says to the group, patting Fallon's back. "I've never–the ingredients for the spell aren't even remotely accessible to the general market. Ashwood, bone of oryx, spindlethrush? The only places that have those herbs in particular are the caverns beneath the royal library, and they're under lock and key every hour of the day. This can't actually be what it is."

Marianna stares at me, her eyes milky and distant. The corners of her mouth tilt into a soft, sleepy smile, and then she closes her eyes for what I hope is a while, at least. She needs the rest.

"I am certain," Minerva says slowly, glancing between the women. "I swear to the Goddess that this is what we're dealing with. This is... this is a death sentence for her, I fear."

"What did you just say?" My voice is a thunderous growl, but Kenna sighs, her silver eyes meeting mine. She looks tired, her slightly curly dark brown hair falling in loose spirals out of the bun she pinned to the top of her head a few hours ago when she rolled up her sleeves and jumped in at the mention of Dark Magic.

"Blake, you need to leave and get some rest. Maddy has been waiting to talk to you."

"I'm not leaving her without an explanation as to what that fucking animal did to her!" I snap back. "You said she's dying? Why? What kind of spell or potion would do this to a person, and why was it used?"

Kenna closes her eyes and exhales, surrendering, but it's Maeve who speaks, her voice tight to shield the same feelings her mother can't help but show.

"Binding is highly illegal and so rare it's been, what, centuries since the last recorded case?" She arches a brow at Minerva and her mom, who nod in agreement, before I slowly turn around to face her. "You said Marianna mentioned to you that Dean imprinted on her before she turned twenty-one. Imprinting is not the same as being fated mates. It's a different kind of bond, surface level. Rejection and the death of a mate wouldn't carry the same kind of weight as it would for those who are fated, whose timelines cross, or however you see it." She waves a dismissive hand in my direction before pacing to the window overlooking the city. Soren hasn't returned yet. It's been hours, and I can tell she's growing nervous. "A binding spell mimics the fated mate bond in a physical way. It binds a couple using magic, turning the act of imprinting into more of a... magically induced bond." She turns back to me, sighing heavily. "It's similar to a blood oath. If anything were to happen to Dean, it would happen to her. She'd feel it in the bond, live it, like a real mate would."

She struggles to find her wording, to come up with a way to explain, then continues, "If he were unfaithful, for example, it would be painful for her. She'd feel it in the mark. If he were to get hurt, or sick, she'd feel it. If something were to happen to him–if he were to... to die–" Her eyes meet mine, heavy and dark. "She'd–she'd die, Blake. She wasn't really his mate. He forced her to be in the most dangerous, illicit way I can think of. He bound her with a potion and a spell, and I'm guessing she's been... she's been trying to escape him for a very long time and couldn't because of this. He was always able to find her again using their bond. This is how it ends. She's going to die."

"I can't accept that."

"You have to," Kenna says warily, shaking her head. "Any kind of treatment is just going to prolong her suffering–"

"There has to be a way to undo this. Misty–"

"Misty didn't train in the dark arts like we did," Maeve says, motioning to her mom and Minerva. "There are no cures for curses like these."

"This is not how she dies!" I shout, and the room falls silent. Three sets of eyes are on me as I pace to the foot of the bed, gripping the footboard like it's the only thing keeping me upright. "This isn't how she dies because I've seen it, okay? How do we fix this? This is wrong. This shouldn't be happening this way!"

"You can cut out the mark," Minerva offers, but Kenna shakes her head.

"We'd risk the curse spreading at an accelerated rate. Right now it's just within the mark."

"It won't stay that way, and you know that," Minerva argues. "It'll spread slowly, killing her slowly, painfully. We have a shot, I believe, to cut it out, but where it's placed on her neck... it would be a tricky surgery. She could bleed out before any kind of healing drafts or spells take effect. We'd need a team of witches at her bedside constantly using their magic."

"That is so risky, Minerva. It hasn't ever been done," Kenna argues.

"It's worth a try. We need to do something," Maeve says.

"We have... minutes to act," Minerva says. "I'll call down to the clinic and prepare to move her–"

"And if we can't dispel the curse?" Maeve asks. "If we cut out the mark, and the curse takes hold anyway?"

Silence settles for several long, aching seconds. I glance between the women, my heart beating out of rhythm.

"We keep her comfortable. She'll have moments of lucidity." Kenna's voice breaks over the words. "She can say goodbye to her daughter and her mom."

"You've got to be fucking kidding me!" I snarl.

"Blake," Maeve says softly, and I whirl toward her, taken aback by the tears clouding her eyes.

"I won't accept this. He put her through hell. I saw it all, Maeve. Every single fucking thing he ever did to her, and you're telling me the reason he was able to do it, to keep her down and under his thumb for so long, was because he fucking cursed her? She's not going to die like this. *I. Won't. Allow. It.*"

"It's not up to you," she says, her voice trembling. "If cutting out the mark doesn't work–"

"Fuck you," I hiss, and Kenna's head snaps up, her eyes wide.

"Blake!"

"Fuck all of you."

Kenna grits her teeth.

"You need to leave, High Lord," Minerva says weakly as my powers begin to prickle to the surface, clawing for dominance, lighting behind my eyes.

I feel a touch on my back–soft and familiar. It makes me want to sink into myself, to fall to my knees and beg for someone to just... help her.

Grandma Maddy is standing behind me. The conversation about my relation to Marianna and Skye hasn't been had yet. It's not that I'm avoiding it, either; I just... can't.

"Misty," I breathe, shaking my head. "Misty can break curses. I'll get her, I'll bring her here, and she'll fix this."

"This is different from the curse Richard of Arcane Umbra used on his people, Blake," Maeve says solemnly. "This isn't–" She licks her lips, shuddering. "She was bound to Dean, okay? He's dragging her into death. She's not–there's nothing keeping her here anymore."

"Then bind her to *me*," I say, my voice edging on pleading. "I will mark her right now–I swear on the Goddess, I will. Save her! Save–"

Grandma Maddy grabs my hand and guides me backward out of the room. I don't fight it. I don't think I have the strength to. Marianna is... fading right before my eyes, her breath shallow and uneven.

In the next room, which I can see into when Grandma silently closes Marianna's door, and I turn around, Leona looks up at me from her perch on a stool next to Skye's bed, her eyes full of tears.

"You need a minute of quiet, I think," Grandma says in a near whisper and walks me away, into a snug living space just beyond the hallway housing both bedrooms.

"I need to get Misty."

"I think it's wise, yes. But I'm not a witch. What do I know?" she chuckles, but her voice is edged with the same hurt currently tearing me to shreds. "I'm the only normal person in the family besides Brie, and maybe Cole, I suppose, but I...." She tapers off as she guides me past the living space and into the corridor. "Why didn't you tell us about them?"

"I made a vow to protect them from everything I saw as a threat," I admit, unable to look her in the eyes as I shatter beyond repair. "I didn't want Skye to be like me. I thought if I–I thought if I wasn't there, if she didn't have someone to guide her, her powers wouldn't emerge. I thought if I gave up on Marianna and let her go, she'd–" She'd live past her twenty-sixth birthday, when our... when her tether abruptly ended, so short. So brutally insignificant. That's what I'd seen back then, that one time I let myself look into her mind. She was just... gone.

But like this? Gone because of that fucking asshole?

"I wanted Skye to have a normal life," I continue after a moment. "I didn't want her growing up in the glare of cameras and public speculation, especially knowing what she could become, and Marianna agreed. I wasn't under the impression I would ever know her. This has all–this has all been very abrupt."

Grandma tilts her head, considering my words. "She's beautiful. They both are. I remember Marianna."

"She came to the castle a few times."

"Now what, Blake?"

"How can you ask me that?" I whisper, meeting her stormy blue eyes. "She's dying."

"That doesn't sound right to me," she says matter-of-factly, her narrow shoulders lifting in a shrug. "All of these powerful people in this family, and nobody can do anything? I've never heard of such a thing."

"This isn't funny–"

"I never said it was, but you're smart. You know her. Would she go down without a fight?"

"No."

"Then why are you under the impression that she's just going to give up now?"

I search her eyes, resigned, but Kenna edges into the room with a rough sigh. "She's asking for you, Blake."

I rise without hesitation and brush past her, crossing the threshold of the bedroom in a matter of seconds. Minerva packs her things and leaves, and then it's just Maeve, who lingers long enough to glance out of the window once more before turning toward the door.

"He'll come back. This is the most freedom he's had in weeks," I tell her dryly, and thankfully, she gives me a soft, knowing smile that falters as quickly as it came.

Marianna opens her eyes to slits like she has a horrible headache as Maeve shuts the door. I sink onto the side of the bed, hanging my head in my hands for a moment just looking at her. Kenna treated the mark and stuck a bandage on it like that'll do anything.

"They told me what was happening to me," she says, her voice like gravel. "I'm not going to let him kill me, okay? They're going to cut the mark out. I asked them to do it."

I can't form words. My throat feels impossibly tight as she closes her eyes again with a shallow sigh.

"Skye is doing better," I tell her, the words a heavy weight on my tongue. "She's going to be fine. She'll wake up soon, I think."

"She killed him, Blake."

"She did."

Silence swells between us for several moments before Marianna adds, "Do you think she knows what she did?"

"Yeah, I do. It's what she wanted to happen."

Marianna smiles softly, her face blooming with pride, but it's weak. "She's stronger than me. She always has been. She's always been so brave. She'll be fine without me, I think–"

"Don't say that–"

"Because she'll have you now."

Chapter 22

Am I Dead?

MARIANNA

I wake with a start in a sun drenched room I find completely unfamiliar. My brain is a dead weight in my skull—heavy and hazy—like someone's been sitting on it, pressing me deep into the paper thin, but incredibly stiff, mattress.

New scents erupt all around me, but they're not as sharp as they normally are. In fact, my senses feel... all tangled. I can't feel my wolf at all. Instead, I just feel... odd.

I try to lift my head off a thin pillow that smells sharply of laundry detergent but can't. A dull ache grips my neck, forcing me to give up.

I grip sheets that don't feel familiar. Starched and stiff, they crinkle between my fingers, and I have a sudden, blurry memory of Skye's birth in that hospital in Crescent Falls.

After a wave of nausea passes, I grunt with the effort of sitting up, using my elbow to lift my upper body into position. Off-white walls and sparkling clean tile floors in a soft gray greet me along with the glare of the sun, where tremors of sound bleed into the room through the window screen. Music and revelry. It must be Saturday, the start of the mating festival just beyond the castle grounds.

I wince. It's been... four days then, hasn't it? Since... Dean...

"Oh, my Goddess." I tilt to the side, my head pounding and body lulling back into submission against what I know are several potent healing drafts. It all comes back to me in a matter of seconds. The fight. Using myself as a shield against Dean's drunken fury. The blurry memory of watching Blake stop Skye from killing herself while using her powers to their max.

And then pieces of that night, when my injuries were treated, but something felt terribly wrong with my mind and body. I was sick with despair over Dean's death, which was unsettling. My body revolted against it, twisting me into painful, violent knots, and then... nothing. Pieces of memories, of murmured conversations taking place around me while I languished.

I remember talking to Blake, thankful that Skye and my mom wouldn't be totally alone when I had to leave them.

Because I was going to die.

I open my eyes again, scanning the room, wondering if this is... it. Death. I thought the Goddess would have better taste when it came to designing Her Kingdom, however. This is all very sterile.

A young blonde woman in a pencil skirt sits in a plastic chair I hadn't noticed when I first opened my eyes. She's toying with a vase of bright red roses on the table beside her, adjusting the blooms, clicking her tongue as she removes their thorns.

"These are not nearly as nice as mine back home," she says, smiling at me, her bright blue eyes flicking in my direction for a brief second before she goes back to her task. "You've seen the rose gardens at the castle in Crescent Falls, haven't you?"

"Y-yeah." My mouth is painfully dry. I watch her, lying on my side and unable to lift myself up again. I feel weak. Stupidly weak, like my body is balanced on a precipice, one side begging me to surrender and just... go, while the other is dead set on keeping me alive.

"I didn't really get to know Blake," she says softly. "Did he ever tell you about his mom?"

"Luna Sarah?"

She nods, her bright blonde hair falling over her shoulders in soft, delicate waves. "Sarah is a good friend of mine. We talk often. She keeps me updated on everything going on with her family, but she had a hard go of it. She was very powerful as a child, like Skye. She was hidden away by her only surviving family, a father now long dead, I'm afraid, but now I consider him a friend, too."

She brushes the thorns into a little pile.

"Who are you?"

"I'm just here to watch over you for a bit."

The room grows hazy. "Am I dead?"

She laughs—a light, musical sound that fills the room. "No. You're not dead. You want to die, I think. This has been awfully painful for you. But your daughter is very insistent on the fact you stay alive. She told me you promised to buy her a bike this summer. She said she wants something with a basket, to carry... rocks?"

"To carry rocks back from the lake," I say, my voice dreamlike as I smile around the memory of that conversation.

"Yeah, that's what she said." She smiles. "She's adamant you get better, and I told her I'd keep an eye on you. I should be keeping an eye on whoever's in charge of the greenhouse here, though. These roses are horrendous." She winks, and I feel a sense of calm drifting through my body and settling in my bones.

I blink, and the light has shifted in the room, a warm midafternoon glow now replacing the bright streaks of golden morning sunlight. The chair by the table is empty, but the roses are still there, thornless.

I sit up, and it's much easier than this morning. I glance around, taking stock of my surroundings with a clearer head, a less hazy mind bogged down by pain. I'm still in the clinic. The scents, while they remain muted, are familiar. Cold and clean, with a touch of herbs.

The door opens, and a trio of witch nurses shuffle in but stop abruptly when they see me sitting up. One of them turns and rushes away while the others pretend not to be totally surprised I'm upright, let alone, I believe, lucid... or alive. After a whirlwind exam and several prodding questions, the two nurses leave, and the third arrives back in the room with–

"Mommy!" Skye launches onto the bed, hugging me tightly. I grunt as her body collides with mine, but my emotions spill over in the form of hot, unyielding tears.

Mom follows her into the room but slower, trying to bite back her smile, and the nurse tells us that she'll bring some food over if I feel like I'm up to eating something.

But it's the two others who enter after a few minutes of telling Skye that I'm okay that make my blood still in my veins.

Maeve, dressed in a casual, flowy linen set, inspects me from head to toe before entering the room, and... her mom, Alpha Kenna, follows behind her, looking equally as unsure.

"I'm going to take Skye to the garden for a while," Mom says against my temple before pressing a kiss to my skin. "We'll be back."

"You should stay–"

But Mom's face as she pulls away tells me everything I need to know. I'm not out of the woods yet, and judging by Alpha Kenna and Maeve's mirrored expression, it's a miracle I'm even alive.

They seem confused about it, to be perfectly honest.

I watch Mom practically drag Skye out of the room against her protests, but when Skye asks, "Can Blake come?" I feel my chest convulse. The door shuts, closing me in with Maeve and the Alpha of Veiled Valley, and silence echoes through the snug room for several painful heartbeats.

Kenna turns to the roses, her brows pinching as she notices the thornless stems, but Maeve steps toward the bed.

"How are you feeling?"

"Fine," I say, and it's somewhat close to the truth. "My head hurts and I feel a little... overall unwell."

"That's expected." Alpha Kenna turns from the roses to face me.

"I wanted to check in on you before you're moved upstairs. The mark was cut successfully, but the damage was... extensive."

"Do you remember taking a potion of any kind or being put under some type of spell?" Maeve cuts in.

"No. I don't."

"It's likely you were dosed slowly over the course of a year, based on what the healers noted during the procedure. There may not have been a spell, but I find that hard to believe." Kenna moves to the window, her hands tucked behind her back. "How old were you when he marked you?"

"T-twenty. I'd just turned twenty." I barely knew Dean at the time. Dating him had been... fun. I felt somewhat free again for the first time since Skye's birth and the unraveling of my relationship with Blake, but my relationship with Dean hadn't been remotely serious, at least I didn't think it was. He marked me in a moment of passion that caught me off guard. I was furious, but things... escalated at that point.

I was a single mom. I was struggling mentally and emotionally. He love bombed me, said the right things, did the right things for a little while. Once he had me in his clutches, that's when things began to change.

"You're not in the clear yet," Alpha Kenna says, tearing me out of my memories. "I'm worried about this immensely. Dark magic is incredibly, if not impossibly, hard to rectify. Even the idea that something like this could have happened to you is hard to believe, honestly."

"Am I going to die?" I ask.

Maeve takes a breath, looking at her mother.

"It's too early to say. For now, you're stable, and with a daily dose of healing drafts, I believe we'll see slow progress, but for now, your wolf is gone, which is... which in an event like this means you're going to be substantially weaker than before. Healing is going to be hard and slow," Kenna explains.

My eyes catch on the roses. I vaguely remember Blake

mentioning Misty's name several times in my haze. She's supposedly a gifted healer, isn't she? I know a lot about her since she lives in Crescent Falls. She's a writer and historian now, but she went through the Great War of Tarsian, the hero, they say, of the war that took the lives of her grandparents. I've read her books. I've seen her picture on the back. I've seen her golden blonde hair and bright blue eyes.

"Will you thank Princess Misty for me?"

Kenna and Maeve stare at me, confused.

"Um, she was here, in the room with me earlier."

Alpha Kenna looks at the roses again and swallows hard, then nods. She quietly excuses herself and leaves the room in what seems like a rush, but Maeve approaches the bed. "How are you feeling, really?"

"Fine. I feel fine." I smooth my hands over the thin blanket.

Maeve arches a brow, glances at the roses, then back at me. "Misty isn't here. She hasn't been in Eastonia for several weeks, actually. You saw Isla."

"Isla?"

"My great-grandmother," she says with a shrug. "She pops in from time to time."

"The–" I taper off, suddenly realizing who she means. "Oh."

"Consider yourself blessed. Only a few of us have seen her spirit. She must have been worried about you." She clicks her tongue, glancing around the room. "Um–"

"Is Blake here? Is he all right?"

"Blake? Yeah, he's–he's fine. He freaked out a bit, understandably so, but Soren and Skye have been keeping him busy. I think Blake and Soren are actually friends now, even though neither will admit it. Blake is a rather secretive person."

"Yeah, I know."

She looks at me, tilting her head while she scans my face. "Can I ask you something?"

I nod but find it hard to swallow past the knot in my throat. I'm under the impression everyone knows about me and Skye at this point. How could they not?

"Why did you end things with Blake? And before you say anything, we know some of what happened. Blake told us bits and pieces–at least that Skye is his daughter. His parents don't know yet, but I believe he's planning on taking his grandma, Maddy, back to Maatua and then going to Crescent Falls right after. I wanted him to go as soon as everything happened, but he refused to leave your side."

"How long have I been out?"

"Four days," she answers solemnly. "Skye has been just fine, though. She's been having a lot of fun. It's been a while since we've had a kid her age at the castle."

I grip the sheets, trying to push past the fog of the healing drafts weighing down my system to answer her original question.

"Blake and I were never really... we weren't boyfriend and girl-friend. We never had that talk before everything happened, but he... I loved him. I had for a long time–an unrequited crush, I guess, but one night, things changed, and we... we realized we had very deep feelings for each other and acted on them, but he suddenly pulled away."

Maeve purses her lips. "Did he ever explain why?"

"I didn't know what he was until shortly after that. I asked him if he'd changed his mind, and we got into an argument, and he was so... so icy and withdrawn. I pushed him, pressed him until I got under his skin, and he just... his eyes lit up, and it scared me to death. He looked horrified that he'd scared me and ended things then and there, with no explanation. I suppose my reaction was enough for him to know I couldn't handle it–"

"That's the dumbest thing I've ever heard!"

I smile despite myself, shaking my head. "We were both young and dumb."

"I've known Blake my entire life, and yet I feel like I don't know him at all. None of us had any idea about you and Skye; that's how well he hid it."

"We had an agreement about Skye when we found out I was pregnant."

"You wanted her to have a normal life?"

"Yes, and so did he."

"And what now? What happens now?"

"What do you mean?"

"The reason you're alive, that the treatment worked, is because your real mate is out there, close by, considering what I was told by the healers who cut out your mark. Is it Blake?"

"He would have told me." I realize how untrue my words are when they leave my lips. I blink, looking into Maeve's eyes. "He would have told me, right, if it were him?"

Chapter 23

It's Your Fault

Marianna

The day drags on with a rotation of visitors, nurses, healers. Unsurprisingly, student witches from the healing academy who were practically foaming at the mouth to get a glimpse of the first person to be cursed with dark magic and survive longer than a day in... a very long time.

I sit through it all. Sometimes my mom pesters me with questions about how I'm feeling, if I'm ready to eat, if I want to go back to sleep. Other times I'm with Skye, who seems to be suddenly in bloom around several other magical, powerful people she doesn't yet know are family.

But Blake hasn't come. I've barely heard his name spoken. I assume he's away in Maatua or Crescent Falls, whatever Maeve said his plan was.

I try not to feel disappointed he didn't even say goodbye.

In the late evening, I'm deemed recovered enough to be moved upstairs to the beautiful, luxurious guest suite where Mom and Skye have been staying. Minerva administers my nightly dose of a very potent healing draft. Then she gives me a rather thorough exam before finally deciding I'm not likely to die in my sleep tonight and leaving. By then, the sun has long set, and in the late hours of the night, even the mating festival has died down, the party moving down to the lakeshore instead of right outside the castle walls.

I can't sleep. I figure that's all I've been doing for four days, so no wonder.

Dressed in a fresh nightgown and a thin satin robe, I slip out of the bedroom on legs that wobble but otherwise keep me upright. I have zero appetite as it stands. The thought of food hasn't once crossed my mind, so I've been surviving on tea heavily dosed with sugar and milk. Somehow, my withered body is able to maneuver through the suite, past the room where Skye is fast asleep in a bed ten times her size, and past a second bedroom where my mom is completely passed out on top of the covers like she simply fell into bed and descended into a stupor before her head hit the pillow.

The suite itself isn't very large. There's one bathroom, which is roomy and clean. I walk in, and one look in the mirror makes my stomach curl. I bunch my hair into a bun at the nape of my neck and brush my teeth, my hands trembling with the action, and begin the trek back to bed.

But I make a wrong turn, I think, because the next door I open leads into a wide, dim, cavernous hallway that marks the exit to the suite.

I should go back to bed. That's what Alpha Kenna and Minerva would tell me to do, right? could take the opportunity to explore....

I step into the hallway barefoot, my steps silent on the soft, crimson carpet runners covering marble tiles that shine in the moonlight drifting through glossy stained glass windows. A staircase appears. I take it down to a second level balcony that overlooks that grand foyer, but the castle is cloaked in a sleepy darkness that feels peaceful to my addled mind.

I turn to the left, exploring while my legs still have some strength, and follow the soft glow of a light cascading across another stretch of carpet. There, I reach a set of short stairs that spiral to the first floor, where a massive set of doors stretches to the ceiling, slightly ajar.

I can't stop now. I have to use this burst of energy, don't I? I slip through the crack in the doors and cover my mouth with my hand to stifle a gasp as the library erupts all around me. Seven levels and... millions of books fade into moonlight dripping down from the domed, glass ceiling high above my head.

The heavy doors close behind me with a push, sending a snap echoing high into the shadowed recesses of the upper floors, where balconies overlook a half dozen wooden tables. Books lay scattered there, and, to my shock, a man sits near a dormant fireplace. It only takes a second to recognize him.

Blake looks up from several stacks of books spread out before him, many of them open and lying at odd angles. His eyes light from within as he peers through the darkness at me.

His chair screeches, cutting through the silence like a knife.

He rounds the table in a rush, knocking over several books in his wake. The sound of the heavy books hitting the ground thunders through the space between us, covering his footsteps as he careens in my direction, his eyes wild but his face set in grim determination. "You shouldn't be down here. You shouldn't be out of bed–"

"I've been in bed for almost five days."

"You need to rest, Anna, for fuck's sake. Who let you come down here?" He reaches me, bracing a hand against the door at my back, panting like he's out of breath as he scans my face. I've never seen him look so... desperate before. He's totally undone as he inspects me for damage maybe I hadn't seen in the mirror before coming down here.

Something heavy shifts in my chest. My heart beats out of rhythm, thumping hard as he caresses my cheek, then calms as I lean into the warmth of his large, calloused hand and close my eyes for just a moment.

"Where have you been?" I ask, my voice just above a whisper, and open my eyes to look into his, into the power still shining there.

His lips part as he searches my gaze. "I–I couldn't–I've been–" He exhales shallowly, his jaw flexing, and then that weight in my chest... snaps.

His mouth tilts over mine, but our lips don't brush. His breath tickles my skin when he inhales. My name is a whisper that leaves his lips in a strained exhale, like he's doing everything in his power not to kiss me.

He leans his forehead against mine and presses a kiss to the corner of my mouth instead, which I chase, but he pulls away.

Frustration bubbles up in my system. He pushes off the door and tucks his hands in his pockets. I notice the headphones strung around his neck then, the soft stream of unfamiliar music drifting between us.

"I assumed you were in Crescent Falls. That's what Maeve told me."

He takes another step away like he can't stand to be in my bubble any longer, which is... crushing, to say the least. He always holds me at arm's length, even when it feels like the only thing that will make me feel even remotely better would be to just... touch him.

"I was planning on leaving in the morning. I took my grand-mother back to Maatua a few hours ago. I didn't–" He grits his teeth, taking another calculated step backward. "I didn't feel comfortable being gone longer than a few hours given the circumstances."

"So sorry to be a burden–"

"You are not a burden, Marianna. You are the mother of my child–"

"Is that all?" I shouldn't have said it. I realize that the moment the words leave my lips. Goddess, the regrets I have. They shine like never before now, like scrubbing Dean's mark from my body was the only thing standing in the way of the feelings I've been trying to hide for almost a decade.

Blake won't ever feel the same way. He won't let himself, for whatever stupid, infuriating reason.

I need to accept that.

He stares at me for several seconds before replying, "You know that's not the case. You mean more to me than anyone ever has, and that hasn't, and won't, change."

He looks so tired. Soul-draining grief etches his normally steely expression.

"Thank you for... for keeping Skye busy while I recovered–"

"I saw everything he ever did to you," he says, like he's not able to stop himself. He flinches, gritting his teeth, and begins to turn away but suddenly decides against it and holds out a hand. I bristle when a thick, angry laugh escapes him. "Gods, if Skye hadn't killed him, I would have. I would have loved to take him apart piece by piece, slowly–"

"Why? Why bother?" My throat feels tight against the words as I shake my head. "It doesn't matter at all to you. We're just–we just exist on the same plane, Blake. Our only connection is our child–"

"You should have come to me when he started hurting you. The moment you felt unsafe, you should have told me–"

"And what would you have done? Saved me?"

"Yes!"

"Then what, Blake? Disappeared? Shoved me away again–"

He takes a step toward me in disbelief. "You were the one who pushed me away, Marianna."

"You broke up with me!"

"I had to! I scared you to death. You screamed when you saw my powers for the first time, and I can't get that scream out of my fucking head. I was just a kid, too. My powers were nothing compared to what they are now. I could twist your brain to my liking or erase any memory of me, of us. I could hurt you, and you wouldn't even know it was happening. I'm like him, but worse because I'm a monster, Marianna, and you only saw a glimpse of it that night. My powers were–"

"You are not even remotely like him. How could you even say something like that? You never put a hand on me–"

"I have spent seven years in hell to keep you safe. To try to make your life easy and normal," he continues, his fury snapping around the room like a million rubber bands. "And I failed to do the one thing I swore I'd do. I didn't keep you safe from him. I thought you were safe *with* him. It killed me knowing you'd found someone else, that you married someone else. It ruined me knowing you'd found your mate, Marianna, and now... knowing the truth of it? Knowing that I could have just looked and seen–" He turns from me, dragging a hand down his face.

"You hide yourself. You've always been ashamed of what you are."

"You don't know the half of it–"

"You should have trusted this with me. Your powers. Who you really are. I was–I *loved* you." My voice shatters around the damning words. They leave my tongue in a hushed whisper that still somehow booms through the library like a death knell. "You used to be kind, shy, and funny. Blake, you used to sit on that dusty old couch with me for hours talking about books, music, and the video games you loved. You should have told me why you had trouble making friends, why you needed those headphones, why you could lose yourself for hours in a game yet could barely stand more than ten seconds of conversation–"

"It wouldn't have changed anything."

"I would have been more prepared when I saw it for the first time."

"It wouldn't have." He turns back to me, his face set in grim determination.

"I loved you. I still love you. That hasn't changed."

"Don't say that to me," he says darkly, his eyes losing some of their luster.

"And Skye thinks you're the greatest thing since the–the invention of rocks." I choke on a laugh, my words blurred by sudden tears. "Your family loves you but doesn't understand because you've never let them. You've never let me!"

"I couldn't–"

"You can–"

"I know when you die, Marianna. I've seen it written in the stars. I saw it the night I ruined everything we had because I was selfish and wanted to know if the girl I loved more than life itself was my mate. Instead, I saw I lost you so young, before your life even had a chance to begin." He takes another heated step in my direction. "I saw your death, and I scared you. The only thing I knew how to do was shut down and push you away, so I did. But then you were pregnant and terrified, and I did *that* to you, too. I put you in that position. Even if you'd wanted me back at that point, I wouldn't have let it happen. I needed you to stay far, far away from me–"

"If any of that is true, then why waste what time we did have?" I shout. "I almost died a few days ago, didn't I? I should have. That's what everyone keeps saying. That's what you saw, isn't it? Now look at me, Blake. *I'm still here.* I'm not leaving this time. Skye needs you. I fucking need you." Tears stream down my cheeks. "I need you. I need–"

His body crashes into mine, his lips tilting over my mouth as he gives himself one single second to hesitate, to think his actions through.

I don't let him pull away. I grip his shirt and pull him closer, and he leans down, chasing my mouth as I look up at him, and kiss him... softly. A light peck.

He braces his hands against the door over my head and growls as he reigns himself back in, turning back into the Ice Lord I know so well. It's a tiny win, but a win nonetheless.

Blake will never be happy until he lets go of the restraints keeping him chained, and that includes acting on his feelings for me, damning whatever consequences he thinks they have.

He shoves away from the door, clenching his jaw, and says, "If you're fit to travel tomorrow morning, you and Skye are going to Crescent Falls with me. I'm abdicating, officially, and my parents need to know why."

I press my fingers to my lips and watch Blake do his best not to unravel. For whatever reason, his utter inability to regain his bearings after the simplest kiss feels... pretty damn good.

Chapter 24

No Regrets

Marianna

"I don't like this plan whatsoever," Kenna says sharply, tapping her foot as she watches Blake gather what I think might just be random pieces of paper into a briefcase just to make it look like he's busy. "No. Nope, Blake, I will not allow it."

"What, exactly, is the worst that can happen?" he asks, arching a brow. "She's already cursed. She has, what, a few months before the healing drafts stop working, and she succumbs to the curse still in her system?" I try not to bristle at the ice in his tone, but Kenna isn't affected in the slightest. She frowns deeply at him as Blake rounds his desk with his briefcase resting at his side, his dark brows still arched, his striking violet eyes shining an even deeper shade than usual. "You've been pestering me to tell my parents. So, I am. I'd like Marianna to be there when I do. Plus, they need to meet their grandchild."

"You're going to spring this on them and abdicate your title in the same conversation?" She raises her brows, mimicking his expression.

To be honest, I'm... slightly surprised by Blake right now. He's far more expressive, more open and less guarded, than I've ever seen him. Even Soren, who's been lingering in the corner of the room with Fallon in a sling across his chest, seems to notice the change in Blake.

Skye, who'd been using Soren to reach the shiny glass globes and crystals Blake keeps arranged on his bookshelves, shuffles over to us carrying one of the globes between her hands. It's a pure, almost flawless sphere of moonstone. She looks around the group before whispering, "Watch this," and the sphere clouds from within, lighting with her powers.

Blake continues looking at Kenna as Skye's powers cast a violet glare between our bodies. My heart thuds against my ribcage.

"My parents can help with her training, and you know it. Plus, you and my mom love to gossip about the family, and this will give you more content to work with."

Kenna scoffs, but Soren snorts a laugh from the other side of the room, which he quickly staunches when Maeve glides into the office. "Ready?" she asks, checking her watch. "It's nearly nightfall. The moon is rising as we speak."

Nerves I've been fighting all day weave through my body, but Blake lightly brushes his hand against my upper arm before turning to Maeve, nodding. "We'll go to Misty's house first. If Marianna is ill after traveling, she'll be able to help."

"She's already aware that we're on our way." Maeve huffs a breath then glances in Soren's direction with a soft, secret smile. He just shrugs, bouncing on his heels to try to keep their almost one-month-old daughter settled. "I won't be gone long. An hour, tops."

Kenna continues to shake her head. Her silver eyes meet mine with a final look of warning. "I have to remind you that you're very weak right now, Marianna. The curse isn't gone."

"I know." My voice shakes. "But I–I need to make sure Skye has help, so... this is the right move." I look at Blake for reassurance. His eyes hold mine for a few seconds before his gaze drops to my lips, then he turns back to Maeve.

"Let's go."

"You should leave Skye here," Kenna grinds out, losing whatever patience she had. She's been arguing with Blake about this all day, and I can, in fact, see her side of the situation. Even Maeve looks down at her shoes–sneakers–that complete her incredibly casual outfit made up of loose fitting jeans and what I believe is a men's sweatshirt. Kenna continues, "Just until–until everything is settled and you've told your parents the truth about both items on your agenda."

"That's what my mom wants as well," I tell Blake, swallowing past my own nerves. "Skye... she's been through enough. If this doesn't go well–"

"My parents wouldn't deny her–"

"If something happens to me," I cut in, holding his gaze, "if I can't make the jump or get sick... I don't want her to see that."

All eyes are on me except for Skye's. She's already back in the corner with Soren, still gripping the moonstone sphere.

Blake chews the inside of his cheek, deliberating, his eyes downcast on the floor. "Fine," he says after a few seconds. "Skye will stay here. My parents can come visit when they're ready."

Kenna seems pleased, but her eyes still scan my face, my paler than usual skin, and the bandage at the base of my neck with an undeniable wariness.

"Misty is going to use her gifts to try to break the lingering curse," Maeve says to her mom, who closes her eyes and shakes her head like she doesn't believe it can be done.

Blake stares at them, his expression tight and guarded.

While Maeve, Blake, and Kenna discuss the jump to Crescent Falls, I look at my daughter. I take her in, memorizing her details. She's... free. Being around these people, her family, it's already changed her on a molecular level. Her powers ping from wall to wall around the room, lighting up multiple spheres at once, and Soren just grins at her, egging her on.

No one is afraid of her. No one thinks she's too much, too strange, too different.

She fits in.

She's one of them. She always has been.

My neck aches. A weakness has started to spread through my shoulder. I've been trying to ignore how nervous Kenna is about it, her comments about the curse still lingering in my body, but Blake is convinced Misty can break it. She's broken curses before. Her grandmother, Isla, shattered a curse but... sacrificed herself to do it. The thought makes my stomach pinch, but then Blake's taking my hand, guiding me to where Maeve is standing in the center of his office.

"The full moon is on our side. My magic won't be completely overwhelming on her system, I'll be able to use less of it." Maeve reaches back to tie her hair into a loose bun on the top of her head.

"Will it hurt?" I ask.

Blake squeezes my hand. "Maybe a little." His tone is soft, laced with what I can only describe as guilt.

"It'll be quick, and the healers dosed you with herbs that'll help with the stomachache and the headache that'll follow." Maeve gives me a tight smile before glancing at Soren, who nods at her. "It'll be over before you know it."

"Let's go. We're wasting time." Blake grips my hand and reaches for Maeve, his fingers closing around her forearm. The room spins out of control.

My legs refuse to hold my weight, but a second later, it doesn't matter. Darkness swells, replaced by starlight that streaks past me in stripes of gold, orange, and purple. It's loud–a deep roar that splits my body into pieces–then... silence swells before the floor beneath me returns, and the soft ticking of a clock fills my ears.

I sway into something stiff and immovable. Blake's arms snake around me, tugging me against his chest as my blurry vision settles on a softly lit foyer in a very suburban home that's definitely not in Eastonia. Crystal sconces illuminate soft blue walls, lighting a stairwell to a loft overlooking the first floor, where family pictures stretch along the wall beside the stairs. Four people are depicted—a man, a woman, and their two beautiful children—through the space of... twenty years or so.

"I was wondering when you'd get here," a delicate female voice says somewhere behind me.

Blake turns with me in his arms. I grip his shirt, trying to focus on my breathing like Maeve told me to do to cut through the spinning sensation still lingering in my system, but Misty takes up my vision.

Her golden blonde hair trails down her back in soft curls. Big, bright blue eyes scan my face before looking up at Blake with a tight smile.

She looks exactly like the woman I saw in the clinic, but a bit older, I think. Misty is probably in her mid-forties, I suppose. Isla showed herself as a younger woman.

Introductions are made while I linger in a haze of herbs and dizziness. Maeve stays long enough for me to find my bearings again before disappearing in a gust of crimson stardust.

But even as Misty sits me down at her kitchen table and inspects the wound on my neck, I feel... strange. My entire body still seems to be trying to knit itself back together while I watch Blake pace the kitchen. I barely register a word Misty says to him, but everyone back at the palace explained Misty's expertise–her healing gifts. I feel them under my skin as her powers work through my body. It feels warm, soft. It's not painful in the slightest.

"She no longer has a wolf," Misty says to Blake, her voice low and uncertain. "You should have called me right away, Blake."

"I wanted to. You know how the witches are about this kind of thing."

"I could have made it more comfortable for her, at least, while they cut out the mark," she sighs, releasing her grip on my hand and moving through the dark kitchen to an electric kettle. "Cole should look at her wound. There may be something he can do."

"Your powers won't touch it, will they?"

"Kenna was right about it being dark magic. We'd need to find a counter-curse, I think, but I never trained in the dark arts."

"You broke Richard's curse a few times, though–"

"That's very different from this. This curse was directly tied to her mate bond, not necessarily her... body. It's deep, Blake. It's in her soul." She shrugs sadly.

I feel Blake looking at me but can't bring myself to meet his eyes. I feel like such a burden. No one has said it out loud, but I know that whatever time I have is limited. Weeks, months, maybe if I'm lucky, a year or two... all the while, dosed heavily with healing drafts to keep myself functioning, but I'm already so tired, and it's only been... what, a week, since the mark was cut from my skin?

Maeve told me the reason I'm alive is because my true fated mate is out there. Blake hasn't said a word to me about it, but he must know by now that's what the witches think is keeping me alive this long.

He would have... said something about it, right?

"I'll do some research," Misty says with marked determination. "We'll figure it out, okay?"

Blake sucks his lower lip between his teeth and nods as moonlight drifts through the windows overlooking me and the kitchen table.

A few minutes later, I'm in a car speeding down familiar roads. I recognize the buildings stretching to the skyline. We pass the performing arts center. Very few people are out right now, seeing as it's the earliest hours of the morning. I haven't even asked where we're going, but we're moving in the opposite direction of the castle where Blake lived as a teenager.

He pulls into a parking garage at the base of a large skyscraper that breaches the stars. My view of the heavens is suddenly obstructed as the car drives down into the depths of the building, and Blake parks, hurrying to my side of the car to open the door for me.

"That was very chivalrous of you," I try to joke, but he looks... withdrawn. Worn thin. "Where are we?"

"My apartment." He guides me toward an elevator, and we wait for the doors to open. "I haven't been here for a few weeks."

He takes my hand as the doors open and leads me inside the snug elevator, pressing the top button–the penthouse.

My body feels light as the little box sprints into the sky, but his hand doesn't leave mine. In fact, he intertwines our fingers. I look up at him, watching his eyes, which are darker than they normally are. Dark and empty—a hollow kind of grief.

Because I'm dying, aren't I? That's the truth of this, the truth no one will say out loud. I've been cursed by a man who's now dead, a man who bound me to him in death.

Blake saw this—saw some version of what he calls my timeline—saw that my time was limited.

For whatever reason, I don't feel sad. I'm just disappointed, I guess. We could have had a lot more time if we hadn't been so... scared.

The elevator stops, opening to reveal a simple, modern foyer surrounded by windows overlooking the sparkling city below, and a single door.

Blake wordlessly takes me inside his apartment, which is exactly what I thought it'd be. Clean, gray, and modern. It smells like him— brisk, icy, with hints of that cologne he's worn since I first met him.

"We'll stay here for the night. I have a meeting with my parents in the morning, and then we'll go from there."

My fingers are still interlaced with his when I turn to face him. I have so many regrets. I don't want to go into death regretting him.

I rise on my toes, letting go of his fingers and taking his face between my hands instead. His eyes meet mine in the starlit darkness.

"I still love you. I've never stopped," he whispers.

"I know," I reply, and press my mouth to his.

Chapter 25

Show Me Your Power

MARIANNA

I wait for Blake to step out of my embrace. I'll let him. It's his choice to make, even if my fingers curl into his shirt, bunching the fabric.

His lips are heavy and full against mine, but they part, and he exhales deeply, trembling as his hand travels up my back to clutch the back of my neck.

"You're doing this because you feel like you have to," he says grimly, but heat laces through the words.

"No," I whisper, opening my eyes. His face comes into view as I look up, searching his gaze. "Blake, I... I wish I could go back and change everything. I would have–I would have let you in."

He shakes his head but kisses me again, harder this time, putting his whole body into it like this is the last time we'll do this. He backs me against the wall in the entryway of his apartment, bracing his forearm just above my head. My hands travel down his chest and stomach before holding against his belt loops, and the kiss ends once more, leaving me breathless and warm.

"I won't go further than this," he says, but his tone is damning, full of tangled desire and grief. "Not like this."

"Why not?"

"Because you were right to push me away. Everything you said to me the night I came to you, seeing you pregnant with Skye for the first time... you were right. I scared you. I lied to you, and I didn't tell you what I was. It was my choice to push you away. You had every right to hate me, and for years I was glad you did. I have regrets–many of them–but I never regretted you. I want you, Marianna. Fuck, I've missed you. I love you, but we–I am not someone who can ever just... exist with someone like you."

I pull away slightly, my back flat against the wall. He winces, closes his eyes as he struggles to find words to convey how he feels that won't rip me to absolute shreds.

"I didn't mean it like that," he amends. "Marianna–"

"I know," I whisper. "I–I don't even remember most of that night, you know. When we fought. I don't remember it. I blocked it out, I think. I regretted everything I said to you, though. I remember that clearly–that feeling has haunted me for almost a decade–"

"I don't want to trap you more than I already have," he says steadily, his eyes glowing softly in the darkness.

"You didn't trap me. You gave me our daughter. I was the one who forced you away."

"I didn't fight it when I should have," he says. "That makes me a weak man."

"You were just as scared as I was," I whisper, resting my head in the crook of his shoulder. I smooth my hands back up his chest until I'm tucked against him, breathing in his familiar scent. Like a winter storm. Like something bigger and grander than me. Something wild and fierce, but mysterious. "Show me."

"What?"

"Show me your powers."

He swallows hard, his chest convulsing. "I can't do that."

"Why not?"

"Because it's–I could hurt you."

"I'm already dying," I whisper.

His free hand finds my hip. He smooths his thumb over my skin where my skirt has come loose where I tried tucking into my pants, and his touch is enough to send me barreling into heat.

"I made a mistake all those years ago," I tell him, but he groans, sucking in a breath.

"Everything was my fault. It was my fault, Marianna."

"I want to make it right. I want to... to see you, Blake. Really see you. Can you show me who you are? Powers and all?"

He groans again, his face just beside mine as he leans forward, closing his eyes like he's in pain. "I've never shown anyone what I can actually do," he says under his breath. "They know enough, I suppose, and I let them use my gifts to their advantage, but..."

"Show me," I whisper, unbuttoning his shirt. I'm unsure why, but I just want to feel his skin. I spread my hands over his bare chest, and he sighs. I drink in his warmth, letting it flood my body, and he finally relents. He leans back far enough to look in my eyes. The world around us shifts as his eyes begin to glow. My vision blurs for several seconds before settling again, and this time, we're in a void of darkness, just me and him.

Stars dance all around us, woven together by threads made of mist and starlight that twinkle overhead, suspended in mid-air.

He touches me, his hand smoothing up my arm to my shoulder, then my neck, until he caresses my cheek. I close my eyes as the heavens fade and are replaced by... a vision. A memory, something I'm witnessing through his perspective. Blake, as a boy of maybe fourteen, hurrying into a shoe-box sized dorm room and promptly throws up blood while it drips from his nose and ears. Blake, standing in front of a massive orrery in Moonrise, fighting for his life to stay upright while voices scream through his head, and a woman in white whispers in his ears to listen, but I don't know what the voices show him, say to him...

He's just a kid. A kid witnessing all the evil in the world, and he's not as strong as he thought he was.

Another vision of him walking out of the temple in Moonrise, the color drained from his cheeks, his eyes dry and hollow, nearly crushes me. This is the Blake I remember. Young, emotionless, drifting through life like his own was taken from him.

He brings me back to the woven stars and says, "What do you want to see?"

"Am I in your head?"

"Yes."

"Does it hurt?"

"Not really," he says with a short laugh. "It tickles a bit."

"Show me your favorite memory."

I feel like I'm out of body when his powers take me to a familiar street tucked between several skyscrapers. Road noise erupts all around us, and I watch Blake, maybe sixteen at the time, look down at a map on his phone, a little lost. He goes to the wrong apartment at first, but then realizes there's a basement level, and walks back outside feeling... dead. Lifeless and empty, like he's felt for the past two years after brutal training with the mystics, after seeing every wrong in the world, every death, every unfairness. That's his gift. Being able to *see*. He can see everything, and it's overwhelming.

He finds the door to my old apartment and knocks.

I answer.

This is his memory of seeing me for the first time and... being able to relive it, watching him looking down at me, perplexed, while I scowl and try to tell him off...

I smile as his powers dance around me, painting the picture of the day the voices in his head finally quieted, all because of the girl who couldn't figure out how to do math.

Blake's apartment returns in fractals at first. I blink to clear my hazy vision, but I realize with a start we're standing in a cloud of mist tinged with stars. His powers take up the entire apartment. The lights flicker out. The strange crystal spheres, which match the ones he keeps in Moonrise, light up with his magic where they're resting on a nearby bookshelf. I turn to the spheres, watching his memories play out like a movie–memories of us. Some things... I don't even remember. Little moments, I guess, that mattered immensely to him but went right over the top of my head.

"My mother can turn back time," he says. "My dad gets the occasional vision. They're similar in that way. Both can scry. I'm different. I can look into the heavens, burrow into any mind I want, and occasionally, I can see the future if I look hard enough." His powers surge, lighting up the room to the point that it's nearly blinding, before they fade in a phantom gust of wind. The apartment goes silent once again, and I turn back to him, my heart hammering.

"How many times have you looked into my head?"

"Just once. Twice, if you count trying to train you on the use of shields."

"Why didn't you show me this before? When we were younger?"

"I was afraid you wouldn't accept me anymore. You were the only person who ever saw me for what I am."

"A nerd?" I say with a laugh, and to my relief, he smiles, looking down at his shoes.

"Yeah. I guess."

"This is what Skye will be able to do one day? Travel like that? Move through... space and time, through minds?"

"Yes, she's already well on her way."

"And you'll be there for her when I'm gone, right?" The words are heavy on my tongue.

"I promise," he says in a near whisper, and the boiling tension between us snaps.

I lunge at him, launching into his arms. He catches me, spinning me toward the open door to his room, which is shrouded in shadow. The kiss is... otherworldly. It's the kind of kiss that would knock me off my feet if I'd still been standing, but my back hits his bed, his scent all around me, and nothing else matters.

He presses a kiss to my jaw, then my neck, sucking my tender skin. His teeth rake across my collarbone while I hastily unbutton his shirt, desperate to touch him—to feel him again, just skin separating us.

Late at night, when I'm alone and hungry for someone's touch... it's him I think about. It's always been him.

But my neck aches where Dean's mark was just sliced from my flesh.

I wince, and he lifts his head.

"I'm sorry," I whisper as tears of fresh pain prickle along my lash line. I can't fight them off.

"We don't have to do anything, Anna. I think we're getting ahead of ourselves—"

I pull him back to me, my mouth on his, and kiss him like my life depends on it because, honestly, I think it might. His touch is like a wildfire spreading through my body, burning away every terrible memory, every echoing, lingering touch left behind by a man who hated me so much he tried to drag me into death with him.

When I bury my face against Blake's neck, dragging my tongue along the column of his throat... the King of Mystics finally bends until he breaks.

"*Fuck*," he growls, low in his throat, and presses me into the mattress. "Careful. I don't want to hurt you."

I drag my teeth along his collarbone like he just did to me, mimicking the movement, and he sighs, rolling his neck like what I'm doing to him is making him unravel.

His hand caresses my breast before smoothing over my stomach, pulling my shirt free of my pants, then lower, unbuttoning my jeans and pulling the zipper down.

And then he's pinning my wrists above my head, his mouth trailing down my body until he kisses above my navel. He lets go of my wrists, and I'm beyond the ability to move. I don't want to break this spell. I can't take it. I can't handle the fire burning through me every time his mouth touches my skin.

He roughly pulls my jeans down and tosses them across the

room. My panties are next, and the cool night air brushes over my skin, awakening my senses. Adrenaline courses through me and pools at my center, and his mouth dips below the apex of my thighs with a resounding growl of what I can only describe as satisfaction.

But, Blake being Blake, he reels himself back in at the very last second.

"We shouldn't," he whispers against my inner thigh, his breath hot and shallow against my aching folds. "Marianna, what have you done to me?"

"Please," I whisper, then suck in a breath, letting it out in a breathy moan when he presses another wet, hungry kiss to my thigh. He lets out a shallow grunt before he nibbles my skin–anything to stop himself from what he really wants to do–what he's desperately hungry for.

"Please," I repeat, more desperate than before.

Blake, the Royal Prince of Crescent Falls, spreads my legs wide, and lets go of the restraints that control his life, giving in to what he wants, for once.

And it's me.

Chapter 26

Writing a Symphony

Marianna

Blake's tongue parts my folds before his mouth closes around me, sucking deep, and thousands of prickles of heat erupt through me, sweeping me into a kind of semi-consciousness that makes the room blur. My mind goes blissfully blank. It's just me and him, nothing else. His groan of pleasure coils through my body, tightening every muscle. I tremble as he releases me, going back to gentle, exploratory licks, little nibbles, and by the time he presses two fingers inside of me, I'm drowning in him.

I lift my hips from the bed, my knees spread wide, and cry out his name while my fingers tangle in his luscious dark hair. I come undone at the seams within seconds, and it's so strong, so completely overpowering, that for a moment, I'm breathless, shaking and moaning without restraint. His lips press against the inside of my thigh. I feel his smile, feel his breathy exhale as he comes up for air, and... then he's here, on top of me, his hands drifting under my shirt, his mouth sucking on my neck.

I'm reminded that the first, and last, time we were together like this was in the back of his car. We were squished together, fumbling,

201

unsure what to do with our bodies. It was a first for both of us–something sacred we were able to share together. We'd chased feelings and instincts that night while rain pounded the roof of his car, and the windows fogged.

This is different on so many levels. We're older, wiser, I think, maybe not, but still. He moves like he's more experienced, like he knows his way around my body even after so many years apart. He sits me upright and helps me pull off my shirt, then my bra. My legs are draped over his while he keeps a hand on my lower back to keep me steady as I toss what's left of my clothes over the side of the bed. Chest to chest like this, I have a view of his face, the starlight dancing in his eyes, the universe at his fingertips, and it's beautiful.

He slides his hand up the back of my neck and into my hair. Our noses brush, and moonlight dances over our bodies. I slowly, carefully, unbutton the rest of his shirt and slide it off him.

We stay like this for what feels like several minutes–just breathing each other in–light touches, the occasional kiss. He presses his lips to my cheekbone, and a tear slides down my face against my will. For years I've wanted this. I've prayed for this. I wish I could go back and change everything.

I look into his eyes as we balance on a precipice of no return. This will change everything. We had a contract. We had everything planned out. We have Skye to think about.

But right now... I'm just thinking about me. Him. *Us.*

"I want you to play for me soon," he whispers against my skin, pressing his mouth just below my collarbone. His hair smells like his cologne–something deeply spiced and woodsy, a sharp contrast to his usual scent.

"My violin?"

"Yes, I've missed it. I've been listening to the solo you played at your last concert in Crescent Falls for days now, over and over again. I want to hear your songs, though. The ones you wrote when we were younger."

I close my eyes as his kisses deepen, and he lowers his head to my breasts. He leans back onto the bed with me in his arms, covering me with his body again, and his tongues... Gods.

He draws a line with it over my left breast before sucking again, then dips lower, taking my nipple into his eager mouth.

I sharply cry out, winding my legs around his waist, and arch to meet him, heat coursing through my veins and settling in my core again. He nibbles, biting softly, groaning while I writhe and whimper beneath him.

His touch is on the verge of being too much, too intense, when he abruptly pulls away and pulls his belt free of its loops. I sit up again, out of breath as I hastily unbutton his pants and frantically help him out of his clothes. The second his pants hit the ground, we collide in the sheets, wordlessly touching, exploring, almost frantic in our desire to just feel each other.

He nudges my legs apart, his mouth pressed to mine, and grips my hips before plunging his hard cock inside of me in a swift, violent thrust.

"Blake!" I cry out, arching my neck back as the stretch hits me, setting my entire body on fire. Pleasure like I've never known curls through my system, drowning me, as he thrusts in slowly, dragging out his own pleasure, his neck bent as he braces his hands on either side of my shoulders.

"Fuck," he rasps, gritting his teeth. He curses something unintelligible under his breath before lowering his body to mine, settling deep between my hips. I gasp at the depth he reaches. I'm full of him. He's buried to the hilt and refuses to move for several seconds.

"Are you okay?" I pant, caressing his face.

"I don't know," he admits breathlessly, his nose brushing mine as he rolls and grinds his hips against mine, making me moan. His eyes are heavy and dark with need, and his skin is hot–almost fevered–as he watches me, watches as I gasp and whisper his name. "I'm just... you're beautiful."

He thrusts in again, hard this time, hard enough my toes curl, and I let go of any reservations I had left. He kisses me deeply, whispering praise against my lips, and curls his body into mine. Every touch is electric. Every movement of his body is honed to mine. We meet like a key to a lock—a perfect fit. It's like he was built for me. Selfishly, I want that. I want him to myself for the rest of my life—even if I only have minutes, hours, days.

He presses me into the mattress as my inner walls tighten. The tension between us coils in my lower belly, tight as a violin string. I'm so close. I feel the orgasm racing toward fruition at a blinding rate of speed when he rises over me, thrusts hard, and holds himself still while I come undone, my vision blurred by stars and my body quivering.

He curses again, my name the last word on his tongue, before pressing his cock as deep as he can go and spilling himself inside of me while my walls clutch and spasm around him, milking him dry.

Blake trembles, lowering himself onto me again, rolling us onto our sides facing each other. He's still inside me, our legs still tangled, and I'm warm. Blissfully, completely heated to the bone.

I fall asleep within seconds. The room blurs with moonlight, and the last thing I feel is Blake pulling the covers over us, turning me around, and cuddling me close. His warmth penetrates my body, making my muscles melt, and I don't fight the rush of darkness that sweeps me into a dream world, into another memory.

The thing is... It's not mine.

I'm watching memories play out from Blake's perspective. Memories of me tangled with his thoughts. Me, sitting on the couch, pulling a pretend bow across an imaginary violin while classical music plays from an ancient stereo across the room. I tuck my toes under his thigh, and he feels... amazing. Blake isn't sure whether it's the sweater he's wearing or my touch that's making him overheat, but he can't take his eyes off of me, and he wants nothing more than to reach out and just... touch me.

Me, jumping up and down in the rain during the ill-fated concert that changed our lives forever. I'm sopping wet, glowing in the haze of flashing rave lights, while he stands two feet away, holding the stick that once contained a cloud of cotton candy I begged for until he relented, which immediately melted in the rain, but he's still holding it, unable to move as he watches me... smile.

It rewires his brain.

I rewire his brain.

Another memory zips past. Him watching my mom place Skye in my arms moments after she was born. He's out of breath, in awe, looking at the two of us like it's the start of a life he didn't have the nerve to even wish for.

Him, years later, drained of all emotion and a bottomless void of who he used to be. He opens his laptop to an email from our mediator, who tells him I've remarried. He sits there for an hour just staring at the email, what's left of his heart shattering like glass.

Him, standing in the hallway in the basement of the performing arts center, seeing me for the first time in seven years–pulled there by the voices in his head, by a force even he, so powerful, couldn't fight.

Then the dream, his memories, fades into... sheer panic. I feel nothing but pain as a room made of stone fills my vision. I'm trapped, weighed down. Soren suddenly appears looking beaten and terrified as Blake's voice fills the dream, begging Soren to let him die, to find me and Skye and save us from whoever... did this to him.

I wake up with a start and a gargled scream, unable to catch my breath. Blake jolts back to awareness and flies out of bed. His powers light the room as he storms into the depths of the penthouse, and a few moments later, returns, wearing nothing but a pair of boxers. He rubs his eyes, heavy with sleep, then looks at me. "Are you okay?"

"I was dreaming. I didn't mean to startle you." I swallow hard, struggling as my words tremble. "Actually, this is your fault."

"My fault?" he asks.

"I was in your head!"

He scratches his temple, his eyes hooded and dark with fatigue, like that... hour or so had been the first time he'd slept in days before I so rudely tore him from his slumber. "What did you see?"

"Soren tortured you?"

"Oh, no," he say, glancing around the bedroom once more before sliding back into bed. "No, but Soren was there. He... he got me out of that mess. I'll be more careful with my shields going forward. I didn't realize I'd let them down."

He looks stiff, uncomfortable, but I shimmy closer to him and nuzzle into the crook of his shoulder. He draws lazy circles over my naked hip, and silence settles for several minutes before my eyelids start to droop, but I will myself back into existence to ask, "Can you see my dreams?"

"I'm sure they'll mingle tonight. I used to purposefully give my brother and our cousins nightmares if they pissed me off."

"That's awful!" I laugh, lifting my head, but he's... smiling. A soft, lazy kind of smile I don't think I've ever seen him wear.

"Liam used to be terrified of this book that had a rabbit in it."

"A rabbit?"

"It was a vampire rabbit, in his defense. I might have forced a few dreams about it. We shared a room for a while growing up, and I wanted my own space. He slept in our parents' bed until he was like, twelve years old."

"You're kind of a menace."

"I'm an enterprising man. There's a difference."

My answering laugh is soft–sleepy. I drift off in his arms feeling weightless and warm, having long forgotten about the curse ravaging my body.

The wound on my neck aches, but sleep washes over me, carrying me back into a land of dreams, and this time, it's all music.

A little gift from him, I think.

Chapter 27

The Only One I Trust

BLAKE

I wake in the dead middle of the night to the feeling of being watched. The voices in my head skitter through my gray matter, whispering, tittering like they're holding conversations with each other that they don't want me to hear. Hushed whispers from the heavens cease abruptly as I sit up, rubbing my eyes, and look down at where Marianna is curled beside me, her head resting between the pillows. Her hand falls down my chest, settling in my lap. The moonlight paints her skin in silver. It's the most beautiful thing I've ever seen.

I run my fingertips over the curve of her bare waist, waiting for the voices to return, but they stay silent, giving me this moment.

Once, I told Maeve to find the thing that turned the dial on her powers to a simmer. That thing that turned her off, kept her level, made it easier to function. For so long, I thought music was what did that for me.

All this time, it's been her.

I didn't anticipate how last night would go. Standing in my apartment with her, my powers lighting the space between us.... Yeah, that had been... life altering, to say the least. The last time I'd done that—let someone else into my head—it had nearly broken me. It did break me, honestly. I was never the same afterward.

Letting her in had fixed something broken. It mended a wound I had let fester. But now, another wound has taken its place.

I slide out of bed, tugging a shirt over my head. The city blinks and sizzles with light below, but it's still several hours until morning. I have no reason to wake her this early, but I have a feeling someone else is awake, and as I pull on a pair of black sweatpants and a matching sweatshirt, I let my powers pull me back to Eastonia, back to Moonrise, feeling confident that Marianna is safe and secure in my apartment.

Soren's sitting in the lounge on the fourth floor of the castle, tucked deep in the eastern wing of the palace away from the suites and private residences used by the family. He looks up from a notebook when I appear, then sighs deeply, leaning back in a well-loved armchair.

"What are you doing up?" I ask, stepping out of the violent swirls of mist hugging my ankles.

"What are you doing back so soon?" he asks, mimicking my bored tone.

I sit across from him, closing my eyes for a moment in preparation to dispel the voices in my head, but they remain quiet, which is happening increasingly more often. I'm not sure what I'm doing differently, but when Marianna walked back into my life, things began to feel... easier. Less loud.

"I have a question for you, and I had a feeling you were still awake."

He arches a brow. "You have an uncanny ability for knowing where I am at any given moment. If my mate weren't sleeping peacefully upstairs, I'd be wondering if you and I were actually mates." He chuckles, thoroughly entertained. I make a disgusted face and settle deeper into my armchair. "What do you want, Blake?"

"Did you ever run contraband over the border into Crescent Falls?"

"Of course I did," he says, turning his head slightly to the side. "What a stupid fucking question."

"Magical contraband."

He stills, then slowly straightens. "Be more specific."

"Potions–and possibly witches who knew how to use them."

"Tonics, potions, and healers are perfectly legal in Crescent Falls. You should know that, given that you're the royal prince."

I lean forward, bracing my elbows on my knees. "Marianna was given a potion and cursed, bound to Dean, and is now slowly dying. I got a glimpse into Dean's head. He wasn't the type of guy who had the mental capacity to think past his next drink, let alone plot out the use of a curse to bind a woman to him against her will."

"I was the Viper's muscle, Blake," Soren says, tilting his head as he scans my face. I'm not sure what he sees, but he softens, exhaling deeply while rolling out his shoulders and neck. "But yeah, she did move those kinds of things into Crescent Falls. There wasn't a huge market for it, but I know for a fact the Alphas who ran underground auctions, breeder auctions mostly, bought in when anything like that was available." He closes the notebook. "And don't worry, I gave everything I knew about her operations to Evander."

"I wasn't worried about that." I feel echoes of fatigue creeping through my legs. I rise, pacing to the built-in bar on the far side of the room. "I'm just trying to piece together how Dean got his hands on the potion and whether or not she was actually cursed."

"What difference does it make? They cut out the mark. Her wolf will return once she heals–"

"If she were, in fact, cursed, she's going to die." I reach for a bottle of scotch but decide against it, curling my hand into a fist instead. "If she were just given potions over a long period of time... she might fully recover. I need to know for sure."

"Look into her head. She should have memories of when she was cursed if that's the case–"

"No."

"Why not?"

I turn to Soren. His face is set in grim determination, and there he is, the cold-blooded killer I met all those years ago—hard, fierce, and cunning.

Sharp as a fucking *blade*.

"Because it's crossing a boundary."

"Did she set that boundary?"

"No, I did."

"Then fucking cross it. Save her life, Blake, for fuck's sake."

"It's not as easy as you're making it sound."

He sits up straighter and methodically crosses his arms over his chest. "You've looked into mine. Hell, you've been using your powers to keep tabs on me for years now, haven't you? You know exactly where I am, where I'll be in the future. What's stopping you from looking into her head and seeing exactly what went down and how?"

"Because if she were cursed with a binding spell, she wouldn't remember. A witch couldn't just do that and let their victim remember the details. And I–I can't–"

"You're terrified of her."

"What?"

"You're scared of Marianna–"

"Shut the fuck up!"

Soren cuts me off with a cackling laugh that continues until he's nearly out of breath. I'm fuming, likely red in the face, when he runs a hand over his eyes, pinching the bridge of his nose. "Have you been with anyone other than her?"

"Of course I have."

"I'm not talking about a drunken one-night stand. Have you wanted anyone other than her, pined for someone, or has she been it?"

"It's always been her." My hands are curled into fists at my sides.

"Why aren't you–"

"Fighting for her?"

Soren takes a deep breath, resting his palms against his knees, like he's ready for a fight. Tension crackles between us, reminding me that this man is, shockingly, one of the few people I trust.

I trust Soren more than anyone, honestly. He has morals aligned with mine. He understands what this is like for me, what it's been like having to push the person I love away to try to save her, to give her a shot at a better life even if it means I'm not in it.

I really don't want to fight him tonight. I just need someone right now, someone to talk to who might understand...

"She didn't know what I could do. She had no idea I had powers. I fell in love with her. It's as simple as that. I willed a future with her into existence but didn't account for what I am when I made those plans. And when... when I looked into her timeline, our timeline? I saw I would lose her, and I... it was because of me. Somewhere along the line, I'd make a misstep, a miscalculation, that would result in her death. I've spent the last eight years trying to stop it from happening, manipulating every timeline her thread crosses, trying to pick out the frays. It hasn't worked. I was convinced until recently that Hannibal had a hand in her demise. Most, if not all, of his marks were connected to her in some way. Fans of her work, people she crossed in the street, neighbors... people Dean knew, people he worked with, people his Alpha was connected with.... Now I know Hannibal's hand is in this because there is no way Dean could have gotten those potions if it hadn't been for Hannibal's den bringing them into Crescent Falls, and I feel like I've wasted so much time."

"Does she know what you've done for her?"

"No, and she doesn't need to."

"You've spent nearly a decade of your life dedicated to keeping her alive–"

"And I'll spend another decade doing so if I have to. There's no question of that."

"What do you want, Blake? Are you happy continuing on like

this, with her in the background, tucked in your shadow while she tries to raise that kid on her own?"

"I'm used to being alone. I've made peace with it."

"But is it really what you want?"

"It's what has to happen for their safety." I edge toward him, holding out a hand in surrender. He has to understand, doesn't he? This ache, this constant knowledge that everything, and everyone, is a threat? "You have Maeve and Fallon now. You know firsthand how dangerous things are for them, both of them, but especially Fallon. If she were to fall into the wrong hands, it would be disastrous. Skye is the same. Maeve and I are similar, you know. Our powers are intense, insanely valuable, and hard to control. Hannibal wanted something from me and was digging through my head to find what I coveted the most, what I was willing to die to protect, and he nearly found them. Putting them beside me... out in the open... it's out of the question until that man–that thing–is dealt with."

"That could be years from now."

"So be it."

"You need to tell her all of this."

"It wouldn't fix anything." I sink into the armchair across from him and hang my head for a moment.

"Is she your mate, Blake?"

My exhale is deep and restorative. For once in my life, holding back a secret, shielding myself from whispers... doesn't feel right. "I'm different from you. I'm a shifter but also something else. I can't feel the bond like you can, but... I wondered. That's why I looked all those years ago. I looked for our bond, found it, and found her death. She could be my mate but–"

"But what?"

Silence hugs the room for several seconds, broken only by the ticking of a clock on the wall. "But it feels unfair. She's all music, light, and sound. I'm the opposite. I suck light from any room. I need sound to block out the voices in my head. I can't just be in the quiet with her. I'll never be able to do that. I'm not–not good with words,

Soren. I can't write her fucking sonnets and tell her how much I love her because just saying the words doesn't feel like enough. When I found out she got married and had a mate, I was... happy for her and devastated for me. I thought what I'd seen had been a fluke, that we weren't mates, and I was thankful for it. Thankful for her, not for myself. And I let myself fall into the darkness, let it twist and fester like an infection until I'd sucked all the light out of the world around me, and I have no idea how to go back."

"I don't think she cares about those things," he replies, his voice a low, rumbling whisper in the space between us. "I think she's been trying to reach you since your... your what, threads? Since those crossed again. She has to know at this point that you're mates. She has to feel something."

"With the curse–"

"You're different now. You seem less stuck in your head." Soren shifts his weight, glancing down at his watch. "Maeve has commented on the change a few times. She thinks it's because you're finally letting the family see who you are."

"They would hate me if they could really see it. Marianna, too."

"What about Skye? She's the same. Is that how you want her to feel? Like she can't be herself, like she has to hide this part of herself?" He rises, moving toward the door. "Fallon's awake. I'm letting Maeve get some rest tonight before I have to go back to Veiled Valley to meet with Ryatt. Go back to your mate, Blake. I think you already know how to fix this, how to save her, but it means being honest about who, and what, you are."

I remain in the armchair until he leaves, soaking in the silence. The voices in my head remain quiet, even when I move through the aether and arrive back in my apartment just as the sun is starting to push back the darkness, and Crescent Falls erupts in shining glass and twinkling, golden light.

Marianna is still in bed, fast asleep, when I take off my sweatshirt and slide in beside her. I curl my body around hers, tugging her close, and for the first time since I bought this penthouse to escape the rest of the world... I lie there and listen to the sounds of the city waking up for the day.

"Good morning," she says sleepily, rolling over and burying her face in my shirt.

"Good morning," I echo, resting my cheek against her forehead, my eyes on the fading stars beyond the bed.

Chapter 28

Trapped in Memories

Marianna

Misty's house looks homey and warm in the light of midmorning. Coffee scents the air as she moves around her kitchen, opening and shutting cabinets. I rest on one of the stools at the kitchen island, nursing a mug of coffee with cream and vanilla syrup she makes herself, while scanning the family pictures on the walls. Blake rushes back into the kitchen, dressed in sleek navy trousers and a light blue button down, a matching navy blue suit jacket completing the ensemble. He presses the quickest kiss to my temple before darting to the garage, his phone already pressed to his ear.

Misty watches him go, smirking to herself, before she continues rummaging through her cupboards again.

Blake drove me over here about twenty minutes ago. He changed his mind about me tagging along while he talked to his parents, and I can't say I mind. I sigh deeply into my coffee, my stomach in knots for him and what the next day, next week, and next year might look like.

"I have a friend coming over to see you today. She studied

healing in Moonrise back in the day and now has a practice here," Misty says over the sound of Blake's car backing out of the driveway. "She studied the dark arts, too."

I watch her dig through a basket of tea packets, noticing the way her eyes seem to be locked on nothing at all, like she's trapped in her mind.

"I'm afraid I've already met with countless witches who studied the dark arts, and they're all under the same consensus–I can't be saved. I'm cursed."

"What I felt when I let my healing powers drift through you didn't feel like a curse, and I know curses–trust me," she says, her eyes finally lifting from the counter to meet mine. "When I was young, a college student, I broke multiple curses. I had to. I didn't have a choice. But what's happening to you doesn't feel the same. It's like... something is there, blocking your access to your wolf powers. It's just... a shield, almost. It's rather hard to explain, but it doesn't feel like a curse. I'd know."

Her confidence makes the knots in my stomach start to untangle. I take a breath–the first full breath I think I've inhaled since waking up in the clinic a week ago–and let it out slowly.

The click of the electric kettle brings me back to reality. Misty says with a slight hitch in her voice, "I understand Kenna's frustrations and her reservations about this–your treatment." She pours boiling water into a large basin before dropping several pouches of tea into the bowl. Steam billows around her, but she continues, "Curses are so incredibly rare. It's not natural magic by any means. It's manipulated, meant to cause harm, and in your case, your wolf was tied to your ex... mate."

"He was never my mate," I whisper, closing my eyes.

"He did this to hurt you, to take something from you that couldn't be replaced in the event of his death. He wanted you to hurt forever, not die alongside him. He wanted you to suffer, and I think that's on our side, however terrible that sounds. We need to get your wolf back, and if we do that, I don't think the curse is going to be a problem anymore."

"Maeve mentioned the only reason I'm still alive is because my mate is out there somewhere, waiting for me. I have a connection somewhere, holding on." I curl my hands around my coffee mug at the thought of Blake. I desperately want that connection to be him.

"I doubt you'd be able to feel the bond as it stands if he were right in front of you," she says, her eyes meeting mine, and she gives me a look that conveys she's thinking about Blake, too. "I believe that was the point of this–to stop you from ever feeling a mate bond–and that goes against everything our Goddess stands for. It's against Her magic, and using potions to rid someone of their fated mate bond is... dark. The darkest kind of magic of all."

"So you don't think I'm cursed?"

"I don't," she says, matter-of-factly, and gives me a tight smile. "But I agree with Kenna when it comes to how weak you are. You can't carry on like this without a wolf. We need to fix this now, before that weakness progresses."

A resounding knock on the front door steals her attention. Her rapid footsteps in the foyer echo through the otherwise silent house, and then a new, soft female voice drifts through the house, and before I know it, there's a witch standing before me, her dark hair flowing in glossy waves down her back and shoulders.

Dark brown eyes crinkle when she greets me, introducing herself as Katie, one of Cole's colleagues at his children's clinic within Shadowcrest. She's gorgeous and peppy, totally unperturbed by the notion she's here to try to break a curse alongside Misty, and within a minute of rushed introductions, I'm being encouraged to chug as much tea as I can to try to calm my nerves.

"Will it hurt?" I ask as Katie unpacks a strange bowl with symbols etched in its depths from a large leather bag she brought with her.

"Just a bit. I need a little bit of blood, but not much, I promise."

Her dark skin seems to glow from within as the sun fully rises, casting the kitchen in a bright, golden haze.

"What can I do?" Misty asks as Katie arranges several packets of herbs on the kitchen table.

"Grind these up for me, if you can? I brought a mortar, but honestly, your coffee grinder would work better and take less time. I swear it won't leave an aftertaste the next time you grind beans," she says with a sunny laugh that immediately calms my nerves.

Still, as the minutes creep by, I feel a sense of dread lingering, covering me like a wet, weighted blanket. I try to keep my mind focused on seeing Blake again, asking how it went with his parents, telling him how I really feel, and how I want to see him use his powers again but...

A pin-pricking sensation travels through my fingers as Katie takes my hand. She pricks each of my fingers, squeezing them, then rests my hand in the bowl.

"Just give it a few minutes," she says, then rises to check on Misty's progress with the herbs, which are now stinking up the kitchen at an alarming rate.

My stomach turns as blood drips from my fingers. I feel suddenly lightheaded. I close my eyes, drifting, letting a memory pop up and spread through my subconscious.

I'm standing in front of Blake in my mom's shitty little apartment. He steps inside, dripping with rain, his eyes narrowed and his expression etched from shadow. "Why didn't you tell me? Marianna, you should have told me you were pregnant from the moment you knew."

"You need to leave, Blake. Please–I can't talk to you right now."

"Your mom had to find me and tell me," he continues through gritted teeth, his eyes so dark I can't see the violet swirling around his pupils. All I can think about as he steps closer is... how bright his eyes shone that night when everything changed. "We're having a girl," he says, almost painfully. "You should have–"

"Should have what? Called you? Like you would have answered?"

His lips press shut as the storm rages outside, water already pooling in the stairwell leading down to our front door. "I would have been here the second you needed me."

"But that's just it, Blake. You didn't want this. You broke up with me. You told me you needed space so I gave it to you. You told me I couldn't handle it, and maybe you were right. I'm scared of you. You lied to me. This whole time, the past... two years? It was all a lie."

"It wasn't."

"Did you actually like me, or was I just an easy target? A plaything?" Even I don't believe it. Blake isn't that kind of person. But the words taste good on my tongue, especially when his expression pinches into a pain so deep I feel it in my chest, like I've stabbed him in the heart.

Good. I want him to feel the same way I've felt for six months. Empty. Hurting. Alone.

"I love you," he says. "I loved you then, and I love you now, and I will make this right–"

"I don't want you here. You tossed me to the side like trash. It was easy for you, wasn't it? Leaving me after I found out your little secret? Don't act like anything can come from this, Blake. You're... not only a prince but some kind of... magical being? What am I? Nothing but a wolf. You made that perfectly fucking clear–"

"What are you trying to say?" he growls, losing his grip on that mask of iron and indifference.

"I was just someone to hunt and fuck until you met someone on your level, right?"

"Marianna–"

I let my fear of him, my confusing, all-consuming agony over losing him, turn to vicious, uncontrollable anger, "I don't want you in her life. I want you out of mine. Leave."

He stands there in the doorway, totally still. His eyes search mine. "What can I do to fix this?"

"You're a liar. There's nothing left to fix."

"I should have told you–"

"It doesn't matter anymore. Just leave. Leave, and don't come back. I'm doing this on my own."

"No."

"Yes!" I step toward him but halt abruptly when his eyes begin to shine in the darkness all around us. Terror creeps over my skin. I hug myself, stepping back again. "Get out of my house and don't return. I don't want you here."

"I never meant to hurt you or scare you–"

"Go find a witch or something, Blake. Someone who can handle what you are. Someone who can give you–give you powerful babies for your fucking bloodline–"

"What the fuck does that have to do with anything?" he thunders in a tone I've never heard him use before. "I love you, Marianna. You're the one I want. That will never change–"

"Let it change," I shout, each word tight and clear. "You ended this, Blake. You told me to stay away from you, and I have. And so will she. It's safer that way. I wouldn't want you hurting her–"

I snap back to reality with a sob that catches Misty off guard, but Katie looks relieved. I realize with a start that my mouth feels numb, and I look down at the well-loved kitchen table where Misty's children have eaten every meal over the course of their lives until they left for college, but instead of a plate catching the light of the sun, and empty teacup rests in front of me, the remnants of an inky black liquid tremble at the bottom.

"One more cup, I think. How do you feel?" Katie asks, lowering herself into the chair next to mine.

"What's happening to me?" I ask as my mind reels over memories I've buried for years... at least, I thought I had. I can't remember why I tucked them away, but now pieces of my youth are sprinting back in startling clarity.

"You're about to feel really sick," Katie warns, glancing at Misty, who looks pale, her eyes shining with her powers at the ready. "But just gut through it, okay? Don't throw up–"

I'm back in my memories, Misty's kitchen replaced by a hospital room in the inner city. I feel the pain like it's fresh, happening in real time. Mom argues with a doctor while I scream in sheets stained with blood. The baby is too big. It's been hours of this. I'm terrified.

"Enough. Give her a minute. She's in pain, so something needs to be done about that."

Blake's voice tears my attention to the doorway as he stalks into the room looking murderous. He shrugs out of a cloak, lets it fall to the floor, and is at my side in an instant, my tear-stained face clasped between his large, warm hands.

I haven't seen him for almost four months. Everything since then was paperwork, lawyers and mediators while he set up trust funds and accounts I, of course, refused. He didn't try to talk to me again after our fight, and I just... crumbled. Spun out of control and let the darkness in while shoving him as far away as possible even if he was the only thing I wanted.

I was scared.

I thought I was scared of him.

Maybe I still am, but now?

I clasp his hand, whimpering through another contraction, and he presses his forehead against mine–silent, but here. Here when I needed him the most.

"I'm sorry for what I said to you. I didn't mean it. I didn't mean any of it," I cry out, but he just shakes his head, and together, with my mom by our side, we guide Skye into the world.

"I don't want–I don't want to do this," I grind out as my body trembles with pain. Katie and Misty fill my vision once more, but the memory of Skye's birth is still within sight, like I'm trapped between the past and the present.

"It's working, isn't it?" Misty breathes excitedly, a phone pressed to her ear.

"Just a little longer, okay? You're doing great," Katie urges, but pain rips through my head like my brain is being torn wide open, my memories flooding out.

I see Blake looking down at Skye for the first time. She's a bundle in his arms, and he looks so... peaceful. So shocked but proud. But then he pauses, tilting his head as his eyes flare with power and... he gives her to my mom, and that's the last time I saw him until... until the concert, years later.

"No more," I beg, but Katie tips another sip of the sticky, slimy concoction into my mouth. I choke on it, but the effects are immediate, and I slip back into my memories again.

"Kenna says to keep going until she finds the barrier–" Misty's voice fades and is replaced by a rowdy bar and a man I just met, who smiles down at me, handsome and tall.

He buys me a drink. It tastes funny. I feel my... my mind loosening, and it feels...

Good.

Chapter 29

Snap

Blake

THE CASTLE GROUNDS are full of sunlight and bees when I step out of my car and squint against the brightness reflecting off the exterior windows. I brush a bee off my shoulder, which gives me an angry buzz and zooms to the nearest group of rose bushes, which are in full bloom now, painting the garden in shades of red and pink.

It's a quiet day, a weekend, which is why I planned to be here this morning. Both of my parents are here and alone.

A flash of platinum blonde catches my attention, and I turn to my mother, who's crouching in a thicket of hydrangea bushes only a few feet away. She pokes her head up, beaming at me, but that smile fades when she sees the dark expression casting shadows over my face. "Blake? I didn't realize you were coming today. I spoke to Kenna, and it sounds like you were very busy in Moonrise. Someone got cursed?"

"Can we talk? Where's Dad?"

"He's inside," she says, her eyebrows pinched together as she dusts her hands off on her gardening apron–a silly thing Dad bought her for her birthday two decades ago that's covered in embroidered radishes with our handprints and names sloppily painted on the front pocket. "Is something wrong?"

"I just have a meeting with him today. I'd like you to be there, too. Please."

She doesn't like my tone but follows me into the castle through the grand front doors. All the windows are open on the lower level to cut through the heat as early spring bleeds into the warmth of the upcoming summer. Her gardening clogs clap against the freshly waxed wood floors as we cross the foyer, then hike the stairs, then move through the narrow hallways of the second floor toward Dad's office.

But Mom grabs my forearm and pulls me to a stop. "Blake, what's going on? Kenna seemed totally out of sorts, more than usual, and your grandma was just in Moonrise, too. Maddy wouldn't tell me a Goddess–damn thing about what happened. Is the woman who was cursed okay? Does this have to do with Hannibal?"

"Is that Blake?" Dad steps into the hallway where Mom dragged me to a stop. "Blake–"

"Can we please go somewhere we can sit down?" I ask, but my voice shakes. I look down at my hands before glancing between my parents, who're wearing similar expressions of wariness.

When no one moves, I brush past them and into my dad's office, where I spent countless hours shadowing him in both engineering and his duties as king. None of that matters now, does it?

I turn when I hear Dad closing the door behind us, but just as my lips part to start explaining myself, my reasoning for leaving all of this behind, he says, "You're abdicating in favor of Liam."

"How did you know?"

Mom sighs heavily, but her eyes crinkle with understanding. "We've had our suspicions for a few years now. Once you started working alongside Maeve, it felt like... it felt like you were finally where you were meant to be."

Dad doesn't seem as relieved as she is, however. He takes a breath before stalking through the room to sit at his desk. My parents... they had a rough go of it. I was born without my dad present. I know bits and pieces about why, but they're a secretive couple. Compared to Dad's twin brother and their little sister, my parents' relationship wasn't something they showcased to the entire family. They have lived a quiet life here in Crescent Falls, away from the rest of the family by hundreds of miles, and even as I grew up, started gaining access to the family secrets and stories they kept from us as children, my parents never shared theirs.

I do know, thanks to Ryan, that my mom kept me hidden, and my dad saved her life–and mine. I know they're mate and both my parents have mystic abilities.

But that's it.

I was the product of what was meant to be a one-night stand. I know that much, at least.

"You're sure about this?" Dad asks, his dark blue eyes holding on mine with an intensity that makes my spine straighten.

"I am. Liam should be king, your heir. I've already spoken to him about it at length. I've made all the arrangements that needed to be made–leaving the firm, for one. My projects are wrapped up and I've cleared my schedule, as well as put in my notice there." I reach up to loosen the collar of my shirt. "I considered selling my penthouse in the city, but Briar has shown some interest in making it her own, so I'll hold it for her until she graduates. Celeste spoke about possibly taking over my position at the firm as well. As for Noah... he's young. He–"

"Your siblings aren't your responsibility, Blake," Mom says, edging toward me.

"I just wanted every piece to fall into place before I made my decision, and it has, so I am officially abdicating my place in line for the throne. I will no longer be known as Blake, Crown Prince, and I will live in Eastonia full time–"

"Why?" Dad asks, his voice echoing through his office like a death knell. He doesn't look displeased, but he's not happy about this, either. He's always been able to hide how he really feels. If I'm like anyone in the family, it's him. He, and his grandfather, Maddox. Sharp, calculated, and cold.

At least on the outside.

"You know why," I say under my breath, my eyes glowing with my powers.

Mom chews her lower lip, briefly brushing her hand over my forearm in solidarity as she moves through the room to Dad's side and leans against his desk. "So you're doing what the mystics hoped you would? Becoming their king?"

"Yes," I answer, biting back the unease trying to break through the word. "They've needed a ruler for a while now, and Ryatt agrees that they should have their own space carved out for them in our allied kingdoms, with someone to control them. That's me. It's been me since I started training with them as a teenager. I will remain in Moonrise, continuing to stay at the castle, at least until the house I designed is completed."

"You're building a house in Moonrise? Why?" Mom asks, smiling, but her eyes darken with confusion. "The palace is big enough for everyone–"

Here we go.

"Marianna and I–"

"Marianna?" Dad cuts in, and for the first time since I arrived, lets a glimmer of emotion show. Shock, relief, maybe a sliver of confusion at the mention of her name–the only person, only friend outside of the family, I've ever had.

"You and Marianna are back together? When did that happen?" Mom asks, excitement lacing the words.

"How long has this been going on?"

"Can you just–please sit down, Mom?"

My parents stare at me while I struggle to maintain my composure.

"What–"

"Please," I repeat. "Sit down."

My parents glance at each other. Mom gracefully takes a seat in an armchair next to Dad's desk and folds her hands in her lap. Dad, however, leans forward in his chair. "What's going on, Blake?"

"I'm building a house for... my family to live in. All of us. Marianna, me, her mom." My chest tightens. "And Skye. I bought a plot of land on the other side of the lake, in Old Moonrise. It's quiet there. I figured, for a kid her age, she'd.... With powers like hers, she'll like the quiet–"

Mom rises, her face washed in shock. "Who's Skye?"

"Your granddaughter," I answer. My mouth feels impossibly dry. "She's seven. She's... she's like us, Mom. A mystic. A powerful one–"

"You have a daughter?" Dad's voice booms through the room.

I close my eyes for a moment. "Yes."

"Blake?" Mom shakes her head, pain etched through the word, my name. "How–"

"We were very young," I explain, opening my eyes, and then... I tell them everything. I have to. Every detail spills out of me like a storm until I'm out of breath. The breakup, the pregnancy, the deal I made with Marianna to stay out of their lives, and the money available to her. How everything I've done, every lie I've told over the past decade, has been for her. For them.

Mom, however, looks absolutely crushed as she sinks deep into the cushions of her chair. She rubs a hand over her face, asking, "Can we meet her?"

"Of course," I whisper, swallowing past the knot in my throat. "As soon as–as soon as you'd like. She's... wonderful. Marianna did a great job raising her thus far–"

"And you've been absent from her life?"

Dad's voice is harsh, but I suppose I deserve it. "It was Marianna's decision, and I agreed. I thought I could prevent Skye from... being what she is if I kept her at a distance."

"Does she know you're her father?" Mom asks, her voice cracking over the words.

"Not yet. We haven't... had a chance to tell her, to be honest. Marianna is...." Now it's my voice cracking. I back up, sinking into the chair beside my mom, and hang my head as the weight of the last week or so barrels over me like a landslide. I don't know how to even begin. "Marianna was cursed, we believe. Kenna and Maeve have done their best for her, but currently, we're running out of options and time." I look up at my mom. "I looked into her timeline all those years ago and saw that I'd lose her young, and I am."

"Where is she now?" Mom asks while Dad remains customarily silent nearby, still seated behind his desk.

"She's with Misty."

Mom looks at Dad, whose eyes are focused on the door to his office while he drops into thought.

"And where is Skye?" Mom asks softly.

"She's in Moonrise with Leona and Kenna at the palace. I wanted to come here and tell you about them, and my plans for the future, before we... made plans with or... without Marianna." It's crushing. My chest aches with a ferocity that would be enough to bring me to my knees if I weren't seated. But the pain is fresh–something I've only experienced once, and alarm bells start ringing through my head as the voices return in warning. I rise, looking around like Marianna is going to jump out from behind the couch bleeding, maimed, and Mom notices the worried look cutting away at the usual mask I wear to keep my emotions hidden.

"What's wrong?"

"I don't know. I need to go back to Misty's house–" I turn for the door but hear Dad rise from his chair.

"I'll go with you. Sarah, go to Moonrise. Make sure Skye is all right."

Mom makes a small sound in her throat that could either be excitement or distress, I'm not sure, but one second I'm standing with two feet on the ground in the castle, and the next, Dad claps his hand on my shoulder and we're in Misty and Cole's foyer and...

Marianna's sharp laugh lifts around me, blurring my senses as I careen down a hallway, Dad hot on my heels, and into the airy kitchen.

A witch leans against the counter, smiling widely, while Misty, looking a bit worse for wear, sprays cleaning solution all over her countertops. A strange, bitter scent hangs in the air, but it's faint.

Much fainter than Marianna's scent, which is now so strong, so sweet, it penetrates my mind, my very soul, and renders me... utterly useless to the scene unfolding in front of my eyes.

Dad looks around, then says, "What's going on here?"

Misty sighs heavily but smiles, chuckling as she replies, "I think you'd better go to Moonrise and tell Kenna to pay up for me. She didn't think we could do it."

I'm looking at Marianna, who's sitting in the sunlight, her hair mussed and her cheeks a deep red–looking more alive than she has in... what could easily be years.

And when her stunning blue eyes meet mine, I feel it. I hear it, smell it, taste it. A rainbow of color and sound, of feeling.

That sharp ache in my chest relaxes as the mate bond snaps into place, just like I knew it would.

But now... we have time.

"You broke the curse," I whisper.

"Kenna owes me a hundred bucks." Misty laughs, and the witch cackles nearby, her reply lost in the voices currently chattering in what sounds like relief deep inside my mind.

Chapter 30

This Family

Blake

It's late afternoon when we finally return to Moonrise. Marianna slumps in my arms as I spirit us directly into my suite, which is dark, the curtains pulled, and the blinds closed to the outside world. Rain pelts the windows. I lay Marianna in my bed, and she groans, blinking wearily up at me while her skin flushes a pale green.

"How do you people travel like that without throwing up every time?" she rushes out, trembling.

"Most of my family members do, in fact, throw up. You haven't yet, so consider yourself one of the strong ones."

She's limp with her eyes shut before I even finish the sentence.

I walk through the fifth floor's eastern wing of the palace, which I normally have to myself, when Leona comes rushing around a corner, nearly knocking me over. I grab her by the shoulders to steady her as she gasps in surprise. "Blake! I heard you were back, and she–"

"She's fine." I slide the keys to my suite into her hand. "She's lying down. Jumping here wasn't easy on her."

"Kenna tried to explain what happened, but it went right over my head. She's cured? The curse is gone?"

"We'll know for sure in a few days when the potions wear off."

Leona exhales, her breath coming in a whoosh. "How? How could this possibly be real?"

"As far as I know, they used a counter curse, and Misty was able to use her powers from that point forward to heal the damage." I purse my lips, shrugging a shoulder. "Admittedly, I know very little about dark magic."

"You and me both," she breathes, her cheeks stained a fiery red. She pats her chest like she's trying to restart her heart. "Oh, Blake, thank you! I–I feel like I've been barely surviving the past few days. Oh, Marianna. Goddess, I need to go see her."

"Where's Skye?"

Leona takes another deep breath, trying to regain her composure. "She's been following Soren around all day. Skye is a bit obsessed with Fallon, I'm afraid. She's... she's really taken to this place and everyone around." Leona looks mildly unsure as she blinks up at me and then quickly glances away, her eyes locked on the hallway leading to my office and private suite. "She has no idea she's related to any of you yet, but... Kenna and Maeve have been incredibly kind. I've been trying to take Skye back to the townhouse, but they won't hear of it."

"I told my parents about her earlier this morning."

Leona looks up at me again with a heavy sigh. "You know I wanted you to do that from the beginning."

"I know, and looking back, you were right."

"Of course I was right. You were nineteen."

I roll my lower lip between my teeth and match her sigh. "There's nothing we can do about it now other than move on. Marianna will probably sleep for a while, hopefully the entire night. I have some notes from the witch who performed the counter curse that I need to take to Kenna."

"Are your parents here? Maeve mentioned more people just arrived upstairs, but I was already on my way down here when I found out you'd come home."

"Yes." The word wobbles. I've been finding it harder and harder to cover my tracks, keep my emotions guarded, lately. Usually it comes naturally, but ever since I found myself in the same place as Marianna again, that damp, poorly lit hallway beneath the performing arts center... I feel like she flayed me open for the world to see.

And now, here I am, rocking on my heels, watching my mate's mother eye me with skepticism. "Did anything else happen when you were in Crescent Falls? You seem different."

"Marianna can explain everything. If she remembers." I highly doubt she remembers much about those few minutes I spent back at Misty's. I scooped her up the second I felt the mate bond knitting between us and brought her here, seeing the confusion and exhaustion in her eyes. I'm unsure she even felt it given the ungodly amount of herbs in her system.

I felt it, however. It's the only thing on my mind other than my immense regret that... my inability to just be honest with her from the beginning was how she ended up with Dean, the man responsible for her shortened strand in the stars. If I'd just been there, none of this would have happened.

It was all my fault.

I turn Leona toward my suite and give her an encouraging nudge. She glances over her shoulder at me a few times before slipping into my darkened apartment, and I wait for the door to click shut before turning toward the recesses of the palace and hiking down the stairs to the fourth floor, which is where the family tends to congregate the most.

The pink room is a family favorite but is shockingly empty other than an enormous amount of boxes overflowing with toys I remember from childhood but haven't seen in two decades. So is the long, narrow room with the massive dining table we use when the entire family gathers, which is rare these days. So are the numerous sitting rooms and studies that dot either wing.

But voices ring out when I find myself back on the balcony overlooking the grand foyer, and several stories below, Soren sprints into view with Skye hot on his heels, shrieking with laughter before disappearing from sight again.

"He told me he didn't know what to do with kids," Maeve says behind me. I resist the urge to jump out of my skin and slowly turn to look at her over my shoulder. She leans her hip against the balcony, Fallon resting in a sling across her chest. "Look at him now, though." She chuckles, shaking her head. "He's been letting her chase him all over the castle. Mom and I actually got some of our old toys out of storage for her to play with, but she wants Soren instead."

I shouldn't feel jealous, should I?

"He's bored," I reply dryly, and Maeve gives me a knowing smile. "He's been stuck in this palace for weeks now—"

"Very bored. Well, that's going to change any minute, I guess. I was just talking to your dad, and he mentioned Grandpa Ryatt is plotting something that involves Soren."

"Soren is his heir to the Roguelands."

Maeve's expression darkens so deeply that the sea-green of her eyes fades to a stormy blue. "I'm... I'm aware of the rumors, yes."

"Don't consider it a rumor."

"You've seen it in the stars or whatever?"

"No, but... who else, Maeve?"

The column of her throat bobs as she swallows. "I don't want to think about what's coming, what changes are coming. Fallon is just over a month old, and you have a kid... a mate, too." She arches her brow. "Your scent changed."

I run my tongue across my lower lip, rolling my eyes back to the now empty foyer. "That quickly, huh?"

"So Misty's scheme was successful, then? Mom had a conniption about it. I was honestly jealous you got to leave and weren't trapped in a castle with her for the past two days."

"I'm not even entirely sure what they achieved in my absence."

Maeve sighs, patting Fallon's back. "A counter-curse. We thought about it, but honestly very few witches ever train in that kind of magic anymore. It's blood magic, you know. One misstep and several people can die."

"Several?"

"Oh, yeah. Counter-curses are always more dangerous than the original curse. What was the witch's name again? Katie? Anyway, she could have easily cursed herself, Misty, and whoever just happened to be walking by the house on a midmorning stroll if she made any wrong moves. The risks always outweigh the rewards."

"In this case, it was worth it."

"This cannot happen again," Maeve says, her eyes still dark and fixed on a random point on the wall across the foyer. "I can't allow this to happen in the future."

"It wasn't your fault–"

"Contraband leaving Eastonia into Crescent Falls, into the hands of someone who doesn't know a Goddess-damned thing about potions and magic? That feels like my fault." Fallon fusses. Maeve plucks her from the sling and hands her to me, which I'm unprepared for. I grasp the baby and tuck her against my chest while Maeve continues to untangle herself from the sling. "Marianna likely won't have her wolf back for some time as it stands. I wish–gods–I wish I could punish someone for this, make an example out of them in public."

"The man who did this to her was punished by death." It's not enough. The look on Maeve's face tells me she agrees.

"Marianna should recover; that's the good news. I'd like to get Katie here in Moonrise to discuss exactly what she did in person, however. It feels awfully unfair that Crescent Falls has a witch trained in counter-curses, and we don't even have one."

"You said it's rare–"

"Nothing feels impossible these days," she cuts in, sniffling indignantly. "And I hate that Soren just–just found his freedom and is now being called, or summoned, or whatever, to be king of the same place that beat him down his entire life. I hate it. He knows it, too. We've talked about it at length. I hate that Brie and Kieran are stuck in Veiled Valley while Logan remains in Emberfyll waiting for the other shoe to drop. She's pregnant again, you know."

"I know. Another boy."

"She's convinced it's a girl, but we know otherwise," she says shortly, throwing me a look. Yeah, I painted Maeve a picture of Brie's life to settle her nerves on Brie's wedding night, but what else was going on during that time wasn't something I let myself see. "Dad's all up in arms, putting his Ghosts through extra training. They're all exhausted. Hell, I brought Lexa here to help train my own forces, and she beat the shit out of all of them, and now my commanders are absolutely terrified of her and her gang of feral warriors she brought with her to 'help'. Now, I have to send her out to Teshka, most likely, during the busiest planting season in Silverhide because we don't know what's coming next, and I–I should know. *You* should know."

"I know something's coming."

"That's not enough, Blake."

"My mind hasn't been–" Fallon sneezes so aggressively both of us jump. She sighs heavily before dropping her head back against my shoulder, her golden blonde curls tickling my chin. I stand perfectly still as the baby falls asleep, a dead weight in my arms, and Maeve... smiles softly, taking a deep breath, calming down.

"Look, Maeve, my mind has been in shambles since Marianna and Skye came back into my life. The voices quieted. Everything I used to see is out of reach now. I'll need the orrery. I have a few mystics I can trust, but not many. Hannibal is like me somehow, which is why we can't find him. He's shielding himself, keeping himself and whatever plot is in the works, hidden."

She stands in silence for several moments, considering my words. "Marianna was the thing that turned you off."

I close my eyes, thankful for Fallon's steady weight in my arms. "Yeah. She is."

Skye's loud screech below forces my eyes open, and I witness Soren and her running back in the direction they came, this time with Skye on Soren's shoulders.

"He didn't have a childhood," Maeve whispers, like she didn't mean to say it out loud. Her voice is smaller and sadder than I've ever heard. She turns to me, her eyes light and shining like polished sea-glass again. "Thank you for this."

"For what?"

"Trusting us with who you really are. All these years, I thought you were just a pompous, arrogant asshole. I'm still not entirely convinced you aren't, but you're not the villain in my narrative like I thought you were. You were just trying to protect them. I get it." She clasps me on the arm before turning to walk upstairs.

"Are you forgetting something?"

She looks over her shoulder, squinting at Fallon, who's fast asleep on my shoulder. "I don't want to wake her up. She's pretty mean if she hasn't had her four or five naps a day. You've got it."

"Maeve–"

She disappears in a haze of crimson smoke, chuckling, leaving me on the balcony with a baby. Her baby. Her baby, who I'm holding for the first time.

"Goddess dammit," I grumble, but Skye sprints through a darkened corridor, skidding to stop a few yards away. Soren, panting, bends over to rest his hands on his knees, weakly waving at me when he notices me standing there.

"Wanna trade?" he rasps, completely out of breath.

Skye edges toward me, her eyes glowing a soft violet as she inspects me from head to toe. "Mommy's back?"

"Mommy's back," I echo. "She's asleep, though."

"We can play dolls then. Soren isn't very good at it."

He snorts a laugh, now bracing himself on the balcony, gulping down lungfuls of air, and I feel... light. Featherlight. Like this is it, regardless of what Maeve thinks and what our future holds.

This family. I didn't think I'd ever have it.

I didn't think it was in the stars for me.

Now, I'm realizing that even the stars are wrong sometimes.

Chapter 31

How Long Have You Known?

MARIANNA

I wake to spring rain and hazy gray sunlight filtering through modern blinds that don't match the intricate stonework surrounding the windows. Gray paint makes the room darker than it should be, maybe even a few degrees colder than I'm sure it is outside. I stretch like a cat, groaning as my body pops and sizzles from lack of movement, then blink at the ceiling–domed, with a crystal chandelier hanging overhead. I realize with a start I have no godly idea where I am, but I've... hell, I'm not even surprised at this point. I feel like I've lived a thousand lives over the past two or three weeks, so what's a strange bed in a strange room?

A room that smells like Blake at his rawest.

The door on the far side of the room smacks against the wall as it flies open, and a dark-haired blur is my only warning before Skye flies onto the bed.

I catch her with a crunch that stifles Blake's rushed exhale as he follows her into the room, but he stops near the foot of the bed, his eyes sweeping across my face. Skye nuzzles my neck, her arms wrapped so tight my vision goes spotty.

"You smell like pancakes," I whisper into her hair as tears spring loose.

"You missed breakfast," she murmurs into my shirt, then sighs, relaxing into my touch, and I... can't remember the last time she was like this. Cuddly. Wanting to be touched, to be held.

Blake notices my shock and edges closer to the bed and sits down near my feet, leaning forward with his elbows resting on his knees and just... looks at us. Looks at me—me, holding his daughter in my arms.

A deeply rooted type of anguish—regret—passes behind his eyes before he shields it from view. I feel it settle in my chest, tight and unforgiving. A single glimmer of what he's felt for years.

"How are you feeling?" Blake asks quietly.

I rub Skye's back. "Weird, to be honest. A little numb."

"It's the herbs. Those should wear off soon, if not by the end of the day."

"What's my bill?" I laugh, unable to help myself. "I feel like the amount of herbs, potions, and tonics in my system is likely enough to fund Skye's tuition at her next school until college."

Blake's smile is brief, but his eyes light with a silent laugh. "It's on the house."

Skye abruptly wiggles out of my arms and gets off the bed. "I'm going to go play," she announces and then darts out of sight. My heart lurches, but Blake pins my hand to the bed, his eyes holding mine.

"She's fine. Everyone here is keeping an eye on her."

"How long has it been since we were in Crescent Falls?"

"We got back yesterday afternoon. You slept through the night. You haven't missed much."

I try to slide out of bed, but he stops me with a hand on my shoulder. His warmth radiates through my skin, reminding me of our night in his penthouse. It's only been a little over a day since then, but everything feels different now. I just can't put my finger on it. I'm dizzy and numb when he guides me back against the cushions, but he lingers, leaning over me, his face only inches from mine.

I reach up to stroke his cheek, and he leans into the touch, closing his eyes with a heavy sigh.

"Have you slept?"

He shakes his head. "Not yet."

"Come to bed then."

"My parents are here. They want to meet Skye. I told them to wait until today, to give everyone a moment to breathe before... that."

"How'd it go yesterday? We didn't have time to talk about it."

He shrugs a shoulder before relaxing against me, bracing himself on an elbow so he doesn't squish me. This feels like... before. Before the festival in Moorn when everything changed. It feels like those quiet afternoons spent on my couch where I tucked my toes under his thigh and we talked for hours... or I talked, and he listened. Mostly, he listened.

He rests his head against my chest. I run my fingers through his hair, closing my eyes against the hazy feeling still gripping my body, my bones. "It went about as well as it could have. Telling them about Skye overshadowed abdicating the throne, for sure."

"Are you sure that's what you want?"

He lifts his head. "Do you want to be queen?"

My body seizes for a moment. I wonder if he can feel the way I stiffen. We haven't talked about... that. A future together.

I keep running my fingers through his hair as I say, "Can you imagine? Us on the throne of Crescent Falls? We've never been able to make a decision to save our lives."

"All I do is make decisions," he counters, and I smile.

"I make bad ones. You'd spend your entire day fixing everything I've messed up."

"We don't have to worry about that because I won't be king. Not of Crescent Falls."

Not of Crescent Falls... but of his kind. Skye's kind.

I exhale deeply, tucking a lock of hair behind his ear. "Do we have that kind of time?"

He lays his head back down, his body going boneless, like he hasn't had a single moment to relax in days, and that's probably true.

He doesn't have a chance to answer, however, because a soft feminine laugh echoes toward us from the doorway, and I shove him off, my cheeks burning the same color crimson as Maeve's robe. She's now standing in the doorway looking smug, holding a breakfast tray.

Blake stands and runs his fingers through his hair, closing his eyes for several seconds before turning his gaze on her in a glare. "Do you ever knock?"

"No, this is my house." She strides into the room, beaming, damn near strutting past Blake to place the breakfast tray in my lap. "Look at you! You look alive again!"

"Thanks," I murmur as embarrassment burrows through my body.

She turns to Blake with a swish of her crimson robe. "Blake, your mom is driving me insane."

"I know," he begins, but Maeve cuts him off, running right over the top of him.

"She's begging to meet Skye. Sydney, thankfully, is busy with Soren but–"

"I wanted Marianna to be there. They haven't seen her yet, either. I told her she could come but needed to hold off until we were ready to make introductions."

I cut into a pancake and stuff a bite into my mouth, watching the two most powerful people of their generation converse. It's odd, really. They're total opposites but so alike in their mannerisms, like having so much power just within reach makes them... stiff. Blake always looks like he's walking on egg-shells around Maeve and vice versa, but they can't help but try to rile each other up.

It's amazing breakfast entertainment, to say the least.

"What, exactly, are you waiting for? Huh? The next lunar eclipse?" Maeve urges, her hands planted on her hips.

Blake glowers. "It's my decision. Her decision." He waves a hand in my general direction. "Skye doesn't know I'm her father–"

"She's not dumb, Blake, for fuck's sake. She might look like Marianna's twin, but those eyes? Give me a break–"

"It will change everything for her. The life she's lived so far will be over. It's been her, Marianna, and Leona for her entire life, and I can't just walk back into it."

"Leona and Sarah have been in knots since dinner last night over this."

"It's not up to them–"

"But–"

"It's not going to affect Skye in the slightest," I cut in.

Maeve and Blake look at me, startled into silence like they've forgotten I'm here. I shrug, taking another bite of pancakes.

"She's not like that. She's not going to cry and throw herself around or jump on Blake acting like her life is now complete, or something, if that's what you think." I focus on Blake with a small, sad smile. "I'm sorry. If that's what you wanted–"

"She really is your daughter," Maeve smirks, clapping him hard on the shoulder. "Whatever. She's in the garden with Soren as it stands. But Blake, you need to at least let Sarah spend some time with her."

"I wasn't keeping her from her in the slightest. It's just been–I had other things to worry about." Blake is on the verge of losing his patience. It's odd. I feel like... I suddenly get him again. Like we're teenagers again, and I can gauge what he's feeling, what he's...

Oh, my gods.

My chest tightens to the point that I struggle to breathe.

Maeve is walking out of the room. Blake continues arguing with her while following her to the door, all while I stare at the back of his head in... utter shock.

He closes the door behind Maeve, locks it, and raises a hand against the solid wood. Echoes of his power drift from his fingertips, violet light shimmering along the walls, the windows...

"We're mates?"

Blake drops his hand and turns to me, his face totally and completely void of emotion.

I sit up straight as the herbs in my system fade, shoved away by the adrenaline now coursing through my veins.

"Blake–"

"You feel it now?"

His scent is overwhelming my senses, turning my... honestly, fury and confusion, into something so heated I feel like my body is suddenly molten. I try to shove those feelings aside, but Blake stalks toward me, his eyes dark as they search my face.

"Marianna–"

"How long have you known?" I clutch the breakfast tray like it's my only lifeline.

Blake stops short of the bed. His power radiates through the room, shimmering along the walls. It's a shield, I realize. It has to be. No one is going to be able to come near this suite while we... have the conversation we should have had almost eight years ago. I slide the breakfast tray to the side and rise. A thin, silky nightgown falls to just above my knees–something I don't remember putting on but... it's the furthest thing from my mind as I square my shoulders and fold my arms under my chest.

"How long, Blake?"

He blinks at me, narrowing his eyes as he scans my set, inspects my expression–grim determination.

"You've known this whole time, haven't you?"

"Not exactly."

"What does that even mean?"

"I looked into your timeline when I was eighteen years old, Anna. My powers weren't mature yet. I couldn't even shift yet, but... I tried, and I saw that you'd die young, and our bond–"

I shove him hard. "You did know!"

"It wasn't something I would have been able to interpret with the skills I had at the time. I quit my training with the mystics after a few months. I didn't even make it a year under their care!" His voice edges on a shout, which startles me. I back up a step, which causes his furious expression to shatter. "I didn't mean to yell."

"What did you see? What does it even look like?"

"I–it's hard to explain–"

"Try."

He swallows hard, his eyes shining like polished amethyst in the dim light of morning. "I quit my training with the mystics a few months before I met you. I was torn to shreds, Marianna. I can't explain what it was like, but it was what I prevented Skye from going through. Torture. Mental and emotional torture. I came home a broken kid, just on the cusp of becoming a man, and had no idea where to go from there. Then I met you, and those voices in my head finally shut the fuck up and left me alone. Every time I was with you, it was just music and light. Your voice, Marianna, was enough to make me whole again. And as the months passed, and we grew closer, and I finally found the nerve to open up to you, to get close, I... I fell head over heels in love with you. I was young and dumb and had to know that you were mine. I looked. I saw our love there, written in the stars. It was just as clear as the fact that you were supposed to die, and it was going to be my fault–"

"How was any of this your fault? Dean–"

"Dean found a binding spell, yes. He put you under a curse, yes. But if I hadn't been the one to ruin everything between us, none of this would have happened. If I hadn't scared you–if I hadn't lied to you from the beginning about what I was and what I was capable of back then.... I should have told you the truth from the beginning. That was where our threads frayed. I ruined us. You left me, rightfully so, and your thread became ensnared with someone who should have never even met you. It was my fault." Blake's eyes are hollow as he holds my gaze, his hands outstretched in a show of surrender. "I gave you up. I gave Skye up thinking I was protecting you, that being with me was the reason you'd die young. I thought it was because of the Spider. I thought everything I had to do over the past five years was to–to keep you alive, but I was the one causing you harm from the beginning."

I can't do much but just stare at him. My heart quakes. "Blake–"

"We're mates, Marianna. Fated mates. I love you. I've never stopped loving you for a fucking second, but if this isn't what you want–"

"Are you fucking kidding me?" I snap then howl a laugh that bounces from wall to wall. Blake looks utterly, completely confused, like I expected. He might be opening up more, shedding that mask, his brain somewhat less busy, but his lack of social cues... yeah, those are still alive and well.

"What's–what's so funny?" He steps toward me. "Are you rejecting me?"

Chapter 32

A Granddaughter

Marianna

"I'm not rejecting you," I rush out, clasping his hands. "Blake–"

He slides his hands from mine and steps back, an unreadable expression shadowing the planes of his face. "Are you–"

"Do you want me here? With you? Me and Skye? Is... is there something here for all of us, Blake, with you?"

His lips part, but no sound comes out. He looks shocked–that mask of indifference slipping just a touch.

"Can we have a life together?" I ask, my heart beginning to tremble.

"We–"

"Can you let me in, for real this time? Everything. I need–I have to see everything. You can't hide anymore. I can't be with just parts of you, Blake. I need it all. The good parts, the bad parts. The parts that scare you, that you think will scare me–"

The magic coating the room quakes–an alert, I surmise, that someone is coming.

Blake ignores it, his hands shaking slightly as he takes hold of my face and leans his forehead against mine.

"I–I do want that," he says with great effort. "But–"

"But I'm not some fierce warrior. I'm not a princess with royal blood–"

"Your great-grandfather was an Alpha."

"I don't have powers," I whisper, but his lips brush my forehead in a featherlight kiss that sends a shiver of warmth licking down my spine.

"I don't want any of that."

"But you could be with someone who–"

"I want quiet," he whispers against my skin, his mouth brushing against my temple. "I want calm. I want to sit on a couch with you, listening to music, watching Skye do her homework. I want to come home to you playing your violin. I want to sit in the royal box with our daughter watching you play for all of Eastonia knowing that you're mine. That's all I want."

Another ripple of energy shimmers through the room. Blake growls against my temple before pulling away and turning toward the door, swiping his fingers through his hair as the mask slips back over his face, blocking what I realize is the real him... only for me to see.

His shields drop. "Are you all right with my parents meeting Skye? I was thinking we could go on a walk in the garden. It's quiet out there."

I turn toward his closet, wondering if there's anything I could possibly turn into an outfit in there but... my clothes from the town-house are already hanging up neatly, arranged by color, cut, and texture...

Blake's hand went into this, no doubt. I feel tears prickling to life but blink them away, wondering if this–if he is what I even deserve after what I did to us.

I pull a shirt from a hanger and turn to him. "Do you want to tell her you're her dad today?"

"I'm not sure how to even begin."

I shrug. "She's going to understand. She's like you, remember?"

His answering smile is soft but unsure. A few minutes later, dressed in jeans and a simple blue top, I follow him into the recesses of the castle where Skye quickly makes her presence known. Instead of the quiet observer she's been for the past year or so, she's animated, talking rapidly as she skips beside Blake to match his long stride when he walks us down to the first level of the palace and through a private, well-lit corridor leading to the massive veranda and garden on the back side of the castle. Beautiful trees cast shade across the mowed lawn. Hydrangeas and roses scent the air as the sun sparkles through the trees, casting the grass in flickering strips of gold.

"Can you teach me how to use the spheres?"

"One day," Blake replies, smiling down at her. She clutches his hand and tugs him toward the rose bushes, talking about the bees, and I... sit down on a bench in the sun, letting it play over my skin for the first time in... weeks, I think, feeling whole, warm and... unburdened as I watch my mate inspect the rose bushes with our child.

"Marianna?"

I turn to the soft, musical voice to my left as the Queen of Crescent Falls floats into view, her shimmering white-blonde hair falling loose around her shoulders. She's dressed casually in slacks and a light gray sweater, but her eyes, that stunning violet, shine with what I can only describe as uncertainty when my gaze locks on her face.

Blake inherited her beauty–that ethereal kind of beauty that radiates like starlight on a perfectly clear night. Then, she smiles, and if I weren't sitting when I first noticed the way her nose crinkles, I'd fall to my knees.

Just like Skye.

I rise, preparing to bow, but she touches my arm. "You've grown up since the last time I saw you."

"It's been a while," I whisper as loud as I can muster, which isn't much. The last time I saw her was the night Blake and I ended things in that knockout, drag out fight in the curved driveway of the castle. I'd been to his place a few times, which had been a shock to my system, of course, but... his family knew about me and that I was

Blake's friend. His only friend. They had no idea we were so much more.

She'd walked out of the garage around the back of the castle at the very moment I told Blake to stay away from me and I bolted.

The look on her face is forever cemented into my brain.

But now, her face is full of relief. She pulls me into an embrace I'm not expecting. "Your mom and I have been talking. There's nothing that needs to be said between you and me, but–" She pulls away, holding me at arm's length as King Sydney steps into view, but his eyes are on Blake and Skye, watching them with glimmers of tears, maybe, in his eyes. "But–I know what it feels like. What you had to do, raising that baby on your own. I'm so thankful you had your mother with you."

My gaze flickers back to her face. "You do?"

She tilts her head, her cheeks going slightly rosy. "Blake and I are the same. I'm sure he's made that known. I... I wiped Sydney's memory of me, however. He had no idea Blake was even his child until... weeks after he and I crossed paths again. I regret it immensely. I'm so proud of Blake for being stronger than I was."

She steps away and turns to where Sydney is cautiously approaching Blake and Skye. My daughter looks up from the roses and watches Sydney close in. She steps closer to Blake on instinct as what she thinks is a stranger begins to speak to them. Sydney's words are too faint for me to hear, but Blake motions to him, likely explaining that Sydney is his father.

"I have to admit that staying away from her the past day has been difficult for us. We've been curious, honestly. I understand why Blake wanted us to wait, and it's a big enough castle, I suppose, to have made that easy enough but..." Sarah trails off as she watches her son and her grandchild lure Sydney closer to the roses, to the bees she's suddenly obsessed with. "I worried about Blake so much. I worried he would never find his person. I worried he'd continue to fall further into himself, but when you came into his life, he changed for the better. Then you were gone, and he..." She can't continue. She looks down at her hands before curling them into fists.

"I never intended to keep her away from you, not like this. I wasn't–I didn't know what to do, and Blake handled everything. He made sure we were both taken care of."

"He said you barely touched the money," she says quietly.

"I... I couldn't bring myself to do it." Shame ripples through me, but I brush it away, closing my arms over my chest. "I wanted to do it on my own, without him. I was angry with him for a long time, but I regret–" A thought strikes me. "Blake said you can turn back time."

She chuckles under her breath, then sighs, "I can, yes."

"If we–if we went back..." I close my eyes.

"It's something I could, in theory, do, but it would change everything for everyone. Other futures would be at stake. Blake and I already talked about it, and he wasn't sure he wanted to go back, to change things. But if it's something you want–"

"It's not," I say quickly, swallowing hard. I look back on my memories and see the scared, heartbroken girl I used to be. I see her clearly, like she's standing in front of me right now. I stayed that way for so long, terrified my daughter would turn into the man who broke my heart, but... I overlooked who Blake really was back then. He would have never hurt me. The fact that he scared me ruined him.

That's the only reason I would go back. To save him from that feeling that warped him into the closed off shell of a man he became.

But now?

He laughs. It's a sound I haven't heard in years. Sarah and I turn to the men at the same time, watching as Sydney and Blake converse, and Skye picks rose petals, stuffing them into her pockets for later.

"He has so much to offer," Sarah whispers, "If he could only get out of his head every once in a while."

Silence settles between us for several long moments before I take a breath, asking, "Do you want to meet her?"

Sarah smiles weakly and nods, trying to hide the excitement in her eyes, and I watch her go. I sink back onto my bench and take it in, smiling as Sarah kneels down and talks to Skye about the flowers, watch as two parents see their son as a father for the first time, even if Skye has no idea that these are her grandparents yet.

I'm leaving it up to Blake.

He doesn't seem ready today, especially when we leave the garden and rejoin the family currently gathered at the palace. Kenna is preparing to leave for Veiled Valley tonight, and Sarah and Sydney debate staying for a few days over the course of the afternoon, but as night falls, and the family parts after dinner, I find myself alone with Skye in the guest suite where my mom has been staying since Dean died in our townhouse.

I run my fingers through Skye's hair as she falls asleep beside me, wondering what comes next. The mate bond, to be honest, and maybe this is strictly because of the hell I was dragged through, raked through coals and then back out of again, felt... easy. Simple. *Warm.* It wasn't the explosive sense of knowing and belonging I expected, but I've always felt off kilter around Blake and all-consumed by his presence, so those feelings weren't anything new.

Mom is already asleep when I ease out of Skye's room. I follow that bond through the castle and find Blake in his office, seated behind his desk in the dark, his laptop casting a blue-hued glow around the far wall of the room.

He looks up at me as I enter. "Is she asleep?"

I nod, giving him the softest of smiles. "Yeah, she was exhausted."

He closes his laptop with a sigh and leans back in his chair, scrubbing a hand down his face. "I have to go to Veiled Valley in a few days."

"What for?"

"War," he yawns, like it's just another day in his life, and this isn't totally jarring whatsoever.

"Is it going to come to that?"

"Probably. I hope not."

"Are you going to work all night?"

"I wasn't working," he replies, rising from his chair and tucking it in. "I was emailing the headmaster of Skye's new school. We have a meeting with her next week, when I'm back from Veiled Valley and I–" He cuts himself off, shaking his head. "I'm getting ahead of myself. There're things we need to talk about first–"

"I think you need to shift," I offer, and he gives me a skeptical look.

"Oh?"

I stretch my arms over my head with a sigh. "I know I do. I want to at least try."

He rolls his lower lip between his teeth as he considers it, then says with a soft, breathy sigh, "All right. Only if you feel up to it."

"I want to be alone with you for a minute. Really alone."

Yeah, that does it.

Chapter 33

No More Teasing

BLAKE

"Take it slow," I urge, concern hanging from every syllable as Marianna removes a robe of glossy emerald green that makes her skin glow a soft bronzed gold in the moonlight. It's nearly a full moon—tomorrow, I believe, which makes sense, seeing as tomorrow is the last full day and night of the mating festival taking place just beyond the palace walls.

I make an effort not to outwardly gawk at Marianna's naked body, but it's hard not to look. She's glorious—all softness and curves—places I want to sink my teeth into the second I have a chance.

"Will someone take our clothes while we're gone?" she asks, clutching the robe to her chest, her shoulders and arms bare.

I look around the quiet, wooden park that backs up to the castle, the delivery gate just within sight. I cleared the guards from the area twenty minutes ago, so we're alone. "If they do, they'll have to answer to me."

She gives me a weak smile before letting the robe drop to the soft grass and kicking it toward a tree. I chew the inside of my cheek when the moonlight hits her skin, and she sighs, trembling like it's the best feeling in the world, and as a full-blooded shifter who hasn't been able to stretch those wolf powers in weeks, I'm sure it is.

My wolf, while incredibly powerful, isn't nearly as needy as some of the other wolves in my family. I think the strain of my other powers keeps it more docile, which I generally appreciate, but seeing Marianna like this, in just her skin? My wolf is now clawing to the surface, begging for release.

My nostrils flare as a soft breeze echoes through the branches, carrying her scent in my direction. I watch her shift, which seems to take some effort, and she's immediately uneasy on her feet.

"I'm fine," she says into my head when she notices the way I'm watching her trot around. *"Just a little numb."*

I blink, meeting her round, glowing blue eyes. While we haven't completely acknowledged the mate bond yet, it's there, radiating through my chest like the threads of her soul are woven through my heart. I hadn't expected to hear her through the mind-link yet, though.

"So, where are we going?" she asks with a deep stretch. She's a beautiful wolf—dark and glossy. Similar in color to my wolf, I suppose, without the underlying red that runs in my bloodline, thanks to my grandma, Maddy.

I take off my shirt and gather her robe, hanging them over a branch before undressing completely. I shift with ease, and a soft burst of violet mist skitters through the woods and dissipates just as the moon peeks out from behind the clouds. Marianna eyes me for a moment before turning her snout toward the moon and closing her eyes.

"I'm worried that you won't be able to hold yourself in your wolf form for very long," I say into her mind. *"So we won't go far."*

A soft sigh echoes through our threads, but she replies, *"That's probably wise. I wouldn't want to be naked in the forest during our trek home, even though I'm sure you'd love that."* She gives me a wolfish smile, and I feel...

"So we're back to you trying everything in your power to get under my skin?"

"Is it working?"

I take off in a blur of dark fur, and her scoff explodes through my mind, but she follows, keeping up at a sprint I hope will truly test her strength after weeks spent under the haze of witches' herbs and potions.

It's a sultry night–suffocatingly so, actually. It rained hard earlier in the day, and when the clouds broke, the heat of summer finally replaced the cool, drizzly days of spring, but that sucking humidity Moonrise is known for is now in full effect.

After a few miles at a steady, fast pace, I slow down, and Marianna keeps up, padding her way around the same trees and rocks I can sail over with ease.

"You never had any training, did you?" I ask.

"Is it that obvious?" she laughs, tripping over her own feet. *"I think you'd be surprised to learn how many average wolves never go through wolf training. That's for the elite, Prince Blake."*

"I'm no longer Prince Blake," I reply, then leap over a boulder as the forest around us begins to thin.

"Oh, right. What are you now, then?"

"To you, Blake. To everyone else... I suppose, High Lord."

A cackling laugh rips through the bond. *"High Lord? High Lord of what?"*

"The mystics. Occasionally the priestesses of the temple call me that, too."

Another laugh, this time more a snort. *"I know you hate that."*

I stop as the trail we've been following fades into a mix of sparse grass, moss, and the beginnings of the boulder fields. I'm too hot in my fur. The heat sinks into my skin, impossible to shake. *"I don't like it; you're correct. There's not much I can do about it. They've been calling me High Lord since I was a teenager. It's something they saw in me, I guess."*

Marianna eyes me for a moment before sighing, her eyes sliding from mine to the landscape ahead of us. I feel the tension tightening through our bond. I know she's thinking about Skye and her future, what the mystics might call her one day. If she'll take my place, trapped inside her own head, losing herself to the powers some people would die to covet without knowing they come with shackles.

"*I won't let Skye become like me,*" I tell her, and her eyes meet mine again. "*She'll grow up with her powers in the open, highly trained. I won't allow her to fall in on herself like I let myself do.*"

"*Is that something we can even prevent?*"

"*I don't know. But we can try. It's all we can do.*"

She scratches the ground for a moment, likely in deep thought. "*If we have another child, would they be... like her?*"

The question works its way through my body, but not in the way I expect. Before Skye, I never planned on having children. I considered my powers a curse, something I wanted to nip in the bud.

Marianna turns and continues up the boulders without giving me a chance to answer the question, and I follow, matching her slower pace. At the end of the field, she pauses, glancing over her shoulder at me as the alpine pool comes into view.

Neither of us says anything, but the consensus is unanimous. I leap off a boulder into the water, shifting back into my human form as the chilled water bites my skin, but it's refreshing. Just what I needed to jog my mind back into focus. Marianna shifts back before easing into the water, shivering, but once she's neck deep, she sighs, closing her eyes as the cool water erases the heat of the night in a single breath.

I reach for her, closing my fingers around her wrist and tugging her toward the shallow end. Just touching her sends a jolt of heat through my body, igniting that ache–that deep, relentless longing I've been fighting for years. The second her toes drag along the bottom of the pool, she wraps her arms around my neck, pressing her naked body against mine and...

I blow out a breath before dipping my head to nuzzle her neck, drinking in her scent, the softness of her skin.

"This is so much better," she whispers around a sigh. "I knew it was going to be hot in Moonrise, but not like this, especially so early in the season."

"Don't worry," I laugh, smiling against her skin. "It gets worse."

She groans a laugh, but I back her against the rocky face of the cliff overlooking the pool. There isn't even a breeze up here to cut through the heat, but the water feels wonderful, and I feel... overcome. The voices in my head are silent, holding space for her, like she is the one thing that can balance me out, giving me room to breathe.

Her fingers tighten on my shoulders, and she presses her lips to my temple.

"I never answered your question," I whisper, lifting my face to look her in the eyes. They're that startling blue—wide and bright, lined with those dark, thick eyelashes that are definitely a blessing from the Goddess.

"About kids? It was–it was forward of me–"

"I'd have another if it were what you wanted."

"Is it what you want?"

"I didn't want it until I met you. I didn't have any intention of having any more after Skye was born."

"Then why say–"

"Because if it wasn't with you, if you weren't their mother, it was out of the question."

She searches my eyes. "What have you been doing all these years, Blake?"

"Rotting," I admit, and she presses her mouth to mine in a soft kiss that... quickly turns to anything but soft.

I can't help it. Years of restraint, years of immense control snap in an instant. Even that night in my penthouse pales in comparison to the way I feel now, like I'll die if I'm not inside of her. She hooks her legs around my waist as I lean up against the smooth, damp rock. I'm already hard. Hell, I've been absolutely rigid since the moment she slid her robe from her shoulders, but now it's almost painful. Her tongue slides over mine, and she moans when I grind my hips against her, my cock sliding against her lower belly.

She reaches between us, dipping her arm under water, and slowly brushes the softest touch to my shaft before curling her fingers around me in a tight embrace. I press her harder against the rock, gritting my teeth in a growl. "Don't tease me."

"I'm making up for lost time," she purrs with a cat-like grin. Another pump and I'm already coming undone at the seams.

"Marianna–" I hiss out a breath that she steals with another kiss, and I know, without a shadow of a doubt, that I will forever be at this woman's mercy.

I'm exactly where I want to be.

I shove her against the rock and thrust hard, parting through her folds in a violent, swift stroke.

"Blake!" she cries out, but I'm beyond comprehension when her inner walls grip me tight, forcing a rough groan from my lips.

My wolf takes over, dead set on claiming her, on bringing her to her knees. But I fight it, at least for now, my mouth on hers and our bodies writhing in the cool sanctuary of the water.

When I push in as far as she can handle, she lets out a sharp gasp, clutching my shoulders so tight her nails leave imprints on my skin. She growls my name, biting down hard on my lower lip.

"No biting," I grind out, but her sly grin when she releases me sets fire to my blood, and I... "Bite me again."

"Where?"

"Wherever you want. Wherever you want to leave your mark."

Her eyes flash with understanding. There's no conversation left to be had, no further apologies, and no groveling. We're done with that. We're not the teenage lovebirds we used to be. This is real now. This moment is forever, and I'll be damned if I don't leave this place with her scar on my body.

"Will it hurt you?" she whispers.

I thrust into her hard, and that whisper turns to a deep, shaking moan as her body locks around mine. She's close. I'm beyond close.

I've been trying to hold back since the moment she so much as touched me. She trembles, leaning her face against my neck. I continue pumping into her, losing myself in the feel of her body gliding against mine. She's hot to the touch for me, her body tight and giving and I...

"Mark me," I whisper into her hair, closing my eyes as my release nears, the tension in my coiling tight.

Chapter 34

It's Not a Dream

BLAKE

Marianna is just as close. I feel it before she can–the way she tightens and begins to spasm around my cock, the way her thighs lock and her toes curl behind my back.

Her teeth graze my neck as she pants, breathing my name as our worlds collide and burst into nothing but starlight, and there it is... the tapestry. Our threads–once frayed, now binding into one. I see our life stretching through the stars.

A long life.

"Please," I damn near beg, and she bites down, sucking a bruise as her teeth sink into my skin and the mate bond erupts into what I can only describe as madness. I slam her against the rock as my release barrels through me like a rogue wave. She comes as well, screaming my name into the night, but I bite down on her neck, holding her still, damning the still healing skin left behind by the mark the healers cut out of her–a mark that should never have been there.

It should always have been mine.

I keep us there, suspended, my feet flat on the bottom of the pool as we drift through echoes of pleasure, through hints of pain, our bond healing what was broken because we finally faced it head on—together.

I'll always regret the years I wasted. I'll always regret not being man enough to tell her how I really felt and showing her who I really was before it was too late, but I'll spend the rest of my life making up for it.

It's deep into the night when we arrive back at the castle—loose and unburdened, holding hands and walking slowly through the dark, empty hallways.

But it's the screech from above that brings me back to startling focus, and Marianna's hand tears out of mine, her body a blur as she runs toward the guest suite where our daughter's screams curdle the air all around me.

It's a familiar sound. My own screams have pulled me out of nightmares most of my life.

The guest suite is cloaked in shadow when I step inside and close the door behind me. The voices in my head titter nervously as they return, igniting my powers as Skye's own gifts fill the suite. Marianna's voice is soft and low as she speaks to Leona in the bedroom at the end of the hallway where dimmed light spills into the shadows, but my focus catches on the two crystal spheres on a coffee table in the cozy living room just before Skye's bedroom, which are lit from within, swirling with childhood memories the nightmare displaced.

I close my eyes for a moment before reaching for one, holding the smooth, moonstone ball between my hands.

Skye screams again in the bedroom, which quickly turns to a whimpered moan, and I close my eyes, setting the sphere down, and turn to the bedroom.

Maeve creeps into view, having slid so silently into the suite behind me I hadn't noticed her opening the door.

I walk into the bedroom and see my mate and her mother on either side of Skye's bed. Marianna's eyes are glassy with tears. She looks up at me, shaking her head. "Waking her up makes it worse."

"I know," I reply, my voice painfully dry. Leona moves out of the way. I edge toward the bed, feeling Soren's presence joining Maeve's in the doorway, Fallon resting on his chest.

I lean down and gently brush Skye's dark hair away from her face, tucking it behind her ear, then take a breath and press my fingertips to her forehead.

My body jerks. My powers rage to full strength, and it catches me off guard. I'm sucked in, past the stars, past the tapestry, past... anything I've ever been able to accomplish before.

Skye is... everywhere, but invisible. Her fear and torment bleed around me as a wide, circular room made of stone comes into view. She's trying to get out, to wake up, but she went too far in her dreams. She can't control them yet. She can't dig her way out of this dreamscape, but then I realize this isn't a dream at all.

She's having a vision.

Hannibal steps into view, his long, pale fingers knitted behind his back. He's inspecting a basin of sorts full of flickering crystals. He picks one up, inspects it, and sets it down as another man, just as tall, lean, and inhumanly good looking, comes to a step beside him dressed in fine clothes made of dark velvet and silk.

I shield my powers immediately, stretching them to their breaking point to cover Skye's presence as well, and the crystals in the basin flicker out, turning to useless, dull rock.

Hannibal lets out a breath in an annoyed sigh, but the regal man beside him frowns, his dark brown hair trembling around his pointed ears.

"I'm growing tired of this," the man says, and Hannibal bows his head in a show of submission. "You said this would be easy. Getting you back to the homeland was incredibly difficult and a strain on our resources, Arachnis, and for what? You failed your mission."

"I did not fail, Your Grace," Hannibal says lightly, his milky white eyes lifting to meet his *king*. "I was correct about a Firestone rising to power. I was correct about an Alpha King returning to the ancient basin of life–what they call the Deadlands now. I was correct about Uvansa being painted red with blood—a baptism to honor us."

Uvansa? I don't so much as blink as Hannibal goes on, "Everything I prophesied happened."

"You prophesied the royals in Eastonia falling with the coronation of their new queen. And yet, they are still as strong."

"They have mystics on their side. The mystics—their king. He's one of them—a family member."

The king turns to Hannibal, his face washed in confusion. "What do you mean?"

Hannibal smirks as he picks up another crystal. He turns and I... I nearly lose my grip on my powers. A glimmer of light distorts his body, his back, and as he turns into the light of the room, wings of silver ignite along his spine.

My heart skips a beat and holds.

"Somehow, in their filthy, wasted bloodline, a true mystic has been born again. The seer of all seers, and I had him in my clutches before that Firestone demon got in my way. We lost the war because the mystics switched sides and aligned with the Moon Goddess. They aided the Firestone Queens in the last battles, and their Goddess rewarded them for it by dropping those veils and trapping our Kings inside that dome of chaos and madness. The mystics refused to help the Kings of Eastonia. But this one... this mystic I've found? He has a dark side, something... deep, and twisted. I saw glimpses of it when I was inside his head, but he's strong. His shields are... worth looking into, if I can get my hands on him again."

"I should be punishing you for letting him go so carelessly. You're lucky the Trials are upcoming—"

"If you want the fae to walk freely in Eastonia again," Hannibal grinds out, edging toward the king. "If you want those filthy mongrels and their witch queens to bow to their real gods once again, we must get the mystic on our side. He is how we win this war. These shifters aren't meant to be free. You've seen what happens when they fall out of the fray. They killed their last king in cold blood. Filthy, bleeding pigs killed a *fae god*."

"The great-grandson of King Tithus was less fae than a Firestone witch," the king growls. "Of course he failed in his mission. He had no powers. He had no strength. He was useless."

"But the new Firestone Queen and her predecessor did what he couldn't do–they dropped the veils. Eastonia is ripe for the taking, and now Emberfyll is open, and the progeny of those escaped slaves can finally be brought to justice."

"And what do you suggest I do?" the king sneers.

"You mentioned the upcoming Trials?" Hannibal's smile is sick and twisted, just like I remember. "How many centuries has it been since someone born on Eastonian soil has bled on ours?"

I'm ripped from the vision in an instant, my veins full of ice. A sharp echo of sound breaks through the darkness funneling into my body, and then Marianna is leaning over me, talking rapidly to everyone in the room. I reach for Skye, but she's safe in Leona's arms. With the last remnants of my powers, I shield Skye, wrapping her mind in starlit magic, then collapse.

"Blake? Oh, Goddess, Blake?" Marianna's voice is sharp and rushed as blinding light explodes around me. I try to sit up, but hands press me back to a bed that smells like... us. Marianna and I. I shove what I realize is Soren away and sit up fully, fighting past a wave of dizziness that nearly sends me under again, but the room comes into view, and the faces looking down at me are familiar–no pointed ears, thank the Goddess.

"I need to speak to Ryatt, Isaac, my father, and Ryan immediately," I shout then fly out of bed where I promptly fall to my knees as the ice in my veins shifts and thaws.

Marianna makes a sound deeply tinged with frustration and tries to pull me upright. "Just lie down–"

Soren, my saving grace, asks, "Why?"

He crosses his arms over his chest as I drag my body upright by pulling on the sheets of the bed until I'm sitting on the edge of the mattress. I turn to my mate, however, asking, "Where's Skye?"

"She's with my mom and Maeve. She's not feeling well, and she's–she's back to being quiet again–"

"She didn't have a nightmare last night, Marianna. She had a vision." I run my hand over my face while trying to make sense of what I saw. "Soren, I need your help now. Gather the men, put out the call to the family. I will meet with everyone in Veiled Valley. I want my mother to stay here, in Moonrise, with Skye. Her training needs to begin as soon as possible. As soon as she's well, but... Maeve needs to use her powers to shield her and Marianna–"

"What's going on?" Marianna asks, but Soren's face is set in grim determination.

"What did you see?"

"Hannibal," I say, his name like acid on my tongue. "Hannibal and his king. I know where they are. I can find them."

Soren stills. Marianna blinks at me. My brain feels fuzzy, and the voices are gone when I need them the most.

"I just need a moment to remember the details," I tell them.

"You need to rest. You passed out." Marianna squeaks. Concern shadows her features. Behind her, the windows are bright with sunlight. I've been out all night. It has to be midmorning by now.

I turn to Soren, weary. "You need to come to Veiled Valley with me tomorrow."

He nods. "I'll put the call out."

"Tell Maeve–"

"About the shields," he says, waving at me in dismissal. "I know." He glances at Marianna and then moves toward the door. Marianna wrings her hands until he leaves then turns to me, but just as her lips part, I cut her off.

"Marianna, there are things I don't think I can explain to you about what Skye and I can do with our powers," I begin, forcing the words into existence. "But you have to know that she is... incredibly powerful for her age. More than I ever anticipated. This cannot happen again."

"Did they–did they know she saw them?"

"I'm not sure, but I'm using my powers to shield her mind from now on. Maeve can help until I've fully recovered, but it took... it took all of my powers to even come close to how far she'd gone in the stars."

Marianna looks utterly confused, and I don't blame her. I've kept her out of this successfully until last night. I don't want this burden on her shoulders. I never did. "What do we do? Is she in danger?" She wrings her hands.

"No. No, I made sure that man–that *thing* doesn't know about the two of you, but when it comes to it, you'll go into hiding. Just like we planned. Just like what's written in the contract."

She pales, but I manage to rise. I take her hand and pull her close.

"Everything will be okay. I promise."

A burst of energy cloaks the room, powerful enough to make the palace tremble.

Apparently, I wasn't the only one who could feel the force of Skye's powers.

Ryatt's voice echoes through my suite, sharp and stern.

Chapter 35

All in the Family

MARIANNA

Blake can barely manage to walk the twelve feet to the bedroom door without needing to brace himself against the wall. I lunge for him but halt mid-step when a tall, broad, and honestly, impossibly handsome man in his mid-seventies barrels into the room looking downright murderous. His black hair is brushed away from his face, peppered with dark gray, but his silver eyes are sharpened and honed on Blake as he braces his hands on the doorframe and scans Blake, then the room, and... softens when he sees me standing in outright terror only a few feet away.

I know him. Not personally, of course, but it's impossible not to know of the ever feared, ever worshipped, Alpha King Ryatt–The King of Shadows, of darkness. The King of The Roguelands and the mystical, secretive Veiled Valley that he passed down to his daughter.

Blake sways but manages to keep himself upright as he stretches a hand toward Ryatt in what I can only describe as surrender. "Ryatt, not now."

"You're Marianna, then?" Ryatt's voice is nearly as deep and dry as Blake's.

I nod, give him a quick, unsteady bow, and refuse to meet his eyes again. I look down at my feet, noticing the way his shadow moves throughout the room despite the fact that he's standing still.

"Where is Maeve?" Ryatt asks sternly.

"She's with–she's in the western wing of this floor, in a suite with–with Skye–"

"The daughter you hid from the family for seven years?"

I bite my lower lip, squeezing my eyes shut.

"Kenna can't keep a secret to save her life, can she?" Blake rasps, but Ryatt isn't even remotely entertained.

"You and I have to talk, Blake. When you're well. Marianna, come with me, please."

My stomach falls to my toes. I take a short step in his direction, keeping my head down, but Blake stops me, grabbing my hand and straightening to his full height, his shoulders squared.

Ryatt arches a brow at Blake, chuckles low, and rolls his eyes– which makes him look entirely casual, not like the demon from my worst nightmares that manifested in the doorway only moments ago.

"Fine. We'll do this now. Can you walk, Blake, or should I spirit you across the castle?"

Blake doesn't say a word. He tugs me along, and Ryatt has to move out of our way. Blake's suite is a blur as I follow him through the hallways of gray modernity, and I can feel the tension pouring off of him. He doesn't have privacy here, not at all. I feel suddenly defensive about it, wondering why his family thinks they have a right to him at any given moment of the day or night.

But one look at him tells me everything I need to know about how he's lived while we were separated. Everything he's done, every-thing he refused to give himself–whether that be peace, privacy, or even a moment to think without the voices in his head running wild– it was for others.

Blake has never lived a single day in his life just for himself, and it guts me.

I squeeze his hand, sending a caress through the fine threads of our bond, praying he can feel what I feel... grateful for everything he's ever done for me, for Skye, and honestly, for them–this strange family I'm suddenly, inexplicably a part of.

Skye is where I left her this morning while Blake was still in his stupor–sitting in a bed, surrounded by her beloved stuffed animals, gripping one of those crystal spheres like her life depends on it. Her eyes don't even lift when the three of us walk into the room, but Maeve rises from an armchair near a window overlooking the city, Fallon bright and fully awake in her arms.

I flinch when Ryatt steps past me, bracing myself for him to launch into an attack on my daughter, but I'm rocked to my core when the most feared man in the Allied Kingdoms absolutely melts as he leans down to smile at his... great-granddaughter, Fallon. My shoulders slump as relief washes through me. I feel... awful, honestly, as I look around the room. Sarah is here, too, quietly rearranging flowers in a vase on a dresser along the far wall. She glances over her shoulder, giving me a tight, but encouraging, smile, and Sydney, who I thought had left for Crescent Falls, lingers in the corner with my mom, his head bent in quiet conversation.

They're not bad people. Just... somewhat scary, powerful, magical people.

And then there's me... powerless, Normal. Maybe even... boring?

I release my grip on Blake and sit beside Skye on the bed, pulling her into my lap. She doesn't fight it but doesn't relax. When I lean my chin on her shoulder, I feel her take a deep breath, her little body trembling as she exhales. She's exhausted but too scared to fall asleep. This has happened before–horrible nightmares. Mom and I used to take turns staying awake with her during the nights when she refused to shut her eyes until the memories of those dreams faded from her mind.

Ryatt finally turns from Fallon to look around the room, and his gaze falls on Skye. He inspects her from afar, his expression gentle, curious, and with a deep breath, he turns to Blake, letting it out in a whoosh. "Your grandfather and I have placed wagers on which of you kids was going to send us into early graves, and I believe he might leave this realm before me at this rate. He thought he had me beat with Maeve's situation."

"Ryatt!" Sarah hisses, narrowing her eyes at him.

Maeve scoffs, scooping Fallon against her shoulder. "Excuse me?"

Sydney smirks, but Sarah looks wildly between the group before her mouth twitches into a smile that shatters the earlier tension. I run my fingers through Skye's hair, watching the family break into lifted, animated arguments that seem completely unserious, but Blake... he's not messing around right now. He looks beyond fatigued, his skin an icy, unhealthy gray. He says, under his breath, "What's our next move?" directing his words at Maeve, who purses her lips for a moment, brows pinched in thought.

"Obviously, it depends on what you've seen," Maeve replies pointedly.

Blake braces himself on the bed before sitting down near my feet. He curls his fingers around my ankle almost absently, like I'm an anchor in the storm going on inside his head, and then he lays it all out for the family, who listens quietly, intently, no one daring to so much as breathe.

"Fae?" Ryatt says after at least twenty minutes of Blake's explanation. "I've never heard that word before."

"They spoke of our old gods, our old kings, saying they were one and the same," Blake concludes, closing his eyes. "Hannibal has... wings."

"Wings?" Maeve narrows her eyes.

Blake nods. "And some kind of a magical shield that can keep them hidden. I'm not sure."

"I'll have Misty and Arthur look into it," Ryatt says before taking Fallon out of Maeve's arms with practiced grace. Fallon looks incredibly small tucked in the crook of his elbow. "Where's Soren?"

Maeve's expression withers with discomfort as she eyes her grandfather. "Why?"

Ryatt gives her a sharp look. "You know why."

"We'll talk about that later." She hisses and then moves like the wind toward the door. "He's downstairs sparring with the warriors, from what I understand. He needed to blow off some steam." She glances at her mom before leaving the room, and Ryatt follows, shutting the door behind him.

Sarah rises from her chair and clears her throat. "Isaac and Maddy have extended an enthusiastic invitation for Marianna, Leona, and Skye to come to Maatua for a while. I think it would be wise, given the circumstances."

My spine straights as I glance at Blake, who's staring at the far wall, his back to his parents. "Not yet."

Sarah shrugs a shoulder and turns to Sydney. "Lunch, then? Leona, we know a beautiful little restaurant on the lake. You should join us."

Mom gives her a soft smile and a nod in reply, but one look at her face tells me all I need to know. This is... way out of our league. We're normal people. People who go to the grocery store and fret over bills. Not... royals.

"Mom, I need you to come to the orrery with us tomorrow–Skye and me." Blake squeezes my ankle but isn't looking at me when he says, "Anna, I don't know if.... If you want to come, please do, but–"

"I'll stay behind," I rush out, tightening my grip on Skye. "That place gives me the creeps, anyway."

Sydney, to his credit, nods knowingly and turns for the door, motioning to his mate. Mom follows them out, and the room falls into silence again. Skye is just... staring at Blake, however, her eyes wide and round, the same brilliant shade of violet as his.

"Let's go walk around the garden," I offer to my poor, forlorn, exhausted mate and daughter, but after waiting several seconds for a reply, neither so much as blinks. "All right... a nap, then. You both could use it." I slowly untangle myself from Skye. She doesn't fight when I scoop her up, bunch the blankets down, and tuck her in a little nest of warmth. Blake, barely lucid on the edge of the bed, simply leans back until his spine is flat against the mattress, and within seconds of me pulling the curtains closed against the sunlight, they're asleep.

I leave the room without even looking over my shoulder.

Skye is safest with him. I feel it in my bones. I don't let myself feel that twang of grief that I've lost a special part of Skye–the sacred bond I shared when it was just me and her.

This is better. This is better for all of us, Blake included.

With nothing to do, I wander the castle. I explore the library, the sunroom on the second floor, and eventually find myself chatting with a maid in the gallery while she shows me portraits of the family I've never seen before.

"That's my mate's parents," Ryatt's voice says somewhere behind me. I whirl, surprised. I didn't even hear him come in. The maid bows low before scurrying out of the wide, echoing room that stretches nearly three stories high to a domed ceiling with an ancient mural painted across it. "Isla and Maddox."

I turn from him. He's still holding Fallon, and that makes me slightly more comfortable being alone with this man–this all powerful creature I can barely wrap my mind around. I look up at the portrait, at the perfect strokes of paint that make it look more like a photograph than a painting. Isla is middle-aged but gorgeous, looking so much like Misty it makes my heart skip a few beats as I scan the blue eyes, the soft glowing skin, and glorious golden hair they're known for.

Maddox, however, is a startling image of Blake, but his eyes are deep green, and his hair is more brown, with no tinges of the dark, wine red Skye has inherited from her father.

But Maddox... yeah. His genetics are strong–stronger than Isla's, I'm afraid. So many of his ancestors carry his high, strong cheekbones. His wide mouth. His regal, straight nose.

"Did you know them well?" I ask Ryatt, who nods, smiling gently as he steps to my side.

"It was a rocky start, to say the least, but they came around. Maddox and I spent a great deal of time together over the years before his death. I miss them, admittedly. My mate, Ella, she painted these."

"She did?"

"Oh, yes. She's brilliant." He scans the wall where more paintings are hung in thick, golden frames. "This one is one of my favorites." He points to a painting of a fox in a dark, treelined clearing. The fox guards a felled... beast of some sort, while the fox glows from within, her eyes orbs of swirling gold. "That's Amanda. You're likely to meet her and her insanely large family the longer you spend time here. She's Ella's best friend and the mate of... my best friend."

Ryatt takes me to the gallery, painting his own picture of a long life lived, of adventures, of war and peace.

But it's a smaller portrait of a group of boys that catches my attention.

"No way," I laugh. "That's Blake?"

"Yes." Ryatt smiles, shaking his head. "Blake was the first boy of the generation–of the grandkids. Hard to believe he used to be as small as Fallon." His voice is wistful with memories that swirl just behind his silver eyes. "He was the leader of the group until Brie took over her rightful place and dethroned him. She's only a bit older. That's Aris, the blond one, and Liam, and the baby is Adrian, Misty and Cole's son. He was probably one or two in this; I can't remember. We're only missing Noah in this one."

The portrait beside it is the girls of the generation–Brie, likely around Skye's age, standing stoically behind Maeve, who's grinning like a little demon while a pair of twins with blonde hair, I assume Blake's sisters, Briar and Celeste, sit in front of them.

"Josie was born about a week after Ella completed this painting," he says, dreamlike. "It feels like so long ago." He moves a few feet away, carefully adjusting Fallon's weight in his arms. "Ella will want a portrait of you and Skye to add to the collection. She's already planning it out."

My heart squeezes as I scan the wall of family–family belonging to my daughter.

Family that belongs to me, now.

Family Blake is willing to die for, to do... anything for.

Chapter 36

Depleted and Refreshed

Marianna

Over the course of the afternoon, I check on Blake and Skye repeatedly, but both are sleeping like the dead. Sarah, Sydney, and my mom return from their lunch in great spirits. Sydney goes off to find Ryatt, and I slink around the castle while my mom and Sarah live in "grandma bliss" together, making up for lost time.

I'm checking on Blake and Skye for the eighth time as the sun sets when Maeve clicks her tongue at me from the entrance of the suite, tilting her head in a motion to follow her.

"Have you eaten today?" she asks as we walk through one of the many upper hallways in the palace, which after today, I feel like I can traverse without getting totally lost.

"Barely," I admit, and she nods.

"Same. Come on." She opens a side door I thought was just a mirror, and a staircase appears.

I guess I should still be careful walking around this place, especially now that I know there're tunnels and corridors within the castle walls themselves.

We reach her suite, which is grand but girly, which makes Soren, currently pacing one of the two living areas, Fallon fussing in his arms, look desperately out of place, especially in fighting leathers and a slightly sweaty shirt.

"She's pissed," he says, patting Fallon's back, but she lifts her head and wails.

Maeve blows out her breath and takes the beautiful, blonde baby girl in her arms, but instead of settling, Fallon begins to scream until she turns a deep purple.

"Oh, jeez," Maeve grumbles, but I notice the uncertainty in her eyes when she sinks onto a couch and tries to nurse Fallon, but it's no use.

I shift from foot to foot, my fingertips tingling with the desire to help, but... this is the queen. That baby? She's the royal princess of Eastonia, Maeve's heir. Fallon will be queen one day.

But Soren and Maeve share mirrored expressions of... straight up confusion as they debate how to settle her. I smile to myself when Soren scratches his head, looking utterly helpless, and Maeve doesn't seem much better.

"Um, can I hold her?"

They blink at me, and within a second, Fallon is in my arms, purple with fury. But I realize when I maneuver her belly down over my forearm, she's not raging for no reason.

"She's a bit colicky," I tell the fresh parents, who are standing stunned as I rock Fallon on my arm. She whimpers for a few seconds before settling into silence, her eyes drooping with fatigue. I pat her back, finding myself swaying–muscle memory, I suppose, after months spent in the same position, but with Skye on my arm.

"How–how did you do that?" Maeve asks, stunned.

"Her belly hurts, that's all. The pressure of my arm is more comfortable for her."

Soren watches as I continue to sway, but Maeve sinks back onto the couch looking defeated. "I had no idea. This whole time..."

"It's no one's fault. Skye was like this for a few months, but eventually, she grew out of it. Is feeding going okay? Nursing?"

"Better than it was, yeah, thanks to you." She smiles at me, but her eyes are slightly wet with unshed tears. Tears of guilt, I realize, and bite my lip.

"Babies are hard." Fallon falls asleep, her cheek pressed against the crook of my elbow.

"My sister made it look so easy."

"Yeah, well, look at her now," Soren chuckles, resting his arms against the back of the couch, leaning his weight against it. "Kieran is... a lot."

"He's a little demon," Maeve agrees and then laughs heartily. "I don't know how she does it."

"Well, it's an old wives' tale, but easy babies tend to make up for it in toddlerhood." I smile, absently running my fingers through Fallon's silk-fine curls.

"What was Skye like when she was younger?" Maeve asks, reaching for the teapot on the coffee table. I watch steam rise as she pours three cups of tea, scenting the air with chamomile.

"Like this," I tell them, motioning to Fallon. "Fussy, for sure. She grew out of that around nine months old, but by then, she was on the move." I smile as memories of Skye as a baby sprint through my head. "She was curious and headstrong as a toddler but generally easygoing. She used to be so bright and animated. She loved to play pretend and sing... dance..." I turn away from them so they can't see the broken expression crossing my features, but Maeve sighs, lacing her fingers over her knees.

"And then her powers emerged?"

"Yep." I turn back to face them, nodding. "She was six when she started regressing into herself. The nightmares started happening, and she just... changed. She's–she's better here. I've noticed it.... She feels like she can be herself." Now, they're seeing my guilt, so similar to how they feel about themselves right now, like they're doing everything wrong.

"I don't know how you did this on your own for so long," Maeve says, and Soren sighs, squeezing her shoulder before the phone in his pocket rings, and he answers it, his footsteps heavy when he retreats into a room down the hall. Maeve picks up a cup of tea and rises, handing it to me while Fallon continues to snooze, the sunlight pouring through the window warming her skin. "Soren didn't know I was pregnant until a few days before she was born. I feel like he was thrown into the fire, so to speak, but he's handled it so well, and I... feel like I haven't."

"You're doing amazing, Maeve."

She shakes her head. "I'm trying. I can't get the hang of it, and then everything else going on is... I should have taken a longer break after she was born, but I couldn't, not when war is on our doorstep." She sips her tea, closing her eyes. "I shouldn't even be complaining. You must be incredibly overwhelmed right now."

"I... yeah, it's been a lot." I can't help but laugh.

The tension breaks. I hold her gaze for several seconds, and she gives me a slight smile, but just as Fallon starts to stir, Blake walks into the suite looking a bit worse for wear but upright, which is progress.

Maeve frowns at him when he stumbles over a carpet runner. "Do you mind? You're interrupting us."

"I was just–just making sure Marianna was still here," he says, his voice uncharacteristically frantic.

My heart lurches, and his eyes meet mine, relief washing through them. Where would I go?

I hand Fallon back to Maeve and go to Blake, wrapping an arm around his waist, and we leave, walking back through the castle at a slower pace than I anticipated. He's cold to the touch.

"Are you okay?"

"I'm fine. I'll be fine by tomorrow," he says but doesn't look like he means it.

"What's wrong with you?"

"We call it a depletion event. I used all of my powers, all of my reserves, pulling Skye out of that vision." He braces a hand on the wall near the staircase leading to the floor where Skye's staying in the guest suite with my mom.

"You should go back to bed," I urge.

"I have work to do–"

"Is my mom with Skye?"

He nods, and with great effort, I help him down the stairs but turn onto the fifth floor balcony, leading him to his suite instead.

"Mom wanted to know when we can return to the townhouse, and I wasn't sure what to say," I tell him, drawing the curtains back to darken his bedroom.

"I want you here," he says gruffly.

I turn to face him. He sits on the edge of the bed, his hands trembling as he takes off his shiny leather loafers. "Are you sure?"

"I want you in this bed, with me, every night and every morning," he replies, his eyes darker than usual.

I furrow my brows. He should be flat on his back, not looking like he wants to eat me, but I can't say I mind.

"Lock the door," he says sternly, and my blood ignites like someone just struck a match.

I obey, then move slowly back in his direction. "You need to rest."

"I can rest when I'm dead. I have too much to do–"

"Lie down," I cut in, coming to a stop between his legs, but he doesn't listen. So, I kneel, brushing my hands up his thighs. He bows his head, his eyes heavy and hooded as I unbutton his shirt.

"You don't have to do that. I can–"

"Let me take care of you," I whisper, looking up into his eyes. He curls his fingers around the back of my neck, pulls me forward, and kisses me. It's a long, slow kiss that makes the bond between us tremble. His mark is already healed on my neck–a glorious, silver scar I feel proud to carry. It tingles, then heats, matching the same feelings in my body. My desire for him reaches a peak, too hot to dial back to simmer.

I smooth my hands over his bare chest, pushing his shirt off his arms. He tugs me close and then pulls me onto the bed. He's weak, which... isn't like him. He slumps against me, panting. I remove his shirt completely and toss it over the side of the bed. "Lie down, Blake."

"No–"

"I said," I whisper, guiding him off me and onto his back, "lie down and let me take care of you, for once."

His hands settle on my hips for a moment until I scoot off him, off the bed entirely. He watches with a predator's intent. I make a show of taking off my shirt, then my bra. He swallows hard, the column of his throat bobbing. I run my fingers down my belly to the button of my jeans.

"Come back to bed," he rasps.

I shimmy out of my pants, and his eyes are focused on my breasts, which bounce with the motion. He sits up, and I can feel the heat beginning to pour through him, thawing the ice clogging his veins. I slowly pull my panties down, and his breathy groan fills me with want so intense I find it hard to focus.

"Come to bed," he repeats darkly, his eyes shining with... powers. "Now."

I step out of my panties and walk the short distance to the side of the bed. He sits up, pressing a wet kiss to my stomach before pulling me onto the mattress. I'm boneless as he rolls on top of me, nudging my legs apart. He fumbles with his zipper for a fraction of a second before pulling his pants and boxers down just enough to free himself.

He's out of his mind over *me*.

"Blake," I whimper, but his mouth is rough on my neck. He bites down over the mark he left there, sucking like he's claiming me again, leaving another mark for the entire world to see. His cock presses through my folds in a deep, swift thrust until he's buried to the hilt, and my inner walls clench him tight.

He grunts in satisfaction, losing himself completely to the feeling of being inside of me, consumed by me.

I clutch the back of his neck and arch my hips to meet him thrust for thrust. He pummels me into the sheets. He's not gentle, but I didn't want that. I want him undone, unleashed, and utterly open to what he really wants for once.

His powers return in full, his body so hot it's fevered. I begin to whimper his name as an orgasm whispers through me, threatening to explode. He raises a hand and shields the room around us.

"Don't be quiet. I want to hear you scream my name," he groans, hissing out a breath. He rises on an elbow and presses my hip to the mattress, grinding inside of me so deep my toes curl, and all I see is stars.

"Gods, please!" I gasp, my body flooding with light and pleasure, and when his name leaves my lips, it's a scream.

We fall asleep together, naked, warm in our bed, our legs tangled in the sheets.

Chapter 37

A Slip of the Tongue

Marianna and I doze in the quiet darkness of my bedroom for nearly an hour before convincing each other to get up long enough to put on clothes and brush our teeth, at least. Within minutes, we're back in bed. Marianna snuggles close while I stare at the ceiling, listening to the... silence, as she drifts back to sleep.

The world is a shockingly loud place, even in the dead of night. Normally, this is when the stars–the voices in my head–are the most annoying. Loud. Chaotic. Constantly chattering back and forth about everything and nothing all at once. But now?

I can hear the breeze coming through the windows. The curtains tremble, fabric brushing against the wall. The palace creaks, settling, pipes groaning and rumbling all around but hushed by the thick walls.

I don't remember closing my eyes. I don't remember a blank, empty kind of sleep washing over me–dreamless. But I wake several hours later to the moonlight shifting across the ground and the bedroom door silently opening, a small shadow stretching over the rays of silver on the carpet.

I open my eyes to slits as my powers awaken, telling me far too late that someone has stepped past the shields I've started using around my suite to give Marianna some privacy. Even the shields I used around the guest room across the palace didn't catch Skye slipping out of bed and tiptoeing across the castle.

I sit up ever so slightly as she shuffles past the door, staring right at me, clutching a worn out teddy bear. Her eyes slowly scan my face before slipping to the side, where Marianna is fast asleep, facing the wall, her body curled around a pillow.

Oh, shit.

"Skye, are you all right?" I whisper just loud enough for her to hear. I dig deep into my memories, sifting through things my mother told me recently about myself at Skye's age. Sleepwalking and night terrors plagued my parents when I was school aged. I was constantly moving around in the middle of night to the point Cosette, recently retired and blissfully married to one of Ryatt's retired commanders, moved back to the manor in Shadowcrest for a few weeks and positioned an armchair in front of my bedroom door, where she sat guard while my parents slept. She never woke me up, but according to my mom, she lured me safely back into bed.

I inspect the look on Skye's face, looking for signs that she might be sleepwalking as she works her way through another dream, another vision, but she turns back to me, blinking, her lower lip trembling just a touch.

Wide awake.

She takes several steps toward the bed before stopping again with a soft, breathy sigh, her eyes on Marianna again.

"Come here," I whisper, motioning to the bed–to the gaping space between me and her mother. Skye doesn't hesitate. She moves like the wind, damn near floating across the carpet, and climbs into the bed to settle next to Marianna. Her mom sighs in her sleep and rolls, clasping an arm around Skye's waist, and curls her body around the little girl without even waking up, like it's a reflex.

Skye, however, is lying on her side... staring at me.

I lay my head back on my pillow and stare back.

Several long, achingly silent seconds pass before I ask, "Did you have another dream?"

"No. I stayed awake."

Because she's terrified of what she'll see next, isn't she?

I roll onto my side. She's an arm's length away, but seeing her and Marianna like this? My stomach tightens as the vision of my mate and daughter, snuggled in bed, washes over me like a tidal wave. I can't fight the current of emotion that comes next. Years wasted. Precious years. Especially precious for Skye.

"I still get nightmares," I admit with heartbreaking quiet. "Some worse than others."

"What are they about?"

"Most I don't remember by the time they wake me up," I tell her before tugging on the sheets currently clamped between Marianna's knees. I cover Skye to the chin, adding, "But mostly bad things happening to the people and places I love, and I can't figure out how to stop it."

Skye exhales deeply through her nose. She doesn't say anything, but I can tell that whatever was wrong is now much, much better, and the antidote she needed, Marianna, is currently tugging her closer, flooding her with warmth.

But Marianna's proximity does nothing for the ache in Skye's voice when she whispers, "I killed someone."

"I know."

"I wanted to do it."

"I know you did."

"Am I–are bad things going to happen now? The stars say so. It's my fault–"

"That was not your fault," I rush out, shaking my head. "You were protecting your mom. I didn't get there in time. I should have been there."

Her eyes glisten with tears that don't fall down her cheeks. She holds them in the same way I do, refusing to give up, to give in, to feel. Feeling makes everything we see and sense more vivid, but I hate this for her.

"Does Mom dream about you all the time because of me? Because you're the only one like me?"

"Why do you think that is?" My chest tightens as she scans my face. Marianna stirs but doesn't fully wake before slumping back into sleep.

"You're my dad."

"I–I am." The weight of the world–her world–falls on my shoulders in an instant. I wait for her tears, for her anger, but she just stares at me, inspecting me, likely deciding whether or not she thinks that's a good or a bad thing.

"Soren said so."

I blink, then narrow my eyes at her. "He did?"

"He said *my dad* wouldn't like me getting fingerprints on his crystals and then let me play with all the spheres in your office."

That fucking bastard. "Oh–"

"And then he felt bad, I think."

"I would hope so."

"Does Mom know?"

"Know what?"

"That you're my dad?"

"Oh, um–"

"Because Grammy said that the Moon Goddess plants a little seed in a mommy and that's where babies grow and sometimes–" she sits up a bit, Marianna's hand sliding down her waist, "sometimes someone says they'll take care of the baby, too, and there's where dads come from–"

"I–"

"But Mommy didn't know that you wanted to be my dad–"

"Skye," I whisper, reaching across the space between us to rest my hand against her cheek. "Your Mommy and I have known each other for a very long time, and you're right, the Moon Goddess gave us a seed because we were very much in love, and–" my voice breaks. "And... I helped it grow but..."

Skye yawns, blinking blearily as fatigue washes through her. I grapple with how to explain this to a seven-year-old girl whose life has just been turned on its head in so many ways.

"But I was very young, and so was Mommy, and we didn't know what to do. I didn't know how to be a dad, and... I scared Mommy. It was my fault."

"Because you can see the stars like me?"

"Because I can see the stars like you can."

She blinks several times, locked in Marianna's warmth, but whispers, "Can you give me a good dream?"

"I've never–" I stop myself, closing my eyes for a moment while absently stroking her cheek. My mother has the ability–displacing memories and adding new ones–fictional ones. She spun countless dreams for me as a boy trying to erase the nightmares, but they were all of... trucks, and... jumping off of high places–boy things.

I let my powers untangle the grief and guilt currently sending me into a tailspin and let them flow into my daughter, painting her a vision of... Maatua. Yeah, that'll work. Of the rocky beach a few miles north of where my grandparents live, where smooth stones and seashells are abundant, and the water is warm and inviting. I place Skye on that beach with a basket and a hammer and turn every stone into an agate.

She falls asleep with the softest sigh, and nothing will be the same again from this moment forward.

"Blake?"

Marianna's whisper pulls me out of a dream about... well, the same dream I made for Skye, actually. I blink into early morning sunlight before turning my head. Marianna is caught in the glare of the sun while Skye continues to sleep between us, softly snoring.

Marianna gives me the gentlest smile before shrugging and looking a bit guilty as she motions to Skye. "When did this happen?"

"A few hours ago, I think," I whisper back, then glance at the watch I failed to take off before falling asleep. "It's only six. You should go back to sleep."

"Are you sure?"

"It's fine. I need to... do something." I slide out of bed with newfound purpose while Marianna lies back down, absently stroking Skye's back.

I'm dressed and walking through the castle a few minutes later, following the scent of coffee spicing the air to the yellow room on the fourth floor where the beginnings of a large breakfast are being laid out, but two people are already gathered by a side table, pouring coffee that must have been just delivered.

"Good morning," Mom says brightly, turning from Leona, who gives me the same kind of cheery smile only morning people who wake up at the crack of the Goddess can muster.

"Good morning," I rasp, eyeing them skeptically as I reach for the carafe and pour myself a cup. The women continue staring at me until I sigh heavily and ask, "What is it?"

"Marianna mentioned through the mind-link that Skye crept into your suite last night," Leona begins with what I can only describe as a smug, but hopeful, smile. "I'm glad she told me because when I woke up and Skye was gone, I thought the worst."

"You should really consider a new suite, perhaps, something bigger for everyone," Mom suggests, and the second Soren, Fallon tucked in the crook of his arm, arrives, I realize I'm in for it now. The whole family is now banking on me to make a decision–to publicly say I'm not the monster they believe I am. That I have a family, something I'm capable of being responsible for. That I'm not the demon that's been haunting this golden palace for over a year now.

Instead of telling my mother and the mother of my mate what

they're desperate to hear... I turn to Soren, following his process toward the coffee table, giving him an icy look even though inside I'm feeling surprisingly warm about the fact he slipped up and told Skye a snippet of the truth. Maybe it wasn't a bad thing after all. I can barely even continue glaring at the man–my friend, I guess–and when he meets my eyes with a sleepy, slightly battered flat smile, I cave.

I turn back to my mother and my mate's mother, and rip off the bandaid they've been fussing about for days now.

"Skye is aware that I'm her father now–"

"Oh, finally," Leona breathes, beaming at Mom, who matches her smile with radiance that lights up the room.

Soren smirks, murmuring an apology as he squeezes between the women to fetch a coffee mug off the table. Mom plucks Fallon off his arm and cradles her, still smiling, but the second she opens her mouth to start making plans, I cut her off with a wave of my hand.

"We will all sit down and discuss the future at a later date. Today, when Marianna and Skye are awake, and once they've had breakfast, I'm taking Skye to the orrery."

"Oh, that's right," Mom murmurs, disappointed. "Are you sure?"

"I need to go and look for something and... yeah, she needs to see it. I want to know if she can use it without training."

Leona pales but doesn't say anything. Soren, however, uninvited to the conversation, in my opinion, says, "She can use your fancy crystal bowling balls just fine. I'm not sure what she's doing with them, but–"

"It's just a way to syphon an image from the heavens to see it with your own eyes inside your head," Mom says. "They're rather fun. Definitely beats using a bowl of water like we used to back in the day."

Soren looks confused for a moment before deciding to just drink his coffee in peace while someone else holds his baby, but I eye him, and he catches my gaze.

"When we return this afternoon, you and I are going to Veiled Valley."

He gives me a curt, knowing nod, like he anticipated this already.

There's an underlying tension in the air that no one wants to acknowledge, but the silence is deafening. Hannibal has been quiet for far too long, and now I've seen him again.

Which means I can find him.

Chapter 38

I'm Leaving

MARIANNA

The townhouse in Wisteria Way is cloaked in shadows I don't remember being there as I follow my mom into the living room. Dust shimmers in the sunlight, highlighting just how long it's been since anyone has been here.

I stare at the foot of the stairs for several seconds, locked in my head as the memory of Dean screaming in my face and punching me hurtles back into clear, unfiltered focus, but then Mom steps into my line of vision, and the present pierces the memory, fading it into obscurity.

"You know," she says, sliding her finger over the dusty mantle, "I think I'm going to stay here."

"What?"

I follow her progress across the room while she inspects the freshly framed pictures now resting on the mantle. New frames, since Dean smashed everything that was once there. Someone came here a few weeks ago and cleaned from top to bottom, scrubbing any hint of what happened here from existence, but the smell of bleach still hangs in the sunbeams drifting through the curtains as Mom replies, "I've been spending a lot of time with Alpha Kenna and Luna Sarah."

"Yeah," I murmur, eyeing her as she fluffs the throw pillows on the sofa and sets them down again.

"You and Blake—well, it finally happened. Just like Sarah and I hoped it would all those years ago. She was just as hopeful about your relationship with Blake as I was, you know."

I feel somewhat defensive for whatever reason. It's an odd feeling, like I'm guarding something sacred. Like we thought... like we thought we were the only people in the world back then, and what we were, what we had, meant nothing to anyone else.

It was ours.

Always, inexplicably, just for us.

"Blake is staying here in Eastonia. You have an opportunity to have a life with him, with Skye, the three of you, and I feel like I need to move on with mine."

I straighten as she brushes past me into the kitchen. "Move on?"

Cabinets open and shut while I whirl to follow her progress through the kitchen, where she gathers a duster and other cleaning supplies. "I don't mean that I'll never see you and Skye again, Honey–"

"Obviously–"

"I just mean...." She sets the duster down on the counter with a sigh, bracing her palms on the smooth, quartz surface. "You and I have been through so much together. It was just you and me against the world after your dad died, Marianna. I tried to keep you out of it —the struggle of it—being a single mother, leaving our pack to try to give you a better future.... Now look at you. First chair of the Moonrise Philharmonic. Skye has a spot at the most prestigious academy for young witches in the world–"

"That's not a sure thing yet–"

"Blake saw to it. He saw to everything while you were fighting for your life, Anna, and I realized then that... he can give you what I can't. You've spent the last twenty years taking care of me. Picking up the bills when my shifts at the restaurant couldn't. Marrying that asshole–gods." She hangs her head.

I edge into the kitchen. "Mom, what happened with Dean wasn't your fault in the slightest."

"I should have tried harder to keep him away from you. I couldn't. I should have tried harder to mend things between you and Blake when you were pregnant with Skye, but... I'm not as good of a mother as you are."

I grip the archway into the kitchen, stunned into silence. "Mom–"

"You have a future here, Marianna. A real shot at the kind of life you've always deserved, that Skye deserves, and it would be an honor to step back and watch." She motions to the townhouse with a soft, wet laugh, like she's on the verge of tears. "I'm keeping the townhouse. Apparently, Blake, with his infinite wealth, bought it for us. It's completely paid off."

I startle, my jaw slack. "When?"

"A lot of things happened while you were cursed and dying," she murmurs, trying her hardest to smile, but she seems just as overwhelmed as I feel. "He made sure everything was in place for Skye– for me–in the event we–lost you." A tear slides down her cheek, but she quickly wipes it away, sniffling. "But you're here, and you're well, and you carry his mark. You're his mate, just like I knew you were back then, back when his world revolved around you, and you hung the moon and the sun in his sky."

I look down at my sandals with a wince. "I'm not sure I even deserve this."

"He loves you. He loves you more than anything. He's... learning to navigate being a father to Skye, but Sarah and I both agree they'll find middle ground in time. They're very alike."

"So alike," I whisper under my breath, meeting her eyes.

"Are you having doubts?"

"Of course not," I rush out, and it's honest, the most natural thing I've ever said. "There isn't a doubt in my mind that this is where I'm meant to be and who I'm meant to be with. I just–Blake is–there's something he's stuck on, something he won't tell me. Something that happened to him that makes it impossible for him to be here with us all the time." I struggle to put my observations into words, wringing my hands as I step closer to the kitchen island in surrender. "He has visions, can see the future, and hear the stars, Mom. They talk to him constantly, and he forces them back, like he's holding his true power at bay, and I think it's because of me. He–he saw that I was going to die and let me put a wedge between us, thinking our separation was somehow going to save my life, and now he blames himself for not being there, and for me turning to Dean. His family is on the cusp of war, and he's the only person who can give them the information they need to protect their kingdoms, and he... can't do it."

Mom holds my gaze as I spill my heart, and it sucks. Goddess, it hurts.

"I feel like I'm the thing in his way."

"Marianna–"

I hold up a hand, cutting her off. "I know how it sounds, but you have to hear me out on this. Blake knows how powerful he is. I can feel it radiating off him whenever we're together. He knows he could single-handedly put an end to all of his family's problems if he just allowed himself to be who and what he is, but he won't, for me. And now... with Skye? She's more powerful than he was at her age. It's weighing on him. I can tell he feels like he's being pulled in several different directions."

"What do you think Blake actually wants? Is it power, Marianna, or is it a simple life with you?"

I meet my mother's gaze, my heart lodged in my throat as I weakly reply, "It's me, but–"

"Then there's nothing else to say. He's in control of his gifts. It's his decision. If he wants to forsake his power and live quietly with you, that's up to him. Isn't that what you want as well?"

"I'm worried about him," I gut out, my fingers curling into fists.

"Too much time has passed. We've only had a few weeks to sort out our issues with each other. He's taking on too much."

"Then tell him how you feel."

"It doesn't matter how I feel when he can't talk to me about this. He doesn't think I'll understand."

"And maybe he's right, and you won't, but Blake is a grown man. He's a strange man, yes, but he has stood by your side since you came back into his life without question. He was devastated beyond recognition when you nearly died. He's carrying that, Marianna. He looks at you and Skye and sees a future that he's desperate to protect."

"I know." My heart begins to crack as I dig my nails into my palms. "I also see a future I want to protect, but that means..."

"Being honest with him?" Mom cocks her head to the side, giving me a pointed look.

I exhale deeply and roll my eyes to the ceiling. "This part of him, his gifts, is something I still don't understand."

"Then tell him. He's in the city today, isn't he?"

"He told me not to go to the orrery or temple without him."

"Well, he's already there," she remarks, crossing her arms over her chest. "So... that counts for something."

Without a second thought, I hike my purse over my shoulder and turn toward the front door, but hesitate, glancing at her over my shoulder. "We'll continue our conversation about your abandoning me and Skye later."

"Me living by myself is not abandoning either of you!" She laughs, but I'm already stalking toward the door, and the heat of the day greets me in a breeze carrying the heavy, floral scent of wisteria and magnolia blossoms–deep and rich–the first real hint of summer in Moonrise.

MY SKIN immediately erupts in prickles the second I pass through the sacred archway of the temple. The air in here is chilled despite the open windows and archways leading to the courtyards that span the length of the massive religious campus. It could be winter still, for all I know, as I scurry through the temple, ignoring the curious glances from priestesses. No one speaks to me, however, which I'm incredibly grateful for, but when I reach the second building–a dormitory, I believe, for those who live here full time–mystics begin to take the place of the more nonchalant priestesses of the Moon Goddess, dressed in white or pale blue robes with veils or masks. They rise from benches, turn their veiled faces, and pause their conversations to stare at me and... bow.

Chills snake up and down my spine as they part to allow me to hurry through the main hallway, past the moonstone fountain where Skye once made her wishes. I can feel their gaze on my skin, burrowing deep. I hate it. I want to crawl out of my body, to wash my skin raw. It's a sensation that's almost impossible to describe, but it's like being looked at under a microscope, like they have the ability to flay me open with just a look.

Blake, to his credit, doesn't make me feel like that, but when I reach the massive glass doors that open to the orrery, I realize that he could. He has used his powers on me. He's seen my life's trajectory laid out on a silver platter.

He's tried to change it to save my life.

The door opens wide, and I realize I've been standing there trying to catch my breath for what could have been several minutes. Blake looks down at me, one of his dark brows raising just a touch.

"I know you told me not to come here without you, but I figured you were already here–" I cut myself off, biting my tongue, and slowly meet his gaze. His eyes shine like polished amethyst in the sparkling sunlight shimmering through the domed glass ceiling.

"Are you all right?"

"I hate it here," I whisper before I can stop myself, and he gives me a half-cocked smile–something small and just for me–a confirmation that he feels the same. He reaches for me, his touch warm and grounding, and guides me through the doors.

Chapter 39

Music is Magic

MARIANNA

Sarah and Sydney are with Skye, standing against the railing around the massive orrery made of copper and glass. Planets spin, tilting on their axes, while the models of stars whirl around on no set course. Blake steps to the side but keeps his hand on my arm, tugging me close, while I gaze in awe at the marvel of magical engineering taking up the entire room. We're the only people here. We have the whole place to ourselves. The room is much warmer, thankfully, than the rest of the temple.

It's my nerves going haywire, I suppose.

I watch as Sydney picks Skye up and swings her onto his shoulders, walking out of sight around the back of the orrery.

Blake sighs deeply but smiles as he says under his breath, "My dad can read the positioning of the stars better than my mom can. They have a small orrery at the castle in Crescent Falls, actually. My grandfather Isaac designed it, and my grandma Maddy secretly had it built for him as a present."

"I didn't realize that these powers run so deeply in your family."

Another deep sigh. "It's complicated." He twines his fingers in mine as we watch Sydney rise on his toes to allow Skye to reach for one of the planets–this one made of glass or crystal, swirling with sunlight. "My grandfather is very powerful. He has powers of manipulation–of objects. He can unlock anything, a talent my father and I also possess. We can break through shields, spirit from one place to another, and while they possess some mystic abilities... I got most of mine from my mother."

"How does that work, exactly?"

He leans back, his shoulder resting on the alabaster wall. "Our family has some theories about where our powers came from, but it's, again, incredibly complicated. In my case, my mother is a mystic, and when it comes to Ella's line... Ryatt is also a powerful being, so Kenna and her children were passed those gifts in one way or the other, but when it comes to my great-grandparents...." He tapers off, staring absently at the orrery, like he's looking past it into the very stars that power it. "Isla was given her powers of healing and light as a child. There used to be a magical waterfall in Maatua, but its powers have waned over the last century. The going theory about how Isla passed her gifts to her children–to my grandfather, at least–is that she died giving birth to him. Both of them died, actually. Maddox had a special diamond–the Diamond of Faith, they called it–and she was clutching it to keep it safe while a battle raged outside the castle walls."

"I learned about that battle in school," I tell him, meeting his eyes, but he's not looking in my direction. He's still gazing at the orrery, his brow slightly furrowed.

"It solidified his position as Alpha King, yes." He finally looks down at me, his stern expression softening. "We believe the diamond brought her back to life, and my grandfather, as well. From there, Grandpa Isaac began developing certain gifts that aligned with Isla–light, healing, but his beast form was... new. Ella kept her powers a secret until she left with Ryatt to Eastonia, but the theory about her, and the Firestone blood in our family's veins, comes from Maddox, actually."

I blink, trying to envision the complicated genetics that now run in my daughter.

Blake continues, "Our family was exceedingly powerful for three generations, but in mine, we've noticed some patterns some in the family find alarming."

"Like what?"

"I am the only child of my parents to possess any gifts at all," he says quietly. "My brothers and sisters are normal shifters–no visions, no abilities to spirit from place to place, nothing. Misty, the most powerful of her generation, didn't pass her gifts of light and mist to her children, but Adrian, her oldest, I believe might be hiding his powers if he has them." He looks down at his hands before curling them into fists. "Lexa, Ryan's daughter, is incredibly gifted in the wolf arts. But she's still young, and if she has a beast form, like Ryan, it hasn't shown itself yet. No one in that line has healing gifts. In essence, the powers Isla passed down to my line of the family are going away."

We both look at Skye.

"She," he says under his breath, "is the exception."

I find it hard to swallow and quickly steer the conversation away from Skye. "What about Maeve's side of the family?"

Blake hums a sigh. "They've only gotten more powerful."

"Why them and not your side?"

"That's a very good question. They're all from Eastonia, for one, where witches and other beings are plentiful. Ryatt has dormant Firestone blood–men don't have Firestone powers but carry the genetics required, which explains Maddox's contribution. He and Isla had Ella, and we believe Isla's powers and Maddox's dormant powers ignited her Firestone gifts, and then she found Ryatt, who made those gifts even stronger in their daughter, who passed those powers to her children."

"If we have another baby, would they be like Skye? Or your siblings?" I feel my body tense the second the words leave my mouth. I press my fingers to my lips as a blush spreads like wildfire across my cheeks. "I–I just mean–you mentioned none of your siblings have gifts, and it seems to be the first baby that gets any powers at all."

He steps a little closer, leaning down to brush his reply over the top of my ear. "Why are you turning bright red, Marianna?"

I don't think I can blush any deeper.

"When we have another baby," he whispers, "it won't matter if they have powers or not. I wouldn't care. That would be the last thing on my mind."

"And what would be on your mind, then?"

"Making up for lost time," he says, and my heart lurches as he slowly pulls away to look at Skye, who's currently using her powers to light up several of the planets, turning the glass a soft violet–just like her eyes.

"I leave for Veiled Valley tonight," Blake says. "But I have a few hours. Let's go back to the castle. They'll be fine here."

"Are you sure?"

"Come with me," he whispers and moves us toward the door, turning his back on the orrery.

BLAKE

Marianna moves through the music shop, her eyes wide while she takes in the instruments strung along the walls. I turn as the shop's owner returns from the back holding a violin case, his dark brown eyes crinkling while he gives me a tight, professional smile. "Your timing is impeccable, Blake," he says casually, lifting the case onto the counter I've been leaning against while Marianna loses all sense of time and direction in a store full of music. He opens the case and steps back, motioning to the glossy black violin resting against a cushion of red velvet.

I can readily admit I have no idea what I'm looking at. The brands and craftsmanship of string instruments go right over the top of my head, but I do know this violin in particular cost me a small fortune. It's nearly as expensive as the entire fucking house I'm designing on the outskirts of Moonrise.

The shop owner, Markus, carefully picks up the violin. The black wood catches the artificial light and glimmers like it's lit from within. A sharp gasp echoes toward me, and suddenly Marianna is beside us, her eyes bright, wide, and a deep blue as she looks at the gift I ordered... weeks ago, when I first found out she was joining the Moonrise Philharmonic.

"It's Simian wood," Markus says to her, holding the violin by the neck as he turns it around. "It's rare, but hardy, and comes from the Simian tree in the Deadlands, which takes over five hundred years to grow to maturity–"

"Blake, don't you dare," Marianna rasps, and I look at her, slightly surprised.

"What do you mean?"

"You brought me here to buy me a new violin? Mine is perfectly fine. I take good care of it!"

"You've been playing the same violin since you were Skye's age." I take the violin from Markus, inspect it like I know anything about violins, then hand it to her.

She hesitates before gripping the neck, her fingers curling over the strings, but the second her skin meets the warm, shimmering wood... she folds with a dramatic sigh and a smile that could light up the darkest night.

"We have practice rooms in the back if you want to try it out. Otherwise, play here, for me." Markus grins, chuckling. "It's not every day the first chair of the philharmonic comes to my old shop."

"I couldn't possibly," she says, shaking her head. "I can't afford this."

"I know," I cut in before Markus can give away that secret that's been in play before Marianna and I even began to discuss getting back together. "That's why I bought it."

"Blake!"

"Give it a go." I encourage her, nodding at the instrument. Again, she hesitates, then slowly perches her chin on the chin rest and lifts the bow from the case–the same dark, impeccable wood–rare, just like her.

Markus and I step back as she begins to play something smooth and slow, testing each string, moving through a random melody like she can taste each stroke and vibration. After a few pulls of her bow, she relaxes, her eyelids fluttering before they close, and the melody drops to a deep, dramatic whine that has every head in the otherwise quiet shop turning to look in our direction.

Marianna pulls her bow across the strings like a long, slow exhale. The voices in my head quiet, honed on her and the sound she can create without a single thought–like this is her power. Her gift. Music–the music that settles me, turning me into a normal man and not some demon from the worst nightmares.

I'm unaware that she's stopped playing. I'm just looking at her, drinking her in, scrubbing my mind of who she used to be and replacing those fractured, painful memories of who she is now–the woman I love, the woman I've loved practically my entire life.

Markus, now a very rich man, sees us out of the shop with promises of attending the opening night of the symphony this fall. The remnants of the mating festival still glisten on the cobblestone streets in the form of confetti that's yet to float down the storm drains, but it's a clear, bright, hot day as we walk side by side through the narrow streets, just the two of us.

"We wouldn't have ever been able to be out like this in Crescent Falls, huh?"

I glance at her, realizing I've been stuck in my head for the last ten minutes or so while we walk in no set direction. "Not without an entourage of security wolves and a sea of paparazzi following our every move, no."

"Is that why you abdicated?"

I take the case from her and replace it with my hand, knitting our fingers together while we walk past the castle and into the quiet, sprawling neighborhoods that hug the city center. "Partly. I never felt like it was a good fit to begin with."

"Maeve has mentioned on several occasions that you're a fantastic delegator."

"That doesn't necessarily mean I'd make a good king," I reply, guiding her down a treelined street directly behind the castle where the forest begins, with only a few homes–large ones–rising above the tree line.

She glances at the violin case. "Blake, how likely is it that there will even be a symphony season this year?"

The road turns from pavement to rough gravel, narrowing into something closer to a trail than what will one day be a driveway. "I'd like to think it will happen."

"But what do you really believe?"

The trees cast shade over the rough path. The heat isn't nearly as intense here, which is a welcome relief. Marianna's mint colored sundress swishes around her thighs as she absently follows me down the trail, never once questioning where I'm taking her. "I'll know more about the situation when I arrive in Veiled Valley."

"Then Eastonia is going to war?"

I suck in a breath and let it out slowly, closing my eyes for a moment as the sun breaks through the trees again, revealing a wide bluff of what used to be woodlands but has been cleared, revealing several acres' worth of leveled dirt. Beyond, a sweeping view of Moonrise's natural, untouched beauty spreads as far as the eye can see–shallow, rolling mountains and green valleys. "Maeve will do everything in her power to prevent that once we know that Hannibal and his kind won't be causing us any more issues." I think of Logan and Kieran, my stomach pinching. There's something there my family hasn't discussed–their connection to Hannibal and Emberfyll's role in all of this.

Marianna huffs a breath, then realizes we've stopped walking. "Where are we?"

"Home. At least, eventually."

She blinks, looking out over the view and… not much else.

"I'm going to build a house here when this is all said and done."

"Do you want me to go to Veiled Valley with you?"

"Yes," I answer without a shred of hesitation, "but it's not… it's for work. I'd rather you stayed here with Maeve, where I know you're safe."

"How bad are things really, Blake? Do you–can you see what's going to happen?"

"I haven't looked in a while."

"Should you look?"

That's the question, isn't it? The one thing I've been avoiding my entire life? Afraid of what I'll see?

"Do you think Skye will like living here?" I ask, unable to answer her question. I can feel her looking up at me. I can't bring myself to look down and see the disappointment and frustration in those eyes I love and see in my dreams.

"She'll love it."

Chapter 40

Origins

Blake

Soren's footsteps slosh through puddles beside me, covering the magical buzz of Veiled Valley's arts district as we walk through the rain. It's pitch black–the night sky clogged by thick, dark clouds that promise the continuation of the downpour that started moments after we arrived in the ancient, veiled city.

Soren pulls his ball cap down to shield his face from the rain, grumbling under his breath as we walk through the city, crossing another bridge. "Couldn't you have just jumped us directly to wherever it is we're going?"

"Spiriting into the Archives is forbidden. It's actually magically impossible," I reply over the incessant, pounding rain. Thunder booms, rattling the awnings suspended over busy restaurants and bars.

"Who exactly is Arthur, and why is he so important? It's midnight, for Goddess's sake."

We step beneath the shelter of an awning for a moment. I peer up at the stone staircase leading to the next level of the city, which is shrouded in almost total darkness. "What *is* Arthur is the better question."

"What?"

I adjust my cloak, turning my attention to Soren, who I'm surprised to find annoyed with the prospect of this trip instead of chomping at the bit to get away from Moonrise for the next few days. "Arthur lives in the Archives–the ancient library here in Veiled Valley. He's... not like us."

Soren rolls his eyes. "Great. That seems to be a theme these days. What is he, exactly?"

"No one really knows. I honestly doubt he knows. He's very old. He was an exceedingly old man back when Ella came to live in Veiled Valley, and she was younger than me at the time."

Soren looks utterly perplexed. "That was like... fifty years ago–"

"Exactly. Come on, we're meeting Ryatt there, and he's going to be furious if we're late."

"It's already late," Soren murmurs behind me, but I'm already halfway up the last hike to the quiet, darkened heights of the city. Veiled Valley is covered by clouds below, nothing but the glow of the neon lights from the arts district to distinguish the kingdom from the storm raging through the valley, but within minutes, we're standing in the foyer of the massive, cavernous library overlooking the city below, shedding our wet coats and cloaks.

Soren shakes out his hat as voices drift down the narrow stone corridor–Misty's voice lifted over what I know is Ryatt, and the man of the hour, Arthur himself.

Ryatt is leaning against a wooden table when we walk into the first room of the multi-level library. Shelves stretch to the ceiling, and the exterior wall is completely made of glass that usually gives a view of the city, but tonight, water pours down the panes and shimmers with blue light as lightning crackles. Misty huffs as she crosses her arms under her chest, her golden blonde hair tumbling down her back in soft curls as she turns from Ryatt to smile softly at me and Soren, but Soren is staring at the small, ancient man standing directly on the surface of the table beside Ryatt. Arthur, dressed in a brown tweed suit that would fit an eight-year-old boy perfectly, twists his snow-white beard around a gnarled finger as he stares down at Soren in the exact same manner, raising a wiry white brown. "Ah-ha. This must be the heir you were talking about. I can see what you mean, Ryatt, about him being *old king born.*"

Soren glances at me before focusing his attention on Misty, who rolls her eyes and plants her hands on her hips. "Well, we're all here now. Can we get this over with?"

"What exactly are we doing here?" I ask Ryatt, who called this meeting tonight. Technically, the family is meeting tomorrow at the castle to discuss war plans if it comes to that. Hours ago, I was walking around Moonrise with my mate and her new violin, talking about a future where I picked up our daughter from school while Marianna prepared for her evening performances at the concert hall. I thought I had the night with her, at least, before getting a rather rushed summons from Ryatt with the command to bring Soren with me.

Ryatt glances at Arthur, whom he can look directly in the eye as long as Arthur, who can't be more than three feet tall, remains standing on the table. "Misty, I want to hear your recollection of your time beyond the portal Richard of Arcane Umbra opened–"

"I'm not doing this again," Misty says with a shiver, shaking her head.

Arthur's head is on a swivel as he glances between Ryatt and Misty.

"Soren needs to hear it. He spent more time with the Viper than anyone, and if the people you saw in the portal are anything like the Viper–"

"They weren't the same," Misty says on a breath, glaring. She turns to Soren, shaking her head. "They didn't have the ears. They weren't exceedingly tall like you described. They had–they had fangs–"

"Not the same," Arthur muses, then slowly maneuvers off the table and hobbles his way to a ladder leaning against the bookshelves.

Soren is torn between Misty's story as she recounts the war in Tarsian and watching Arthur scale the wall. I don't blame him. Even Ryatt positions himself beneath the old man–the ancient being, by all accounts–in the event he falls to his death.

"They were normal women. Kind women," Misty continues hotly. "But one of them had pointy teeth."

"And the other?" Ryatt asks even though I know he's already heard this story.

"She was a shifter, for sure."

"That's because shifters are everywhere," Arthur says from the ladder. A book thuds to the ground. He continues his search, pulling down two more thick, dusty books, before continuing, "You're a rather resilient bunch."

Soren can't decide where to look but settles on Arthur as he slowly moves down the ladder.

"Misty, we've spoken about the portal. You know my stance," Arthur says while Ryatt picks up the books he let fall to the ground. "You didn't go to another realm. Our world is large. Crescent Falls and Eastonia share a continent, but there are others. Other kingdoms. Other undiscovered worlds. Other... undiscovered beings."

Misty, also a historian, frowns at Arthur. "We have no proof."

"We have these," Arthur says, patting the books Ryatt just placed on the table.

"Myths and legends aren't proof," Ryatt argues, but Arthur shakes his head.

"Eastonia and Crescent Falls have long been considered the cradle of the wolf kind, yes, and while our history spans thousands of years, there's a lot we don't know about the time before the Firestone witches. Misty can attest to that," Arthur remarks, cracking open one of the books and blowing the dust from the pages. "Anything before the dawn of the Firestones is lost to time, I'm afraid, but their own legends and folktales were passed down through the generations, stories about immortal beings with fangs–vampires–who require blood to survive. And... faeries, also immortal but in a more mystical way."

"And what are you?" Soren asks without restraining himself.

Arthur looks directly at him but doesn't answer. I honestly doubt Arthur knows what he is or where he came from, old as he is.

"Misty traveled to another place, not another time, that's all," Arthur says to the room at large. "And your Spider, Hannibal, also came from another place, but I believe he's been trapped in Eastonia for a very long time–likely from a time before the fall of the Firestone Empire–"

"He cannot be that old," Ryatt says. "I saw him. He's young. Younger than the boys here." He points to Soren and me.

"Well, faeries were rumored to be very beautiful, that's true. They were gods, according to the Firestone legends."

"Why are you only telling us this now? We've been coming to you for guidance since the Spider started playing his games with the family," I grind out, but Arthur waves his hand at me in dismissal.

"We had no proof, but when Ryatt came to me shortly after Queen Maeve's stand against the Viper, I remembered something. Something from the time of the Firestone era, the banshee scream she described. Yes, that was it. You see, there are dozens of types of faeries, or at least, in the myths about them–water fae with their siren songs and elemental magic, fae with the ability to fly, to make flowers bloom, to paint the sky with stars and... rewrite memories." Arthur looks directly at me. "Yes, just like you, High Lord of the Mystics."

"So you're saying these... these children's tales," Ryatt says with effort, his eyes narrowing with frustration as he waves down to the ancient books now littering the table, "aren't tales at all?"

"There's always truth in fiction."

Ryatt's nostrils flare in annoyance, but I step closer to the books, gently flipping a page. The text is in a language that predates Firestone. It's looping scribbles–symbols I don't recognize, and even Misty, who excels at this kind of thing, looks perplexed.

"What is your theory, Arthur? Are we right to assume my grand-daughter's mate and their son are fae?" Ryatt's voice silences the room. Even the rain outside the ancient walls ceases the pounding against the windows as his words settle.

This is the real reason he called this meeting—this secret meeting of a select few.

I know the family has had questions ever since Kieran's birth. I know Brie and Logan have been uneasy, and that things in Emberfyll haven't been smooth, so much so that Logan is seriously considering moving his entire pack to the Deadlands, if not here, to Veiled Valley.

There's so much he doesn't know about his own history, about his son's history.

And now, after everything that happened with the Viper and Hannibal... if they're like them, what do we do?

"No. Not entirely. You must understand that fae, when they existed here in Eastonia, were gods to people like us. They may have walked among us, but they were not like us, and according to the legends, they are simply described as the Old Gods—those who lived during the time of our Moon Goddess's mortal life. It's likely that Emberfyll may have been a fae kingdom at some point, and over the generations, perhaps fae and wolves had... relations... that resulted in a kind of hybrid society. Emberfyll is likely as old as Veiled Valley from your own research, Misty. It's highly plausible, in my opinion, that Logan and his pack carry fae blood, which would explain the physical characteristics—the height, the ears."

"But not the powers," Soren cuts in. "The Viper could turn anything she touched to silver."

"Yes, I am aware." Arthur sighs heavily. "Again, based on the myths, there were dozens of different kinds of fae—high fae, their beautiful rulers—the gods of old. Immortal, winged beauties. But also lower fae—creatures of the water and the sky. Ugly beasts—some winged, some not. The oldest written texts that describe our own Goddess recount Her in Her... winged form as a woman with moon-white hair and pearlescent skin. Her wolf, however, did not have wings."

"Then she was also fae? Or a... a hybrid of both?" Misty shifts her weight.

"That's a question to ask when your time in the realm of the living ends, my dear," Arthur says to Misty, who looks pale and uncomfortable.

"What are we up against, Arthur?" Ryatt asks.

"Hell," he answers honestly. "If they're still out there, if the legends passed through millennia weren't correct, and they didn't ascend to the heavens after all like the gods they were rumored to be, but were simply displaced... hell. They're powerful creatures. Hard to kill. In the legends, they are the gods, so their will was law."

I look at Misty, whose eyes are locked on one of the books. She's lost in thought. She eventually meets my eyes and tilts her head toward the hallway leading out of the library and back to the foyer, her voice a soft whisper inside my head as she asks if I'd like to take a walk.

Ryatt lifts his head from his conversation with Arthur but says nothing as the two of us walk away. He begins to grill Soren instead, asking about the physical characteristics and powers of the Viper, all while Arthur murmurs his agreement that fae are, in fact, what we're dealing with.

Outside, huddled beneath a pair of columns holding up the exterior facade of the library's entrance, Misty turns to me, stuffing her hands in her pockets.

"You have to find them."

"I know."

"You don't have a choice anymore, Blake. You're the only one who can see that far–"

"I don't know where I'm looking." I think of Skye's dream with a wince. "I don't know how far or how close these people are."

"I've been doing as much research as I can," she says. "We're still finding bits and pieces of the Firestone empire but nothing before that. We know so little about the Old Gods–their stories, yes, but that's it. We know about the blessing of the falls in Maatua and the Goddess's hand in that, but not Her origins. We know nothing, but if Hannibal is... fae, then what can we do? He disappeared from the island. Maeve couldn't get close to him. It was like the Viper was strategically put there as a buffer. And if Kieran–if Logan and Kieran are fae, and everything that happened in Emberfyll was because of the fae..." She tapers off, shaking her head. "I'm tired, Blake. Everyone is tired. I almost wish something would happen so we can all move on with our lives and put Hannibal behind us–"

"I'll find him. I'll put an end to it." I meet her eyes in the rain-soaked darkness. "You have my word."

"Will there ever be peace, Blake? Can you see it?"

"I've never looked that far, Aunt Misty."

But I will. I have to.

Because I'm a wolf... aren't I?

Or are there... pieces of us, my family, that the fae are to thank for? Our powers?

Voices from inside the library drift toward us.

Misty reaches out to clutch my forearm in silent solidarity. "You're the only one who can do what you do," she whispers. "I'm sorry."

She must know the cost, doesn't she? She must be able to feel it– the limits of my powers. I slowly step out of her touch and look out at the rain.

"Blake?"

I turn slightly to the side, staring at her over my shoulder.

She takes a shallow breath. "We thought–I thought it was over when Cole killed Richard. I thought what I saw–the people I saw– didn't matter–"

"This isn't your fault, Misty–"

"It could be."

"It's not. I'll fix it. I'll fix everything."

Chapter 41

A Message From the Goddess

Blake

I barely slept that night. The voices in my head were louder than they've ever been but totally unintelligible, like they're trying to scream loud enough that I'll finally understand but can't quite get to me.

The spirit of the castle in Veiled Valley lays out a large breakfast spread barely anyone touches. Aris, seated at the end of the long table in the dining hall, toys with a strip of bacon in silence, his head tilted toward the flickering chandelier. I'm sitting across from him next to Soren, who told me last night, when I found him seated in an upstairs sitting room with every single light on, that he has a thing about ghosts and isn't a fan of this castle for that reason and is currently staring at Aris so intensely it makes me wonder what his deal is.

Aris nods to himself, then smirks up at the chandelier, which flickers again.

"Are you talking to that thing?" Soren spits, practically snarling.

Aris startles, blinking at Soren across an array of fruit and a large platter of scrambled eggs. "What?"

"The thing," he replies, waving a hand around the room with a shiver. "The ghost."

"The spirit? It's not a ghost." Aris stuffs a piece of bacon into his mouth. "It doesn't like when you call it that, either."

A rush of cold wind rushes around our feet, and Soren leaps out of his chair, growling, "I've had enough," before stalking off, leaving me and Aris alone.

He sighs heavily, shifting his position in his chair, and serves himself another helping of eggs.

"Are you hazing your new brother-in-law?" I ask under my breath, and he smirks.

"You can't fault me for taking advantage of the opportunity that's been practically served to me on a silver platter."

"You can communicate with it, then?"

His sharp silver eyes, just like Ryatt and his mother's, meet mine. "Can you not?"

I eye him warily. This is the first time I've heard of anyone being able to speak, let alone hear the spirit of this castle. "What does it say to you?"

"It gossips." He takes a bite of eggs, shrugging. "About the family. It knows everything about everyone." Aris seems totally unbothered, like this information isn't anything new, but it's the first I'm hearing of it.

"You're the only one it talks to, aren't you?"

"What can I say?" he drawls with a boyish smirk, rising. "It likes me best." He leaves his plate on the table and begins to saunter off but pauses, turning on his heel to face me again. "Actually, it needs you to go to your room and lie down." He scratches his head, looking up at the ceiling like whatever entity inhabits this place is currently dangling from the chandelier.

"What?"

"It says you're missing something, and someone has been wanting to talk to you for a long time, and that person needs you to... take a nap."

"Are you drunk?"

"Not yet." He winks then swaggers out of the room, whistling.

I remain in my seat for several seconds, scanning the room for any inconsistencies. The air is unnaturally still, like the entity followed Aris out, but then a chill snakes up my spine like a thousand little spiders, and I grunt against the horrific feeling of it, jerking out of my chair. "Fine," I murmur, adjusting my suit jacket as I stalk down a hallway toward a dark stairwell. Sconces flicker to life, and air rushes around my ankles, leading the way. "I know where I'm going. This is fruitless anyway, given Maeve and the rest of the family will be here within the hour to discuss next steps." I shake my head at the stupidity of the situation at large. There's nothing that can be done besides waiting like sitting ducks for Hannibal to make a move.

I enter the tidy guest room where I failed to fall asleep last night. I drew the curtains back this morning, but the entity snaps them closed and dims the lights the second I breach the threshold. "Why do you only talk to Aris?"

Silence.

I shake my head as I shrug out of my suit, slipping out of the loafers I polished last night out of sheer boredom and the inability to sleep. "What are you?"

More silence—the still, unnatural kind.

"Who are you?"

A soft shudder plays over the room. The comforter on the bed pulls back, and something—someone—slaps my pillow, leaving an imprint, a silent but stern command.

Sleep. Not just rest. Not just doze.

"Sleeping isn't something that comes naturally to me, even with my mate nearby. I don't know what you want from me."

Another ripple of air scurries through the room, disturbing the curtains. The voices in my head titter excitedly, somewhat frantically, and a single, intelligibility sentence laces through the noise.

"He's afraid of what he'll see, always has been." Laughter follows.

I shake my head, trying to loosen what feels like a thousand beads stuck within my skull, and finally submit.

"I don't have time for this," I warn out loud, but the second my back hits the mattress, the comforter snakes up the bed, covering me to the chin, and a supernatural force presses... down... "HEY!"

Pressure envelopes my entire body. I find it hard to fill my lungs as the weight of what feels like six wolves bears down on my chest. A dizzying sensation sweeps through my system, rendering my panicked senses useless, and before I can even reach out through the mind-link for help... Darkness snatches my vision. My body relaxes, numbing, falling into a stupor I haven't felt since Hannibal tried and failed to dig through my head. I'm swept away on a dark current, my body rocked into a forced slumber, and there's nothing I can do about it.

Hours, minutes, or seconds later, I wake up face down in a bed of moss. Fog snakes over my arms, which are sprawled in front of me. I cough as I fill my lungs with wet, chilled air and blink rapidly, trying to clear what has to be a dream. Fog is... everywhere. It burrows over an uneven landscape–a small valley full of gray cliffs and boulders. Dead, gnarled trees surround the clearing, and as the fog parts, I see fragments of what has to be stone pavers leading into a wall of thick mist that partially obscures a building tucked beneath the cliff, trapped in the shadows.

I have no idea where I am, but I do know this is a vision. There are no voices in my head. My powers are totally gone, useless. This isn't real. None of this is real.

I ease onto my knees, panting, feeling the wet fog penetrating my shirt. A bellow of pain captures my attention, then two men fighting to the death burst through the fog, toppling over each other. It's... me. Me–and a man I don't recognize at all. Me... dressed in clothes that don't belong to me. Me–

Not me.

Maddox drives his fist into the man's jaw, ending the fight, then rises, turning his attention to the temple directly behind me.

Maddox is young. My age, or close. His sharp, dark green eyes scan the temple with fervor as he wipes his bloody mouth on his sleeve and takes off toward the entrance with a limp.

I look back at the unconscious man and rise, cautiously turning to follow the vision of my great-grandfather into the temple, but when I cross the threshold, I find myself alone.

Alone, but in awe of what's laid out in front of me.

A statue is carved into the farthest wall from the entrance. It towers over the altar–carved out of what I believe might be a dark kind of marble–ribbed with white and silver against a sea of onyx. The Moon Goddess in Her human form looks down at the altar, one hand raised, the other lowered to where two massive, beautiful wolves are depicted, curled around her legs. The Goddess wears a diadem of moonstones spun around a central jewel–a diamond.

And I know that diamond.

I know this story.

This temple.

I turn and race back outside, but the temple door snaps shut, barely missing my nose.

"Do you know how long I've been calling out to you, angel?"

It's a voice both young and old, male and female. It booms through the temple. I feel a presence behind me but refuse to turn. I can't. *I won't.*

"Do you think I have infinite time to scheme and chase you down? I gave you a gift, which you've proved unworthy of, which you've deemed to ignore–"

I sink to my knees.

"Look at Me," the Moon Goddess says only feet away. "Blake."

"I can't."

"Then hear me because this is the only time I will deign to say it. You must act before all is lost. You must let go of your inhibitions and your fear before you ruin my kingdom forever!"

"What will you have me do?"

"You are looking for answers as to why your family members are my chosen ones. It's not that simple. My blessings were bestowed long ago. Fate has been on your side, on all of your sides."

"I don't understand—"

"Then hear this and remember, angel. Your gifts, your talents, are not of my doing. Long ago, during the time when the gods walked, I made the shifters my chosen people. I gave them this land, this cradle of magic and peace, and the others were threatened by my actions. They were threatened by the power and devotion my worshippers possessed because it was out of love, not fear. They created the fae in their own image—hatred, disgust, and greed. The war that followed was brutal. The fae believed themselves to be gods, so they were. They enslaved their own kind, ruined their own women, and destroyed the lands the Old Gods gave them out of the need for more and more power. I shielded my people. To the witches, I gave my powers, knowing I'd fade into insignificance the other gods couldn't fathom. To the shifters, I gave my blessing that they would find their mates and feel my love through those bonds. The Firestones were commanded to protect my glorious kingdom, and they sacrificed themselves to do so, but the fae... remain. My veils have been broken. They will come and kill everyone they can't enslave. I have worshippers on the other side, fae and shifters alike. What you've refused to see, what the stars have been begging to show you, is that war will not touch the Allied Kingdoms."

Silence sweeps through me, through the temple, as my mind reels around what She's saying.

"You want us to... invade?"

"You will invade. Tell your kings."

I make the mistake of turning my head. I can't help it.

A sleek, pure white wolf stands only feet away, her eyes glowing white. Without moving at all, Her voice laces through the air, carried on a phantom wind. "You will determine her outcome. Do not fail, because she cannot fail."

"Wh-who?"

"The warrior's daughter," she says, and bright light explodes behind my eyes.

"What in the actual fuck are you doing?! We've been waiting for you for an hour!!" Maeve screeches as she pulls the curtains back, flooding the room with violent, midday sunlight. I jolt upright, panting, unable to catch my breath. "What's the matter with you?" she shouts, furious, but then stills when she sees the horrified look on my face. "Blake? What–what happened? What did you see?"

"Nothing," I rasp, sweeping my hair away from my face. "I–I don't know. *I don't know.*"

Chapter 42

No One's There

Marianna

Morning sunlight still plays over the garden at the townhouse when my mom walks out onto the back porch with a mug of coffee in each hand. She passes one down to my perch on the steps, squinting into the sun, where Skye is lost in the glare. She's playing with her rocks again–the rocks she left behind when we abandoned this house, and our lives changed forever.

I couldn't sleep last night. Blake has his meeting in Veiled Valley today, apparently, but he told me he'd be back tonight–hopefully.

I sip my coffee, watching Skye carefully inspect each little pebble before dropping them into a to-go container Mom's letting her keep to carry her treasures back to the castle.

"How was your first night of freedom?" I tease, and she smiles.

"Quiet. I languished on the couch and watched all the shows you think are boring. I ate chips and drank wine until I went to bed."

"Mmm hmm..." I smile at her, noticing the color in her cheeks. "Were we really all that bad to live with?"

"No, of course not, but I realized I haven't been alone since I met your father all those years ago. I forgot her."

"Who?"

"*Leona*. I've been Mom, or someone's mate and wife, practically my entire life. It'll be quite the adventure getting to know myself again."

"Do you think that adventure can start tomorrow?"

She arches a brow. "What do you need?"

"Can you hang out with Skye for a few hours? I got an email from the director at the symphony. I have a meeting today with the conductor and what sounds like the entire board. I assume it's to go over the music for this season."

"This early? You have weeks until the season starts."

The knot of dread in my stomach that's been there since I woke up this morning tightens. "I'll find out."

"I'll watch her. Don't worry, okay? Everything will be fine."

Later, I can't help but think she's wrong as I walk through the city, my fingers curled around the handle of my violin case. People huddle in cafes, lost in tense conversation. Warriors stalk the streets, and everyone gives them a wide berth. Moonrise has lost its undercurrent of magic and light over the past few weeks.

Do the people know how precarious things are, or can they just sense it?

The performance center is a massive, ancient opera house situated toward the edge of the city. It overlooks the lake, which sparkles in the morning sunlight. I have an hour to kill, so I walk along the bike trail that weaves along the shore, then up to the wide arena of alabaster, where a training session is taking place below. The base of the arena is too far down to see, but I can hear the sparring–the clash of weapons, the snarling of those in their wolf forms.

I wade through a group of locals sitting on the benches along the curved wall of the arena while they sip coffee, and I climb the wide stairs to the performing arts center, which rises low and wide, casting a long, cool shadow over my body that's a welcome relief from the heat.

"Hey, you're Marianna, right?"

I turn to the deep female voice calling up to me. Lexa jogs up the steps with a dancer's grace, her rich brown hair curled tightly around her face and falling loose in a glorious mane down her back. She's not dressed in leather armor like the last time I saw her. Jean shorts and a burnt orange tank top make her look younger, less hardened, and she smiles when she reaches my side.

"Hey," I reply, giving her a wobbly, slightly shy smile in return. She's young–maybe twenty? For some reason, I can't sense a wolf in her yet, but it's obvious she's powerful... and tall. Taller than Maeve by at least an inch.

"I haven't had a chance to come back to the castle to formally introduce myself or anything, but I'm Blake's cousin. I wasn't sure if you knew. I doubt he said anything." We reach the top of the stairs, locked in the shadow of the arts center. "My dad is his dad's twin brother–the younger twin."

"Blake did tell me about you," I chuckle. "You're... from the Deadlands?"

"Yeah," she breathes, then turns her head back to the arena. "I'm actually going back in a few days. I've been here since last fall."

"Why?"

"Maeve brought me here to train her warriors and guards." She shrugs, looking back down at me with a smile. "But I have shit to do back home. I've already missed the spring planting."

"Lexa!" A young man at the base of the stairs calls her name, waving, his dark blond hair catching the sunshine.

She winces, grits her teeth, and turns her back to him. But he calls out her name again, and I notice a shudder rolling through her.

"Are you okay?"

"Yeah, fine," she rushes out, but now the man is walking up the stairs, skipping two steps at a time. "I just–ugh, okay, that's Captain Austin, and he's–I'm technically skipping–"

"Lexa, for fuck's sake," Austin pants, lunging up the final steps. He's handsome, clean cut, but scarred along his jaw. His soft green eyes inspect Lexa's scowl before he turns to me with a tight nod, gruffly introducing himself. "Captain Austin of the Royal Commander's Ghost Reserves," he says and... bows. Not deeply, to his credit, but still. It confuses me greatly.

"Uh–I'm–"

"Marianna Abbot–he knows," Lexa cuts in with a hint of annoyance.

"Why–why did you bow?" I ask.

Now Austin's the one looking confused. "You're Prince Blake's mate."

Well, word travels fast.

"Is it... in the news?"

"No, no," Lexa replies quickly, but her eyes slide to Austin with a glare so intense I feel the temperature in the space between us heat by several degrees. "Blake has managed to keep it quiet." Lexa throws another glare at Austin, and for a moment, I swear I see his mouth tick into a secret smirk, and his eyes... well, it's painfully obvious Austin, whoever he is, has feelings for Lexa.

And she's either oblivious or entirely uninterested.

Or shy.

Maybe a bit of all three.

"We're in your way," she says. "I'm sure I'll see you at the castle tonight, though. Maeve's hosting a dinner for us there before my regiment heads back to Silverhide." She glances at Austin, who is still looking at her like she hangs the stars for him every night. "Just us. Not your regiment of fucking idiots."

My lips pop open in a perfect O. Austin just smiles at her as she whirls and continues on her way.

He follows like a lost puppy.

I watch them go, making a mental note to bring this up to Blake, not that he'll give me any juicy insight into Lexa and her strange connection to the captain, but still, the conversation would be a welcome break from war, strife, and hardship.

I walk into the performing arts center, weaving through

employee only hallways and stairwells until I reach the practice rooms in the basement.

I've been here a few times since moving–mostly to sign paperwork or when meeting the directors and the conductor–my boss. But the practice room listed in the email is empty when I arrive. I look around, resting my case on the cheap plastic table, and just when I'm starting to sit, the door opens, revealing a frantic young woman I know as one of the many secretaries who work here, keeping the gears turning for the directors.

"The meeting was canceled and rescheduled for Thursday," she breathes. "Just now."

"Oh–"

"I'm sorry you came all this way for nothing!"

"It's really all right," I reply, wondering why she's so shaken. My lips part to ask if everything is okay, but she slips away, leaving the door cracked.

I stand in the quiet solitude of the practice room, alone, for what feels like several minutes before reaching for my violin case. I'm not sure why, but it feels like a fine time to just... play. I'm alone. It's quiet. I don't have to worry about disturbing anyone at the castle even though Blake told me it was fine... Still, this is what I used to do. I'd drop Skye off at school and close myself into a room just like this something–snug, sound proof. I'd play every song I knew and ones I made up until my fingers were sore, and my neck felt like lead.

The new violin feels like a foreign entity on my arm, anyway. I should get used to it, find a new rhythm against its weight, so I do.

Music fills the practice room. I close my eyes, relaxing my body until every muscle loosens, and I begin to sway, to move with each note. I imagine Skye's laugh and create a song that sounds like it–soft, giggly, and playful. I think of Blake and his calculated expression–hard, hollow–and the secret smiles that play behind his eyes–soft and curious. I weave them into the music. At this point, I don't even hear it, but I can feel it, and it feels... it feels good. Like I'm finally myself again after everything that happened this summer, and before.

A ripple of energy coasts through the room, but I keep playing. Blake's footsteps are silent, but I can feel him here, the threads that bind our hearts tugging tight as he slowly, silently, closes the door behind him and leans his weight against it. I keep playing, turning a few scratchy, even notes into a melody, then a sonnet, then a full-blown symphony. I play until I'm sure my fingers will bleed.

Minutes pass, I'm sure. Maybe hours. I wouldn't know. I lose myself to it completely.

I pull the string across the neck one last time–slowly, softly, a quiet end–before turning to my mate.

Blake's sitting on the ground with his back to the door, wearing a thick black cloak despite the summer heat. He's leaning his head against the door, his face tilted to the ceiling, and his eyes are shut, his face... relaxed, but shadowed by an emotion I can only describe as pained.

I lower my violin, resting it on the table, and move in his direction. He doesn't move. He doesn't open his eyes as I slide down the wall beside him. But his fingers curl around mine when I weave our hands together. He leans his head against mine when I rest my cheek on his shoulder and breathe in his scent.

"How'd it go?"

"Horrible," he says in a rasp, like he hasn't used his voice in a very long time.

"Really?"

He shrugs one shoulder. "I'm not sure how to describe it."

"You could try?"

A small, unenthusiastic laugh is his reply. "I wish it were that easy."

"What happened, Blake?" I lean into him, smoothing my thumb over his fingers. "Please, tell me."

"Fae are real. What Skye saw in her vision is real. Where they are is still a mystery. I... Had a dream I'm struggling to decipher. Maeve is mad that she had to spend the entire morning in Veiled Valley because of me. I left before the meeting, so I don't know what my family is planning to do with me, but I assume..." He tapers off with a sigh. "Marianna?"

"Yeah?"

"Remember that night you nearly convinced me to steal a ferry and sail into the unknown with you?"

I smile, my eyes watering. "Of course."

"What if we just... left?"

There's something in his tone that gives me pause. It's not a sound I've heard before. It's... shattered. Absolutely, utterly broken. Like he's given up.

"Blake?"

"I don't think I can handle this," he admits so softly I almost miss it. "What I'm being asked to do."

"What are you being asked to do?"

He grits his teeth. I... I hate this. Something's wrong, I can tell. I can feel it in our bond.

"I may be going away for a while. I don't know how long or when I'll have to go, but... I need Skye's help with something. I need her powers."

I straighten, and he turns his head to look me in the eyes. He appears... battered beyond belief. Exhausted. Worn thin.

"I need her to... look for Hannibal. I need her to find him, because I can't."

Chapter 43

Enemies Within

BLAKE

It's quiet in my office. The air is still and empty, scented with coffee and fresh ink. I move from my printer and sit at my desk, fanning through the papers I've just printed, which are still warm. The door leading to my suite opens with a squeak, revealing Marianna, who peeks her head in and says, "She's asleep."

I can't do more than nod. "Will you let me know when she wakes up?"

"I will. Um... the moonstone sphere? I put it on her bedside table. Is that where it needs to be? Or, like, under her pillow?"

For the first time in days, I feel a single slice of calm pierce the roiling mess of emotions currently taking up all the space in my mind. It's simply because of her, the image of her clutching the door, her dark hair swishing around her shoulders and her eyes... so blue. The perfect blue. I don't deserve this. I never have. "That's just fine."

Marianna's gaze holds mine, scanning, deeply inspecting, but I've trained my entire life to keep people at arm's length.

Including her.

It's killing me.

It's killing her.

She doesn't hide the disappointment shadowing her expression. She gives me a tight nod before wordlessly slipping out of sight, the door closing behind her. I close my eyes for a moment, resisting the urge to lock the door.

To lock her out.

It would be safer that way for all three of us.

I turn my attention to the documents now littering my desk. Misty sent copies of the texts from Arthur almost immediately after I didn't show up to the family meeting in Veiled Valley. She did her best to translate some of the fables, but large gaps render them useless. Her notes say as much.

We're damned.

I'm damned if my vision of the Goddess means anything other than me effectively losing my mind.

"Please," I say as the main door to my office opens despite it being locked and shielded against intruders, "I'm busy."

"As your queen," Maeve replies hotly, "I have the right to be here. You still live in my castle, by the way."

"By next spring, you'll rarely see me." I pull several highlighters out of a drawer, glancing at Maeve. Fallon isn't with her. I'm sure Soren returned to Moonrise with her after the meeting. I'm sure he's upstairs with her right now. I'd rather he be the one stepping into my space instead of Maeve. He'd at least try to joke, to tease in an effort to break the tension threatening to suffocate the room. He'd tell me to snap out of it and maybe that'd be enough, but Maeve is here, already digging in her heels.

"I need you to tell me what you saw."

"There's no point."

"There is. I just spent the last three hours going over every scenario with your father, my parents, and our grandfathers in the event our shores are invaded. We have plans in action; we're just waiting for a spark–"

"There won't be war on Eastonian soil."

She stops in the center of the fine carpet, her arms slack at her sides. "Why?"

"Why? What kind of question is that?"

Her eyes narrow to cat-like slits. "I see the old Blake is back."

"What is that supposed to mean?"

"You really think no one else can see? That *she* can't see it?" She motions to the door to my suite with a scoff. "What's wrong with you, Blake? You hid your mate and your kid from us for seven years and then suddenly there you were, surrounded by family, and we had the real version of you for a few weeks before you–you turned into this again."

"This is just who I am."

"You're a liar. You always have been. A fucking brilliant liar."

I methodically rise from my chair as tension crackles between us.

Maeve continues without skipping a beat, "You've been lying to your parents. You've been lying to Marianna, and you've been lying to me."

"Do not bring my mate into this–"

"Soren is the only person you're remotely honest with and–"

"Soren is the only person who has ever seen me as something more than a monster!" I shout, and she startles. I... flinch, my throat tightening, like it's unused to the level of volume I summoned. I tug at the collar of my shirt, which is suddenly tight enough to strangle me.

"What's wrong with you? I'm asking that from a place of concern, Blake. What the hell is the matter with you?"

"I'm not talking about this with you."

"You'll lose them, Blake. Both of them. Marianna knows how precarious this situation is. I saw her this morning when the two of you returned to the castle. She looked heartbroken, and it's your fault, isn't it? What kind of game do you think you're playing with her? Is it because she's your mate? Do you think she'll just allow you to be like this, to shut her out–"

"If you say her name again," I snarl, my vision going red, "I'll kill you. I swear on the Goddess."

"Marianna," she croons as her powers crackle. "Marianna, Marianna, Marianna!"

I take two determined steps in her direction before her powers flare at their full strength. Heat blasts through the door, a promise of painful, slow death, but I raise a hand.

That's all it takes. Maeve's eyes flash violet, her powers snapping, failing, falling to specks of embers all around us.

I am, and have always been, more powerful than her.

I lower my hand, swallowing past a knot of guilt, resisting the urge to vomit.

Maeve sways before righting herself, her hand flying to her chest like her heart is about to shatter in her chest. She whirls to me, tears wetting her eyes. "Blake?"

"Do you not see what I am?" My voice is like ice—frigid, bitter. "You've known this entire time, Maeve. You knew. You told me we'd be enemies one day. That we'd be the reason our kingdoms fell, and *you were right.*"

Maeve's horrified expression shatters to something dripping with pain. I ignore it, ignore the anguished look in her eyes while I pace to the window overlooking the city I swore to protect and serve—the only place that has ever felt like home.

"I had a vision directly from the Goddess this morning." My voice carries in a whisper. The air feels like it's being forced from the room, so silent I can hear the breeze rippling through the trees just beyond the window. "I am not in Her good graces as it stands."

"Why?"

"Why did She come to me in a vision, showing me Her true self? Letting me, a mortal, see Her image?" My sneer rattles through the room. I finally look into Maeve's eyes. "Because I'm ignoring the powers She said She gave me, but I think... I *know* She's mistaken. She's either mistaken or terrified I'll turn on Her because even She sees what I am and what I can do... and it rivals Her own power.

These powers aren't from Her. This curse? This is something else. Something dark, Maeve. Look at what I can do to you just by raising a hand. I'm the only person who can stand toe-to-toe against you, and you wouldn't stand a chance. She only came to me in a frantic attempt to keep me under control. Keep your enemies closer, right?"

Her silence is deafening.

I step toward her, and she takes a step back. I chuckle darkly. "Hannibal didn't just want something from me. He wanted *me*. I am more than a threat to him. I am something he's been searching for, maybe that his people have been searching for, for a very long time."

"You have no proof."

"I know that mystics have been easily swayed to switch sides over the course of our history. The Draven coven is a prime example. Hell, even Richard of Arcane Umbra had–"

"They were forced–"

"They were not."

Her back straightens, shoulders squared. "You've lost your fucking mind!"

"I am not meant to be a hero, Maeve. I was never meant to be an Alpha King. I was never meant to stand here, in this fucking room, working for you."

"What are you trying to say?" Her voice cracks, and I hate it. I hate the panic in her eyes as she curls her fingers into fists at her sides, and her powers begin to simmer through the distance between us.

"I've been fighting against what I am my entire life. Since the day I came to Moonrise for training and saw what I'm capable of, what kind of world I could create with just a thought, a fucking flick of my wrist if I willed it. The chaos, destruction, and pain I could cause. I am the harbinger of death, Maeve. A fallen fucking angel. The Goddess confirmed it. I am death itself in the shell of a man, and I've spent my entire life trying to fight my way toward something better, something–" I weakly point at the door to my suite–to my mate and daughter–but tears... tears fill my eyes, blurring my vision. "They are the only things keeping me grounded, and I'm–I'm losing the ability–to keep myself–here."

I press my finger against my temple, squeezing my eyes shut as I lose myself to emotions I've spent my entire life controlling but no longer can. "The voices in my head won't shut up, even when she plays her music. Even when I'm with her, Maeve, I can still hear them. They're begging me to act, but they argue about it–about whether I should burn this entire kingdom to the ground and rise as the Old God I am or sacrifice myself to you–your people–the very people men like me tried to exterminate during the fall of the Firestones three thousand years ago. I am a monster, Maeve. And I'm being called *home*."

"You're not–"

"Do you know what they call me at the temple? *High Lord*. Do you know where that originates? The courts of the Old Gods and the Old Kings that followed–the Kings that enslaved Eastonia–enslaved your great-grandparents and your grandfather. The very kings your grandparents fought against to give Eastonia a chance of becoming this! *The fae!*" I motion all around me–at the palace Ella pulled out of the lake. At the peaceful, serene city beyond. The souls going about their days not knowing a beast from hell lingers here, in this castle.

Maeve reads between the lines of my total mental breakdown. She turns her withering expression to steel, her eyes going bone dry. "What are you planning?"

I laugh darkly, my eyes still blurred by tears.

"This whole time.... You knew what you were capable of this entire time, didn't you?" She doesn't move from her spot on the carpet even though I pace toward her. She has a shield around herself, and I don't blame her. I can now sense Soren's presence in the hallway–frantic–but he's locked out. She's locking him out–not me. That's telling, to say the least.

This is the showdown we've been inching toward since childhood. A make or break moment that will define the future of the kingdom we share—and love. The moment that could fracture a family forever.

"You knew what happened to Brie. You knew where she was, what she was going through, that entire time."

"No."

"But you could have simply looked, and you didn't. You pick and choose how and when to use your powers, and you've... never used them to their full extent. Not even close."

I stop pacing a few feet from her.

"You knew Marianna would be cursed, that she'd die without intervention, and you still kept her at arm's length. You saw that, didn't you? Or did you choose to let fate take your own mate instead of using your gifts to—"

"To dictate a future of my own making? To weave those threads into existence against their will?" I ask, and she pales.

"Because you can do that, can't you? You are the decider. You can... change the future. You can do it. You've always been able to do it."

Silence sweeps through the room. Soren pounds on the door, but Maeve doesn't look away from me, her eyes locked on mine.

"You hid it from everyone so easily."

"Hannibal and his people will come back to Eastonia for me if I don't give in to them, Maeve."

"I don't care about that right now. I care about you." Her voice breaks. "You were going to—to die. Soren told me you were begging him to just let you die—"

"He should have."

Her lower lip trembles. "Blake—"

"If I allow myself to use my full powers, I will not be the same. It will consume me. Your powers are nothing in comparison," I tell her as steadily as I can manage. "If I had used my powers to rewrite Marianna's fate, I would have lost her regardless because I would have been brought to my fucking knees, Maeve, and culled. I don't know how else to describe it. It would have killed me at a soul level.

Only darkness would remain, and that's the one thing I'm trying to prevent. Because if I lose this part of myself–the shifter side, the side capable of having a mate–capable of being loyal and loving–of understanding what it means to live–I will kill everyone. I will enslave Eastonia. I will turn the mystics against you. I will kill you and sit on your throne, taking back what the Old Gods believed our Goddess took from them. The family has been asking me to act, to help, for years now. You have to see that I've done what I can. You have to know that I've been holding myself back to save everyone we love."

"And now what? You what, Blake? What are you trying to tell me?"

This is the moment. The confirmation she's been looking for. The spark.

"I can find Hannibal. I can find the fae and stop a war you already know we can't win. I can do it."

Her eyes soften with dismay.

She understands what I'm trying to tell her–why I told her everything. The secrets I've been holding onto since I was fourteen, when I saw my future split into two lifelines. One life spent hiding, pretending.

One... spent in darkness, but for a much, much shorter period of time.

"I can go to them and stop them, stop the war from happening, but I will not return." I edge toward her, my eyes lighting from within with my powers. "And if I do, Maeve, ever step foot on Eastonian soil again... you have to kill me. You have to promise."

"No."

I grab her forearm, our powers mingling against her will. She winces, baring her teeth as a blood oath crackles between us. "Kill me if I come back. I will not be the Blake you know."

"Does she know?"

The thought of Marianna cuts me to my core.

"She will. I'll tell her. Swear you'll take care of them."

Soren kicks through the door. Wood shatters around the room as he barrels toward us, but it's already done.

"I will," Maeve rasps, tears shining on her cheeks. "You're a fucking bastard, Blake."

Soren forcefully separates us, shoving me back several feet. He stares at me in both awe and fury. I don't blame him as he smooths his hand over Maeve's forearm, which is now marked with fading swirls and unintelligible patterns of violet and crimson that sink into her skin, shimmering before they disappear.

"What have you done?" he asks me in a broken whisper.

But it's the soft, shallow exhale that truly breaks me. I close my eyes for a moment before turning to the door to my suite. Marianna stands in the open doorway, clutching the door I didn't lock.

Chapter 44

I'm Not Afraid of You

Marianna

Soren meets my eyes through what I can only describe as a haze. The room looks and feels distorted, but that might be my mind trying to shield me from what I just heard and saw.

Blake remains in the center of the room while Maeve backs away, her eyes wet with tears and her gaze darting from me to Soren, who looks livid as he tells his mate, "We're done here. Come with me."

Maeve jerks into sudden awareness and turns her back on Blake. She leaves the room first, tearing into the hallway, her rapid footsteps the only sound in the vacuum of silence spreading through Blake's office. But Soren turns to look at Blake over his shoulder with a rough sigh. "We're going to talk this through. Don't do anything stupid until we do."

I wait for the door to click shut. Blake doesn't move from his spot in the center of the office, but... I have to do something. I have to *say* something.

He beats me to it. "How much did you hear?"

"It doesn't matter. I wasn't supposed to hear any of it, was I?"

"This is a complicated situation, Marianna–"

"Don't patronize me." My tone is like a sharpened blade. Blake flinches, calming himself by running his fingers through his hair, but gives me his back as I step deeper into the room. "Look at me, Blake."

He braces his hands on his desk, lowering his head.

"*Look at me.*" I edge toward him like he's a wild animal loose from its cage. "Blake?"

"You heard everything, didn't you?"

"Are you–do you not want me to know who you are? I'm your mate–"

"And I'm a monster." He finally turns to look at me, his face just... broken. His eyes swirl with power but are lined with aggressive dark circles. He's exhausted. I can feel it leaching through our bond–like he's on the verge of collapse.

"You need to sleep," I say, my voice cracking. "When was the last time you slept through the night? When was the last time you slept at all?"

He just stares at me, shaking his head. "You need to leave."

"I'm not going anywhere, and you're going to fucking bed!"

"I can't. I can't–"

"Because you'll get visions? You're terrified of your powers, Blake! You have to stop! You have to sleep!"

He moves toward the door to leave his office, but I leap into his way, extending my hands. Fury flashes behind his eyes as they narrow. "Marianna, get out of my way."

"What's wrong with you? What happened in Veiled Valley? You came back to Moonrise and immediately found me at the arts center. Why? You looked like you'd been to hell and back, and you said you needed Skye's help. You directed me to bring those spheres into her bedroom, for fuck's sake. Why? What are you planning? Blake?!" Panic cuts through the numbness, rendering my senses useless. "BLAKE!"

"I can't talk to you about this–"

"You can!"

"I can't!" he shouts, his eyes wild, and his power simmering between us. I can feel it, taste it. It consumes me and spits me back out in warning, but I... I will not turn away from him and run like the first time.

"Go to bed," I rasp, tears in my eyes. "Now."

He gives me a dry smirk. "I have too much to do."

"Before you leave? That's what you told me, that you were going away for a while. You're going to try to find Hannibal, aren't you? Why? What's the fucking point, Blake?"

His jaw tenses, but his eyes soften just a touch–just enough that I know I might be getting through to him. It's like he's trapped in his own head right now–like everything is barreling out of control, and he's boxing everyone out. He can't help it, I realize. It's too much. It's always been too much. He's always been at war with himself, torn between the man he wants to be and the powerful being he is.

"You showed me what you can do with your powers so I wouldn't be afraid anymore. So I'd understand, and I do. But you're lying about... how far you can actually stretch those gifts. I heard it all, Blake. I saw you extinguish Maeve's flame with zero effort. And I'm still here." I motion to myself, desperate. "I didn't run. *I'm still here.*"

His chest rises and falls like he's struggling to take a breath. Electricity crackles between us like the room is full of it–his power–with nowhere to go.

"I shouldn't have left you in the first place," I admit. "I was scared. I didn't know–"

"You were right."

"I wasn't. We both made mistakes back then; I know that. But I'm your mate. I have always been your mate. You knew. I know you knew. I know it's been eating you alive for almost a decade. I know you've been shielding yourself from your own powers since you were a kid and realized what you were actually capable of, and it's too much. You need to sleep, Blake. You need to just... give in."

He closes his eyes, shaking his head.

"Please," I beg, taking a step toward him. "Please, just sleep. For me. For us. Skye needs you. She's like you, remember? She'll either grow up without you or be damned to a life where she believes she has to be afraid of what she is because the man who gave her these gifts hasn't ever allowed himself to just be who he is."

Blake opens his eyes but doesn't say a word.

I take another step, then another, reaching past the shields buzzing around his body–shields the naked eye can't see but that I can feel ripping through our bond, like he's doing everything in his power to keep me away.

"I love you," I croak, sniffling, as I place my hand against his chest. "Please. Go to sleep, Blake."

"I don't know what I'll see."

"I'll be there. I'll go with you."

He shakes his head, but I press my body against his.

"I know you can do it. You did it for Skye. You let yourself into her vision. Let me into yours. You don't have to go alone."

My wolf senses prickle, alerting me to another presence in the room. A quick glance toward the door gives a glimpse of Soren standing in the doorway beside Lexa, of all people, but their faces are cast in mid-afternoon shadow. I ignore them, praying Blake is also ignoring them.

"Skye is napping. She'll be asleep for a while longer. Just take me with you. Please."

Soren steps into the room, and that's enough for Blake to turn, snapping back to reality. He stalks to the door to our suite, leaving me standing alone, shaken.

He slips through the open door, not bothering to close it. I release the first long breath I've taken since hearing him and Maeve scream at each other and going to investigate, only to have my heart torn from my chest.

"I'll talk to him," Soren offers, his voice dripping with what I can only describe as concern. He tries to step past me, but I stop him, shaking my head.

"Just... leave us alone for a while. He needs to rest. He doesn't sleep."

"I'm aware of that," Soren replies, and when I look up at him, I notice the slightest lost look in his eyes.

"He trusts you, you know. He wasn't going to hurt Maeve. Blake... he's not like us. He doesn't know how to talk about these things."

"These things?" Soren chuckles but seems to understand what I'm trying to convey.

"He's never been able to show people who he really is. He just showed Maeve."

"Yeah," he breathes, crossing his arms over his chest. "He sure did."

"I'll send Skye up to you when she wakes up if that's okay."

"That's fine. I'll take her out to the garden or something."

Lexa remains stoically in the doorway like she was brought here to try to subdue Blake, but when I catch her eyes as I move toward the suite, she's watching me intently, a slightly confused, unsure expression passing behind her lovely dark blue eyes.

Blake is in our room, sitting on the edge of the bed. His shirt is untucked from his trousers, his hair ruffled. He looks generally undone, one shoe already off but the other still laced.

I'm not sure what to say or do, to be perfectly honest. I climb into the bed and lay my hand on his forearm in silent invitation.

"Marianna, I'm sorry. You shouldn't–you shouldn't have to go through this with me. You've already been through so much."

"You're a little rough around the edges, sure, but you have to remember I spent seven years raising your daughter. If you're trying to compare yourself to Dean, you're going to have to try harder than that."

He finally turns to look at me. I simply shrug a shoulder and lie down, beckoning him to join.

"You're not scared of me?"

"You've never hurt me. You never would, and I trust you. I also know you're hurting. My music... used to help, didn't it? Now it doesn't shut anything out."

He runs his tongue over his lower lip, his eyes downcast on his lap.

"You need to sleep. Please, just try. *Please.*"

He holds my gaze for several seconds. I wish I could get into his head right now to decipher what he's thinking and feeling. For a moment, I get a single glimpse, and if I weren't already lying down, it would have brought me to my knees. It's the same look of fear that Skye wore the night she killed Dean–the night I think she realized what she's capable of–death.

Blake has been weighed down by that knowledge for at least twelve years.

He finally takes his other shoe off and lies beside me. I wrap my arms around his waist and snuggle close, my head resting on his chest, pressing my body against his like a dead weight. I knit my fingers in his, close my eyes, and wait.

Blake falls asleep almost instantly, like his exhaustion was so extreme it would have only taken the act of sitting down to send him into a stupor. He makes good on my plea to take me with him, and my vision fades into darkness I can't control, and I'm swept into a dreamworld that's both foreign and shockingly familiar because I can feel him here–everywhere.

At first, it's a jumble of images and voices–stars and light. Then, I'm on a coastline somewhere south, where the water is just being touched by the sunrise, and the sky is a deep, angry red. Turbulent waves crash along a blood-soaked beach–weapons scattered. Bodies everywhere. Slaughtered. A woman screams into the sunrise, a glint of pure gold reflecting off what I believe might be a bow strapped to her back, before the vision fades, and I'm swept to another place.

An arena. Something ancient and massive. A hazy crowd blurred by unforgiving sunlight. Then, another place, a thick forest where mist snakes between trees. A white wolf darts through the brush, chased by a black wolf with silver eyes. They sprint out of sight before I can get a good look at them.

I have the sudden sensation that what I'm seeing isn't the full story–like Blake is purposely keeping me out of the visions that plague his mind when it's at rest and his powers have full authority. Like the beach, the arena, and the forest were manipulated–details missing. *People* missing.

But then I'm on another beach. Perfect, flawless turquoise water laps the shore in smooth, gentle waves. A stunning sandcastle only an architect and his daughter could create rests just along the tide line.

This is where he keeps us, and when I wake up, it's fully dark beyond the windows in our room, and Blake is still beside me, fast asleep.

Chapter 45

My Only Friend

Blake

I wake to full darkness, a nearly full moon painting the bedroom in strips of silver. Moonlight illuminates Marianna and Skye, the latter stretched out like a starfish between us, one fist resting against Marianna's cheek while the other clutches my wrinkled shirt in a death grip. My body feels heavy, and my brain takes several seconds to register the room around us. I've been asleep most of the day, and well into the night, which hasn't happened in many years.

I'm still not fully awake as I untangle Skye's fingers from my shirt. She opens her eyes to slits but quickly succumbs to a deep slumber again before I've loosened her fingers enough to slip free.

Everything that happened in the last day or so barrels back to me the second my feet touch the floor. I slump on the edge of the mattress, hanging my head in my hands as the visions I saw ripple through my head.

The stars are now quiet, like they've done their job and can now rest, just like I have. Bastards.

I change my clothes and splash cold water on my face. I move through the suite on autopilot like my body knows what to do and where to go even though I'm still stuck in my head, still fanning through the damning visions Marianna begged me to give in to, and I did.

Visions of a... crimson future. A bloody, violent future. A future I have to let play out if the visions can be trusted.

Before I know it, I'm in that little study again on the fourth floor. Emerald walls and ceiling height bookshelves lock me in a familiar embrace. This room was generally off limits when I was younger, just a boy let loose in this palace whenever the family gathered. This is where kings met for drinks, for quiet conversation about their families, about succession, war, and trade. I shake the image of Ryatt and my grandfather Isaac sitting in the twin armchairs near the windows before walking to the long, built-in shelving unit on the far side of the room, turning on a rather complicated espresso machine, letting the hum of the appliance yank me back to full awareness.

I'm not the only person in the room, and I knew that the second I breached the threshold, but Soren hasn't said a word yet. He hasn't even looked in my direction.

I make a cup of coffee. It's methodical–movements I make on a daily basis. A mug. Coffee. A perfect pour. No cream, no sugar, no frills. Everything happens exactly like it should–

"You really hurt Maeve's feelings," Soren says into the silence.

"I was unaware she had those."

"Don't be a dick. This is serious."

I turn, downing the coffee without so much as feeling the temperature, and set the empty mug on the counter. Soren is splayed out in an armchair, casually, almost lazily, like he's been here for a while. Waiting for me, I suppose. "What do you want me to say, Soren?"

"You might think I know very little about Maeve. I haven't had almost a decade of experience with her like you've had with Marianna, but she's at least honest with me. She's always been wary of you, and for a while, I didn't really get it. Sure, you lied to her. Sure, you lied and continue to lie to everyone, but I kind of understood why. You're a simple man, Blake. That's the meat of it. You know exactly what to do and how to do without getting anyone else involved, but that's not how this family works." He taps his fingers on the armrests, arching a brow in invitation to debate his observations.

"Say what you want to say, by all means—"

"You hurt my mate, and now I'm dealing with the consequences of that. I should, in all honesty, kick your ass into oblivion for what you said and did to her, but I... won't. I get it, okay? You and Maeve have been at odds for years and have had some kind of truce the last year or so, but she truly didn't know what you were actually capable of."

"She knew—"

"She did not. Maeve told me she always wondered if you'd end up the enemy, if there would come a point in time when you turned on your family and went dark. She told me she often worried in the years leading up to her coronation that you'd rise to the throne in Crescent Falls and undo everything your great-grandparents accomplished. But you abdicated for her. You came here, for her. You've been running this kingdom like a well-oiled machine while she rests with Fallon, all as you're actively losing your mind while the family has been leaning on you, begging you to do the one thing you knew would send you over the edge into that darkness." He takes a breath, pausing, before asking, "Am I right?"

I find it impossible to swallow. I manage a short nod. It's all I can muster.

"And then Marianna came back into your life."

I close my eyes. "I don't need you to narrate the last few weeks for me—"

"I have to, Blake, because you can't put these pieces together, can you? You are hanging on by a thread."

"You and I are not—"

"What? Friends?" He rises, exasperated. "We're past that. I know that side of you–the dark side, the side you hide from everyone you've ever allowed to get close to you. I've seen it with my own eyes, Blake, how calculated and manipulative you can be, how dangerous you are. And I remained by your side, regardless. Call it what you want, but I'm the only person who has truly been in your corner for five years without questioning you–"

"Don't—"

"Marianna," he says steadily, pointing his finger at my chest, "came back to you. You did your best to keep her at arm's length, thinking you'd somehow save her life, but what you were really doing was trying to keep her away from a life of misery with you."

"Soren, please."

"You're destroying yourself trying to be something you're not."

"You have no idea what you're talking about."

"I'm mated to the most powerful woman in our world," he rasps, his eyes bright and honed on mine, silently begging me to understand. "And you're the most powerful man, and you're my friend. Do you think I don't see the similarities between you and Maeve? Your undying loyalty to your family? Your shared fears of your own powers? The difference between you, however, is that Maeve has accepted what she is and her fate. You haven't."

"I will lose everything, Soren. That's the difference—if I accept who I am. Not just that, but my fate? All of this–my family, my life– goes away. I will be gone. What remains isn't something this family can trust. Do you understand?"

"I understand that you don't think you're capable of controlling your gifts, but I've seen you do it. I saw you, just hours ago, silence Maeve's flame in a single second. Do you realize how much power that takes? And how easily you controlled it? You're not giving yourself enough credit, man."

"I am a god, Soren." I step toward him, losing my grip on my restraints. "Do you get that? I am a god reincarnated–the God of Death, all right? What am I supposed to do with that knowledge? I want to be able to walk my fucking daughter to school, okay? I want to make dinner for my girls at night without seeing their lifelines splattered all over the walls, okay? I want–I want to go to bed with my mate and be able to hold her in my arms without seeing every Goddess-damned injustice coming her way, but I can't."

"You can control it!"

"I don't know how!"

"Then learn!"

"It's not that simple–"

"You say you're a god," he shouts, his tone bordering on anger. "Act like one, Blake. Maeve says the stars talk to you, so... tell them to shut the fuck up? Maybe? Make them listen. Make them bend your will just like you made me bend to yours for five fucking years."

My breath comes in short, frustrated rasps. "You don't–"

"Understand? Fuck no, of course I don't. I don't have voices pinging through my skull every given second, but I know, for a fact, I wouldn't just sit there and allow it to happen. You have two choices, Blake. It's clear something is happening, that war is coming. I can tell just by the look on your face that you've seen it clear as day, and I won't ask for the details because, honestly, I don't want to know. But," he continues, taking a deep breath, "you can either sit here and lose your mate and child by driving them further away, losing yourself to your gifts, or you can finally accept what you are, and who you are, and make that work to your benefit. Fight the darkness, twist it, turn it into something you can continue to use, or you will lose it all. But you already know that."

I let the silence settle for several long, tense moments. I let it fester like a virus. My mind is a pool of knotted thoughts and tangled decisions. But I meet Soren's eyes, accepting a fact I've known for months but wasn't ever going to admit.

He is my friend, whether we like it or not. Whether we want it or not.

"You will be Alpha King of the Roguelands. Ryatt was correct when he said that the Roguelands will always choose its king, and it chose you years ago, long before you were even in the Viper's embrace. It chose you as a kid–a starving, sick, violent kid. You will be king, and every Alpha in that forest will rise when you call on them for aid in the next weeks. It will happen. You will ascend to Ryatt's throne."

Soren pales slightly but doesn't break eye contact.

"Maeve will make the right decision in the coming weeks. She'll debate it, but she'll know in her heart she's making the right choice. Remind her of that."

"What choice is that?"

"It's not mine to say."

Soren tilts his head in confusion but doesn't press me, which I'm thankful for. The images of the visions I had lace through my mind in vivid detail, along with the guilt of what's to come, and who will have to bear the brunt of the violence involved.

"Has Lexa been sent back to the Deadlands?"

Soren narrows his eyes. "Why?"

"I'm just asking."

"She left this afternoon." He moves toward me. "What's going on? What have you seen?"

"I need you to do something for me. To promise me something."

"Another blood oath?"

"No. Just... take care of Marianna in my absence. Skye loves you. Marianna trusts you. If I return, I might not be.... Maeve will decide my fate, and she's the only one I trust to be able to see if I'm still Blake or if I return as something–or someone–else. But take care of Marianna."

"You know I will."

"I can find Hannibal, Soren. If Skye's dreams are correct, I can find him. I can... go to him, his people, and I have to, because if I don't, the war coming our way will not be one we win, and..." I taper off, having a hard time putting the meaning of my vision into words. "It has to be me."

He takes several sharp breaths. "You're sure you want to do this? I could go with you."

"You wouldn't survive the jump."

A light flickers on in his head, and it's a relief. "How far away are they?"

"Very."

Chapter 46

It's All for You

MARIANNA

I wake up alone in the haze of another bright, sunny day. Summer heat pours over Moonrise as I slide out of bed and pull on a thin, silken robe over the tank top and shorts I fell asleep in late last night, after putting Skye to bed and rejoining Blake. He hadn't woken up since I forced him to sleep yesterday, sometime in the early afternoon, but he's gone now..

I blink back fatigue still clogging my eyesight and open our bedroom door, where soft voices drift toward me, carried on a warm breeze scented like maple syrup and freshly brewed coffee.

Skye kneels beside the coffee table in the living room, a plate of half-eaten pancakes resting beside her. She looks up at me with a sugary grin before her gaze locks back onto the chessboard on the table. Blake turns his head and follows my progress across the room to where a breakfast spread has been laid out–pancakes, eggs, fruit, and an assortment of juices, but I reach for the carafe of steaming coffee, trying to will my hands to stop trembling as his gaze works through me.

I'm not scared of him. I'm scared for him. Terrified.

But the scene in front of me is undeniable.

"You're not very good at this, are you?" Skye titters, knocking one of his pieces from the board.

"You're just exceptionally good at chess," Blake replies under his breath, slightly taken aback, I think, at her level of skill. So am I, admittedly.

"Where did you learn how to play chess, Skye?"

"Dad," she shrugs, waiting patiently for Blake to make his next move. "Just now."

"About twenty minutes ago," Blake replies with a soft growl. He moves a knight, and Skye doesn't even need to think through her next move. She steals his piece within a second.

I hang back by the breakfast table, slowly bringing my coffee to my lips. Blake shifts his weight on the carpet, muttering something under his breath as they lean into the game, his eyes flashing with restraint and Skye absolutely glowing under his undivided attention, which makes my heart sing but also squeeze so tight it nearly takes my breath away.

He looks about as relaxed as he possibly can, but I can feel the seconds ticking by like a timer is somehow woven into our mate bond, like every moment that passes is a moment closer to when he makes the decision that will change the course of our life forever.

I think back on our first moments together here in Moonrise while they finish their game. Seeing him at the temple. Our chance meeting at the alpine lake. The afternoon he spent with Skye in the backyard of the townhouse when he'd told me her powers were extreme, and she needed training.

But she's been better with him around. She's easier on us and herself—like she finally feels like she has a place to stand in the world because her world is now surrounded by magic, just like her own.

But the man at its center, the man who's been tucking her in at night and slowly, cautiously getting to know her, is going to... leave. Again.

"Your great-grandfather is very good at chess," Blake says as their murmured conversation breaks through my thoughts. "His father, Maddox, taught him how to play when he was your age."

"Is he better than me?"

"I'm not sure. Are you using your powers to cheat?"

She tilts her head to the side while he gives her a sharp, but still playful, look that screams he knows exactly what she's doing, what she's seeing behind those violet eyes.

I sink into an armchair for the rest of the morning, a silent observer to their conversations, to the next game of chess they play– which she also wins. Time moves slowly, and I'm grateful for it, but I know what's coming. I know what he's planning.

I just hope he gives me some time to prepare, to really let it sink in.

"Skye?" Soren calls out. His voice reaches us before he comes into view. Fallon wiggles in the carrier on Soren's chest, and he's dressed in shorts and a ratty old T-shirt with his favorite hat slapped backward on his head.

Skye pops up from her spot on the carpet with excitement shining behind her eyes. Blake, however, seems to sink against the foot of the couch while he runs a hand down his face.

I sit up a little straighter as I watch my mate roll his neck, his eyes pinched shut like he has a blinding headache.

"It's our lucky day, kid. I'm busting out of the castle, and you're coming with me," Soren booms.

"Where are we going?" Skye asks, bouncing on her toes.

"We have a royal escort to the lake. We're going to the beach and having a picnic. Jane and Patton will be there, too."

Skye's head whips in my direction. "And Dad and Mom?"

My heart sinks to my stomach. "Um, not today, honey."

Skye looks at Blake, but he has his head in his hands. I rise from my chair, trying to hide my concern, but Soren also catches on and quickly says, "Let's go. We'll be back by dinner, okay? We're picking up your grammy on the way…"

I remain in place while Soren talks Skye out of the room, closing us into silence, but I realize quite quickly that we're not alone.

Maeve had been hanging back, just out of sight, while Soren fetched Skye. She's a tangle of shadows as she edges into the living room, glancing at the breakfast spread before settling her sights on Blake.

He looks up from his hands, his eyes tired and slightly hazy with his powers. "Next time, can you just come in instead of standing right against my shields? It gives me a blinding migraine."

Maeve's mouth twitches, but only a ghost of a smile remains, and I quickly realize I don't need to be here for whatever conversation is about to take place.

"I'll be at the lake as long as both of you can promise not to kill each other if I leave," I say, cutting through the tension between them.

"I think that's wise," Maeve says under her breath, but Blake looks at me, really looks, and I see nothing but mingled heartbreak and determination in his eyes.

He's made a decision. He knows what he needs to do.

And he's not ready to tell me.

It takes all of five minutes to catch up to Soren and Skye, the latter ecstatic that I'm joining them. Within an hour, we have a small picnic spot on the coarse, but warm, sand, with warriors in their wolf forms lingering nearby but some privacy, nonetheless.

Mom is on the shore with Skye looking for agates, of course, while I sit on a blanket with Fallon resting between my tights, her tiny fingers clutching my thumbs while she blows raspberries.

Soren and I have been sitting in silence for several minutes at this point. We're both watching Jane and Patton pace the beach, obviously locked in deep conversation.

"They're delaying the wedding," Soren says with a soft sigh.

"Why?" I know why. I shouldn't have even asked.

"The war, whenever that'll be. Every territory under Maeve's control is tightening up, all warriors accounted for." He draws his knees up to his chest. "Patton would take her to the temple today if it were entirely up to him, but Jane... wants more for him. A real wedding. All the fluff. He'd love it, and she knows it."

"They're great mates for each other."

Soren's soft smile doesn't reach his eyes. "I wanted this for him. Something easy. Someone he doesn't have to put on a show for and who loves him regardless of what he went through with the Viper."

Fallon yawns, blinking into the shade of the massive umbrella casting us in shadow. Her curly blonde hair ripples in the breeze coming off the lake as I rock her from side to side on my thighs, her body a comforting, grounding weight. "Blake told me bits and pieces about the Viper. But... she's whatever Hannibal is, right?"

"She was. Maeve killed her, and it wasn't easy." His tone gives me pause. His voice is tight, controlled, but laced with what I know are horrible memories.

"Blake... he's going after Hannibal, isn't he?"

Soren stares at the water. He rolls his lips between his teeth before nodding, stealing a quick glance in my direction. "It's personal for him."

"Why?"

"Because of you."

I shake my head, releasing a bitter laugh. "No—"

"He was willing to die to protect your memory. He was dying in Hannibal's hands, shielding the memory of you, Marianna." He takes another deep breath, his tone even more bitter as he adds, "No one messes with our mates and gets away with it."

I stare at him, suddenly, finally, understanding. "This is all because Blake feels threatened by Hannibal when it comes to me?"

"Of course it is. But it's also so much bigger than that. The whole family is being called to attention right now, everyone making moves, everyone lying in wait. Blake is the one who can tell them when to strike, but he won't, because it means..."

"Giving in to his powers."

"Yes."

"He talked to you about it then?"

"Last night."

I look down at Fallon, a weight lifting off my shoulders. "Good. I hoped he would."

"He... did he talk to you about what he has to do?"

"He mentioned leaving."

"It's not that simple."

"But leaving for where, exactly? And when? I can't get that out of him. All for a vendetta against a man who had already left–"

"He has to finish this. I don't think he has a choice."

"But if he could just ignore it," I counter even though I already know it's not even remotely close to the truth, "and we all just move on, would there be a war?"

"I don't know, but I feel it. Something... unsteady. Blake feels like he's the one that has to right it."

Neither of us speaks again for another hour, which bleeds into another, then another. The day stretches into late afternoon, then early evening, quiet and uneventful. We all have dinner together at the castle. Even my mom joins us, but over the chatter and occasional laughter, Blake's silence and inability to even touch his food drenches me in dread. I miss him. I feel like I just got him back, and then this shift happened, ruining everything.

But as I watch him carefully, dutifully, tuck Skye into bed, I feel a sweeping calm drift through me. Whatever he chooses... whatever he feels pulled to do, he's doing it for us. For his kingdom. For his family. For me.

I just wish I could hear him say why out loud. Just to silence my nerves.

But Blake has always been a man of few words.

He wasn't planning on coming to bed with me, that's clear, but I guide him to the bed regardless in a quiet command, a siren's song, a gentle plea to be here for a moment with me, and he does.

I kiss him like my life depends on it. I pour every ounce of love I feel into the kiss, which turns into one more, and then our clothes fall to the floor, and it's just the two of us against a world of unknowns, but in our room, it's... beautiful. Safe and warm.

I fall asleep in his strong arms, drinking in his scent. A scent that reminds me of winter and the cozy security of Solstice.

I tell him I love him.

He presses his lips to mine one last time before I fall asleep.

Chapter 47

Shattered

BLAKE

Moonlight plays over Marianna's naked skin. She's like a painting–flawless, almost airbrushed. Ethereal and all-consuming even at rest. The moon is full and high in the sky as I trace my fingertips over the curve of her breasts and down to her navel, then lower, where I flatten my hand between her hips, closing my eyes against the anguish soaring through my body, through my wolf. Even the stars go silent, giving me space to grieve the life I tried and failed to give her–them. Marianna, Skye, and... the two boys currently nestled deep in her womb. Boys she won't know about for weeks still.

Maybe this knowledge is a gift from the Goddess, a little snippet of the lives that will move on without me if I fail. I've made promises I'm not sure I can keep. I've sworn vows in silence, betting my life on an outcome that I already know is out of reach, but I have no choice but to try to save my family and my kingdom from a war we would never recover from.

I was too young to remember my great-grandmother's face. Her voice has been lost to time. But I remember her story. I know she laid her life at the Goddess's altar in exchange for ours—for mine. She used her powers to save a kingdom.

Now, I have to use mine.

I press a kiss to Marianna's stomach and whisper a silent apology. I dress in the dark—black pants and a black shirt along with my favorite black cloak and boots. The city is quiet and calm, the air just starting to cool after another incredibly hot day. The temple rises above me, light pouring from windows where shadows drift as priestesses and mystics get ready for bed, but...

Calliope is already waiting for me in the grand foyer of the temple, flanked by a dozen mystics in their masks and white robes. They know. They would have seen it, sensed it in the murky fabric their powers can't quite pass through.

I pull the hood of my cloak down and scan the bodies shrouded in white and command, "Evacuate the temple and all of its buildings. No one remains. Just me." I look down the line. No one moves; no one so much as breathes. I continue, "Bring every sphere into the Orrery. Every single one. You have thirty minutes."

The mystics move, disappearing in every direction. I remain in the foyer, closing my eyes as rapid footsteps and murmurs of confusion fill my head, mingling with the incessant chatter of the stars. I only open my eyes again when the temple falls into complete silence. Calliope is the only person remaining. She turns to me, standing in front of the door leading out to the city, and bows her head ever so slightly.

I lower my head as well, and when I rise back to my full height, she's gone, and Moonrise is still sleeping beyond the rolling front garden of the temple.

I spend the next hour moving from room to room making sure everyone made it out. I open every door, pull every mirror from the walls and carry them deep into the recesses of the temple, where the Orrery expands around me, gears moving on their own accord. I arrange the mirrors along the walls, leaning them against the stone.

Moonstone spheres cover the floor–every single one, just like I commanded.

Everything is in place.

I pick up one of the spheres and walk to a table where mystics in training–acolytes–would normally take notes about the prophecies the orrery gave them. I hold the sphere between my hands and dig deep, letting specific memories flow into the crystal orb until it's full of light and images from my head.

Marianna and I in her old living room in that shitty little apartment. Me, smiling up at her as she plays her violin so aggressively that the strings snap and she laughs. Marianna, pregnant, her eyes full of tears as I grip her hand and pull her close, embracing her, grounding her, the last time we'd touch like that for over seven years.

The moment Skye came into the world. The tears of joy in Marianna's eyes. The moment I held my daughter for the first time and saw the powers brewing behind her milky, newborn gaze already, just moments after she entered the world.

Recent memories. Waking up slowly with Marianna in the morning a few days ago, tracing her skin, drinking in her scent like it's my life's blood. The night Skye snuck into our bed, and I saw myself mirrored in her tired eyes.

I bleed my hope for their future into the sphere. My girls and the boys that will follow. A warm, inviting home. Solstice celebrations. School graduations. Weddings to their mates–fated, of course. Grandchildren I may never meet. Seeing my mate as an old woman, gray, and beautiful still.

But there's so little I can do to manipulate the future, which is hazy at the moment. It's in my hands–those fine threads with no beginning and no end. I have the power to weave them to my will but... at what cost?

I already know the answer to that question as I rise, letting my powers flow into every sphere. The mirrors reflect the violet light beginning to glow beneath my skin, mingling with the silver glow of the full moon. My wolf is restless. Little does he know that we're about to go on the adventure of a lifetime.

Because I will not return until Hannibal, his king, and all the fae that would threaten us–the shifters–are dead.

By my hand or... *hers*.

I close my eyes, raising my hands to the ceiling. The orrery creaks painfully as it begins to move faster than it ever has before. I'm not a witch. I know no spells. There's nothing I can say to protect myself as I let my powers surge further than they ever have before.

For the first time in my life, I let my shields down. I let the voices in–let them take full control. I allow myself to feel. Every emotion. Everything beautiful, painful, and heart-wrenching.

The only words I utter are simple. Concise.

"Show me what you want me to see."

Pain like I've never felt before tears me to shreds. The mirrors shatter. A deep vibration rattles through the orrery as the spheres splinter, and the voices in my head begin to scream.

And then I... pull apart at the seams. The pain is immense. I let the darkness I've been so afraid of sweep in, consuming me.

A roar explodes all around me. My scream of pain shatters through the sound of the orrery breaking into slivers of hot metal and the glass dome above my head shattering, and then... quiet.

The dead kind.

MARIANNA

Skye's rapid footsteps sprinting through the suite wake me up with a start. I reach for Blake, startled into alertness, but dread washes over me when I feel nothing but the chilled sheets where we'd fallen asleep together only hours ago.

"MAMA!" Skye screams, her voice ragged with fear and despair. I pull the sheet around me and leap out of bed, colliding with my daughter as she drags me to my knees, tears streaming down her cheeks while her eyes light from within with violet power.

"What's wrong?" I plead, panicked. "What—"

A roaring echo funnels over the castle, replaced by an eerie stillness that makes every fine, downy hair on the back of my neck stand on end. I feel like the world is moving in slow motion as I slowly turn toward the windows over the bed, where a bright light stretches to the sky.

"What is that?" I whisper, but the words turn to a rough, rattling scream when a shockwave hits the castle, strong enough to break through the magical shields Maeve keeps around the fortress.

Skye screams, and my eardrums nearly burst from the impact. Glass showers over us. I drag her to the ground, covering her with my body. The room fills with light for several seconds before the darkness returns, but I can't catch my breath. My body is locked tight around Skye, and I'm trembling so badly my teeth clank together.

That feeling of dread returns, drowning me, pulling me into its current. I blink past tears and dust hanging in the air all around us, trying to clear my vision. Cracks creep along the walls of the room as sirens blare in the distance. The door to the bedroom was blown off its hinges, and the shadow rushing into the room isn't the man I want right now. Not even close.

Soren scoops us up like we weigh nothing, rushing us into the living area of the suite just outside the bedroom. The windows are nothing more than shards of glass shimmering in the moonlight, and beyond the tattered window frames, Maeve's powers dance through the sky like ribbons of crimson.

"What happened?" I cry out, but I can't hear Soren over the wailing of sirens and shouts of alarm rising from the streets several stories below.

"Are you all right?" he shouts over the chaos, setting me down on a spot of carpet not covered in glass, but holds tight to Skye, who has her trembling arms wrapped tightly around his neck.

"Where's Blake?" I bellow, but the look Soren gives me answers for him. "No. No—where is he? He couldn't have—he was just with me—"

"We have to go now," Soren says steadily, calmly, but his eyes betray his tone. There's pain there—something heavy and damning, like he knew this was coming in one way or another. Blake was his friend. He's the only true friend I think Blake has ever had. He knew. He had to have known.

"What did he do? Where is he? Soren, where is Blake?!" I can barely get the words out between sobs. I can't breathe. My body refuses to function.

"You and Skye are going to Veiled Valley, right now. Please, we need to move," he says, yanking me into the hallway outside of the suite, which is so thick with dust I can't see more than the darting shadows of the workers and maids trying to take stock of each other and the castle at large.

Soren brings us to the sixth floor—the private floor he inhabits with Maeve and Fallon. I drag him to a stop, trying to pull out of his grasp. "My—my mom! I have to get my mom!"

"I already sent warriors to find her—"

I free myself from his touch and race down the hallway away from him, making a beeline to a set of doors that opens to a narrow balcony that overlooks the city.

I'm not prepared for what I see.

I gasp—a guttural sound full of despair and confusion—as Moonrise comes into view. A city of dust and moonlight.

The temple, that grand, opulent building that once stood in the center of the city, is gone. Nothing but a black void remains, smoldering with embers.

"No." It's the only sound I can make as my heart shatters in my chest.

"He evacuated everyone from the temple."

I flinch, clutching the railing as Maeve's tired, stunned voice reaches me. She's standing only a foot behind me, Fallon squirming against her chest. Maeve's eyes are burning crimson with her powers as she looks over her city, tears welling along her lower lashes. "He got everyone out before he went."

"Went where?" I sob, and her eyes slowly meet mine.

Chapter 48

Bursts of Chaos

MARIANNA

I get dressed, and then we're ushered down to the basement of the castle in short order. Soren doesn't set Skye down until we reach the web of hallways leading to what I thought were storage rooms but end up being an intricate, absolutely unreal, training facility built levels below the main floor of the castle. There, we enter a small arena of sorts, where several guards are already waiting for us, as well as... Sydney.

Blake and I haven't married yet, but Sydney is as close as he can be to a father-in-law at this point in time, and that's written clearly on his face when Skye runs into his waiting arms, but his eyes remain on mine. Silent. Hollow with both grief and startling understanding. There's no room for anything else, but I... I feel nothing but anger.

Soren's talking, but I barely register a word he says as I stare back at Sydney, my hands curling into fists at my side. I want to say what's on my heart—that he should have known that Blake would become this, that he could see it clearly in his son's eyes, that he knew Blake was struggling—had struggled his entire life—with these powers and not because he didn't understand them..

Blake knew what he was capable of this entire time, and it weighed on him until he broke, and did something so reckless I could scream.

I turn from Sydney before I can spit the venom simmering on the tip of my tongue that he doesn't even deserve, but I just need someone... anyone, to take it out on.

"Oh my gods, Anna!" Mom bursts through a group of warriors clogging the doorway, her arms outstretched. Skye screams for her grammy behind us, and then her little arms are wrapped around our waists, her face buried between us. I let the tears fall. I let them drown me, soaking in the dusty collar of my shirt–Blake's shirt that Soren swiped for me, along with a pair of joggers. I fell asleep in Blake's arms last night, totally unaware of what he was planning to do.

That's the part that hurts the most. The secret he kept. That last night, when we were tangled together, and wrapped in each other's arms... that he kissed me, whispering what I realize now were broken promises of a bright future ahead of us, where everything is always warm, always good, and always easy.

"Marianna, I need to speak to you," Sydney says over the hushed voices of the guards and the whimpering cries of my mom and Skye. I turn to him, letting him see the acute pain behind my eyes, but I let my family go and walk to him, slowly, wading through the guards waiting for Soren's directions, I believe, because Maeve isn't down here with us.

She's dealing with everything above–her broken city.

Sydney takes me by the shoulder and guides me to a quiet curve of the indoor arena–training grounds, I realize. "I'm here to take you, Skye, and your mother to Veiled Valley."

"Why?"

"It was what–what Blake wanted," he says with a perfectly straight face. Gods, he looks like Blake right now. Stern, emotionless, but his eyes are a torrent of things left unsaid, feelings he can't or won't voice.

He might think he's lost his son. I let the knowledge sink in, mingling with the dread, confusion, and utter grief I feel.

I press my hand to my chest without even realizing it, like I can feel the strings of our bond just beneath my skin–still intact.

"He's not dead."

"No, he's not."

"Is he coming back?"

Sydney takes a shallow breath, his lips parting with the exhale, but Soren's voice rips over the murmurs in the crowd. "Security at the castle is being tripled as of right now. Find your leaders and regroup to be assigned to your new posts here and throughout the city. Go."

The guards move out silently, and Soren turns to me, but I look back at Sydney. "I'm not going to Veiled Valley. I'm going to stay. So is Skye, and so is my mom. We're going to stay here."

Sydney glances at Soren.

I lick my lips, finding them dry. "I can't go. If he comes back–if something went wrong... I need to be here. I can't hide from this. He's my mate. I don't understand why he did this, or why he didn't even tell me goodbye, but I know with my entire heart," I breathe, tears welling in my eyes, "that he wouldn't do something like this to... hurt anyone. He went to find Hannibal, didn't he? He told you, right?" My voice cracks painfully as I look over my shoulder at Soren. "He only trusted you. He told you what he was planning. You knew?"

Soren's eyes are glassy, but he lowers his gaze to the floor. It's confirmation enough.

"Let me take your mom and Skye to Veiled Valley, just for a few days, until this blows over. Until we know more. You can remain, of course. Maeve could use the company." Sydney's voice is raw, but he's not here to argue. "Skye will be with family. It's going to be chaotic here for a while."

I nod, too torn to shreds to even process the next minute, let alone the new few days.

My mom doesn't argue. She holds tight to Skye as I walk back to them and kneel, taking Skye's hands in mine. Her face is damp with tears, and her eyes shine violet, just like Blake's. It kills me.

It gives me a single shred of hope.

It brings me to the ground.

I caress her cheek and lean my forehead against hers. "You're going to go with your grandpa on an adventure for a few days. We've never been to Veiled Valley before, but I've been told it's beautiful. And there's a friendly ghost in the castle who can make toys out of thin air."

"Can the ghost bring Daddy back?"

Daddy. I haven't heard her call him that before. My heart crushes under the weight of my grief. "You can ask, and maybe the ghost will bring you a dream about him. What do you say? Can you be strong and brave for me? For Grammy?"

She nods, straightening up, her shoulders squared.

"That's my girl."

I rise to speak to Mom, but Skye squeezes my hand, her voice a low murmur–a brief, breathy whisper. "Daddy gave me a dream before he left for his trip. It's upstairs, in the sphere in your room. His favorite. He said it would be there for you when he left. You just have to look."

"What?"

"You need to go, Sydney," Soren says over the top of us.

I feel my soul being torn from my body as Mom clutches me close, pressing a wet kiss to my cheek. "It's just a few days. I'll bring her back, okay? Just give it a few days."

"Mom–"

"Maeve wants to speak to you," Soren says, and I'm effectively torn between what needs to happen and the reality that everything I know is swirling down the drain.

I watch my mom and daughter disappear into the aether with Sydney. Then, I spend the climb back to Maeve's office wondering if my mom arrived in Veiled Valley desperately ill from the jump. I think of how Skye must be feeling, how it was selfish of me to ask her, a seven-year-old, to be strong. Guilt riddles my senses useless as I move on autopilot into Maeve's office.

The queen stands behind her desk, her eyes cold and serious as she speaks with several very important looking older men in uniforms—the commanders of her royal forces.

"Commander Andrews will station his captains and their regiments along our borders with the Roguelands and the Deadlands, while you, Commander Ashwood, will be moving your forces into Tarsian. The Royal Guard of Tarsian already has their naval fleet waiting off the coast, but you will aid their ground operations along their shores." She sighs, drawing in a breath, before continuing, "Alpha King Soren will base his operations in–in Twin Cities and aid Alpha King Ryan in the Deadlands, if it comes to that."

I blink, and beside me, Soren straightens as his mate meets his eyes with a brief glance. I've heard rumblings of Soren possibly being Alpha King of the Roguelands, but I've never been there, and I've never heard anyone call him that.

But his mate, his queen... she just did. It's a momentous moment that quickly gets swept away on the tide as the commanders leave hastily with their orders.

"You will go to the Roguelands immediately. Ryatt will meet you there. He still has sway with some of the larger packs. No trained warrior will be spared. Everyone with training must report to Twin Cities," she tells her own mate in a voice I find foreign. It's icy and stern, but the look on her face....

Soren moves toward her desk as she begins to shatter, but she quickly regains her composer, waving him away. "Will you please go check on Fallon? She's with Jane and Patton. She's getting Fallon packed to leave for Veiled Valley shortly."

Soren grits his teeth like he's biting back whatever he wants to say, but nods, glancing at me before leaving the room. Maeve sits behind her desk and briefly hangs her head. I barely breathe as the Queen of Eastonia rolls her neck and looks right at me.

"I didn't know he was going to do this."

"That's not why I wanted to see you," she says under her breath. "I just–things are moving quickly now, Marianna. My sister and her son are in Veiled Valley already–my mother went to fetch them. My brother-in-law is moving his pack to the Deadlands officially, and I've just given the order for my father to prepare to launch certain factions of his Ghost army to Emberfyll, using it as a base, and for what?" She laughs darkly, a cruel sound that rattles my bones. "You knew Blake better than anyone, and even you didn't know what he was capable of, did you?"

I can't tell by her tone whether she's accusing me of something, but I can see the lines of stress stretched across her face. Shadows dance below her eyes as she turns her sea-green gaze on mine, shaking her head. "He's more powerful than me."

"He doesn't want to be."

"You were there when he made me vow to kill him if he set foot in my kingdom again. It was a blood oath. I have to do it, Marianna, if he returns."

My heart sinks into my stomach.

"You don't have to–"

"What was he thinking?" she says, more to herself than to me, as she runs her fingers through her hair, disrupting the neat updo. "What the fuck was he thinking?"

"I think you should go upstairs and be with your mate and daughter," I whisper, but she's staring blankly down at her desk like I'm no longer in the room.

I see myself out without another word to her. I have to, because of what Skye told me before she left, because of what he left for me. The castle is in an uproar as I rush to the fifth floor, ignoring the maids and staff who clog the hallways, unsure what to do or where to go as their normal routines spiral out of control.

I lock myself in Blake's suite–my suite, by all accounts. I think about our conversation last night in the shadow of the moon, when it'd just been us talking about a wedding, about eloping, about taking Skye to Maatua and forgetting the world all around us.

That conversation had tasted so sweet—a sharp comparison to the bitter taste in my mouth when I open the door to the bedroom.

Sunlight makes the glass still embedded in the carpet glimmer like sparkling diamond shards. The shattered windows let in a rush of heat. Glass covers the bedspread. It's a mess, but one thing remains untouched, because it hadn't been there when the temple exploded hours ago.

A moonstone sphere sits dormant on the edge of the bed, like Blake somehow placed it there before he got lost in the aether of his own design. It shines in the sunlight, beckoning, but I'm paralyzed in the doorway.

It takes several minutes to find my nerve, and when I finally do, I pick my way across the glass covered room and sit on the edge of the bed with the sphere in my lap, and there's only one thing I can do.

"What did you want to show me?" I whisper into the silent heat.

The sphere flares with light and then images. Memories that take my breath away. Memories from his perspective, like he bled his mind into the stupid glass ball before ruining our lives, and I... hate him for it. I don't understand. I can't understand.

But then the images fade into something... new. Something that hasn't happened yet. Things that are all sunshine and warmth. A pristine, white sand beach. Skye in a little bathing suit running around, her hands full of shells that she leaves at our feet while we lounge in the sand. His hand intertwined with mine, his thumb tracing my wedding ring—the ring he slipped on my finger in another image, where I was dressed in white in a forest of... flowers, and he was there, looking down at me, and we married in the sun, on a warm, spring day...

An image of a grand house in the woods nearby, with that startling view of Moonrise's forest. It'll be quiet there, according to this last gift from him. The... kids. They'll love the backyard. He'll spend an entire weekend with his brother Liam building a play set, only for one of our... *boys*–gods–to fall and break his arm within three days because he jumped off the top of the slide onto his brother–his twin.

The final image is so far in the future I can't fathom it. That same house cloaked in snow. A bitter cold evening warmed by a fire. A grandchild on his knee with violet eyes and a huge, gummy smile while the others–many others–play with the toys they got for Solstice, our living room a wash of colors and random sounds.

I blink back tears as the sphere goes dark and empty, but I've found the answer to the question that's been plaguing me since this morning. Why?

That future is his *why*.

Chapter 49

A Week of Not Knowing

MARIANNA

A Week Later...

Some mornings, I can barely drag myself out of bed, but I do. I put on the brave face I have Dean to thank for–a face that hides the internal anguish and dread ripping me to pieces.

But I'm being strong for Skye. I have to. I promised Blake I would be. Some nights when I can't sleep, I go to the empty, quiet ballroom and fill the space with the sound of my violin, praying he can hear the music through our bond. It's all I have to hang on to–the only thing keeping me from falling into myself, from giving up.

Now, morning sunlight drifts through the curtains in Blake's suite as I gather what belongings I'll need for the day and stuff them in my purse, along with a few snacks and drinks for me and my daughter. She's in the main living room when I walk out, sliding my sunglasses into my hair while double checking I brought everything we'd need for a day out of... here. Just away. The palace walls have felt like a grim reminder of who won't be joining us today and why.

She returned from Veiled Valley three days ago. She's quiet again, falling into the same patterns that used to consume her when we lived in Crescent Falls, before Blake opened her eyes to a world and a family we'd denied her before.

"Ready? I was thinking we could go to the park at the school, but there's something I want to show you first."

Skye just looks up from the moonstone spheres she arranged on a coffee table and nods, her eyes heavy and dark—lacking their usual luster. I motion for her to follow, and she obeys without a fight, her fingers sliding into mine as we leave the suite and lock up tight before turning into a maze of hallways and stairwells we both can now maneuver without a single thought.

Staying here instead of returning to the townhouse with my mom... it felt right. Skye is comfortable here, especially given that Maeve and Soren are usually around. It's safe and quiet. Skye spends most of her time in the garden these days, more so when Sarah and Sydney visit, which is often, but lately I've been feeling more than a little lost. Like this place is too big, too wide, and too much of a reminder of what Blake was willing to sacrifice to ensure Skye was safe and our kingdom wouldn't be going to war.

I'm stuck in my head when we turn onto the balcony with a sweeping view of the first two stories of the castle. Skye gasps, her fingers slipping from mine as she pulls away and begins to dart toward the grand staircase leading to the foyer. For a single second, I let myself hope. I feel that hope shimmer through me, igniting a warmth I haven't felt since Blake slipped from our bed that fateful morning and never returned.

But I prepare myself for the disappointment and barely feel it wash through me when Skye darts right into Sarah's open arms.

"How's my girl? Are you excited for the summer festival? It starts tonight, you know. I thought we could go, all of us." Sarah squeezes Skye before lowering her to the ground, but her violet eyes are on mine as I slowly ascend the stairs one step at a time, my heart lodged in my throat. "Hey, sweetheart."

"I didn't know you were coming," I say, but I doubt my voice lifts higher than a murmur. The same kind of pain and uncertainty currently tearing me to pieces lingers behind her eyes, but she's much stronger than me. She beams down at Skye, but her eyes remain sad and hollow. She can hide parts of her feelings, at least.

I just let them out at night, silently screaming into Blake's cold pillow.

"I wasn't planning on it but woke up this morning with an urge to come visit. I hope that's all right."

I reach her side, and she opens her arms to me, gently gripping me in greeting. "Of course it's all right," I reply. "We were just going to go to the park and... take a walk. I didn't really have plans but..." I look down at Skye, who's swinging her arms while gazing down at the flickers of light dancing across the floor at our feet–a colorful mural made by the sun reflecting through the stained glass windows. "Come with us, please," I offer.

Sarah runs her fingers through Skye's hair and nods, and before long, we're weaving through the quiet, slightly traumatized streets of Moonrise as the morning sun lifts over the highest buildings, flooding the streets in golden light.

Skye's school playground is totally empty, much to her disappointment, but she begins to busy herself by collecting smooth stones from beneath the swings while Sarah and I sit beside each other in the shade of a large oak tree.

Sarah folds her arms in her lap while I wind my arms around my knees, tugging them against my chest. Silence settles between us for several minutes as we watch Skye play by herself.

"What is she doing?" Sarah asks, her white-blonde hair lifting in a soft, cool breeze, which is a welcome relief from the stifling mid-summer heat already reaching a near boil.

"She's been building what she calls faerie houses in the garden back at the castle," I admit with some effort. "Before he left, Blake read to her some of the old myths Arthur was able to find about... them." I close my eyes, resisting the urge to bite my tongue. With a deep breath, I continue, "She builds little huts made of pebbles, sticks, and flower stems in hopes the faeries will come at night and return Blake to us."

Sarah's lips barely twitch into a smile. "Yeah, Misty said those fables were rather tame in their recollections of what these people are."

"They're not small by any means."

"No. Well, maybe some. But what do we know? Nothing until Blake comes back." She stretches her legs out in front of her.

I rest my chin on my knee, my eyes still on Skye as she climbs up the side of the play set, her pockets weighed down with rocks. "Did Ryatt talk to Logan and his people yet?"

"Yes," Sarah breathes, her eyes suddenly downcast. "They... Logan, obviously, remembers very little about his childhood in Emberfyll, and what he does remember is marred by war and strife, so, it doesn't help us much, but the elders in his pack have some fleeting memories of legends and stories told through the ages about the fae. There's a song from Emberfyll, an old folklore, that's meant for children. I heard Brie singing it to Kieran once and thought it was strange but didn't think about it after that. She heard it from Logan's people, obviously." She shifts her weight, relaxing a touch. "It's meant to deter children from going near still bodies of water. *Don't go to the shore, dear one. She lives beneath the quiet, in the dark, where her teeth shine like diamonds and her nails like polished bone. Stay in the grasses, the marshes, the forests and hills where the wolves roam.*"

"She sang that to Kieran?"

Sarah smiles weakly, chuckling, "Admittedly, most nursery rhymes are shockingly sinister and violent, aren't they?"

I can't help but agree. "What do you think it means?"

"I think, and the rest of the family agrees, that wherever the fae are from, shifters are... lesser. Maybe even hunted, or enslaved, or worse–outright killed. Ryatt and Ella are under the impression that Emberfyll might have become a kingdom of shifters who tried to leave the land of the fae, and if that's true, and the legends about the Great War of the Gods is remotely correct, then they were cut off from their own kind by the same Goddess we worship, and I have a hard time believing them."

Another soft breeze ripples through the branches high above our heads. I let the silence sneak in, let the conversation drop off, and we both watch Skye–our connection to Blake–continue her hunt for stones.

Several minutes later, Sarah takes a huge breath and looks at me. "Marianna, I actually came here for a reason and... there's something Sydney and I would like you to consider."

I meet her gaze as dread weaves between my ribs, tightening like laces. "What?"

"I know Skye is going to start school this fall, and your season with the philharmonic begins around the same time but... that's weeks away, and I wonder if you'd be–if she'd be happier, perhaps, coming back to Crescent Falls for the rest of the summer."

I swallow past the lump in my throat. I can't form words. Not yet. Not now. Of course, I've been going over our options lately. How could I not? I'm living in Maeve's castle–Maeve, who's preparing for war if it comes to that. I'm in Moonrise, which is, by all accounts, shut down completely. I don't know if Skye's school will even open for the fall semester at this rate. I don't know if the philharmonic season will begin on time. Everyone is holding their breaths, waiting for the first shoe to drop, and we're stuck in the middle of it.

"Leona would come too, of course. We have plenty of room in the castle. In fact, we have too much room," she says with a small but pained laugh. "I'm a mother of five. I used to pray for silence, but now that my kids are grown, I often wonder what I was thinking back then."

I take another breath, then another, while my mind reels.

Sarah continues, "Blake may have abdicated the throne, but Skye is still a princess, Marianna. He's still a prince of Crescent Falls, and that'll never change."

"Even if he doesn't come back?"

Sarah exhales deeply, squinting into the growing sunlight now stretching into our haven of shade. "To be completely, utterly honest, I worry about the two of you being in Moonrise. Blake told no one of his plans. If he's not successful in whatever deranged plot against the fae he cooked up in secret, you and Skye will be in serious danger. That's not something Sydney nor I can easily ignore. Maeve can keep you safe, yes, but Moonrise is the capital of Eastonia, and if Eastonia goes to war... Blake would want you as far away from the violence as possible. I want you away from it." Her voice cracks, but Skye runs in our direction while we both hastily wipe tears from our cheeks. My daughter hands me a flower she swiped from the garden along the playground fence, and Sarah gets a handful of shiny little rocks.

Skye doesn't even look up at us before darting back to the playground as two families appear at the gate with six children all around her age. She skids to a stop and watches, waiting, I suppose, to see if the friends she made recently are joining them.

"I worry about disrupting her life here. I already moved her from Crescent Falls once."

"I understand completely."

"She's made friends." The words wobble off my tongue. "I don't think—I don't think I can take her away from that."

"Think about it, okay? Maybe talk to your mom and see what she says—" Sarah cuts herself off abruptly and rises so quickly I feel my body tighten with a sudden sensation of nearby danger.

"Skye!" I call out, and Skye whips her head around, then runs in my direction.

"We need to go back to the castle," Sarah says under her breath, narrowing her eyes. They glow from within with her powers.

But a blaring siren rips the air to pieces all around us. I look up as Maeve's powers suddenly stretch across the sky—painting the perfect blue heavens a sparkling crimson before it fades—a shield.

Sarah grabs my wrist as Skye jumps into my arms.

The castle is chaotic and loud when we arrive.

"My mom," I rush out, setting Skye down in the foyer, but Soren sprints into view, sliding around a corner, breathless.

"Patton is already fetching her," he pants, but it's his clothing that catches me by surprise. He's totally outfitted in Ghost armor from head to toe.

"What happened?" Sarah barks, her voice dropping an octave and dripping with conviction.

"The Deadlands," Soren pants, adjusting his gloves. "There was an attack in the Deadlands, on the shore of Teshka." His eyes slide to mine, then back to Sarah. "Have you spoken to Ryan?"

"No?" Sarah searches his eyes. "Soren, what the hell is going on?"

"Lexa and her regiment are missing. They were taken."

Chapter 50

Epilogue–In the Deadlands

Lexa

Summer sunlight sweeps across the trembling fields of wheat–a wash of pure gold against the emerald face of the mountains just beyond. I lift my face to the sun and breathe in, letting the scent of what will be another prosperous harvest fill my lungs. It smells like... bread. Bread and apples. Bread and roasting meat. Bread and the ever burning fire at the center of the village, where lively chatter rises above the crackling embers, above the stretch of a laundry line being raised, above the sound of shutters opening and mothers calling out for their children to come brush their teeth before running off to play.

Goddess, it's good to be home.

"Lexa! LEXA!" Chessie's voice rips down the road, followed by her pounding booted footsteps as she races in my direction. I turn, catching her in the glare of the early morning sun, her wild blonde hair tousled from sleep–unbrushed–and her dress–the first dress I've seen her wear in over six months–wrinkled, like she picked it off the line and failed to hang it up in her closet afterward.

Six months spent training what most would consider Eastonia's finest warriors—the Ghost army—definitely took a toll on all of us. She skids to a stop at my side, panting, brushing her glorious golden locks away from her sun-kissed face. "What are you doing? Where are you going? Can I come?"

"CHESSSSSSSSSSSSIE!"

She winces as her mother's voice echoes from the village proper, where her parents have a stately little cottage right smack-dab in the center of town—a coveted spot, honestly. It's a testament to the fact that her father is one of my dad's oldest friends, one who has memories of a time before the Silverhide pack came to the Deadlands.

Chessie grabs my forearm, and we set out in a brisk walk away from her mother's voice. "Seriously, what are you doing today?"

"What's her problem?" I rush out, but Chessie rolls her eyes, dragging me off the gravel road leading away from the village and into the winding forest that eventually drops into Endova, the territory of my mother's people.

"Me, I'm her problem," she gripes as we disappear into the wheat, which brushes my stomach but is nearly to her shoulders. "You remember how she bitched and moaned about me leaving for Moonrise last fall? Well, now that I'm back, all she wants to talk about is me getting married and bride prices. Apparently, she knows someone who knows someone in Teshka whose friend has a cousin with a son who's had his eye on me for some time now."

I sputter a laugh. "Oh, please, it can't be that bad."

"She's already sewing my wedding dress for the Harvest Festival. It's horrendous, Lexa. I'd rather get married naked."

I give her a playful nudge, and thankfully she laughs, her green eyes crinkling against the sharp sunlight as we weave through the wheat. She's not alone when it comes to overbearing mothers. Meg, Hara, Analise, and Jen are all hiding out at the base of the mountain where the wheat turns to sparse evergreen trees, all dodging equally annoying mothers and their plans for their of-age daughters to get married this fall.

When we reach them, Hara says, "Jaime's already paid my bride price," with a shrug as I follow the group through the trees, taking the long way to the lake, where they apparently plan to hide from their moms until further notice.

"Well, you like him and hoped for the match," Jen replies with a flick of her wrist, her dark brown hair braided tightly down her back, swaying back and forth. "Jaime is also *hot as fuck.*"

"He has a brother," Analise chimes in behind me, giggling.

A few titters of laughter cut through Chessie's moan. "You guys don't get it, do you? We just had the best winter of our lives, and now we're home, and our moms think it's totally acceptable that we sit back down at our looms and bat our eyelashes at every Endovian or Teshkan warrior who comes to visit? Get real."

"I don't mind the attention," Meg says slyly, which earns her a rough nudge to the shoulder by Jen.

"They don't want us marrying any Ghosts and moving to Moonrise or Veiled Valley," Annalise says, and the girls balk, making disgusted faces that force me to hide a smile.

"Ugh! Ghosts? Who do they think we are?" Jen complains.

"Us? With Ghosts? Gross," Hara hisses, and I smile even harder.

Yeah, I took my girls with me when Maeve sent me to Moonrise. Why not? The queen hadn't cared. She even encouraged it. I had my own townhouse, and the six of us split the three bedrooms, spending our days at the arena or training center in the basement of the palace and our nights totally and completely... exhausted. We had certain freedoms that were impossible to fathom here in the Deadlands, sure. Bars, nightclubs, the works... but we were always beaten to shit after our training sessions, and most nights, we were lucky if we were able to make it up the stairs before falling asleep.

It was the best time of my life.

I've also never been so tired, and I still am.

I fight the urge to rub my eyes as the lake comes into view, sparkling like polished sapphire in the sunlight. While Meg, Hara, Jen, and Analise race to the shore, dropping their baskets and towels, and strip down to bikinis they wore beneath their clothes, I hang back on the dock with Chessie, who slumps beside me, dipping her legs in the water next to mine.

"You don't have to get married, you know. My dad did away with that custom years ago. It's your decision. Your parents can't force you into it."

"I know," she sighs, kicking her legs. She lifts her face to the sun while the rest of our friends splash each other or float on their backs nearby, oblivious to our conversation. "I hate to admit it, but part of me is happy about it. Getting married. Not the moving somewhere new if my future husband is from a tribal pack but... yeah. Being settled. Having kids. I'm looking forward to that." She rests her cheek on her shoulder. "Don't get me wrong, I love being a warrior. Moonrise was a dream. Watching the lives of the Ghost warriors we beat up every day flash before their eyes. I'll remember that forever, but..."

"But it was exhausting?"

She smiles, nodding. "The first thing I did when we got home was sleep. I slept for two days straight."

"Same," I breathe, then I lean back until I'm flat against the dock. I didn't come here to swim. I'd just been... aimlessly walking around... not, like, looking for cell reception or anything...

"So..." Chessie says, kicking water at my legs. "Did you and Austin..."

"Did Austin and I what?"

She shrugs. "You guys seemed pretty cozy after that last training session before we left."

Meg backstrokes in front of us. "Austin totally has the hots for you, Lexa! I could see his hard-on through his leathers every time you coached his battalion through a training session!"

I kick at her, and she giggles, swimming away.

"That's not true!" I call out, but she flips onto her belly and dives beneath the surface, popping up several yards away where Hara and Jen are treading water. "It's not true," I repeat to Chessie.

"I dunno. He definitely watched your every move for months."

"He's a captain. That was his job. We were training his guys."

"You're a captain, too. What's the issue?"

"There's no issue because there's nothing going on." My voice is a tad sharper than intended, but Chessie is used to it. These are my friends, sure, but I'm their leader. Their captain. The one they watch, obey, and heed. It's been that way since we were little, back when the girls of the village separated into two factions. Faction one: dolls and playing house.

Faction two: beating the absolute shit out of the village boys during their war games.

Guess which one my parents encouraged?

"I can't stay up here for long. I'm going hunting with my mom this afternoon." I sit up and hug my knees to my chest, wondering if the phone in the bag slung over my shoulder is ever going to ring.

Chessie pouts. "Come on! Stay. Let's swim!"

"Meg is going to harass me about Captain Austin if I stay. I can feel it."

Chessie turns to me, leaning close. "Come on, Lexa. It's me. What really happened? You've been off since we got on the train to leave Moonrise, and Austin did, in fact, come to say goodbye to all of us. To *you*."

"Sporting the black eye I gave him—"

"During a training session!"

"We kissed."

Chessie gasps. I wince, turning away from her and looking down at my hands.

"And a little *more* than that."

"You did not."

"Unfortunately, yes, we did, and it was quick and meant nothing."

Chessie rolls her eyes back to the water, blowing out her breath. "That doesn't mean nothing—"

"In this case, it meant... nothing. A little fun before coming home." My stomach curls as I look out over the water at the woman acting so carefree, so unburdened. Austin fills my mind, his sun-bleached hair golden blond in the glare of a neon sign taking up my vision. His scent–thick, sharp, and woodsy–some cologne I'll never be able to scrub from my memory. The way it felt when his arms curled around me, pressing me against the stone exterior wall of the shitty bar in Old Moonrise where we'd been meeting for drinks for months, late at night, when our battalions had long gone to bed.

"What's your bride price?" Chessie asks under her breath, pulling me out of my memories.

"I doubt I have one," I chuckle, and she squints up at me in disbelief.

"You're the Alpha King's daughter."

"So?"

"Your dad paid your mom's price with a golden elk pelt–the last golden elk by all accounts–"

"My dad said, jokingly, that if a man can beat me in a fight, he can marry me. So far, no man has ever beaten me in anything." I rise, dusting off my thighs, and hike my bag over my shoulder. "I gotta go. I'll see you at the pack house for supper."

"LEXA! DON'T GO!" The rest of the girls whine, but I catch Meg's sharp look as I turn to face the shore–curious and cutting. She's one of the best warriors. Mom agrees. We're the top warriors under her command. Meg could easily be a captain one day if she ever lets go of her last-man-standing attitude. She's not what I'd consider a team player, but she's working on it, at least.

The village is busy and bustling when I walk out of the forest and take the trail to the large wooden house rising from a thicket of trees, perched just above the rest with a view of the village below. I wasn't born here, but I grew up within the warm wooden walls that greet me. Nora looks up from the couch where she's sprawled out, her sketchbook in her lap. She inherited Mom's fiery red curls but has a knack for taming them that neither Mom nor I have been able to master, even with her guidance. They dance around her shoulders in tight, glossy, perfect coils as she shimmies to an upright position, her amber eyes searching my face before narrowing. "What's up with you?"

"Me?" I drop my bag on the worktable where Mom has been priming arrows in anticipation for our hunt. "Nothing. I thought you were packing to go back to Moonrise today."

"Sydney was supposed to come get me like, now, but he grabbed Mom and Dad instead, and they haven't returned."

I slowly look at my little sister, noticing the fine lines of concern creasing the sides of her eyes. "What?"

"Sydney came and went in a hurry. Dad told me to stay here. Mom was worried because you weren't here, but Sydney said they couldn't wait."

I glance at the clock on the wall, furrowing my brow. "When did they leave?"

"Half an hour ago, maybe."

I look down at the scattered arrowheads Mom abandoned in haste. The stomach-curling feeling returns. "Nora–"

A burst of energy explodes through the room. I flinch, even after being around this kind of magic my entire life. The tang of metal fills my mouth as Mom steps out of the mist, and Sydney appears behind her, looking grave, his face cast in shadow to the point I can't make out his expression.

Mom's amber eyes are grimly set with determination as she focuses on Nora, asking, "Are you packed?"

"Yeah." Nora slowly slides off the couch, looking from Mom to me. "What's going on? Where's Dad?"

Mom motions to Nora to grab her bag off the floor, and she does, her grip tight on the leather handle. "Uncle Sydney is going to take you to Veiled Valley now–"

"I thought I was going to Moonrise–"

"We have to go, Nora," Sydney says, his voice cool, steady, and monotone, but his eyes... pain radiates there in the wells of stormy blue, a color we share. I look like my dad, Ryan. I have his coloring, his dark brown hair and big, stormy blue eyes. I have their shared height, their strength, and I can see past the stony expression, and I know, without a shadow of a doubt, that something is terribly wrong.

Nora rushes past me, but Mom stops her, pulling her in for a tight hug that hollows out my stomach. Mom looks crushed as she slowly releases Nora, whispering that our dad will meet her in Veiled Valley, and when Sydney and Nora wordlessly disappear into the aether, she turns to me.

"Blake did something reckless, didn't he?" I ask, and Mom closes her eyes in confirmation.

Thank you for reading! Book 16, Lexa's story, is coming soon!

Also by Bella Moondragon

The Alpha King's Breeder series:

Bought by the Alpha: The Alpha King's Breeder Book 1

Loved by the Alpha: The Alpha King's Breeder Book 2

Lost by the Alpha: The Alpha King's Breeder Book 3

Luna of the Alpha: The Alpha King's Breeder Book 4

Legacy of the Alpha: The Alpha Kings's Breeder Book 5

Daughter of the Alpha: The Alpha King's Breeder Book 6

Descendants of the Alpha: The Alpha King's Breeder Book 7

Shadow of the Alpha: The Alpha King's Breeder Book 8

Son of the Alpha: The Alpha King's Breeder Book 9

Spare of the Alpha: The Alpha King's Breeder Book 10

Claimed by the Alpha: The Alpha King's Breeder Book 11

Atonement for the Alpha King: The Alpha King's Breeder Book 12

Rejected by the Alpha: The Alpha King's Breeder Book 13

Abducted by the Alpha: The Alpha King's Breeder Book 14

Abandoned by the Alpha: The Alpha King's Breeder Book 15

Wolf Shifter Fairy Tale Retellings series

Beauty and the Alpha Beast

Sleeping Beasty

Tangling With the Alpha

The Luna's Vampire Prince series:

The Culling

The Kingdom

The Conquered

Pregnant With Four Alphas' Babies

Chosen As the Breeder

Mated to Four Alphas

Threats Against the Breeder

At War for the Breeder

The Stolen Breeder

Four Alphas, Four Babies

Becoming the Luna Queen

Descendants of the Breeder

Desired by the Devil series

Whispers of the Devil

Banter of the Devil

Murmurs of the Devil

The Mafia Kings series

Indebted to the Mafia King

<u>Loved by the Mafia King</u>

Claimed by the Mafia King

Secrets of the Mafia King

Burned by the Mafia King

Kidnapped by the Mafia King

Dark Stalker Romance series

Tempted by Sin

Fated to Sin

Secret Billionaires series

Finding the Secret Billionaire by Olivia Bhelle Kildare

Falling for My Secret Billionaire by Bella Moondragon

Driven by the Secret Billionaire by ID Johnson

Wolf Shifter Alpha Kings series

Ravens and Ruins

Sundrops and Shadows

Snowflakes and Sabotage

The Vampire King's Feeder series

Claiming the Alpha's Daughter

Loving the Alpha's Daughter

Finding the Alpha's Daughter

Bewitching the Alpha's Son

Writing as B. Moon

The Boy Who Died

Sign up for Bella's newsletter here.

Or get a free novella from The Alpha King's Breeder series when you sign up here: The Beta and the Maid

Follow Bella on Facebook here.

Follow Bella on Bookbub here.